I0788001

hangovers
and
HOLIDAYS

For all my prickly bitches.
You're stuck with me.

Foreword

Dear Reader,

Thank you for picking up *Hangovers and Holidays*. If you haven't read the first four in the Untouchable series, I caution you to go and grab those right now and read them first.

There doesn't seem a lot I can say after reaching book five before you read it, so I've left you a note at the end. Still, this series remains a labor of love for me. I adore Frankie, the boys, and Rachel. Oh, Rachel. She's a girl after my own heart with all the tripwires and barbs to her personality.

The best part of found family and friends is they accept you for who you are and encourage all your eccentricities. They push you to be you and support you to make your life all you could want it to be. And yes, they will give you no small amount of shit along the way because really, who would we be without a little hassle and a whole lot of laughter?

This series wouldn't be complete without the enormous support of Blake Blessing, Rebecca Royce and Sara Vermillion. They've been tremendous as cheerleaders (and in Sara's case, cracking the whip), as sounding boards, and sometimes even telling me to take a break because I was pushing too hard. I flove them to pieces.

I'll be honest, I'm always pushing too hard so these folks keep me in check :D You should thank them, too.

Thank you to every single reader who has given this series a shot and to those who left reviews. Thank you to the readers who recommend the series to their friends and to every single person who has reached out to me about it. I see and hear all of you. Thank you to the readers who make the beautiful collages and cast who they see as the characters in this series.

I get such a thrill for every single one I see.

Thank you. Thank you. Thank you.

One last thing, for those who are not on my newsletter or in my group, this series is slated to be ten books long. We're at the halfway point here. So buckle up, it's going to be a fun ride.

And as always, the housekeeping notes:

For those of you who have never read a reverse harem before, first let me thank you for picking this up and giving it a shot. Second, a reverse harem means the heroine will not make a choice in this book or any other between the guys in her life. It may take her a while to reach that conclusion, but it's the journey that drives it. There are many ways to frame this kind of relationship, currently reverse harem fits it very well.

Also, this is the fifth book in a series. If you haven't read the first four, I encourage you to pause here and go grab them. While there may be no specific happy endings at the end of each of these books, there will be one to the whole series, that I promise you. Some of these books will have cliffhangers, largely due to the size of the story, but the happy ending has to be earned as part of the journey.

Thank you again for reading Frankie's story and I truly hope you enjoy it!

xoxo

Heather

Chapter One
WHITE KNUCKLES

COOP

"Water or beer?" I asked Jake as we moved closer to the makeshift bar Kaplan and his buds had set up for the party. The whole point of coming tonight had been to get out and just enjoy being together. It had also been about having fun without the constant demands on our time or hers. Normally, Archie threw the best ravers and we would be the ones hosting. None of us wanted to do that. At least here, we could party and ditch when we felt like it.

"Water," Jake said firmly, his gaze fixed on the ice chest where the water bottles were. "You can have a beer though." He was driving. Made sense. Frankie hated beer anyway.

"I'm good with water." If we wanted something, we could head over to Archie's place. Though, to be honest, we hadn't missed having access to it at all at Frankie's for the last three weeks. I'd rather be with her than drink anyway.

The line was taking for-fucking-ever. Why didn't they just set it up to grab and go? Then again, there were two guys handling the service and they looked like catering, so maybe that was better. Either way, we were verifying her bottle hadn't been tampered with before we gave it to her. There was water in a cooler in Jake's SUV, we could just go grab it and fuck this line.

Archie pushed through the crowd and ignored the scowls as he cut right to where we were. "You guys setting up camp over here?" He had to pitch his voice louder to be heard over the throbbing beat. Kaplan's stereo system was killer. He scratched at his jaw and rolled his shoulders with a rasp of the dry straw protruding from the wrist of his costume.

"Service with a smile," Jake retorted drily with a nod to where the pair of caterers took their time passing out drinks. It wasn't a fully open bar. Cash was exchanging hands. Archie wrinkled his nose.

"Fucking cheap bastard," he muttered, and I snorted. There was something vaguely amusing about a guy dressed up as a scarecrow bitching about money. Then again, Archie had never had a cash bar at his place for any party he hosted.

I twisted to glance back toward the dancers where I'd last seen Frankie and Bubba. But I couldn't spot the blue gingham dress or the oversized terrier— the fact that Bubba had put on the furry ears and whiskers had been hilarious. Course, he hadn't had to take a bath in silver body paint. At least it wasn't itching so far. I wasn't holding out hope that would last.

Maybe I could talk Frankie into helping me wash it off later. Granted, she only had one hand, but we could take our time...

"They went outside," Archie was saying, and I snapped my focus back to him and Jake as the line finally fucking moved and we got four people closer to scoring our drinks. "Cooling off and taking a break from the crowd."

That made sense. And Arch was giving Bubba some time with Frankie. I'd give him credit, he'd been firm and steady in proving he was in. The attention he showered on her without smothering required walking a fine line, but it was there in his eyes every time he looked at her. I was pretty sure Frankie was the only one who hadn't noticed, at least not at first. She also had a damn good reason to be distracted, so we didn't give her shit. Let her forgive Bubba on her own schedule.

"Ten minutes is plenty of time, right?" I snarked, and Jake snorted.

It was more like fifteen by the time we finally made it to the bar and got waters all the way around. Archie dropped a twenty in their jar so they'd give us bottles from the bottom. I wasn't the only one who double-checked the seals.

Paranoid. That was going to be us from now on.

Drinks in hand, we pushed our way through the crowd toward the door. How many fucking people had Kaplan invited? It was like the entire senior class, a good chunk of the juniors, and plenty of the sophomores were here. It was wall to wall people.

Greg Sanders stopped us on the way to the door. His Dallas Cowboys football jersey serving as his costume made me snort. He was a wide receiver for the team. "Jake, man, I was looking for you."

"Yeah?" Jake raised his brows, made almost more amusing by the addition of the faux furry ones he wore.

"You should watch your back. I heard that Shawn and Jackson are looking for you and Bubba."

Jake smirked. "Let them find me."

I frowned, but it was Archie who asked, "Why the fuck are they looking for you?"

With a shrug, Jake said, "'Cause we called the fucks out for their behavior. They're friends of Mitch's."

At the mention of that asshole's name, I scowled. Really not who I wanted to discuss at a party, unless it was funeral plans so I could go piss on his grave.

Greg made a face and shook his head. "Yeah, just watch your back." Greg gave him a pat on the shoulder. "Not all of us are dicks."

"Just a little dickish," Jake retaliated, and they both laughed. Archie rolled his eyes, but I pushed back against the surge of people to head for the door.

I caught sight of Rachel on the far side, and she raised her eyebrows, but I just shook my head. We were good. We finally made it to the damn door, and the first wash of chilly, October air was a relief against the rising humidity inside from the press of too many bodies and the dancing. At least the paint wasn't melting off of me.

Some of the party had spilled outside onto the drive. And likely other places. The distinct sound of grunting was hard to miss, as were the moans. I rolled my eyes. They were definitely not in that direction. A quick sweep of those visible didn't reveal Frankie or Bubba.

I glanced at Archie. He jerked his thumb to the side. "Covered porch this way." At least he knew the place. I hadn't been to Corey's since sophomore year. I think we all did a party here then, too. Maybe.

Jake's strides picked up speed, and we cut around the corner of the house in time to see someone yanking Frankie back off the porch and Bubba lunging at…

"Fucking Mitch?" The words fell from Jake's lips, even as he raced forward. He flung one of the water bottles he was carrying, and it struck the guy holding Frankie. She stumbled sideways as her assailant tossed her to the ground, but Jake was already on the guy.

"Get Frankie," I told Archie, even as I leapt the railing to plow into the asshole Bubba was pounding on. There were easily a half-dozen others on Bubba, and I grabbed the first one of those and darted around the fist he threw at me before I slammed my fist into his jaw.

It fucking hurt. But I jammed my knee right into his crotch and then shoved him into the guy behind him. Then I peeled into the next guy. Someone nailed me right in my kidneys.

How many of these fuckers were there?

A feminine shriek cut through the air, and I twisted, even as I tried to get the asshole on me into a headlock.

Where the fuck was Frankie, and why hadn't Archie gotten her out of here?

JAKE

The air outside was a balm after the cloying humidity of all the bodies dancing and pressed together indoors. Fucking costume itched. But it was worth it to see Frankie laugh each time her eyes focused on me. Granted, the 'cowardly' part of the title wasn't my favorite, but maybe I could talk her into letting me make her purr later.

I was still half-grinning about that idea when we hit the corner of the house. I had just enough time to see the bag get yanked over Frankie's head as she was hauled backwards over the railing and off the porch. Ten guys—maybe more, maybe less—faced off with Bubba and surrounded him.

Rage poured through my system. A distant part of my mind recognized what happened in these situations. They were the kinds of things that Diane wanted to dissect during anger management. At the moment, I didn't give a flying fuck.

Three things were abundantly clear.

Some asshole had his hands on Frankie.

A series of assholes were pounding on Bubba.

And I was going to beat the living hell out of all of them.

The water bottle in my hand became a projectile as I flung it. It struck the side of the jerk holding Frankie's head, and he tossed her away. I narrowed my target to tackle him and wrenched him to the ground *away* from her.

Coop shouted something, but I wasn't listening. I slammed my fist into the asshole I tackled, then grabbed a fistful of his hair to slam his head against the ground. He tried to stick his thumbs in my eyes, and I choked the motherfucker until he didn't move

On my feet, I shot a look to where Frankie had been as Archie lurched past me, striking another asshole with two fast jabs. A fist slammed into my face, and I tasted blood as the inside of my lip split. Turning my head, I met Jackson Taylor's gaze and bared my teeth. He wanted to fight me?

Yes. Fucking. Please.

I caught the next fist he threw at me and wrenched his arm down. After that, it was all flying fists as a second guy launched into me. I took a pair of jabs to the kidneys before I slammed my elbow back and caught his face. The crunch of buckling bone was like music to my ears.

I didn't know what these assholes had planned, and I didn't care. They weren't laying a finger on Frankie. As soon as I knocked one down, I collided with another. Some dim part of my brain trying to take notes on all of this registered Mitch's face amidst the crowd. Mitch, who Bubba had knocked right through the railing and currently scrabbled with, even as others whaled on him.

Coop waded in without regard, his fists flying. While he didn't fight often, we used to box back in middle school and in the early part of high school. We'd only stopped because he decided he liked his nose unbroken and I was an asshole.

Both were fair assessments.

A fist caught me in the solar plexus and knocked all the air out of me. I didn't even try to figure out who or what or why. I just grabbed his hair and slammed his head down against my knee, then worked my way toward Bubba. Mitch was in that mess.

I wanted my pound of flesh from that asshole.

I wanted Frankie's pound of flesh.

Bubba broke his jaw, but I wanted to break his legs.

And cut off his dick.

Fuck reasonable.

Then a feminine shriek cut through noise and jerked me out of the red haze.

Where the fuck was Frankie?

IAN

Mitch popping up like a damn devilish jack in the box was not on any bucket list or bingo card for my plans tonight. Tonight had been about Frankie, and for about thirty seconds there, I thought we'd done it. She'd re-opened the door she'd closed.

"You know I want to trust you?"

I wanted her to trust me.

She wanted a promise to talk to her if stuff started bothering me again? Yes.

She wanted to establish rules and be one of the people making them? Agreed.

She wanted a night of dancing? Sign me up.

Karaoke? Anytime. Anywhere.

I meant it when I said I would do anything for her. Then Mitch walked his ass up with half the damn team at his back.

The fucking dick.

I'd put myself between him and Frankie. No way in hell would I let them get through me to get to her. I'd already broken his jaw once. If he wanted me to take the rest of him apart, sign me up. Even blocking them from getting to her didn't stop someone from yanking her away. I twisted to go after her, and that earned me a flurry of blows.

Every single one would leave a mark, but I was too pissed to care. Somewhere between the fist slamming into my ribs and another catching me just behind the ear, I landed a fist right into Mitch's shoulder. He had a bad one. Wrenched it in junior year.

A dislocation.

Real bitch of an injury.

His sharp scream pressing out between his teeth was a sweet sound, even as the taste of copper flooded my mouth. Another blow had my eyes watering, then Coop was there, wading in next to me. We were trading guys off.

If Coop was there, then Archie and Jake were there.

They would get Frankie.

I locked my sights on Mitch. I was going to rip that asshole apart. The railing buckled under us, and the sound of wood tearing ripped through the night air as we went down in a hail of fists, elbows, and kicks. I rolled away from the first blow that caught me in the ribs.

Thank God for adrenaline, because the faint crack, audible over the grunts and explosions of air left me gasping for a breath. But I managed to wrench the guy kicking me down with an arm around his knee. Two sharp blows to the side, and he was screaming as the kneecap popped.

Asshole.

I spat blood out as I rolled to the side. Coop had another guy down, and Jake tackled a third. We weren't alone out here. Some of the guys from the party poured out. Some teammates.

How many were on our side, I wasn't sure.

But I caught sight of Mitch, and launched after him. I made it the three strides through the broken railing and onto the porch before I landed on him as he tried to stagger away. He managed to land another punch, but I ate the blow before gripping his arm and twisting it back and up. That shoulder I'd popped earlier had to be screaming now, because he was.

I hauled him backward and threw his ass off the porch.

Anger boiled inside of me as I glared at him. My right eye was already swelling shut, and I couldn't breathe through one nostril. My ribs ached, my lungs burned, and my fists felt like I'd put them through a cheese grater.

All I wanted was to completely rearrange his face.

Mitch stared up at me, our gazes locked.

Fear flickered in his eyes.

Even in the half-light cast by the pair of bulbs on the porch, I could read the pain and terror in the other guy's expression.

"Not so fucking tough now, are you, asshole?" Good.

I wanted him afraid.

I wanted him to beg, too.

I wanted him to feel helpless.

I'd seen her when I got in that room. I'd seen her flailing, even as she lost the battle against the drugs in her system.

I'd listened to her whimpering in her sleep.

And I'd seen the absolute agony in her eyes.

But the worst of it all—when she'd cried at the hospital. Those terrible, gut-wrenching sobs.

Fuck this asshole.

Then a girl's cry ripped through my fury.

Frankie?

ARCHIE

Were they fucking kidding me? What was with all these assholes? The night had been going well. Now there were what, a dozen jocks here to deliver a beat down? Hope they weren't planning on winning. I'd dropped the bottles of water I'd been carrying the minute Jake launched forward. He'd gone after the guy who'd had a hold of Frankie, and Coop cut toward Bubba, even as he told me to get her.

No problem.

Getting Frankie the fuck out of here was at the top of my list. I cut across the yard, heading to where she struggled to pull the bag off her head. I had to narrowly avoid a couple of the fights. Jake wasn't holding back, and the sound of fists pounding flesh was a lot louder than the techno beat carrying from inside the house.

I just caught sight of her blonde hair as she tugged the bag off when a body slammed into mine. We went down, and I hit the grass with a painful explosion of air. I wasn't a football player. Didn't pretend any interest in sports beyond the casual. But I was no fucking lightweight. I twisted with the guy, rolling him over. Rising up, I slammed one fist into his face. One. Two. Three.

With a grunt, the guy went still and his eyes rolled back.

Pussy.

Snapping my head up, I stared at where Frankie was supposed to be.

She wasn't there.

I scanned the fighting. The only blonds I saw in motion were Bubba and Coop. Where the fuck…

There.

Oh.

I was already on my feet and striding in her direction as she caught a handful of Sharon's hair and yanked the other girl's head back. Any other time, a chick fight sounded like fun. Rumor had it that Frankie was no slouch in the fighting department. Coop and Jake were forever telling stories about it.

Then again, I hadn't really seen her in any fights, and I didn't want to see her in one right now. I could just toss Sharon on her ass and get Frankie the hell out of here.

The last thing I expected was Frankie cracking Sharon right across the face with her cast or Sharon's shriek of pain as she went down, blood spurting from her nose.

Another shadow loomed up behind her, and I was on the move. I yanked Frankie to me and away, just in time for the latest assailant to take a face full of pepper spray.

His shrieks were even louder and more high-pitched than Sharon's had been.

Rachel prowled forward, a can outstretched in her hand, and she scowled.

Arms around Frankie, I swept her from head to toe. "Are you all right?" I demanded.

"I'm fine," she muttered, more anger in her voice than fear. She glared to where Sharon rocked on the ground, clutching at her face. "Bitch tried to sucker punch me."

Was it any wonder that I loved her? A grin pulled at my mouth, then I glanced to where the guys were almost done taking out the trash.

Rachel stalked forward to stand next to us, just as red and blue flashing lights lit us all up.

"Well," she said. "This is a shit show."

That was one word for it, but Frankie was safe.

Right now, that was pretty much all I cared about.

Chapter Two
BLOODY KNUCKLES

FRANKIE

"You and your boyfriend were just talking when the others arrived?" It was the fourth time I'd been asked the same question.

"Yes," I told him flatly, arms folded together. We'd been outside long enough that I'd actually gotten chilled, and my arm was killing me. I couldn't see Ian or Jake anymore, since they were both placed into the back of police cars. Coop was standing near the police cars also being questioned. The whole area was lit up in flashing lights.

Mitch had been carted away by an ambulance. He wasn't the only one. The only saving grace? A cop had also gone with him. Sharon had also been loaded into an ambulance, crying hysterically.

I should have hit her harder.

"Are we done yet?" Rachel demanded. Archie was also being questioned, and they'd separated all of us. Rachel had managed to stick with me. Hell, I hadn't even had a chance to ask her where her girlfriend went. If nothing else, Corey Kaplan's party would go down in infamy, and I had zero doubt about whether we were all featured in posts online somewhere.

Dread curled in my stomach as the police officer who'd been questioning me focused on Rachel. His name was Talbot. Or at least, his last name was. He seemed nice. He also seemed vaguely familiar. Like he'd been one of the detectives who questioned me at the hospital. Some of that was blurry. He wasn't dressed in a blue uniform, but rather a button-down shirt and a jacket.

"Almost, Ms. Manning. I appreciate your patience. You don't need to stay here for the questioning. It's my understanding you've already been released." She'd also surrendered her pepper spray. Rachel had been the one to call the cops. I owed her for that. Big time.

She looped her arm around my shoulders and glared at the cop. Seriously? I wanted to elbow her. The last thing I needed was her getting arrested, too. My stomach was in knots. Archie had pulled out his phone and fired off two text messages before the cops had swarmed in, and he'd stuck with me until they made us separate for questions.

I'd barely gotten two words in with Ian or Jake, just a couple of long looks. They, along with a good half of the football team, had been cuffed almost immediately.

"Rach," I murmured. "Don't borrow trouble."

"I'm not borrowing trouble," she argued. "You're freezing. Your arm hurts. You were assaulted *again*, and you're being interrogated and asked the exact same set of questions over and over. Could you guys get together and share notes? I'm pretty sure you're not getting graded, so no one will fault you for copying each other's work."

I groaned. "I'm sorry," I managed to say, trying to get the detective focused back on me. "It's been a long night."

"I know," Talbot said. "Part of the reason I want to clear up these questions here is so I don't have to ask you to come down to the station. I think you've been through enough.”

Yeah, he was definitely one of the cops who'd come to the hospital. My stomach bottomed out. I wasn't sure whether I should be happy about that or not. “I appreciate that.”

“Hmmph. Well, let's get this over with,” Rachel said, and I bit back a sigh. She bumped me with her hip, then rubbed my back gently. “You're freezing.”

“I'll live.” All the adrenaline from the fight had drained out of me. The sudden terror. The panic. Then the anger. I was still pissed. When Sharon lunged at me in the middle of all that chaos, I'd locked on her as something I could do something about. My arm ached from the impact.

Worth it.

I'd definitely broken her nose.

She deserved a lot worse. I was so over her shit.

“Walk me through it,” Talbot said, and I just sucked it up and got on with it.

“Ian and I were talking. We were minding our own business, when Mitch and the guys walked up on us. Mitch said he'd been looking for us, and Ian got in front of me. The next thing I know, there's a bag over my head and someone is yanking me backwards over that railing.” My back still hurt from where I'd scraped over the wooden railing. “You know, before it got broken. Anyway, I was struggling against someone, and I could hear them hitting Ian. Then someone knocked the guy away from me, and I hit the ground pretty hard.”

Probably going to bruise from that impact, too. That just added a fresh log to the anger burning away in my gut.

“Um, I got the bag off my head, and there were fights everywhere—there were a lot of guys piling onto Ian. Coop and Jake were trying to help get them off. Then Sharon—she tried to hit me, ran at me from out of nowhere. I ended up hitting her with my cast, broke her nose.” I almost smirked, but I swallowed it back.

Rachel didn't bother. “Damn good hit.”

Yeah, I wasn't sure that was the help I needed at the moment, but I spared her a faint smile, and she grinned.

"She deserved it."

Hell yes, she had. "Anyway…then Archie was there trying to pull me out of it, 'cause another guy was running at me."

"Jimmy Trainer," Rachel supplied. "He didn't make it 'cause I pepper sprayed his happy ass and put him down. The last thing she needs is to get hit again." Pride resonated in her voice.

"Yeah you did." We shared another grin, then looked at Talbot who, while not smiling, did manage to look a bit amused. "Then the cops showed up and started arresting everyone, including Ian and Jake. They were the ones being assaulted and shouldn't have been arrested."

Raising his hands, Talbot said, "I understand that, but there was a lot of property damage and injuries. We're going to sort this all out. Is there anything else I need to know?"

"You mean like the fact that Mitch already assaulted her once, and you assholes haven't actually charged him with anything?" Rachel demanded. "He drugged her, broke her wrist, tried to rape her…"

"Rachel," I said, and she frowned, fiercely, but went quiet.

"That's an ongoing investigation, Ms. Manning," Talbot told her, but he gave me an apologetic look. "Did you feel threatened tonight?"

"Yes."

"Did he touch you in any way?"

"Tonight?" I shook my head. "Ian didn't let him get anywhere near me." I actually had no idea who dragged me off the porch. I was pretty sure he was one of the unconscious guys they'd loaded onto stretchers. No regrets there. I hope he hurt a lot when he woke up.

Asshole.

"Okay, but did you feel threatened by him?"

"He showed up and said he'd been looking for me and Ian specifically, and he was pissed. So yeah, I felt threatened." What a stupid question.

Talbot didn't comment on my sarcasm, he just made a few more notes, then said, "Do you feel you may have antagonized him in any way?"

Was he serious right now? "I haven't seen him since Homecoming." My gut churned. "But then again, I didn't antagonize him *that* night either."

He gave me a small smile. "I have to ask these questions, Ms. Curtis. I understand they're uncomfortable."

"Do you?" Rachel demanded, and I nudged her lightly with my elbow. I appreciated her defense, but I really didn't want this to take any longer than it already had.

"Actually, I do. Now it's my understanding you have a restraining order in place for Mr. Hooper." Hooper? Was that Mitch's last name? A part of me felt like I should know that, but I honestly didn't know him beyond the fact that he was on the football team with Ian and Jake.

"Um…probably? Mr. Wittaker was taking care of a lot of things for me." It sounded like something he would do.

"Can you give me his information?" Talbot's tone had changed to something far more solicitous. "If the restraining order is in place, then Mr. Hooper violated it tonight."

Well, whoop-de-doo. "Does that mean you'll do something about him?"

He sighed. "Ms. Curtis—can I call you Frankie?"

"Yeah, that's fine."

"Thank you, I'm Rick." He waited a beat, so I nodded to acknowledge what he'd said, and he continued, "I understand how difficult it is to think we're sitting on our hands and not doing anything. I wish investigations in real life were as fast as they are on television, but there's a process. We're going through the process. You've done everything right. You made your statements. You released your medical findings. You told us you wanted to press charges. These are all important steps. I know it's a lot to ask for your patience, but we do need it right now."

"And if he shows up again?" Because he'd done it once. Twice if you counted Homecoming. At this point, I never wanted to go to a party again. So far, they'd all sucked.

"We're going to work on that so he doesn't."

I sighed.

Movement beyond him had me shifting my weight. Archie was on his way straight toward me with Mr. Wittaker. Where was Coop?

"My lawyer is here."

"He is?" Talbot turned as Archie and Mr. Wittaker got there. Mr. Wittaker didn't waste any time introducing himself, shaking Talbot's hand, and drawing him away from me and Rachel.

Rachel let me go when Archie wrapped his arms around me. "You okay, babe?"

"No," I said. "I'm really fucking mad."

He grinned a little. "That's my girl. Hold onto that, 'cause it's going to be a long night."

That was what I was afraid of. "Did Coop get arrested too?"

"Detained. They're taking him to the precinct, too. There was blood on his clothes."

Rachel snorted. "Of course there was blood on his clothes. Did they not see the carnage out here?" Thankfully, she didn't shout the words, but Archie just shook his head.

"It's procedure. They probably won't be charged. All of it is self-defense. They're also going to have to get Bubba looked at. He had a lot of guys whaling on him."

My stomach bottomed out. Jake wasn't eighteen. They were probably going to call his mom. He'd gotten hauled down to the precinct a month ago. "We need to go get them."

"We're going to," Archie said. "I've got Jake's keys, so we're going to take his car. Mr. Wittaker is going to meet us there as soon as he takes care of the detective."

"I'm going to go get Skylar and take her home," Rachel said. "Then I'll meet you guys at the police station."

"Rach…"

"I want to," she told me. "Besides…you know the after party is always more fun than the party itself."

I snorted, then pulled away from Archie to give Rachel a hug. "You're a badass."

"Yes, I am," she agreed, squeezing me gently, but she didn't miss my wince. "And you need to get looked at, too."

Suddenly, Archie was in my space. "Did they hurt you?"

"Bruises." But I didn't really get to object as he hauled me toward the paramedics. I glared at Rachel, and she blew me a kiss.

Every once in a while, I remembered why we'd had a love-hate relationship for so long. I just stuck my tongue out at her before I flipped her off, and she finger-waved as she strolled back toward the house where Corey Kaplan was getting reamed out by his parents.

Yeah, this hadn't been a good night for anyone.

The paramedics made me go to the hospital. I wanted to kill Archie. I didn't want to go get x-rays, I wanted to check on the guys. But he was unmovable. I swore we had our first real relationship fight. Only we would save the argument for later, since I wasn't speaking to him right now.

Or at least I hadn't been, right up until he told me that Mr. Wittaker was going to the police station immediately. While we waited for a doctor to look at me, Archie took my left hand in his and examined the knuckles. I was already in a stupid hospital gown. No one even batted an eyelash about the Scarecrow bringing Dorothy into the E.R.

If anything, we were right at home with the other monsters, ghouls, and vampires. The guy who had to get a glass bottle removed from his rectum, however, was now permanently etched into my brain. Who did that?

"I'm sorry," Archie said quietly, and I frowned at him.

"You didn't do anything wrong." So much for a fight. "I know why you said we had to come here first." But I didn't think my ribs were cracked, even if my chest and back hurt. Archie said there were red scrapes along my back when he'd helped me out of the dress and into the gown. His voice had been clipped and angry.

Probably because I'd just gotten rid of some of my bruises and now I had new ones. Yay.

"Not for that," he told me, almost patient as he gave me a long look. "I'm sorry that the party went to hell. We took you out to have fun."

"That wasn't your fault either." They weren't responsible for Mitch.

"Still…"

"Archie, it wasn't your fault, or Ian's or Jake's or Coop's. We didn't do anything wrong. They are the assholes."

"Well, on that we can agree."

My phone buzzed. Rachel had been texting us. She'd gotten to the police station and kept us up to date. She hadn't been able to talk to the guys, but she could see them. So far, they weren't in handcuffs and they were talking to different officers. A medic had also seen Ian. The picture she sent through didn't make me feel better.

Half of his face was bruises. It looked a thousand percent worse than when he and Jake had beaten the crap out of each other.

I was sick to my stomach thinking about it. Coop had a few bruises, an ugly one on his jaw, and Jake's hands were a wreck. He also looked *pissed*. I really didn't envy anyone who had to talk to him. I just wish I was there.

"Wittaker's there," Archie reminded me.

"I know. I just wish the doctor would hurry up and tell me I'm fine so we can go be there for them."

Rubbing his thumb in gentle circles against the back of my hand, Archie said, "How are you feeling?"

Bruised. Battered. Angry. Sick. "Fine," I lied, and he gave me a look. "Well, if you're not going to believe me, why ask?"

He snorted, a grin pulling at the corners of his mouth. "Because it's how I can measure how you feel. When you lie to me, I know you hurt but it's not terrible. When you tell me you really feel bad, I definitely worry."

I didn't laugh.

Well, mostly.

Archie slid an arm around me and pressed his forehead to mine. "I'm just glad you're alright, babe. Glad we got there."

"Me, too." For me. For Ian.

For all of us.

There wasn't much more to say as we waited and got the blow by blows from Rachel.

It took hours, but they finally discharged me with the advice to take my pain meds, because I was going to hurt more in the long run. It didn't look like I'd done further damage to my wrist, but the doctor was worried about my shoulder and my hip. They'd taken the brunt of the fall, and he warned me that they were going to be stiff.

He also wanted me to check in with my regular doctor. Yeah, I'd get right on that. The worst part of how long it took to get done at the E.R. was I had time to see Sharon *and* her parents. Sharon was furious and sobbing. She made up a bullshit story about how she got hurt, right up until she saw me. Archie pulled me away rather than say anything. I saw a couple of the other guys who'd been with Mitch, too. Thankfully, I didn't see Mitch.

Back in Jake's car, I sank back against the seat and stared at the clock. It was the middle of the night. It wouldn't be long before dawn. The guys were still at the police station. Coop had been 'released' thankfully. He hadn't left, instead, he had joined Rachel in texting us updates. They were also sniping at each other over text while sitting next to each other.

I rolled my eyes but let it go. I just wanted to know they were all okay.

Archie diverted to grab fast food, including about four-dozen tacos and burritos—I forbid bean, because I was not having all four of them in my room after eating bean burritos. I adored them, but I'd known them too long. We were not having fart wars.

Ever.

Ugh.

"You know, you used to be more fun," Archie teased.

"I also didn't used to be your girlfriend."

"So, girlfriend means no more farting around you."

I snorted. "That would take a miracle. I'll just be happy if you don't bomb me out of my own bedroom."

He laughed his ass off, but the bean burritos were off the menu for the night. After he'd packed in all the food, along with some desserts and five drinks, we continued on to the police station. He also made me eat something in the parking lot before he'd let me get out of the car. The reason why became rapidly apparent when he nudged me to take a pain med.

"I'll wait."

I didn't want to fall asleep on them, even if I moved with more stiffness after sitting in the car for so long.

"Take a half."

"Oh my god, will you stop being so bossy!"

"No," he said flatly. "You got hurt. Again. You're hurting now. I want to take care of you. You're going to let me do it. If you don't think all three of them wouldn't agree with me…"

I held up a hand. No, I would never dream of that. "A half."

He nodded and snapped one in half for me. I stuffed down another taco, then took the half with a long drink of soda. Hopefully, the caffeine and sugar would help. As soon as I'd taken it, Archie turned all solicitous again, and I felt a little bit like an asshole.

"Sorry I'm so grumpy."

"It's okay," he murmured, pressing another kiss to my cheek as we walked toward the building. "I know you love me."

I chuckled.

"And I'm your favorite," he added the last bit with a sly wink before pulling open the door.

Coop was already on his feet, and he crushed me to him as soon as I got there. Half the paint on his face had been wiped away, but he looked rumpled, bruised, and angry. At least, he did until he cupped my face and searched my eyes. "You're really okay?"

"Promise, just bruises. I have to call the other doc, but that can wait. Archie just made me take a pain med, and there are tacos in the car."

"You're the best."

"Ahem," Archie said. "The tacos were my idea."

"Yeah, but Frankie is still the best."

"Agreed."

Rachel made a gagging noise, and I laughed at her. It hurt but it was funny. We all took a seat and kept waiting. I couldn't see Ian or Jake, but Coop insisted Wittaker was in with them. Ian's parents had arrived. I winced at that announcement. Jake's mom was there, too.

I really didn't want this night to get any worse.

I ended up walking back out to the car with Coop and Rachel so they could have some food. I split my soda with her because we hadn't gotten her a drink. We sucked. She didn't care. Coop suggested I go home, but I shot that shit right down, even when Rachel offered to drive me.

Until Jake and Ian were out, I wasn't going anywhere.

It was almost six when Alicia emerged from the back with Jake. They both looked weary. Worse, Jake's bruises had definitely mottled his face and his knuckles were raw. But the smile on his face chased my own exhaustion away. He scooped me up carefully for a hug, and Alicia gave me a tired smile.

"I was going to ask if he wanted a ride home, but I'm guessing he's heading to your place." Guilt stabbed at me, but she just gave me a gentle hug, then studied me. "You're all right, yes?"

"Just bruises," I assured her, but Jake kept an arm around me, and I studied him. "Are you okay?"

"Just bruises," he told me with a wry smile. "Looks a lot worse than it is. Sorry you got dragged down here again, Mom."

"I know," she said. "I'm proud of you. All of you boys," she added glancing past me to where Coop and Archie waited. "You did good. Just—let's not make the police station a habit? We don't need to host reunions here." She gave Jake a hug, then me, whispering, "You should come over to dinner with the girls. Let's make that happen."

I didn't really know how to respond to that, so I just gave her a smile. After she left, Jake wrapped me in another hug, careful as hell. "You're really okay?"

"Tired," I admitted. The half pill hadn't knocked me out. If anything, it had just relaxed me. Archie kept shooting me looks, especially after Rachel commented it was probably because I was hurting a lot more than I was letting on.

Yeah, didn't need that added to the plate. She just smirked at me. Rachel was never going to change. She was blunt to the point of painful, but she was also still here, waiting for the guys to get out, and she hadn't hesitated to jump into the fight. Though of all of us, she had zero bruises.

And I was really glad about that.

"Worried about you guys."

"No charges," Jake told me. "They really just wanted to ask a lot of questions, and Wittaker sat in with me and made them wait to ask Bubba anything until he could sit there, too. Bubba's parents are here."

"Are they pissed?"

Jake gave a little shrug as he moved us back over to the chairs and settled with me between him and Coop. "They aren't thrilled," he said. "But I think they are more concerned than anything else. They wanted to know why Mitch was running around instead of sitting his ass in jail where he belongs. Which is a damn good question."

When that earned Archie's and Coop's equally vehement opinions, I tuned it out a little. Talbot had tried to explain it to me. I wanted to understand, but I didn't. He'd attacked me twice now. Granted, he didn't lay a finger on me this time, and I could at least remember all of it, but still… Did we have to wait until he did something even more horrible for them to do something about it?

The cats were gonna kill me when we finally got home, whenever that was. At some point, Archie brought in the food and Jake ate his way through a half-dozen of the tacos, but we were still waiting. My eyes had begun to drift shut when the doors opened, allowing Mr. Wittaker, along with Ian and his parents out into the lobby.

Ian looked like hell, but Mr. Wittaker looked pleased. We were all standing, and I made a beeline straight for Ian, hesitating only because of the bruises on his face and the fact that his parents were right there. "Are you okay?"

"I'm fine, Angel," Ian told me and held out an arm. I didn't need any more encouragement, I wrapped myself around him carefully. "No charges," he murmured. "Just a long night."

I damn near sagged with relief.

"You okay?"

"Just bruises." It was becoming our motto, and he rubbed his uninjured cheek against my hair. "Tired, too."

"And we need to get her home," Archie said. "I think we need to get everyone home."

Ian glanced at his parents, and I flushed when his mom eased over to give us both a hug. "You want to go with Frankie?" she asked, and I didn't dare look at his dad.

"Yeah," Ian said. "Thanks for coming down."

"Of course," she murmured, then swept her gaze over me. "If it's too much, you two come back to the house and I'll look after both of you, okay?"

I was pretty sure my face was on fire, but Ian saved me by saying, "We got it, Mom. Thank you."

"Love you," she said, and he answered her with another hug. Then Ian's dad clasped his shoulder gently.

"You kids take care," he said. "Get some rest. We'll get this all sorted."

The relief that he looked at us with kindness rather than reproach was profound. Thankfully, everyone started moving and we shuffled out of the building. It was like all the tiredness of the last twenty-four hours crashed in on me. Rachel gave me a quick hug in the parking lot and headed for her car as she waved off my thanks.

Then we were climbing into Jake's SUV. I sat in the back, sandwiched between Coop and Ian, while Archie took care of the driving. Jake didn't even complain.

I was half-asleep before we were even out of the parking lot, my head on Ian's shoulder and my left hand clasped in Coop's. They were all okay.

Bruised. Battered. Tired.

But okay.

When Ian brushed his lips against my forehead, I smiled. "Don't forget," I reminded him sleepily. "Rules. I get to help make them, too."

"Yes, you do," he said. "I promise. I didn't forget."

There was a beat of quiet in the car, and then Coop said, "Yeah?"

I couldn't get my eyes open to see what he was talking about, but Ian said. "Yeah."

"Thank fuck," Jake muttered from the front seat, and Archie chuckled.

"What?" Ian asked.

"You are now subject to the same boyfriend rules as the rest of us."

"What are the rules?" Coop asked, the tired in his voice dragging at me.

"Well at the moment, it starts and ends with boyfriends don't get bean burritos and we don't get to have fart wars."

There was a beat of silence.

Then all four of them cracked up.

Asses.

Each and every one.

Chapter Three

THE TRICK IS TO KEEP BREATHING

Once we got back to my place, we stripped and showered—everyone one at a time except for me. Archie helped me because he was the least battered of all of us. His argument, not mine. His right hand was definitely bruised, and the knuckles had split in two places. He dismissed the concern, however, and the guys all sided with him.

After, he insisted I take another pain pill, not a half this time, but a full. I didn't even bother to argue against it. I was kind of hurting everywhere. Jake and Ian got the bed with me, and I wanted Coop to at least take the sofa, but he just gave me a smirk as he settled onto his pallet on the floor.

"Bigger bed," Archie told me. "That's on the list this weekend."

I groaned but nodded. At this point, we needed to do a lot of things.

Jake and Ian both had ice packs on, and I was torn between looking at one or the other. When Ian let out a little hiss as he laid down, I studied the bruises forming on his chest. More than one fist had struck him, and I was pretty sure there was a kick mark or two in there.

"Stop worrying," Ian insisted with a slow exhale. "Cracked ribs are not fun, but there's nothing I can do for them."

I winced. "You're sure they're only cracked?" My irritated cats had all been fed, and they'd already settled in different spots around the room. I tried to roll onto my side. The stupid cast made that tricky. Jake caught my hip gently and turned me until my back pressed against his chest and I could face Ian more easily.

"Mom checked, Angel," Ian promised me, pressing a finger to my lips when I opened them to argue. "She checked. The medic checked. They're cracked. They're sore. I'll live. I'd take every damn one again if it meant I got between those bastards and you."

My heart squeezed, then I slid my hand over his and kissed his fingers. He tangled our fingers together and smiled.

"Now go to sleep. The bruises under your eyes have bruises."

"Are you saying I need my beauty sleep?" The tease came a little more easily, so many of the hastily erected stones in the wall between us crumbling away. Even if he'd been there, I'd missed this. The ease of talking to him, of playing, and not worrying if I was saying the wrong thing. Worse, if I was scared to say something because it still hurt.

"Nah, you're gorgeous," he said, his one open eye twinkling. "Jake, on the other hand…" He just sighed.

"Not enough sleep in the world to make him beautiful," Coop said in a half-asleep voice. Jake shifted next to me and there was a thump. "Ow." Coop deadpanned. Then chuckled. "My pillow now."

"Keep it," Jake muttered and tucked his face against me. "I'm sharing Frankie's."

I smiled, and Ian gave my fingers a squeeze, though his smile looked more like a grimace. His poor face. "Stop," he whispered. "Go to sleep. I'll be fine."

Even closing my eyes, I remained aware of them. Aware of Jake's hand on my hip, the soft brush of his breathing evening out, the steady thump of Ian's heart under my hand where he tucked my palm against his chest, the gentle snore from Archie, he'd dropped off so fast and likely deep, and Coop's half-muttered groan that told me he was stretching before he settled into quiet.

I was aware of all of them.

No way I would go to sleep, despite how tired I was. I didn't want to miss a moment of this. Miss them.

It wasn't until I opened gritty eyes hours later to a room dappled half in shadow because the blinds were still closed that I even realized I had gone to sleep.

The room was quiet, I lay there for a moment, trying to get my bearings. I needed to pee in the worst way. Even my teeth ached. The bed behind me was empty. Jake had to have gotten up. Ian was still asleep in front of me. His poor face was really black and blue. Puffy and tender looking. It made my heart ache.

I should get up and get him another ice pack. Maybe offer him one of my pain meds. He wasn't sleeping facing me anymore, but lying on his back. I eased upward, trying not to jostle him.

The pallets on the floor were both folded up, the blankets and pillows stacked in the corner. Even the cats were absent. I bit my lip as I glanced back down at Ian. It looked so much worse than it had the night before.

Fuck Mitch and his friends.

With care, I bent down and brushed my lips to his forehead. My bladder protested, and I forced myself to slide out of the bed. Oh, my back let me know it hated me. So did my hip. My shoulder apparently joined the Frankie sucks club, because it throbbed a little with each halting step I took. Fuck, I was walking like I was eighty not almost eighteen.

Stiff didn't begin to cover it.

The door wasn't all the way closed, so I just eased it open and headed for the bathroom. The apartment was pretty quiet. There was every chance the guys had to go home and deal with things. It took me a minute, but I'd gotten good at going to the bathroom with only one hand to pull my panties down and up—

thank God. I never wanted to have to ask the guys for help on that one again.

No thank you.

After, I brushed my teeth and pulled a comb through my hair. My eyes still had bruises, and I looked like slightly warmed-over crap.

Ugh.

I checked the living room, but it was empty save for the cats. Tiddles looked up from his perch on the sofa, but he went back to staring out the windows and I left him to it. There was a note on the fridge.

Went for food and errands. We'll be back soon.

Okay, so I wasn't wrong. I grabbed a glass and filled it with water. I was hungry and there weren't any leftover tacos. The guys had probably decimated anything left and I didn't feel like fixing anything, so I just headed back to the bedroom.

Maybe I should do homework or text the guys or something, but three things hit me on the way there. One, I was still really freaking tired and I hurt. Two, I had zero idea where my phone was. I probably left it in Jake's SUV. Third, and most important, Ian was still in my bed.

It wasn't until I set the glass of water on the nightstand and eased back into the bed that I realized Ian's eye was open. One eye, the other was mostly swollen shut. I winced, and he reached out a hand to me as I slid back down to the pillows, shifting to shove one under my right wrist before rolling onto his side with a wince of his own. I stared up at him and frowned as I touched two fingers to the puffiness on his cheek.

"I should have gotten you ice."

"I can get it in a minute," he told me. "I'd rather have you here."

A smile pulled at my lips. "I'm glad you're here, too."

"Yeah?"

I nodded slowly.

He glanced from me to the room then back. "Where are the guys?"

"Errands. Food. Note on the fridge said they'd be back." There hadn't been an actual time on the note, and I was pretty sure it was almost five, based on what the clock on the stove said. "I don't know when they left."

"Jake went home at noon," Ian told me, his deep, melodic voice soothing. "He said he'd be back, but he wanted to make sure he and his mom were okay. She didn't give him any kind of hell for the fight."

Relief swarmed through me.

"Don't know about Arch or Coop, they were both asleep when Jake left."

I nodded. We hadn't gone to sleep until after eight in the morning. I couldn't remember the last time I slept most of the day.

"What about you?" I asked.

"What about me?" He tried to lift his eyebrows, then winced, and I cupped his bruised face gently. He leaned into my palm. "Your hand is cold. That feels good."

I chuckled. "Usually it's my feet."

"No, your feet are usually blocks of ice, but your hands vary some. Right now, cool feels good."

That was something. "You said Jake wanted to check in with his mom. I was asking about your parents. They didn't seem mad but…are they really okay with…?"

"Me getting into a fight with a bunch of bullies who wanted to hurt you?"

They'd wanted to hurt him, too, but I just nodded.

"They're fine. Dad usually gives me his try to talk people down speech or at least try a diplomatic approach first. He didn't bother. Not after he heard my full statement." Ian rubbed his bruised cheek against my palm as he gave me a wry grin. "Mom was a little more bloodthirsty, she asked me if I kicked their asses."

It was hard to picture Sara asking that question or even being bloodthirsty. She was a nurse. Still… "I think the answer to that is yes."

"Yeah," he said. "So, they're good with me. Not thrilled I had to be questioned, but right now, I'm not facing any charges and they say it looks pretty clearly like self-defense. There are more people to be questioned. Archie's attorney is pretty great."

"I like 'im," I admitted. "He's done really right by me. Did you know he got a restraining order for Mitch?"

"Nope, but glad to hear it. He violated it."

I sighed.

"Angel, you need one of your pain meds?"

I shook my head. "No, well…probably yes. But I haven't eaten, and I don't really want to take one right now."

He frowned, then winced. That had to suck. Those bruises would get worse before they got better.

"Ice." He opened his mouth, but I shook my head and pointed at him. "Ice. You're hurting, and those are swelling."

"Stay here?" The question melted me. "I want… I like talking to you like this."

"I promise. I'll be right here when you get back."

The heartbreaking smile on his face had me curling my toes under the blanket. With care, he pressed a kiss to the corner of my mouth. It was a blink and you miss it kiss, and then he sat up with a hell of a lot more ease than I had. "I'm holding you to that."

He glanced back at me before he disappeared up the hall. A little thrill went through me. The shift between us had become tangible. It was different from before, deeper somehow. I couldn't really put my finger on it. He wasn't gone long, but he'd made a stop in the bathroom on his way to the kitchen. He came back with his own glass of water, a couple of sodas, and a package of Pop-Tarts.

I was surprised. I didn't think I had any left.

"I hid these," he told me as he settled back on the bed, and I squirmed to sit up next to him. "Tucked them up with the tea. Figured the guys would never look there."

I snickered. Because, he wasn't wrong. He popped open the sodas and offered me one. I took a sip and set it on the nightstand next to my water before facing him again. He got the foil open and passed one of the strawberry frosted ones to me, and I took a bite, grinning at him as he took his own. When I nodded to the ice pack, he didn't quite roll his eyes, but he did lift it up to his face, and I nodded.

"Better."

"Okay, now that we're done fussing over my face, can we talk?"

"I thought we were talking," I teased before taking another bite.

He snorted. "Angel…"

"I'm right here."

"Yes, you are."

I sighed. All things aside—beatings, nightmares, Mitch, the cops, therapy—I was feeling pretty good right now. "You said you'd do anything for me." I enunciated each word carefully. We'd been talking before everything went to hell, he agreed to the rules, to a night of dancing and even to karaoke—though admittedly, Ian singing was no hardship for either of us.

"I did. I know I have a lot of ground to make up with you, but I meant it when I said I'm in. I want to go out with you, buy you flowers, spend time with you, whether it's in the studio doing vocal work or on the bike when you're healed up. I want *you*."

Heat swept through me.

"When I told you I'd do anything for you, you were about to say something when that asshole showed up."

I had.

He stared at me intently. "Tell me what you were going to say?"

"It seems kind of awkward now." I stuffed another bite of Pop-Tart in my mouth to buy myself some time. During his confession, I'd wanted to believe him so badly. But I was scared. I hated that feeling of uncertainty and fear that it would all just blow up again. It really fucking hurt the first time, and it had been so damn hard to try and stay friends.

I really didn't want to lose him.

"Nothing you say to me is going to be that awkward, I promise."

I snorted. Then, you know what, fuck it. "I believe you, but the thing is… you said everything you've written lately has been inspired by me."

He nodded, watching me closely. Unlike me, he wasn't eating his food, he wasn't doing anything—just studying me. "It has been."

"You gave me that song."

"I did."

I swallowed, 'cause this was the awkward part and it really sucked that I had to tell him this. "I've been too chicken to listen to it."

"Okay."

That was it. Just okay? I focused on him again. "You're not mad?"

"C'mon, Angel. I recorded that for you as a gift…and maybe a bit like a personal plea. Would I have preferred you listen to it? Sure, but…you're listening to me now."

He shifted and put his Pop-Tart away and got another drink, and I took a bite as I turned that over in my head. Then he faced me again with his phone in his hand.

"And I can play it for you, if you want to hear it."

I did.

But what did it say about me that my stomach bottomed out at the offer? Even as the butterflies in my gut started beating their wings at supersonic speeds.

Fuck being afraid of it.

"Yes, please." Course the crumbs escaping when I spoke had me clapping a hand over my mouth as Ian chuckled. His eye softened, and his other eye opened a little wider. The ice was definitely helping, but it wasn't working a miracle. He was going to need more than just that. Easing closer to me, he lifted his arm and eyed me. "This okay?"

It took me a beat, more because I was kind of embarrassed about spitting out food than I was anything else, but I leaned forward and he wrapped his arm around my shoulders. Mindful of my new bruises, he curled me back against him, and I sighed as I settled in. He found the list of songs on his phone and then cued up the one he sent me.

The title got me.

Keep Breathing.

The opening bars of the music strum beautifully on the guitar. Having been to the studio, I had to wonder if he recorded it there, because there was a second base line just below the guitar, like he was playing both parts and laid the tracks down together. It was a sweet invitational, almost folksy in the way it beckoned a person to sit down and listen.

Gradually though, it gave way to something deeper and almost haunting. Then his vocals came through like liquid gold, his voice deep and mesmerizing. Those haunting melodies turned almost enchanting with the song he wove about waking every day a little bit darker, like the light was gone. It would be almost too much, except the light wasn't a person, it was what that person did for him.

She saw the light in him and encouraged it.

She.

Me.

I was the one who encouraged his music and loved to listen to him. Now that he was alone with the notes, they were the only thing he had to remind him of what she'd seen in him. The song took me on a journey, but at the heart of it, was the fact that I'd broken up with him.

Tears burned in my eyes as he admitted it was his own fault, but he wanted the light back. He wanted me to believe in him again. He wasn't perfect. He might never be. But he would be the best he could, if it would get him a second chance. Until then, he'd just keep breathing.

I had to suck on my upper lip to keep the tears from falling. It was beautiful.

Oh, I didn't know if I could have handled listening to this before when he'd given it to me. It about broke my heart now, and I'd already said yes to that second chance, maybe not in those exact words but…

The song ended, and I sniffed. My throat ached as I swallowed around the lump and then looked up at him.

"Yes," I said before I could overthink it or he said anything else. He clicked the screen off on the phone and dropped it into his lap. "Yes, I'll give you a second chance, if you give me one."

He closed his eyes, and a whole body shudder rocked him. I didn't know if he curled me up to him or if I tugged him down, but he kissed me. His lips were as warm and firm as I remembered, even if one corner of his mouth was still a little swollen.

When he winced, I started to pull away. "I don't want to hurt you."

"Fuck that," he whispered. "Hurt away." Then he clamped his mouth down on mine far more firmly as he slid his battered fingers around my nape. I shifted and clung to him. It took some maneuvering, and we were both wincing.

"Ow," I said as I managed to half straddle his lap. My Pop-Tart ended up somewhere. I'd find it later. He grimaced as he adjusted me, and my cast landed on his battered shoulder. "Sorry."

Chuckling, he kissed the tip of my chin. "I'm not." Then he kissed me again, slow and lingering. It was like our first kiss in the pool, without the sun and the damp but with the addition of the bruises and the cuts. Laughter swelled through me as he groaned, and I wanted to nip his lower lip, but I didn't dare. He gripped at my hip, and I let out a hiss of breath, so he slid his hand up my side.

When he sucked against my tongue, I hummed a little happy note, and he dragged his other hand up into my hair. With care, he angled my head so he could deepen the kiss, and I dug the fingers of my left hand into his chest. Another pained groan escaped him, and I pulled back. "Sorry."

"I'm not," he repeated in between little huffs of laughter. I met his gaze, and we both cracked up. "This is not how I imagined kissing you again."

"No," I told him. "I didn't dare imagine it. Even when I wanted to." A little part of me felt like a hypocrite. I'd missed the hell out of him. Missed being close and having the right to kiss him or to hold him and just be. But I hadn't been alone.

"Whatever you're thinking," he said in a throaty voice. "Stop."

"I just—"

"Stop." Then he tipped my chin up. "I mean it. I missed this. I missed you."

"Even though you were right there," I agreed with him. "I missed you, too."

He sighed and then rested his forehead against mine. "No more missing each other."

A lopsided grin stole across my face, even as I fought to suppress it. "Kind of hard to miss you when I'm sitting in your lap."

The slow grin curling the corners of his mouth had me shivering. That, and the erection very quickly firming beneath my ass. If I wasn't so damn sore and achy and he wasn't so bruised, I'd be tempted to tease him a little. As it was, it seemed like a very nice promise for the future.

"Hurting?" he checked.

"A little." As much as I was loath to admit it. "You?"

"Yeah, a little." He dipped his gaze to my lips, even as he combed his fingers through my hair. "We could just sit here and rest."

"You do need to ice your face." The ice pack was currently somewhere on the bed, probably hanging out with my abandoned Pop-Tart.

"Absolutely," he agreed, then ran his tongue over his lower lip. "You should be elevating that arm and eating something so you can take some pain meds."

"Probably, though…" I traced a finger against the collar of the t-shirt he wore. "The guys are bringing back food."

"True."

We considered each other. "They could be back any minute." It was heading right in to evening.

"Could be hours," Ian countered.

"Could be," I leaned in and pressed a kiss to the uninjured corner of his mouth. His lips twitched. "Does this hurt?"

"No."

Another kiss. "What about here?"

"No."

"Here?"

"No."

I grinned and nuzzled his jaw. "This looks like it's a safe spot." I worked my way to his ear, but he tugged my hair and I leaned back, only to have him swoop down and kiss me, all lips and tongue. A groan vibrated from one of us.

Maybe both.

When he let me up for air, I said, "We could just make out until they get home."

One moment, I was on his lap, and the next, he had me lying down and stretched out next to me. "This okay?"

I slid a thigh up so he could settle more firmly against me. He stuffed a couple of the pillows so they were supporting us better, then we fixed on each other.

"This is perfect," I sighed before he kissed me again. He strained against me, and I winced, scraping his lower lip with my teeth.

"Ow," we said in unison, and then his laughter chased mine as he kissed me again.

Perfect.

Chapter Four
POCKETFUL OF SUNSHINE

Monday arrived way too soon, and I don't think any of us were ready to go to school. I wanted to insist Ian and Jake stay out and rest, but they both just gave me a kiss and headed out for practice, bruises and all. At least Ian's other eye was open now.

"Don't worry," Coop said as they walked out the door. "The other guys look way worse."

Archie groaned. "Fuck the other guys."

I wrinkled my nose. "No thank you."

They both glared at me, and I stuck my tongue out at them before I limped my way to the bathroom to finish getting ready. My hip and shoulder hated me way more today than they had the evening before. Somehow, we'd managed to have a really good evening, and I got a solid hour of just making out with Ian. Thankfully, whatever ration of crap the guys might have given us, they saved for when I was out of earshot. Or maybe they were as relieved as I was.

For the first time in what seemed like weeks, it felt right. Bumps and bruises aside. I'd slept without a single nightmare.

Who knew that breaking Sharon's nose could be therapeutic?

When I made the mistake of mentioning it aloud, laughter followed me along with Jake promising that if I wanted to keep belting people, he wanted to make sure I had the right technique. Coop rolled his eyes and insisted I knew exactly what I was doing. I didn't need any lessons, even if Ian looked thoughtful and Archie suggested a bodyguard. That launched Ian and Jake both into insisting they would be more than happy to guard my body.

It was kind of adorable.

The cherry was when Rachel texted me that a new Torched single had been released. I paused long enough to download it. In the car, Archie synced my phone up to let it play, and I was singing along with it before we hit the first chorus. It was a cover, but Torched did that. They covered a couple of popular songs to tease a new album, then the album would drop and I almost always loved every single song on it.

The girl group had a great rhythm, and I loved their melodies. Even more, I loved their lead singer because she had my kind of voice. Sometimes raspy. Sometimes not. I could dream of having her range.

"We should check their tour schedule," Archie said as the song looped to play again and he nudged the volume down a little.

"The last time they were near here, the tickets were astronomical." I'd been desperate to go. They'd actually been on tour over the summer. I sighed.

"So?" he said. "You love them, and it would be a blast."

I chuckled. "It would be amazing, but they've already been here. They're probably in Europe. The new album is gonna drop right around Christmas." At least, that was the rumor. Torched never advertised when they planned their releases. They just dropped them.

Like this morning's cover.

"So, we'll check it out. Who else do you want to see?" Archie eyed me as we pulled into the parking lot.

"Uh uh," I told him with a shake of my head.

"Aww…c'mon, you can tell me. I know Broadway is on that list somewhere. Top three shows you want to see."

"Nope." I mimed zipping my lips. "You're already spending a fortune on me."

He grunted as he pulled into his parking spot. "I have no problems with a challenge."

I snorted. That was one way of putting it.

"Hey," he said as he released my seatbelt. I bit my lip as he leaned in close. "You good?"

"Yeah," I told him. The concern wrapped in affection in his eyes made me want to tell him anything he wanted to know.

"Good," he whispered. "Before we're officially out of the car and on school property though…" He nuzzled a kiss to the corner of my lips, cupping my face with one hand and then deepening it slowly as he teased my tongue with his. It was enough to leave me panting and overheated. Nose still brushing mine, he whispered, "You like dance shows, too, right?" The soft whisper made me laugh.

"You think you can just kiss the answers out of me?"

"Maybe," he said with a grin. "Sure is fun to try."

A knock on the passenger window made me jump, and he scowled over my shoulder.

"To be continued," he said as he leaned back, and I glanced over to find Rachel grinning like the cat who caught the mouse and the canary. She wiggled her eyebrows at me, and I groaned.

"Morning, Rach," I greeted her as I stepped out.

"Morning, hot lips," she grinned. "PDAs back on the menu?"

"No," Archie scolded. "Leave her alone."

"Pfft," she grinned and flicked her fingers at him before looping her arm through my left. "So," she continued as we headed toward the school. Coop was already loping toward us from where he'd parked. "Mitch was officially arrested and charged over the weekend *after* he woke up in the hospital. He also has a broken arm to go with his broken jaw."

I didn't gape, but holy shit.

"Also…" She paused for dramatic effect, as though waiting for Coop to catch up to us before continuing. "He's been expelled. There was an emergency meeting yesterday. Half of the football team is on probation and suspended, but Mitch was expelled, and it looks like Cheryl will be too." The last part was offered with a grimace. "Sorry about not realizing how truly cracked she was."

"It's okay," I told her. My stomach churned at the news. Not because they'd been expelled, but because the relief was so profound. "I didn't know either, I just thought she was a little too ditzy." Which had always seemed dramatically unfair on my part. Looking back, it made me view every interaction we had differently.

And far creepier.

"Still, I like to trust my instincts. She totally bypassed them. Going to have to rethink everything." Rachel shook her head. Neither Coop nor Archie said a word about it, even to tease her, and that was a relief. She didn't deserve to catch hell for it, even if she could be epically hard on them.

Not over Cheryl.

That betrayal stung.

I squeezed her arm sympathetically.

"Anyway," she emphasized the syllables. "There's more."

"Oh God, I don't know if I want to hear more." We were inside and on our way to the cafeteria. More than one student glanced our way, speculation in their eyes. Yeah, I didn't need to know what that was about. I hadn't looked at any social media at all. I had no idea what they were saying about the party or the fight or any of it.

"Drumroll please… Jackson rolled on Mitch and Cheryl, among others, and they were behind condom car."

I stopped walking and stared at her. "For real?"

"Yep," she said with a grimace. "It was their way of letting you know they wanted to run a train. Disgusting pervs."

Coop and Archie's expressions chilled.

I didn't think it was possible to loath Mitch more.

I was wrong. I fucking hated what they'd done to my car. How it made me feel.

"It kicks the assault charges up and adds menacing and vandalism to it, so maybe they'll throw the whole book at him." Snarky tone or not, Rachel's expression was nothing but sympathetic for me. "They're gone. You don't have to see them again."

Unless I had to testify, but I'd rather not bring that up at the moment.

"Last, but really not least, the football season here is officially over. All the rest of the games have been forfeited."

Oh. Shit. My stomach dropped.

Ian and Jake had gone to practice this morning, and they hadn't texted yet. While they'd already discussed being good with the season being over, I hated the thought of what they might be missing out on.

"That's pretty much the rumor. I figure it will be announced later today after they inform the remaining players," Rachel continued while I got lost in my thoughts. We'd made it to the cafeteria, and the gazes turning in our direction were numerous. Coop slid up beside me while Archie fell in on Rachel's other side.

It was kind of sweet.

Ian and Jake were already at our table.

"And on that note, I will leave you with the boys. You good for today?" Rachel said, thankfully in a far quieter and less abrasive voice.

"You don't have to take off." I didn't want her to think she wasn't welcome.

"It's good. I actually need to go do a make up test, so I'm going to get that out of the way. I'll see you in French." She winked.

Archie handed her a coffee before she could leave and she stared at it a beat then smirked slowly. "This does not make us friends, Rich Boy."

"I wouldn't dream of it," he drawled.

"Good." She took a sip, then nodded. "Thanks."

"You're welcome."

With a chuckle, she strolled off, coffee in hand.

And it didn't even kill them to be polite. Coop snickered as he dragged out a chair for me. Sitting, I glanced between Ian and Jake. "How bad is it?"

"Eh," Jake told me with a shrug. "No more crack of dawn practices."

"No more staying late Wednesday and Thursday," Ian added.

"And no more games on Friday," Jake said as he toasted us with his cup. "I for one am fucking relieved."

I wasn't the only one who looked at Ian, but he scooted his chair a little closer to mine as he said, "Ditto. More time to hang out with you and work on my music. Coach was right, half the team is gone, and those of us left weren't really feeling the love. He's going to start tryouts for next year early, keep the junior and sophomore players in the rotation, and let them figure out how to be a team before they have to work together."

"I'm sorry," I told him.

"It's fine, Angel. Really. I used to think this was all I wanted to do, but priorities change."

"Well, here's to everyone having their Friday nights back," Archie said, kicking back in the chair. "It's still mine though with Frankie, so let's not get ahead of ourselves."

They all laughed.

"Speaking of which," Coop said. "We are seriously behind in our gaming schedule. With the new free time, we can set up a game night."

That turned into a debate on what game to play, which inevitably led to shit-talking each other over who was better. It was…nice. Normal. Despite the sudden cessation of football, Jake and Ian were both relaxed. Ian's leg rested against mine, and he kept shooting me these glances with a hint of a smile pulling at his mouth.

I got Coop to dig out one of my books for lit so I could read, because I was firmly neutral on what level of chaos they were going to get to in their gaming war. I was also out of it with my wrist still broken and a cast on. Archie kept one-upping Jake, who in turn issued flat challenges to Coop and Ian, both of whom retaliated in kind.

The good mood buoyed me through the day. Even if I was definitely hurting by lunchtime, I'd had fun in government with Archie making a list of bands and performances where I could see it, then studying me as he added each name. Trying to keep my face neutral became a true challenge, especially since he was cracking me up.

Ian helped with everything in math, including taking notes to share with me. When the teacher hit us with a quiz, he made a face. Fortunately, she gave me a pass on taking this one since my grades were high, but that wouldn't work when it came time for an actual test.

The best part was when he walked me to French, he carried my bag with his arm around my shoulders and we didn't have to thread past anyone. They all got out of our way. "I think they're afraid of you."

He shrugged. "As long as it means no one is hassling you, I'm fine with it." He left me at my desk with a wink.

Rachel moved to grab the desk next to mine in French, snagging me for a group project like she knew it was coming. You know, considering Rach, she probably did. Madame included another cooking component with this project, and I had to roll my eyes. What was it with her and cooking assignments? Mathieu grinned when he passed out the pages with the recipe suggestions.

Opera cake was on the list, and I snorted at him. He winked and kept moving.

"Down girl," Rachel snarked. "You threw that one back, remember?"

I rolled my eyes and stuck my tongue out at her. She snickered. We spent the rest of the hour divvying up the project and setting up a time for her to come over so we could cook. Well, in all likelihood, she would cook and I would direct.

And referee, because no way would the guys miss out on a chance to tease Rachel.

Maybe I really had gone crazy, because that sounded like fun, even if they all ended up aggravating each other.

After school, we reconvened back at my place, but homework planning wasn't the number one item on the agenda. No, apparently, the date schedule was.

"Okay, with Bubba back on the board," Jake said, flashing a grin at me, "we need to iron out our days."

I groaned. "How about we work on making sure we're all caught up?"

"Actually," Archie said. "We need to discuss the master bedroom." He gave me a look. "We need to clean all of that out."

That was another thing I really didn't want to deal with. "I can't just throw her stuff out."

"Fine, I'll have movers take her shit to her. But I want you to get any items in there you want out first, fair?"

It was enormously fair. Tiddles wandered back and forth under my left hand as he demanded pettings. Tabby had settled in Coop's lap like she owned it, and Tory kept a wary eye on all of us from the hallway. I think she was really getting used to having all the guys there, but she still got jumpy when we were all being loud.

"That's easy, we can do that tonight. We'll help you go through while we box all that shit up, and Archie can wave his wand and get the stuff removed while we're at school tomorrow." Coop gave a little wave. "Poof. Last vestiges gone."

"We can decide what you want to do with the room after," Jake tacked on.

"If you want to do anything at all with it," Ian suggested from where he sat on the floor right in front of me. He had pulled one of my legs over his shoulder and he gave my foot a squeeze.

"Well, my vote is bigger bed," Archie drawled. "We can put it in there *or…*" He pressed on, even with me making a face. "We can shift stuff so that we can make like, a study room or something, and put your old bed in there and the bigger bed in your room."

"A bigger bed in your room would be a tight fit," Coop mused. "You thinking queen or California king?"

"Actually," Archie said as he leaned forward from where he sprawled on the sofa and held up his phone. "I was thinking this."

Jake burst out laughing when he saw it, and Coop's eyebrows climbed. By the time he passed the phone to Ian, I was curious and leaned forward. Then I just stared. "That's not a bed, that's a football field."

"Hardly," Archie said with a grin. "But there's more than enough room for all of us *and* your cats."

Heat flooded my face. "Okay, before we discuss new beds and sleeping arrangements." Because yeah, the thought of all of them sleeping there regularly and not just spread around the room with two in bed with me was insanely hot and distracting. "We still need to do rules."

"Rules?"

"We got no bean burrito rule," Coop teased, and I flipped him off. Unrepentant, he continued, "What rules specifically do you want to make? The rules on our screaming orgasm competition?"

Yeah, okay. My face caught on fire as both Jake and Archie chuckled.

"He kind of has a point. Angel." Ian shocked the shit out of me when he tipped his head back to eye me. He had an ice pack held to his face at my insistence. "You will, of course, be the final judge of that contest."

"Et tu, Brute?"

He grinned. "I know I'm behind, I'll take any advantage I can get." I didn't think my face could flame any hotter. Particularly with our recent make-out session punctuated by little bites of pain or not. "Not that I'm rushing anything.

I'm just a big believer in how thorough you like to be in your research."

"Fuck me, that is the nerdiest flirting ever," Jake said. "I don't know whether to be disgusted or impressed."

Archie snorted. "She's red as a beet. I think impressed, because he's definitely getting to her."

"I hate you all," I muttered.

"No you don't," Coop chuckled. "Not even a little bit."

Asses.

"Rules," I said, ignoring that last bit. "We need rules because I don't want to hurt anyone's feelings or, you know, run into what we did before."

"That was my fault," Ian reminded me as he squeezed my calf as though an apology.

I stopped petting Tiddles for a moment and ran my fingers through Ian's hair. "You had rules before, right?"

"Yes," Archie admitted. "Not sure those are the kind of rules you're talking about."

"What are they?"

The fact that no one answered right away and they looked at each other only served to make me more curious.

"C'mon, spill. You made rules about *me*. What were they?"

Jake made a face. "Only if you promise to not get pissed if you don't like what the rules were."

I stared at him, and he didn't back down for an instant. "Fine," I conceded, more curious than irritated. "I will not get pissed if I don't like what the rules were, emphasis on the word *were*. If we're establishing new rules that get my input, that means I can veto an old rule and toss it out so it no longer applies. Fair?"

They did another one of those long looks at each other, and I didn't even have to see Ian's face to know he was in agreement with me right now. Maybe we were both going to be trying too hard for a while, and I was okay with that. I was just damn happy to have him back. I didn't want to screw it up, and neither did he.

"Fair," Archie said as both Jake and Coop nodded. "They didn't start out as more than some loose guidelines," he admitted. "Rule number one—don't text us when on a date. Whoever was with you deserved to have your undivided attention."

That wasn't so bad.

The corners of Jake's lips tipped up in a half-smirk, and that coupled with his bruises added to the bad boy element he rocked without trying. It also sent a shiver up my spine when he focused on me, like I was the only one in the room. "Rule number two—Sunday nights are *mine*."

"Rule number three," Coop chuckled. "Don't step on another guy's date."

"How is that different from rule number one?" Wasn't that the point of the no texting rule?

"I don't have to text to show up when Coop is over here," Jake said flatly. "That steps on another guy's time. Same with when you go out to eat with Archie or I take you to the drive-in. That's our one-on-one time."

Okay. "Fair."

"Rule number four," Archie said, stretching forward to snag his coffee off the table. We'd stopped for fresh on the way home. We all had a lot of homework. With Halloween behind us, the race to the holidays was on. Thanksgiving in three weeks and the winter break two weeks after we got back from that. Every single class had a major project due, and we'd have all the tests. Yay. "No competing with each other."

That jerked me out of my homework musing, and I stared at him.

"What? No competing?" I glanced from him to Jake, to Coop, and then down at the back of Ian's head, before looking at Archie again. "Seriously? You four? No competing?"

"We managed," Coop actually sounded offended. "But the important one was you, so we all focused on our own strengths, not trying to one up each other."

"Screaming orgasm contest doesn't count," Jake said with a grin. "That's *friendly* competition."

And I was blushing again, but Jake only laughed at me.

Still, no competing. Wow.

They were all laughing, and I plowed on, heading back to the subject at hand. "So just four rules?"

The laughter faded, and Ian sighed.

"Nope," Archie picked up the thread. "Rule number five—no one else, just us."

A shiver went through me at the possessive look in his eyes. That rule didn't surprise me. I licked my lips and nodded.

"Rule number six," Ian volunteered. "Don't hurt Frankie."

That got a sharp nod from all of them.

"We fucked that one up some," Jake admitted, and Coop sighed.

"But we're working on it," Archie insisted. "I like to think we've gotten better."

"So do I," I agreed, and some of the tension went out of their shoulders.

"Rule number seven was mind your own business. We only talk about what we want to talk about. We don't butt in to each other's relationships with you." Ian tilted his head back to look at me again. "Unless we see someone messing up like I did. The guys nailed me for that, and rightly so."

"And we worked it out," Coop clarified. "Because we're still friends, and friends have to communicate."

"Okay, Dr. Phil," Archie teased. "Dial it back. She gets it. Rule number eight was no fighting."

"We did a shitastic job with that one," Jake declared wryly. "But I stand by slugging Bubba. He deserved it."

"So did you," Ian retorted drily. "Not that I'm disagreeing with the fact that I deserved it."

They shared one of those nods that meant they were in accord, and it took everything I had not to roll my eyes.

"That just leaves rule number nine, " I murmured. "I think, unless you added any more."

"Rule number nine?" I had all of their attention, except for Archie, who just laughed softly.

"No, I think we're at nine, and I think that one should stand. Naked worrying is not allowed."

Immediate assent came from all the guys on that one, and at least the blushing had calmed enough. Naked worrying had nothing on screaming orgasm contest.

"So, Baby Girl," Jake said. "Any of those rules you want to toss out?"

"I don't think so, though I'm confused why Sunday nights with you got a rule, but all the other date nights didn't."

"'Cause Jake is a territorial ass," Ian told me. "And he wanted to make damn sure he had time with you locked in no matter what else was going on."

"No lie," Jake admitted. "We can amend that one, within reason. To maybe…all four of us get an evening with you to ourselves, at least once a week?"

"Schedules and school and work permitting," Coop suggested. "Some weeks are going to be tougher than others."

"Fair," Archie mused. "But we're all staying here, so we can just rotate on those nights so your families get off your asses about how much time you're over here."

His family didn't give him grief, and I frowned.

"No one is irritated with us," Coop argued. "Mom wants Frankie to come over for dinner though."

"Ditto," Jake and Ian said in unison.

"Okay, *that* is an issue for another day." I needed to think about this some.

"Done," Archie said. "But just so you know, Jeremy would love to have you over, and so would Grandpa the next time he's in town."

I liked his grandfather. Really, I liked all of their parents, except for mine and Archie's directly, so this wasn't really a problem.

"Did you want to add any more?" Ian asked, shifting to look at me. "You did say you wanted to make rules."

"I do have one… It's kind of one I asked for before, but I think we need to make it a real rule."

I had all of their attention.

"Name it," Ian said.

"Rule number ten…" I labeled it because we had a list, and maybe we needed to print it out. I could do that later, too. "We talk to each other when something is wrong or we have questions or we're worried." I held Ian's gaze the whole time. "Even if it's hard to talk about. We agree that we don't make assumptions or decisions for each other without consulting the other person." That went for them as well as for me.

He didn't hesitate. "Done."

The other three followed suit.

We had to shift gears at that point, because homework wasn't going to do itself. They took turns helping me with mine if I needed anything handwritten out, otherwise, they set me up with my laptop and I henpecked away left-handed.

The rules had been easy. Splitting up tasks for homework, then for getting food together, and finally for packing up Maddy's room—I found one box of items I planned to keep and it wasn't much, but they were some old things of mine—the guys kept it easy and light.

They'd moved all the furniture to one side so it was all ready to be hauled out, and Coop had even run the vacuum. The room smelled better, though it still reminded me of Maddy, but it would probably be better after it aired out. Coop and Ian had cleaned out the bathroom together so it sparkled.

"Rule number eleven," Archie suggested as he set the last box in place. "We make big decisions by vote. Democratically."

"Maybe," I said. "But you're not going to get the football-sized bed by going around me with the guys to vote."

He grinned slyly. "Don't think they'll side with you?"

"No, I think you guys have a fantasy about me in a huge bed." And considering I had a couple of my own, I could say it with some authority.

"Oh, I think you're underestimating us," Coop said, arms folded where he leaned against the wall. His eyes were scorching as he raked them over me, and I had no doubt what he was thinking about because that memory wasn't far from my mind either. "We have a *lot* of fantasies."

"All about you," Jake agreed. "Not all necessarily needing a bed."

Yep. That did it. The blush I'd managed to fend off for the conversation won, and my face caught on fire. "I hate you all," I muttered as they laughed at me.

64

How Does That Make You Feel?

"**I** feel like I should know the answer to that," I told Erin. It was only my second appointment, but it was easier this week. Or maybe I was just distracted. A lifetime had happened since our last appointment.

"Well, if you feel like you should know the answer, what do you think it is?" Her quiet question prodded me, and I lifted my shoulders with a wince. The bruises and stiffness only seemed to worsen each day. The fact that Jake had found some liniment to rub into my hip and shoulder the night before had helped, but not enough.

Now they wanted me to ice it as well as stink to high heaven with the various bio-freezes. Could be worse, I supposed. It was that, or they wanted me to take the pain meds.

I was over those, even if the pain grew teeth clenching. Jake and Coop would argue with me. Archie had just stopped and put the pills in my hand and stared until I took them. I had a feeling after Coop and Jake witnessing that earlier this morning, I was going to get more of the same.

"A part of me is happy that they're gone from school. That their expulsions mean they are excised from my life. But…" I didn't know how to phrase it without sounding like a total idiot. "I kind of miss Cheryl. I miss…who I thought she was?" Was that even a thing? "It's like with Maddy. A part of me does miss her, even if I would be happy if I never spoke to her again. At the same time, it makes my stomach hurt and it's so fucking…sorry…"

"Cuss away, don't edit yourself." Erin's calm acceptance made it easy to push forward.

"I miss her. I miss what a mom is supposed to be. What I kind of thought we had, or maybe I just lied to myself about. I can't tell the guys that. They really hate her. And I don't."

"You don't what?"

"I don't hate her. She just makes me sad. She makes me really, really sad."

"And you don't think you should feel sad?"

"I should hate her. I should hate her for always choosing everything that isn't me."

"There is no *should*, there is how you feel. Your feelings are your feelings."

"Okay fine, I get Maddy. But why Cheryl? Why… We weren't close but…" I sighed. "I thought she liked me. I can't in a million years picture doing to the people around me what she did—even the ones I don't like."

"I'm going to say this again, and I need you to spend some time with these words and to make yourself comfortable with the thought and the emotion. You are allowed, entitled even, to feel how you feel. There's no right or wrong. Your emotions are yours. Acknowledging them, it's the first step toward understanding them."

"That sounds really great," I said with a sigh. "But I feel a lot of things."

"And that's okay, too."

I nodded, but it was more an acknowledgement than anything else.

"We're getting close to the end of our session, and we've talked about a lot of disappointments today. Can you tell me one good thing that's happened since we last spoke? Something that made you feel good?"

"Archie said he loved me," I admitted and let myself smile. The warmth that evoked helped to fill in some the empty and aching places those other disappointments left in their wake. "Ian and I are in a good place again. We made up."

"How does that make you feel?"

I laughed, even as I blinked back some tears. "You just asked me what made me feel good."

"And now I'm asking how those two things make you feel?"

I sucked on the inside of my lip. A blush warmed my face. "I feel wanted, valued…seen." Wry smile in place, I lifted my shoulders. I was almost afraid to admit it because I didn't want to jinx anything.

"I feel good."

Chapter Five
IT'S THE LITTLE THINGS

Jake and I cut out of school early on Friday. I, because I had an actual doctor's appointment, and Jake, because he was my ride. The guys had actually rock paper scissor'd it the day before, even though Jake said it would be easier if he did it since we had seventh together anyway.

Some arguments I just refused to wade in on. Particularly when PMS seemed intent on making me miserable and pissy. Just easier to eat my ice cream and let them figure it out on their own.

Jake won in a run-off with Coop that lasted eight rounds with the two of them choosing the same damn item every time, until Jake switched it up and rocked Coop's scissors.

All hilarity aside, I was both dreading and looking forward to the doctor's appointment. The follow-up from the emergency room visit was a pain in the ass, but I liked Dr. Robbins. She'd been my doctor *forever*. It was the one thing that I didn't mind going to see her about all this because from the age of eight onward, she'd been my doc.

Mostly because Maddy had gotten irked with the pediatrician who argued with her, and the next thing I knew, no more peds for me. Just Doc Robbins.

As we pulled into the parking lot, I reminded Jake, "You can just sit in the car or the waiting room, but you're not coming back with me."

He chuckled. "I'll be good."

"Uh huh, and you'll be good out here. It'll go faster if you're not there." And besides, I had thing to discuss with her that I did not want to discuss with Jake. Or any of them, at least not right now. I gave him a quick kiss. "If I need you, I have my phone. I'll call, and you can play Super Jake."

With a gentle snort, he caught my nape and pulled me back for a far more thorough kiss. "I'll hold you to that. You still feeling a little off?"

"Shark week is imminent. That means chocolate."

"Got it," he said, then winked. "I'll make sure I let the guys know they better come bearing gifts if they want to hang out this weekend."

I grinned. "I'm not that bad."

"Nope," he said. "You're perfect. Even when you want to be a monster." He gave me a perfectly innocent smile, even if his pale blue eyes danced with mirthful teasing.

I smacked his shoulder, but I was still laughing as I got out of the SUV.

Inside, I had to wait fifteen minutes before they took me back. I texted him to let him know I'd been called, and he told me to take my time.

Doc Robbins didn't make me wait long. She hustled in the room as soon as the nurse was done with my vitals. I'd already turned my temporary emancipation paperwork over at the front desk, so all these decisions would be mine. Not that Maddy had been to a doctor's appointment with me since I got a driver's permit.

Wearing a hot pink dress that looked stunning against her dark skin and a paler cream colored sweater over it, Doctor Robbins gave me a smile as she came in. "Well, it's about time you came to see me. I keep getting reports from you seeing other doctors."

"Sorry, I seem to be spending a lot of time at the E.R. lately, and then they have me seeing an orthopedic doctor for this." I motioned to the cast on my arm.

"Hmm-hmm." She studied me. "You doing okay? Doing follow-ups?"

"I am, and I'm seeing a psychologist, trying to get my head straight."

"Good." She settled in a chair. "Tell me what I can do for you today."

I took a deep breath. "I need some advice," I told her on the exhale. "About birth control." Then I laid out what I wanted and why. We discussed all the options, from the IUD to the implant to shots. The side effects weren't a fun list to go over, but she had pamphlets on each of the different contraceptive methods.

The great thing about Doctor Robbins, she talked about all of this like it was perfectly normal. The best time to change methods was around my period, and since shark week was about here, this was the best time.

"Okay, let's get you in a gown, and I want to do a pelvic and go over your other injuries, then we'll get you set up after we check the insurance coverage." That was actually a valid concern for me. There was a real chance Maddy would kick me off her policy, considering how pissed she was at the moment, and since re-enrollment was this month, I wanted to get this done while I still had it.

No way I was asking Archie for the money to cover this.

It took about forty-five minutes total, including the blood work, the pelvic, and the quick check of my shoulder and hip. Both sets of bruises looked colorful, but they were doing better. I had a Band-Aid on my upper arm for the implant.

"Seven days," she told me, having shocked the hell out of me that I could go ahead and do it today. "Seven days before it's fully effective, so this is good. No more pills. Just remember, that implant isn't going to prevent STDs, so if you have unprotected sex, make sure you know they're clean."

Yeah.

That was another fun set of conversations.

One big step at a time.

"Thanks, Doctor Robbins." The best part of all this though was it might make the cramps more tolerable. They weren't the worst thing ever, but I was already sore before we did the pelvic, and I was getting more uncomfortable as time passed.

Jake had only texted me once after I got back to the exam room. Outside, I found him taking a nap in his car. The wind had definitely turned brisk, and there were storm clouds rolling in. He had his seat back and his feet up, and there was the hum of music from inside. I stood there like a creeper for a minute and just smiled at him.

Then I fished out my phone and snapped a picture. He looked adorable, especially with the way his hair fell over one eye. He'd been letting it grow longer and longer. I liked it. Sooner or later, he'd cut it. The bruises on his face were as mottled as the ones on my shoulder and hip, but at least the swelling had gone down for him and Ian both.

He sat up as soon as I opened the door, going from asleep and adorable to rumpled and adorable as he swept a look over me from head to toe. "All good?"

"Yep," I said as I climbed in. He reached past me without a word and snagged the seatbelt. As soon as he clicked it into place, he kissed me gently and I sighed against his lips. "What are you going to do when I get my wrist back and you guys don't have to do everything for me?"

"Enjoy the hell out of driving you nuts by doing it anyway," Jake said with a grin.

Rolling my eyes, I touched my fingers to his cheek and then sighed as he settled back in his seat. "Can I ask you a kind of awkward and potentially invasive question?"

Eyebrows raised, he said, "You had definitely better ask whatever it is now."

"Have you ever been tested to make sure you're clean?" I'd never really asked before. I kind of assumed, and Jake was pretty clear about *always* wearing a condom. I liked to assume the other guys had been as careful, but...

"Specifically?" He shook his head. "Do you want me to be? Or better phrased, do you need me to be?"

I glanced down a beat, this was kind of embarrassing. I'd given him a blowjob—more than once now. So it wasn't like I hadn't been up close and personal. "I'd like to be one hundred percent sure. Or as sure as we can. I got blood work done and it's part of the panel she's going to do so I can say I'm clean."

"We know you're clean, Baby Girl," Jake stated firmly. Even though the engine was running, he made no move to pull out of the parking spot. All of his attention was focused on me. "I had a physical right before school started. Bloodwork and everything. I'm clean. I'd wager Bubba can say the same, he had to get the same physical I did."

Made sense. Football.

"Thank you."

"Hey," he said, threading his fingers through mine, and I leaned toward him to rest my head against his shoulder. "No thanks required. Though…can I ask what brought this up? You're okay, right? All the guys have…"

"Everyone uses condoms," I told him in a rush. "And no one gave me anything."

Some of the tension went out of his arm.

"I just want to make sure we're all covered. I mean you guys and me." Since I was having sex with all of them, well, not Ian yet. But hopefully, maybe soon.

I froze. How insatiable was I that I had Jake, Coop, and Archie, but I was really anticipating Ian, too?

"Wow, I'm turning into a—"

"You be really careful about the word you choose," Jake all but growled at me, and I lifted my head to meet his fierce gaze. "Nobody talks bad about my girl, not even my girl."

A shiver raced up my spine. "Got it." Then I stuck my tongue out at him, and his entire expression shifted as he cracked a smile.

"You're adorably the worst. You know that, right?"

"So you have told me." This time, he kissed my fingers before releasing my hand and shifting the car into gear.

"By the way, Coop and Archie hit the grocery store on the way home. There is a chocolate feast waiting for you, weepy movies, heating pad, and some kind of back massager thing that Archie insisted on buying. We might need a bigger boat for shark week just to carry all the crap they got."

I busted out laughing.

My guys rocked.

The weekend flew past, and the guys spoiled me rotten. Shark week was never fun, and the first two days inevitably sucked. Not only did they get me a chocolate feast, they ordered in all my favorite take-out foods and coordinated with the movers Archie brought in to empty out Maddy's room while the cats and I hid out in my own.

In between rom-coms and dramas, Archie continued his campaign for the bigger bed. He kept showing me different ones and even suggested we all go to the different stores to test the beds to find the one we all wanted.

There was something awkward and yet utterly natural about that. The guys had all but moved into the apartment with me. A part of me wondered if I should be pushing back on that or not. It was something I'd probably end up discussing with Erin. We hadn't touched on my relationship with the guys as much. Not when we'd focused on Maddy to a great extent and on Mitch and those events.

Ian had brought over one of his guitars and asked if he could just keep it there rather than take it back and forth. Archie and Jake stole my car Saturday afternoon to change the oil and the fluids in it, and I only found out after the fact. Before I could discuss testing with Archie or Coop, Jake announced over dinner that they needed to get it done if they hadn't.

That earned me a pair of speculative looks from both of them, and I just tucked into my food and focused on that. I wasn't one hundred percent ready to discuss all of the whys and stuff. Not yet. There were other conversations I needed to have.

Things we needed to decide between us and with everyone. A lot of things I didn't want to leave up in the air or to chance.

Monday, we kicked off a new routine with Ian and Jake no longer having practice. They decided of their own accord to go running before school, and Archie went with them. Coop hung with me, both of us a little bemused by this running.

Even more when Jake said I could go with them when I was feeling better. Um, yay?

"So, Trina has a date on Wednesday."

I stared at him. "He actually still asked her *after* you guys talked to him?"

Nose wrinkled, Coop stared at me. "No, Auburn is out. Walked away. Smart."

I didn't roll my eyes, but it took actual effort. "Then who does she have a date with?"

"Kid in her grade."

"Okay, that's better, right?"

"Same problem, kid's just shorter." Coop grousing had to be one of my favorite things ever. Wasn't going to tell him that, though. I slid my feet over to rest in his lap, and he dropped a hand down to wrap around my ankle. "She asked if we'd do the double-date thing."

"Uh huh."

"So, I told her I'd talk to you." He didn't quite meet my eyes as he took a large swallow of his coffee. "And if you were feeling up for it, we could go with them. But if not, she'd have to reschedule."

I took a bite of my chocolate covered donuts—the guys had seriously not been kidding about the chocolate shopping. We had chocolate everything at the moment. It was a little bit like heaven. "Okay." After waiting a beat for him to continue, I curled my toes against him. "Are you going to ask me?"

"Nope," he told me, a grin curling his lips. "First, I said I'd talk to you, which I have done. Second, our next date is *not* going to be double-dating with my sister and the boy she likes. Mom can go keep an eye on them, she already said she would if I didn't want to do it."

Propping my chin on my fist, I studied him. "You're adorable."

He snorted.

"Has it occurred to you that Trina wanting us to go on the double-dates with her is a way to get you to spend more time with her?"

The scowl reappeared. "Don't try to use your logic on me."

I chuckled. "Coop, she adores you, and you're always over here. She might be feeling a little ignored."

His shoulders dropped, and he tilted his head back. "You want to go on the double-date with them?"

"Not particularly, but I will."

I poked him with my toes gently, and he gave my ankle a squeeze. "I'll think about it and see how you're doing tomorrow. You were not comfortable yesterday."

"The first two days are always the worst." But I appreciated the sentiment regardless.

Cutting a look at the clock, he glanced back to me. "The question about whether we've all been tested—is that because I almost forgot the condom that one day?" Genuine worry reflected in his eyes. "I'm not going to risk you. You know that, right?"

"I do," I assured him. "And it's partially because of that, and partially just…I'm having sex with three of you, and there's a real chance Ian and I might start having sex too—that's me having sex with four guys on a fairly regular basis."

"You're worried about us." He nodded once. "Fair point. Also, very you." I rolled my eyes, but he leaned forward. "It is very you. You start worrying about all of us. You're worried about whether Bubba is all in, you're worried that we're going to make you choose. You're worried…"

"I'm worried about a lot of things." I could admit that. "But this is just one thing we can all do something about. All of you say you don't want to risk me. Is it so bad that I don't want to risk you?"

"No, it's not so bad," he confessed. "I like that you care. I mean, clearly, I'm your favorite."

"Clearly," I said, tone dry and he grinned, and it was impossible not to smile back at him.

"You jest, but I know you." He tapped his head, then pointed at me. "I get you."

I laughed. "You're terrible."

"And you like me this way."

Yes, yes I did.

"Also," he continued, easing my feet from his lap as he stood and gathered up our breakfast dishes. "Mom has invited you over for dinner later this week. If we go out with Trina, I'll ask her if we can do it next week."

Dinner with Carly wasn't a novelty, well, it wasn't a standard anymore. I used to eat over there all the time when we were younger. But his mom wasn't the only one insisting on inviting me over. I had invitations from Alicia and Sara, too. Jake and Ian both said I didn't have to worry about it, but with everything going on, keeping the peace with their parents needed to stay higher on the list of things we needed to do.

The back door opening saved me from responding as Jake, Archie, and Ian all entered, sweaty, and breathing hard. In their tank tops and shorts, despite the chilly temperatures, they all looked really, really good.

"Now that's a good look," Jake said, then he dropped a kiss on my lips as he swung past on his way for the shower.

Archie followed him, then tucked my chin up with a wink before he gave me a kiss. "Don't drool." I swatted him, and he laughed.

Ian snorted and then planted a hand on the back of my chair and another on the table, before he delivered his version of a good morning kiss. Tongue sweeping in, he made a little satisfied hum before he lifted his head. "You taste like coffee and chocolate."

"There are more donuts," I told him.

He chuckled. "We'll save those for you." Then he gave me another kiss, one that had me gripping his neck for balance as he thoroughly explored my mouth and sent my pulse racing. "I can always just do taste tests right here."

"Shower's open," Jake yelled.

"Damn," Ian murmured. "Raincheck?"

I laughed and gave him a gentle shove, but he was already on the move. Settling back in the chair, I met Coop's amused gaze and raised my brows at his smirk. "What?"

"Happy looks good on you." His eyes darkened a notch.

"You're picturing pinning me to the fridge right now, aren't you?"

Grasping my left hand, he tugged me out of the chair, then spun me around to pin me against the fridge. "Nope," he said, gentle as hell when he settled his hands on my hips. "I'm just going to do it."

Then he closed his mouth over mine, and the vague notion of cramps faded as he teased, nipped, and sucked at my lips.

Yeah, happy felt good, too.

Chapter Six
NOT ALL DAYS ARE GOOD

COOP

Fortunately, Trina got herself grounded before the date became an issue. Unfortunately, she got grounded because Mom busted her for smoking again. That meant Dad got called, and he showed up to have a 'talk' with her. As usual, the 'talk' began and ended with him taking Trina's side, and though he tried to soften the punishment, Mom wasn't having any of it.

I spent the whole 'lecture' leaning against the wall next to the hallway, arms folded and ready to leave. Personally, I'd rather be over at Frankie's or working or, hell, going running. Well, no I'd rather not be running, definitely rather be with Frankie.

"Two weeks," Mom said. "Final answer."

"Carly, we could make it one… It's only her first real rebellion."

I stared at Dad and barely swallowed back my scoff, but Mom didn't even give it that much effort. "We can make it a month. Do you want to keep negotiating for her Thomas?"

Oh, she used the full name. Dad finally noticed the graffiti on the wall and shut the fuck up, much to Trina's chagrin. She cast a hopeful look at me, but I shook my head. I told her the cigarettes were bad for her. Phase or not, it was a terrible habit. I'd tried them exactly once. Not that I planned to share it. Frankie and I had both split a pack of smokes with Jake when he got back from Germany.

She threw up, I had a headache from hell, and Jake had been disgusted enough that he tossed the rest in the trash. Our rebellions could stick it out with sharing Frankie between us and alcohol. That worked for us. We'd done a little weed over the summer, sans Frankie, but the smoke stunk, even if it was fun.

"I hate all of you," Trina yelled, tears filling her angry eyes as she stormed away. She slapped my arm as she passed me and muttered, "Jerk," before disappearing up the hallway. The slam of her door added the final punctuation mark to that tantrum.

Good times.

Dad sighed. "You didn't have to be so rough on her, Carly. She's acting out."

"I called you over here to back me up. If you can't be bothered, then you don't need to be here." With Trina out of the way, Mom's expression went to stone. She rose and avoided Dad's hand when he went to touch her arm. "Thanks for nothing. Feel free to let yourself out."

This was the shit that I hated—the icy wall between them and the fact that Dad fucked it up with Mom. I'd heard her cry herself to sleep. I didn't care what he had to say on the subject, he hurt her. He could go. I pinned him with a look as Mom headed to the kitchen.

"Coop."

"Dad."

The old man sighed as he straightened. Sometimes, I forgot what it was like when I was younger. When Dad and I hung out willingly. How he taught me to throw a baseball, or when he took me and Frankie to baseball games. "You got a minute?"

"Nope."

Another aggrieved sigh left him. "Cooper, I'd like to talk to you."

"I'm good with the whole let's pretend the other one doesn't exist. It's been working for me." Mom wanted him out of here, and Dad's jaw set. Fuck, he wasn't going anywhere until he talked to me. Fine. I'd split the difference. "I'll walk you to your car."

Instead of heading to the door, though, he moved to the hallway where I was standing. What the…

"Trina?" he called. "I'm going now."

Sis didn't answer him. He waited a moment, jaw flexing, then grunted as he turned away, and I pushed off the wall to follow him to the door. Most likely, Sis had her earphones in. I rather doubted she even heard Dad's farewell. Even if she did, she probably didn't want to talk to him after his betrayal anyway.

I caught Mom's eye where she watched our exit from the kitchen. I mouthed, "I'll be back," to her, and she gave me a small smile and a nod. The pain in her eyes just pissed me off at Dad all over again. I didn't know exactly *what* he'd done. It had to have been an affair. I didn't think it was money. But whatever it was, it was bad enough that he'd tried for years to win Mom's affections back, and she had nothing to do with that. She talked to him about us, and that was it.

It had just been an ugly year, and nothing I'd done had made it better, though I sure as fuck tried. Keeping my distance from Dad was the least I could do. Even when she tried to tell me he was still my father and I was allowed to have a relationship with him.

Nope, I was firmly #TeamMom, and Dad could go fuck himself.

While she'd never actually said anything, the relief in her eyes about killed me. Trina had been the complete opposite and a lot younger. She didn't see how much pain Mom was in, or how Mom just took all of her rebellion and tantrums and kept going. Even when Mom wouldn't say anything to her, I had.

Still, it had been tough.

Dad didn't say a word as he headed for the parking lot. He'd parked in the open parking where Frankie used to park her car and right next to mine. Arms folded, I faced him when he turned. We were the same height, so I could look him dead in the eyes. We had the same build, and where his looming presence had been both a comfort and a bit of a terror when I was younger, he just seemed kind of sad now.

I waited him out. If he wanted to have the conversation, he would have to be the one to start it. At least out here, away from Mom, I didn't have the driving urge to shove him out the door. I could keep it cool.

"Your mom said you're dating Frankie."

That was what he wanted to talk to me about? I raised my brows. "Does it matter?"

"Yes and no," Dad said, not remotely clearing it up. "Just—she said you haven't been serious about anyone, and you've known Frankie for years."

Mom might have said that, but I doubted they'd had some kind of heart to heart about me. "Dad, what do you want?"

Raking a hand through his sandy blond, yet sporting more than his own fair share of gray hair, Dad leaned back against his car. "We've never really talked about…girls and stuff."

"Sex?" I didn't scoff. I didn't snort. I didn't do much other than keep it bland. "I'm familiar with sex. Safe sex. Also with STDs and pregnancy. I know about condoms. I also know how to treat a girl right and not fuck around on her. Anything else you want to cover?"

He stared at me a beat. "I always wondered if you knew."

"We're not having *that* conversation." Some things I wished I didn't know.

"Coop, are you ever going to not be pissed at me?"

"Ask me in ten years."

"Look," Dad said, studying me with the same eyes I had. Sometimes, I wondered if it had to bug Mom how much I looked like him. "I screwed up. I accept that I made mistakes. I owe your mother, more than I'll ever be able to repay her. I want to make it up to her, but she wants nothing to do with that."

He wasn't telling me anything I didn't know.

"But, Coop, I want to know you, too."

"Actions speak louder than words, Dad," I told him, unwilling to change my tune at this point. "You hurt Mom. Then you left."

"She told me to get out." He let out an exasperated sigh. "Can you understand that I want to fight for her, but I can't fight her and hurt her again?"

"Why did you hurt her in the first place?" As much as I didn't want to have this conversation. I had to know. "Why do that to her? You guys always seemed…happy, she always had your back. Hell, she had your back even after this crap. She's never blamed you. She's never talked down about you. She's *encouraged* me to give you a chance."

"Because your mother is a much better person than I am."

"Well, on that, we can agree." It was my turn to rake a hand through my hair, and the moment it hit me that I was mirroring his gesture, I dropped my hands to my side again.

"I was a fool," Dad told me. "That's what happened. I let some soft words and compliments go to my head. I let myself think I deserved more than I did. Your mother worked. I worked. We were always busy, and she never seemed to have time for me anymore. There was always something with you and Trina." He shook his head. "Look, I was a fool. I can't change the past, I can only try to do better in the future. Maybe—maybe if you give me a chance, maybe your mom will too."

I didn't tell him I wouldn't hold my breath, but at the same time… "Dad, I'm eighteen. I graduate this year. I'm going to college. This isn't like six or seven years ago. Focus on Trina, she needs parents." I didn't need him. Mom was doing just fine where I was concerned.

"Then how about a friend?" Dad offered. "Maybe we can start small. I'd offer to take you and Frankie to a game, but the series already wrapped for the year. Maybe in the spring. You know, if you two are still together…"

If? Frankie and I were connected, period. But I let that go because I didn't want to have that conversation. "Maybe. Look, I gotta go." I backed up a couple of steps and then hesitated, because Dad hadn't moved. "I'm not promising anything, but text me and maybe we can…grab a burger or something."

"I'd like that." Dad straightened, the relief coursing through him almost palpable. Yeah, I could do a burger. I'd make it up to Mom. "Bring Frankie, if you want a buffer. I haven't seen her in a while, and it'd be good to get to know her again." He hesitated. "Unless you think Maddy wouldn't approve."

It didn't matter what Maddy approved or not, but I wasn't having *that* conversation with Dad either. "I'll ask Frankie."

"Okay," Dad said with a nod. The weirdness of it though stuck with me, even after I said night and headed back toward the apartment. I paused at the corner of the building to glance back. Dad hadn't moved. He wasn't looking at me, but he was staring over at where Frankie's car was parked, and I frowned.

Thankfully, he didn't linger long. After he climbed into his car, I continued on and shook my head. I didn't need a relationship with him, but if he meant what he said, then maybe giving him a chance wasn't a bad thing.

Mom had a cup of tea in hand and sat in her chair with some crocheting while watching some program when I came in. She glanced at me. "Heading over to Frankie's tonight?"

"That was the plan," I said. "Unless you need me to stay here."

"No," she said with a wry smile. "I get wanting to be with your girlfriend." There was a beat of hesitation. "Everything all right with your father?"

I debated how much to say. "He's feeling guilty. Wants to get to know me again." I shrugged. "Asked about Frankie. Wants to take us out to eat, and I said we could try to get food at some point."

She nodded, the yarn flowing over the hook without hesitation or slowing.

"That okay with you?" I knew the answer. Or more accurately, I knew what she would say, but that didn't mean I wasn't going to ask her.

"I'm never going to tell you to not see your father," she said, her voice calm and even.

"I know." Dropping to sit on the coffee table, I made sure I wasn't blocking the TV before I focused on her again. "You never have. Not seeing him and not speaking to him has been my choice."

"You're a good boy, Coop, but I can fight my own battles."

I gave her a shrug. "You don't have to fight them on your own. Besides, I told him, I'm firmly #TeamMom."

That made her laugh, which was exactly what I hoped it would. "Well, in that case, I better get dinner with Frankie before he does."

Yeah, we could do that. "Next week? Pick a night. I'll make it happen."

She grinned at me. "Good, and tell her she's invited for Thanksgiving."

Oh. Right.

"I'll tell her." Then I rose and pressed a kiss to Mom's cheek. "It's going to be okay. Trina's going to come to her senses. She got over the terrible twos."

The corners of her mouth twitched. "You were an easy teenager."

"I was hell on wheels, Mom, I just kept it out of the house."

She gave me a knowing look. "But you have always known what you wanted, and when you acted out, it was to get her attention."

Yes and no, but we could agree to disagree on that one. "I'm going to grab my stuff. Text me if you need me?"

As soon as I got to Frankie's, I boosted her from the sofa where she, Bubba, and Archie were watching a movie. Jake had gone to work. After stealing her back to her room, I filled her in on what went down with my dad. Like always, she just listened, head tucked against my shoulder and her hand in mine.

"So, I get to have dinner with both of your parents?" Her tone didn't reveal whether she was fond of the idea or not.

"Mom for sure. Dad, we can blow off."

She wrinkled her nose. "How often do girlfriends have to have dinner with their boyfriend's parents?"

My expression must have been as blank as my brain at that question.

I had no idea.

Archie and Bubba both cracked up when we asked them, but it turned out the insufferable bastards didn't know the answer either.

The week blew past us like we were sitting still. Frankie's restlessness only grew more intense with each passing day. She hated the cast. Hated that we had to help with so much. But she'd been getting better at using her laptop for ninety percent of her assignments.

I took her to work with me a couple of times. Jake took her another night. Archie dragged us all out to mini-golf just to cheer her up, and it could have gone hilariously wrong because she couldn't hold the club correctly, so we all shot one-handed.

The tears in her eyes were more from laughter than sadness, and that worked for me. After her session with the therapist on Friday though, she was in a worse mood. I'd gone to get my blood work done, as promised, when Rachel texted out of the blue.

Queen Bitch of the Universe

Taking Frankie home. Gonna hang out with her after. She's not happy.

What the hell?

Me

Did she tell you what happened?

We'd all been careful to not ask her or push her on the appointments. The point of therapy was to let her work through the issues with unbiased assistance. Did I want to know? Hell yes. But we couldn't demand to know. It was none of our business until she chose to share.

Rachel took her sweet fucking time answering me. I'd had my blood drawn and I'd gone over the paperwork and then had a quick exam before my phone buzzed again.

Queen Bitch of the Universe

Idk. At apt. She's lying down. I'll stay
till one of you gets here.

As irritating as she could be, I appreciated it.

I checked my watch. I could ditch now with the doctor's appointment finished. They'd email me the results, then I could give Frankie the all clear she'd asked for.

Me

Heading that way now.

I hesitated a second before adding.

Me

Need anything?

I was in my car before she answered with a succinct 'no.'

I fired off a text to the guys to let them know where Frankie was and that I was on my way there.

Unsurprisingly, they blew up my phone before I was even halfway to her place. I didn't answer them until I parked.

All were in a similar vein, what was wrong? Did I need them to ditch? Whose ass did they need to kick?

The last was Jake's, but that also fit.

Me

Don't know. Maybe just had a bad appt.
Can happen. Finish class. I'll text after I
see her. Might be a minute.

Then I shoved the phone in my pocket. In the apartment, Rachel stood as I let myself in. The television was on, and she had a notebook in her hand. Apparently, she'd killed time doing homework.

"She's still in her room," Rachel told me, pitching her voice low. "You good?"

"I'm good. Hang out a sec before you take off?" At her surprised look, I shrugged. "She may not want me for company. She didn't throw you out so…"

With a faint smirk, Rachel dropped back onto the sofa like she belonged there and went back to her spiral bound notebook. What the fuck was she writing? Poetry? She cleared her throat, and I jerked my gaze up.

"Her room is that way." She pointed with her pen.

Rolling my eyes, I said, "If I'm not out in five minutes, go ahead and take off—and Rachel?"

"Yep?"

"Thank you."

"Didn't do it for you."

"Don't care." I mimicked her snotty tone, but I didn't miss her faint smile as she kept writing without looking up. Leaving it with that, I headed back to the bedroom. I tapped the door once before letting myself in. Still dressed in the jeans and sweatshirt she'd worn to school, she was curled on her side, facing the window with her back to the door. Her right wrist was propped on a pillow.

Closing the door behind me, I crossed to the bed. "Want your shoes off?"

Her shoulders lifted, then dropped. A faint shrug.

"Okay, I'm going to call that a yes." I tugged them off one at a time. "Need me to get rid of the jeans, too?"

No movement.

"So, no." I moved so I could see her face, the wan look made my heart fist. What the hell had they discussed in that session? "Can I get you anything? Chocolate? Pizza? A hug?"

The last word had her gaze tracking to me, and she let out a little sigh. "I could use a hug."

Toeing off my own shoes, I moved over to crawl onto the bed behind her and then eased her so her back was to my chest and I was wrapped around her. "Better?"

"Tighter," she requested in a small voice, so I bundled her up tighter and pressed my face into her hair. Her little relieved sigh allowed some of the tension to relax in me.

"Anything you want," I promised. After a few minutes, the sound of the door closing in the front carried through the house, and Frankie huffed out a sigh.

"Crap, I left Rachel out there…"

"She wasn't worried about that," I told her. "She texted me that you were feeling bad, and I told her if I didn't come out, she could go ahead and take off."

Frankie groaned. "I need to apologize to her, I was just…"

"You had a moment," I reminded her. "You're allowed. Besides, I'm glad she looked after you."

"You still don't like her."

"Eh," I grunted. "She's growing on me. Kind of like a fungus."

"Mean," she accused me, but it lacked any heat. Then, she added, "Thank you for coming."

"Where else would I rather be? Hmm?" I pressed a kiss to the skin behind her ear. "Do you need anything else, or do you just want to lie here for a while?"

"Can we just…be for a bit? We had to talk about Maddy today. A lot of things came out, and I feel all kinds of stupid at the moment."

Not willing to touch that currently, I simply said, "You're not stupid. And I have no problems lying here with you for a while. If you want me to get you naked and do some naked cuddling, we can do that, too."

That got me a little laugh.

We were still cuddled together when the guys got home. Jake dropped in first. He took one look at us and had me scoot Frankie over, then he settled on her other side. When Archie and Bubba got there, they brought food, someone fed the cats, and we all took turns sitting with her and coaxing her to eat.

Jake got her to eat a couple of pieces of chicken, and she finally let me strip her down and get her into some sleep shorts—my old boxers—and a tank top before I cuddled her back up in the bed. By unspoken agreement, the guys carried her television back in there from the living room, and Jake dug up some action movies to watch.

Halfway through the second one, she let out a real laugh and a groan. I caught Archie's look as he studied her from where he sprawled on the floor. He gave me a nod, and I let myself relax further. Some days were not going to be all fun.

I texted Rachel after Frankie fell asleep.

Me

She's better. Sleeping now. Thanks again.

While I wasn't expecting much more than a passing acknowledgement, Rachel did me one better.

Queen Bitch of the Universe

Good. Let me know if she needs anything. Thanks for telling me. Ur not so bad for an asshat.

Lips pursed, I debated my response, then went for it.

Me

From the biggest bitch I know, I'll take that as a compliment.

Queen Bitch of the Universe

That's how I meant it. Take care of my girl.

Me

Always do.

Jake eyed my phone as I clicked off the screen, and I gave him a shrug. She really was growing on me.

Hopefully, I wouldn't need a shot or something if it turned out to be toxic.

Frankie's bad dreams came back, but we kept chasing them away.

It was a long night.

Chapter Seven
A NEW KIND OF NORMAL

FRANKIE

By Sunday, we were getting on each other's nerves. Okay, correction, they were getting on my nerves. When I said I was gonna drive over to Mason's to talk to Marsha, I suddenly had four offers for company. I kind of felt like an ass when I didn't want them to go with me. If anything, I just wanted to breathe a little and kind of figure out what I was going to do for work.

It had been a month, and while they might not have noticed it, the sharp decline in income versus the steep increase in spending had been a sock to the wallet. I still needed to transfer my payment for my car to Maddy's account, something I hadn't brought up because I really didn't want to talk about Maddy.

Especially not after Friday's session with Erin. In fact, better to not think about it at all.

"Guys," I said. "I'll be fine. I can drive. I know it's a little awkward to get the seatbelt on and to start the car, but I can handle it."

"Of course you can, babe," Archie offered in a soothing tone. He'd already snagged his keys. "But you don't have to."

I closed my eyes for a beat, fisting my temper. "I *want* to go on my own." Despite my attempts, it came out snappish. Touching my tongue to my teeth, I sighed at Archie's frown, Jake's worried eyes, and Coop's guarded posture. No surprises there. Intellectually, I got it. They just wanted to help.

They *had* been helping.

Even my heart got that. But fuck, I needed some space.

"Okay," Ian said, shocking me. "Call if you end up needing a hand? Even if it's just to start the car so you can drive on your own?" Just like that. No arguments or pushing.

The other three glared at him, and I blew out a breath. "I will. And I won't be long, I promise. I just…I just need to talk to Marsha and figure out how the schedule is going to work. The holidays are coming, and you know it gets busier there."

With the premature end of football season, the Friday crowds would thin out. So would the post-practice crowds during the week. Still, there had to be something I could do.

Coop compressed his lips. It had to be killing him to not say whatever he was thinking, but he just gave me a nod. Though he scowled, Archie set his keys down before he dropped back onto the sofa and picked up the game controller.

"Suck up," he muttered to Ian, who just shrugged and gave me a small smile.

"Thank you." I mouthed more than spoke the words to Ian, and he winked. Warmth eased through some of the anxiety tying a daisy chain of knots in my gut. "I'll text when I get there." I could make that concession. "And when I head back."

The overprotective I got. Of course, it was also stalking me to the door and all the way out to my car in the form of Jake. He didn't say a word until I unlocked the car and opened the door. It was a gloomy freaking day out here. I hadn't paid much attention to the weather. There was just enough bite in the air that my nipples went peaked to hardened tips, even under a bra and sweatshirt. I should probably have grabbed a jacket. Even my jeans felt kind of thin against the damp breeze.

I'd be damned if I admitted it though, especially when I turned to face Jake's tense expression. The earlier worry was still very much present in his pale blue eyes. "I get it," he said in a low voice. "You need to do things on your own."

"But?" Because there was definitely a but.

"I need to know you're okay," he said, tracing a finger down my cheek. His and Ian's bruises were all ugly yellow and green as they faded, the swelling having long since gone down. Personally, I couldn't wait until they were all gone. His knuckles were still split in a couple of places, like they would try to heal and then the scabs would crack on them.

Archie and Coop both had similar marks on their hands, but they seemed to be healing faster. Maybe Jake was doing something with his? I made a mental note to follow-up on that. "Jake, I know you do. I adore that you guys are doing everything to make me feel safer. I know…" I sighed and leaned back against my car. "I know I've been kind of a mess. But I need to do this for me. I need to breathe."

His frown deepened. "Are we smothering you, Baby Girl?"

"A little," I admitted, but gripped his shirt when he would have backed off. "But I don't think it's just you guys. I think it's me."

"Not sure I get that totally."

"That makes two of us." Then I glanced toward the apartment. None of the others had followed us out. "On Friday, when I was talking to Erin, one of the things we discussed was my need to please Maddy." I couldn't quite look him in the eyes. "Even when she did shitty things, I made excuses for her and I did what I could to make up for her. And the worst part is…"

Pushing these words out were hard. It had been almost impossible on Friday, this last part. It was why I'd been in such a bad mood when I left that appointment. Erin insisted that my feelings were valid, no matter what my opinion of them was. But…

"A part of me still misses her, and I keep trying to figure out what I could have done differently."

"Frankie." He exhaled my name, and there was so much *caring* in the way he said it that I had to blink back tears.

"I hate her," I told him, finally dragging my gaze up so I could look him in the eye. "I love her. I don't know why I was never good enough."

"Baby Girl, the problem is one thousand percent hers," he told me, the growl in his voice sending a shiver up my spine.

"I want to believe that," I told him. "My head kind of does, but my heart?"

"Is too fucking big, and she doesn't deserve it." He pressed his forehead to mine. "I wish I could fix this for you."

"I know." I gave him a small smile. "You know you make my life better, right?"

"Fuck, I hope so. We managed to screw so much shit up for you."

I licked my lips. "Maybe we needed to… I don't know, maybe we needed to be apart and I needed to see what life was like without you guys in it."

"Yeah well, I knew what life without you in it was like, and I fucking hated it then." When he slid an arm around me, I leaned into him and tucked my face against his neck. He massaged my nape as he said, "And maybe that's why I hate the idea of you being out there on your own."

"Well, to be fair," I tried to inject some lightness into my tone, "the last couple of times I've 'stepped out,' shit has gone sideways."

He made a noise of agreement, but finally stepped back, hands on my shoulders. "Text when you get there," he said firmly. "Text when you're leaving."

I nodded. The worry hadn't left his expression at all.

"Are you going anywhere else?" He flexed his fingers against my shoulders, and a part of me hated what this was doing to him—the worry, the concern, and the fear eating at him. It made me want to offer to let him just come along.

But that would kind of defeat the purpose. I needed to do this as much for them as for me at this point.

"I don't think so." I scrunched up my nose, before I offered him a smile. "If I do, how about I text that, too?"

He blew out a breath, then brushed a kiss to my lips. "Thank you."

"You shouldn't have to thank me for being considerate." I got it. They were worried. But they also weren't fighting me on this, which was a win for me.

"You shouldn't have to coddle my feelings," Jake countered, then gave my ass a little squeeze. "Go on, go do your thing."

"Jake?"

"Hmm?"

"Thank you."

A wry smile twisted his lips, and my heart gave a little flutter. Sometimes, the way he looked at me just knocked all the wind out of me. "Get out of here before I change my mind," he said. "I'm already hating every minute you're going to be gone."

I laughed, but the minute I was in the car and got it started—it took a little twisting with my left hand and the same for the gear shift—I found myself missing them, too. Not how I had that summer, but the little things. The touches. The teasing comments. The smiles.

Then I glanced to where Jake waited on the sidewalk, hands tucked into his pockets and looking very lickable. I blew him a kiss and then focused on driving. It wasn't until I got to the edge of the parking lot, waiting to turn out, that I let out another long breath and turned up the music.

It was awkward as fuck driving, no lie. But it was also nice to just be me. For a little while.

Yes, I was pathetic. I couldn't wait to get back to see them *after* I talked to Marsha and maybe straightened out what work I could do, if any.

Marsha, though thrilled to see me, was not interested in me coming back to work until I was one hundred percent. Even if I could run the register just fine, there were too many things I needed both arms for, and personally, she wanted me to focus on me.

In fact, she suggested that I wait until after the holidays to come back. When I gaped at her, she confessed she had hired someone temporarily through the holidays to cover for me. It was a blow. I got it, she couldn't just keep my job indefinitely. Even if she promised my job wasn't going anywhere. However, until I was better, she wanted me looking after myself.

The woman still gave the best hugs, and she sent me off with a chocolate shake, which I sat in the car and drank as I tried to figure out what I was going to do. Mental math told me I had more than enough to cover my expenses through the holidays. There wouldn't be much in the way for Christmas shopping or for Jake's birthday. I could probably splurge a little to make sure I got them *something*.

Head back against the seat, I stared at the flow of traffic outside. I loathed spending the money when I didn't have more coming in. I needed to go over how much I had left owing on the car. The guys were spending money on food, since they were half living with me, so maybe if we worked out a budget, I could pare back what I was spending on all fronts.

I'd originally planned to figure out how to pay Archie back for the rent, but I had a feeling that was not going to happen anytime soon.

Exhaling, I stared down at the phone. I'd texted the group chat when I'd arrived—as promised—but I hadn't said anything about heading back yet.

I needed a plan.

Logging into my banking app, I stared at the number in my account, then the number in my savings. After Christmas, there was about five months until graduation, give or take. If I added a shift, I might be able to make up the difference of what I spent...

Or I could just do a different job in the meanwhile. I glanced around the car and then down at my arm. I really wanted to do something for the guys for Christmas. I wanted to do something for Jake's birthday. Chewing my lower lip, I debated it. Coop and Jake alternated their shift nights, mostly so one of them was always around for me, but we all needed to get back to a more normal schedule.

Dating was definitely on the table, or should be.

My heart raced abruptly, and I had to take several long, deep breaths to calm it down. Dating was on the table with Ian, and it hadn't been off with the other guys. Okay, I said I needed a plan. I took a sip of my shake, then tabbed over to the group chat message.

Me

Done here. About to head back.

Jake

Still feeling okay?

Coop

How did it go?

Archie

We were just debating what to order for dinner. Thoughts?

Ian

Drive safe.

I chuckled.

Me

Sorta. Not great, but not bad. Not hungry—yet. I will. I'll be home soon.

It was still awkward to get the car started and to shift the gears, but it was also getting easier. Maybe I just needed the practice. If I started taking the car to school again, I'd get the practice. The chances of the guys not fighting me driving myself every day weren't great.

And on a little selfish side, I kind of liked riding with them.

It started raining before I'd even made it a block. It turned into a torrential downpour as I turned into the apartments. I was practically crawling, because of how the rain came sheeting down. I'd barely parked under the carport and gotten the car shut off when Jake and Ian appeared, both sporting umbrellas and rain ponchos—Ian even had one for me.

Okay, I'd needed a minute. I admit it. I'd needed to go and talk to Marsha on my own. But it was stuff like this that reminded me why I wouldn't trade any of them for anything.

Homework finished, we sprawled in the living room while the guys pounded each other alternately in racing and fighting games. I had a book open and earphones in, though I wasn't actually listening to anything at the moment. Ian had sent me four more songs he'd been working on, including an updated version of his audition piece.

They were good.

They were really good.

I'd listened to all of them a couple of times, biting my lip as I grinned, aware that Ian watched me closely. When he raised his eyebrows, I grinned wider and hit play again on the beginning. The way his shoulders relaxed as he leaned back against the sofa made me grin wider. I bumped him—gently, because seriously, I was still worried about his ribs, even if he had started running and said it didn't hurt that bad.

"I love them," I'd murmured quietly, and he gave me this delighted little grin. "Now focus, or they're going to kick your ass." Not that my advice helped, because when he jerked his gaze back to the screen, Jake had run his car off the road.

"Ass," Ian snarled, almost cheerfully, and Jake just gave him a smirk before his gaze collided with mine and he winked.

Shaking my head, I went back to the book. One thing about our lit class, we had a lot of extracurricular reading to do, so I might as well get that done while I couldn't do other stuff. It was just nice to hang out with all of them.

Except for the part where I'd brought up budgeting for food. Coop and Jake got it, but Archie just shrugged and said he'd cover all the extras. I didn't want him paying for everything. They settled it by figuring out how much we'd spent the last few weeks they'd more or less been here, then Archie asked how much I wanted to budget. Since the actual amount kind of left me nauseated for how much money we'd been spending—not four times what was normal, but more like ten—I thought about my dwindling bank account and said if we actually went shopping instead of ordering out all the time, I could probably get through the week on fifty.

"Okay, so you put in fifty," Archie said. "We'll take care of the rest."

Translation—I'd budget, and Archie would pay for everything anyway. He wouldn't budge on it. I'd kind of hoped Coop or Jake would back me on this, but all they did was volunteer a hundred each, that Ian then matched. Which at the rate they consumed food, was not going to be enough.

I'd figure something out.

"Hey," Ian murmured, and I dragged my gaze off the words I hadn't been reading. *Invisible Man* by Ralph Ellison was a good book, the problem was me, not the book itself. "You're sighing again. What's wrong?"

"Nothing," I told him, and when he gave me a skeptical look, I shook my head. "Really, I'm just overthinking everything."

"You're still on the budget."

I made a face. "No, well, yes, but that's not quite why I'm sighing."

"C'mon, babe, I can afford it. Use me for my money," Archie said, his grin teasing.

"That is the *last* thing I want to use you for," I snapped, glaring at him. Jake elbowed him, and Archie let out an oomph.

"Hey, I know that." His car, like Ian's, crashed, but neither of them focused on the screen. Instead, they were looking at me. Coop hummed as he zipped past Jake. "But, Frankie, the expenses you're worrying about are bad because we are here, and I for one, *want* to be here."

"Me, too," Ian chimed in.

"So do frick and frack over here," Archie said, motioning to Coop and Jake. "I also like ordering in because I don't cook."

"You could learn," I suggested, much to his skeptical, if semi-horrified expression. "Seriously, you can build robots, you can learn to make an omelet. You have good hands and excellent control."

His slow grin at my declaration had me beet red in a second. Someday, I would not blush when he looked at me like that. Someday. That day was clearly not today. "Good to know you like my hands."

Coop snorted. "She likes mine, too, *and* I know how to cook."

"Pretty sure she likes mine best, and I can cook and clean," Jake threw in, then tossed a look at me. He could also do hair, but we didn't discuss that in mixed company, even if they'd seen him brushing my hair before.

"Nope," Ian interrupted as he stretched his legs out and draped his arm along the sofa so he could stroke his fingers against my bare calf. "I know Frankie prefers the fingering I do."

"You finger your guitar," Coop deadpanned. "Not Frankie. When you get that far, we'll discuss whether you're in the running."

Oh. Hell. No.

My face was on fire, and I squirmed to get up from the sofa and escape this discussion, but Ian slid his hand along the underside of my calf and began to massage it. That alone was enough to send shivers ascending my spine. The very last thing I needed was this to turn into an open discussion about sex.

"Depends," Jake said. "We don't know that he didn't get that far."

I closed my eyes. "I hate you all."

"No you don't," Coop told me, wicked laughter dancing in his eyes. "You do realize the screaming orgasm contest is still on the board."

"Speaking of which," Archie said as though it had just occurred to him. "We need to set up that board."

"No we do not," I snapped and dragged myself into an upright position. Ian shifted to drop his controller on the table and then lifted himself up with his arms before he scooped me up and settled me in his lap as he took a seat. The speed at which he moved reminded me of why he was on the football team in the first place.

Jake cocked an eyebrow, the quiet question in his eyes muting any humor. Was I okay with Ian putting me in his lap?

Despite my preference for a subject change, I didn't mind curling against Ian. He had an arm around my waist, and my ass was more firmly on his thigh than anything else, the heat scorching the back of my neck and likely contributing to the almost sunburnt effect on my face. I gave Jake a little nod, and he relaxed back to lounging on the stack of pillows he'd dragged into the living room.

I opened my mouth to say something when a little humming sound distracted me, and I glanced over toward the hallway leading to the bedrooms as a little circular robotic device rolled out with Tiddles sitting on the back of it, staring down at the machine as it began to hum its way across the carpet.

"What the hell is that?" Not even needing to guess, I switched my glare to Archie.

He wore an absolute unrepentant smirk as he said, "Jake's and my robot project."

Bullshit was the first word to come to mind. Coop snickered, but Jake gave me the most butter wouldn't melt in his mouth smile, eyes twinkling. Even Ian couldn't mask his laughter. If the shaking of his chest against my back didn't give him away, the little huffs of breath against my throat would.

"We're running live tests," Archie continued, though his own smirk betrayed him. "It covers the vacuuming so we could call it chores, too."

I rolled my eyes. "Archie…"

"What?" Yeah, not buying the innocence. "I said I'd work on my life skills. Cooking is definitely not there, and why run a vacuum on a schedule when this little guy can do it for us?" He didn't bat an eyelash as I stared at him.

When I transferred that same stare to Jake, he raised his eyebrows without a trace of a smirk in sight. "It's our project," he promised. "It's not store bought. Nor is it just 'repurposed.' We built it."

I narrowed my eyes. "Before or after Archie bought one and took it completely apart to deconstruct it?"

Not missing a beat, Jake shrugged. "We call that research and development."

A snort escaped me before I could stop it, swiftly followed by a laugh. Archie spread his hands and then grinned at me. "You're welcome, babe."

Chuckling, I shook my head. They weren't fooling me, and at the same time, it was wildly sweet. "Thank you, Archie."

He grinned. "My pleasure." Then he twisted to sit back down, game controller in hand. "Who's in for the next ass whipping?"

Ian plucked one of the earphones out of my ear and tucked it into his as he shifted me on his lap. It let me elevate my cast arm on the sofa behind him while he balanced me, and then unplugged the headphones from my phone and slotted them into his before he opened the music app. "You guys go ahead, Frankie and I have some homework to do."

"Thought we were all done with homework," Coop said, cutting his gaze between us. I gave him a little shrug because I'd been reading. Still, I didn't move my book as Ian tabbed down to a new list, and I stared at the tracks that had no names.

When I glanced at him, he grinned, then pressed his lips close to my ear without the earbud in it. "I want you to listen to these with me. I think you've got the range for all of them. Pick your two favorites, and those will be the ones we practice."

I grimaced. I couldn't help it. I was still a little in shock that he'd gotten me to sound so good for Archie's birthday present song. At the same time, a little thrill curled in my stomach as he hit play. The stretch of his lips as he smiled against me tickled, then he pressed a kiss to my earlobe. It was the simplest thing, and it set off a dozen butterflies in my stomach.

Sprawled out on the floor around us, Jake, Coop, and Archie gave each other hell as they sped through the streets of some European city. I could still hear the game, but I was mostly focused on the soft strumming of the guitar that promised a ballad before the riff of chords took it to another level.

How many songs had Ian worked on over the last few weeks?

When I glanced at him, I found him studying me with a small smile, and I grinned. The song was magic, but then I was pretty sure I'd grown biased. I loved Ian's voice. He could sing rock, country, old folk songs, and modern pop, and I'd just soak it up.

The first two songs were magic, but the third one?

I blinked up at him, and he grinned slowly. "That one," he mouthed, and what else could I do but nod? If I could sing any of them, I'd love to sing that one. I wasn't a singer though, even if it was fun to pretend.

He let out a little hum and began to rub my back gently as we listened. There were tears in my eyes before it was over. Tucking my head against his shoulder, I sighed. We were still waiting on college letters. I'd been wait-listed by two schools, both in the Ivy League. I had a feeling that would be Harvard's response, too. Of all of us, only Ian hadn't heard anything yet.

NYU seemed to be a yes for four of us, but we needed Ian to get in there, too. Not that we were set on it. The programs he'd applied for wouldn't respond as swiftly. The auditions made a difference.

But how could they tell him no?

The fourth song was even better than the third, and my cheeks ached at the fast pace. It was hard to hold on to the melancholy with the beat he set. He needed a band.

He needed… Holy shit. On the fifth song, I jerked my head up and stared at him. The smug grin on his face made me laugh, but it didn't alleviate my shock.

He'd covered one of my favorite Torched songs, right down to the keening wail the lead did in the third stanza.

His chuckle warmed me to my bones, and then he pressed a kiss to my forehead before I tucked my head back down. Coop caught my eye. He was grinning at us, looking all kinds of pleased. I stuck my tongue out at him before I grinned back.

I'd avoided one conversation with them all weekend. Not on purpose, but more because we'd been having fun, and after my meltdown on Friday, I'd wanted the warmth. Now would be as good a time as any to have it, and I still didn't want to disturb the mood.

We had time.

We'd make time.

The fact that the last song Ian recorded was "The Rainbow Connection" and he even mimicked Kermit's voice set me off laughing. I barely got to hear any of it for the wheezes of laughter escaping me. Ian just smiled, as I buried my face to try and smother the sound.

"Okay," Archie announced. "All in favor of making Bubba share whatever the hell made her laugh, raise your hands?"

Ian snorted at them.

That lasted about twenty seconds. Jake plucked me right off of Ian's lap as Archie and Coop tackled Ian. I winced—because of his ribs. But they were all laughing, and Jake had a smug look as he held up Ian's phone, but I managed to click the screen lock before he could get the song playing again.

Before he could call me on it, the vicious crack of wood split through the noise as the coffee table broke and scattered game controllers and textbooks.

All three hooligans paused to look up at me and Jake.

"I replaced the last one," Jake told them drily.

Archie and Coop both pointed at Ian. "It's his fault." '

For his part, Ian just laughed. "Oops?"

Chapter Eight
THE SOUND OF TWO VOICES

IAN

"You should have her home by ten," Jake told me, smirking like an asshole.

"I was thinking more nine-thirty," Coop countered as he waved a French fry in my direction. "It's a school night. Our girl does need her rest."

Archie snorted as he pocketed his keys. "Or you can just drop her off at my place," he said. "Since these two jackasses think they are so funny."

"And you're not?" Jake drawled, but I just ignored them. Frankie had ridden home with Coop, but I'd headed to my house on my bike and cleared some chores I'd been ignoring. Neither of my parents had given me hell about it, but I also wanted to check the mail while I was there. Mom had been the only one home, and she had what I wanted in her hand when I walked in the door.

Her grin had been giddy as she handed it over, and then she eyed me, "I want to ask you a question that is probably none of my business, and at the same time…"

"I'm not having sex with Frankie, Mom." *Yet*, I'd added mentally, and when Mom let out a slow breath, I knew I'd hit the nail on the head with that statement. "That doesn't mean we won't," I continued. Fuck knew I wanted to, but I'd screwed up so many things, I wasn't going to try and dictate anything along the when and the where. I'd wanted to earn her trust before, and now I *needed* to earn it. Needed to be worth the second chance she'd given me.

"I just want the two of you to be safe," was her only comment.

"Me, too."

It took me twenty minutes to pack clean clothes into a duffel. Jeremy had been by a couple of times and done laundry at Frankie's, picking up everything including my stuff, washed, dried, folded, and returned. It was a bit unnerving. I appreciated it, but I was on Frankie's side about the idea Jeremy shouldn't have to do our laundry.

Rather than admit that I didn't know how to do my own either, I'd gotten a couple of lessons from Mom. Thank you, I'd skip that teasing. Jake and Coop were professionals, and Archie had eaten up the teasing as they, along with Frankie, schooled him on doing his own damn clothes.

Now I could honestly say I knew how to do it, too. Cooking though?

Yeah, apparently, he wasn't the only one screwed in that department. I'd fucking learn, though. I'd learn whatever I had to make Frankie's life easier. Fortunately, meal times when we didn't order in had become impromptu lessons with Frankie directing us. I'd always known she had a lot of skills, but I had no idea how many things she knew how to make off the top of her head.

It was both amazing and a little intimidating.

Of course, Mom was after me to make sure Frankie came for Thanksgiving. Since she already had at least two other invitations that I was aware of, chances were unlikely she'd make it, but I promised I'd let Mom know.

Mom swore Dad would be on his best behavior. So, we'd see.

Now, waiting for Frankie, I stared at the new coffee table. It looked pretty close to the old one, but it was bigger and had fatter 'legs' on it.

"Yeah," Archie said without me asking. "I fixed it. Next one is yours though."

I snorted, but didn't argue. Since we'd managed to smash two of them now, and no matter what they said, it hadn't been *my* fault, I had no trouble believing we'd wreck a third. My phone pinged, and I shifted to pull it out of my pocket.

The others were doing the same, except for Archie, who had his phone in his hand. It was another bed. It had to be ten feet across and eight feet long. They'd lose Frankie in there.

"Think the mattress is one piece or two?" Jake mused. "'Cause that's gonna be a bitch to get around the corner."

Coop snorted. "I'm trying to figure out where in her room it goes. It's damn near as big as the room." A mild exaggeration, but he wasn't wrong. It wouldn't leave her a lot of space in there. "And so we draw straws for who gets to sleep on the outside?"

"Definitely rotate," Jake muttered, then checked his watch. "But she isn't a fan of this big of a bed yet."

I closed out the message and pocketed my phone. My guitar case was ready to go, and I had my backpack with a couple of surprises and my notebooks in it.

"She's not a fan of change," Archie countered. "We'll get there."

Some days, I wish I had his confidence. He just set his eyes on something and went for it. I could joke that it had everything to do with his money, but it really didn't. The money didn't make Archie, Archie. His determination and self-confidence—which most people dismissed as arrogance—set him apart. When he wanted something to happen, he just didn't give up. Whether it involved arguing, coaxing, or in some cases, sneaking, he got it done.

Did he ever think it wouldn't work out for him?

"So, nine, right?" Coop pulled my attention back to the conversation, and I just smiled slowly.

"You do realize she doesn't have a curfew, and if you want to give her one, you're on your own." No way in hell would I back that.

"Nah, Jake would take my side."

Predictably, Jake just gave him a thumbs up.

"See?" Coop's grin softened, and his eyes warmed. I didn't even have to look to know Frankie had just come up the hallway.

Her hair was pulled back in a simple ponytail, and she'd changed into a heavier sweatshirt. It was huge on her, and it took me a minute to realize it was one of mine. My own lips pulled into a wider grin. I had no issues with her stealing my clothes. They kind of dwarfed her more slender frame, but I liked seeing her in my clothes.

"Sorry," she said, her gaze skipping from me to the guys then back. "Rachel and I were talking." She held up the phone. "And it went a little long."

"It's all cool," I said. "We have plenty of time." I'd booked the studio for the next four hours. I'd struck a deal with the owner because the studio time was getting pricier by the day. "You ready?"

Those startlingly green eyes of hers warmed when she fixed on me again. "Yep. Just need my coat."

Jake rose, but I beat him and stripped off my own letterman and held it up for her. He snorted before he dropped back on the sofa. Once she was in the coat, I grabbed my guitar case. "Don't wait up," I suggested as I motioned Frankie ahead of me.

"Remember, home by eight-thirty," Archie said, his grin teasing.

"Eight," Coop tacked on. "Then we have time for a movie before bed."

Frankie didn't slow a step, but she did raise her middle finger and flipped them all off as she walked, and I grinned. Their laughter followed us out the door. It had definitely turned cold and damp. We'd get back to the seventies, but it would not be this week. It was a balmy fifty-two and dropping at the moment.

Current forecast said we'd have freezing rain the following week, just in time for Turkey Day.

At her car, she opened the back door for me, and I slid the guitar case inside. Like me, she glanced over at my bike. I'd thrown a plastic cover over it for the rain. "You should put it in the car port when I pull out."

"Nope," I told her. "It won't melt, and I'd rather you parked your car here." I tried to keep my tone soft, because at the moment, telling her no took actual effort on my part. I never wanted to tell her no to anything again. "But thank you, Angel."

The smile she gave me sent all my blood pumping south, and I started doing scales in my head or this would be a real short trip. "Is it hard?"

Yes it was, but no way she was asking about my dick. "Is what hard?" It came out a little thicker than intended, but without any wavering. So, point to me.

"Riding the bike with your ribs."

"My ribs are fine," I told her. They still twinged and would. I'd had bruised and cracked ribs before. They sucked. As long as I could take a mostly deep breath, I just ignored them. I slipped around her to open the driver's side door for her. "And it's fine to ride it. Not really riding for fun at the moment, anyway." At least my bike was fixed. "I'll save that for when you're up to riding with me."

Turning, she stepped right up into me and rose up on her tip toes. She didn't have to ask, I slid a hand to her hip to brace her and then dropped my head and met her kiss with my own. The first brush of her lips was cool on mine, and I almost ruined the moment by grinning.

The minty taste of her breath told me the other reason she'd been running behind. Angling so I could block her from most of the cold breeze, I teased my tongue along the seam of her mouth. She opened more fully to me, and I had to swallow a groan.

Frankie kissed with her whole body. It wasn't just her lips. She planted her left hand on my chest to balance herself, pushing into me as if she wanted to be as close as possible. Damn, it was like that first kiss in the pool, all the bare skin brushing me as we kissed.

Curling my fingers against her hip, I tugged her into me as I twisted my tongue around hers. The barest scrape of her teeth washed heat through my system and chased away even the potential of chill. It didn't matter that layers of clothes separated us, the claim she had on me went far deeper than skin, and I'd be damned if I'd fight even an ounce of it ever again.

I dragged out her lower lip slowly as I lifted my head. We were both panting, and I hadn't imagined the little gasps that had escaped when our mouths were connected. I licked my lips, savoring the taste of her still on them.

"Hi," she said, the pink tinge to her cheeks making her all the more adorable.

"Hi." A sigh escaped me like I was some eleven-year-old with my first crush noticing me.

But wasn't that exactly what Frankie had been? Sixth grade, and she'd been the prettiest girl in the classroom. I'd thought Coop was firmly established as her boyfriend. Took me forever to realize that wasn't the case.

"Okay," I said slowly, getting my brain and libido back in check. "It's too cold to stand out here and make out, as fun as that sounds, and I have to share you if we go back inside."

"Besides," she said, then bit her lower lip as she grinned. "We have a date."

"Yes, we do." I cleared my throat and forced my hand to unpeel from her hip so she could get in the car.

Once she was inside, I closed it and turned around. Exhaling a long breath, I glanced down at my very hard and very interested dick. "Save it," I muttered, running more scales in my head, not that they could remotely compete with Frankie in the car. I had to adjust myself as I circled the car. Once inside, I waited as she pulled her seatbelt on and grinned. "You're getting good at that."

Her eyes practically sparkled, something we hadn't seen in a while. There were days that were almost normal, and then days like Friday happened. Her first visit to see a therapist a couple of days before that hadn't been so bad, but the next one? That had just knocked her down.

While Jake had done his best to bury it, the need to pound something flat had been seething in him. Archie and I had dragged him out running, and we'd keep doing it to get the edge off.

"Can I run something by you without you telling the guys automatically?" She held out the car keys to me, and I slid them in and started it for her, but she handled the gear shifting.

"You can tell me anything," I promised. "I'll be a vault." Then, because it only seemed fair, I said, "To be honest, we don't talk about what you talk to us about unless it's something you've said to all of us. Or we're picking on each other, and even then, we don't talk about what you say." The guys kept the details of their dates pretty close to the vest, too, particularly after she broke up with me. "We don't talk about dates, either."

"So they don't know where we're going?"

I nudged the heat up and grinned. "They know we're going to the studio, but probably not why or for how long."

"Huh," she said, then chewed on her lower lip, and I leaned my head back to give her the space to work it out. That was the thinking face, where she tossed ideas back and forth in her head before she hit us with them. I knew better than to interrupt. She waited until we got to the first traffic light we had to wait for before she said, "I'm thinking about getting a different job for a few months."

I slanted a look at her. "You love Mason's." The job ran her ragged, but Frankie loved it. You could tell when she was at work, she liked the people and she was good with them.

"I do," she admitted. "I like being able to put money in my savings account, and I adore Marsha. But she doesn't want me to even think about coming back before January. She hired someone in because I had to miss so much, and she really wants me to heal."

Fuck. "That sucks."

"It's worse than that," Frankie said, shifting in her seat. "I have enough in savings, but part of the deal with emancipation is being able to show I can support myself. Not working until January is not going to help that."

I bit back another curse. "What kind of job are you looking at?" She was in that cast for at least another two weeks, possibly three. It was going to limit what she could do. Not that she'd ever let limits stop her.

"Jake and Coop do food delivery, and I can clearly drive my car. And I can make two trips if I have to for big orders—you know back and forth to the car."

I grimaced. "I could help with that, you know. You take the shifts, and I can run and fetch and carry."

She laughed. "Ian, I wasn't telling you so you'd have to do the work for me."

"Eh, wouldn't hurt my feelings any, and I'd get a chance to spend more time with you. Who knows, maybe I'll like it and want to do the same thing. Then we can all time our shifts so that someone is always off with you when you need it."

Frankie rolled her eyes, but I didn't take it personally. We pulled in behind the music school, and I put the gear in park for her. "So you don't think it's a bad idea?"

Studying her, I swallowed back my kneejerk response of 'of course I didn't think it was a bad idea.' She wasn't asking me to just placate her, she was asking to settle something in her own head. "If you're doing it because you need the independence yourself, in addition to proving to the court you're self-sufficient—and let's be honest the fact you probably have enough in savings to see you through this means you are." I raised a hand to ask for her patience. She sucked her lip between her teeth and nodded for me to continue. "Then fine. If you want to do it and it's important to you, then I'm all in."

I had to take a minute to consider how to phrase the next part. I did not want to come off as an asshole again.

"If you're doing it because you're genuinely worried about your financial stability because the four of us eat so fucking much or we need to do more than just budget for food, then I want to confront that and step the hell up before we make you crazy. I've got a job lined up for after the holidays, and the savings I put away over the summer will see me through Christmas."

I'd never needed to work. My parents were far from wealthy, but we were pretty damn comfortable and I had next to nothing in expenses. I could do more.

I could do a lot more.

"But call me a little selfish, I kind of wanted to spend the holidays focused on you and not work." We had enough to do after the first of the year. I'd have some decisions to make then, too.

Her smile relieved me. "It's not just about being worried about my financial stability. I think I'll always be worried about that." The curve of her lips faded away, and those gorgeous eyes sobered. "I've gone hungry before, and I've never really told anyone but Coop."

Anger fisted in my chest. Coop had never said that.

Not once.

"Maddy used to forget to shop. Sometimes, we didn't have the money. It would be really tight, and sometimes it would just be she forgot to pick things up. When she was dating, especially, kind of how I'd notice." She chewed her lip. "And I'm not telling you this to feel sorry for me. It was one of the things that came up on Friday. I hadn't really thought about how self-involved her pattern was when there was a new man in her life." Then she gave a little shake of her head. "The point is…I save every dime I can because I want to get out of here. I want to get away from Maddy. Now I'm getting away from Maddy, and it's a little scary, but a part of me thinks I need to do this on my own and not just rely on you guys."

"Fair." Even if I hated every part of it. "But you know you can rely on us. Even if you thought you couldn't rely on me, you can rely on them. They'd never let you starve or lose your place or anything."

"I know," she said, touching the side of her head. "In here? I know it. But here?" She touched her heart. "And worse here?" She touched her stomach. "It just makes me sick thinking how easily this could all get screwed up. I have a job that I can't do, and my boss won't let me do while I'm injured, and I know she means well but…"

"You're scared." I sighed, then reached over to take her hand. "I'm sorry, Angel. I'll back you on whatever you want to do and whatever you need from me, you say the word. It's yours."

Her smile reappeared. "I'm so glad we made up." Then she flushed, and I had to grin. "Okay, that sounded a little weird."

"Nah, it sounded magical to me. And while I'm totally willing to sit here with you all night, you ready to go in?" I wanted to cheer her up for real.

"Are you seriously going to make me sing?" She made a face.

"I'm not going to make you do anything, though I might beg," I teased gently. "But you have a gorgeous voice when you stop thinking about it."

She scoffed and rolled her eyes. "Okay, I already said I'd go on dates with you again. You don't have to butter me up."

"I am not buttering you up." I chuckled, then caught her nape and pulled her in for a fierce kiss. It wasn't gentle or slow like our kiss before we got in the car. This was a lot more teeth and heat. The little bite she left on my lower lip had me panting. There was a confidence in her kiss that was sexy as hell, and at the same time, the blush turning her cheeks a deeper pink delighted the hell out of me. "It's the fucking truth," I told her, keeping our faces close so she couldn't look anywhere but at me. "But I'm not going to make you."

Another kiss, and I slipped out, but not before she let out a slow exhaled, "Okay," that quivered a little and went right to my dick, who stood right the hell to attention. This was my penance for being an ass.

I would suffer it gladly. Especially since we were making progress and I got to have the time with her.

Once inside the school, I picked up my keys for the practice room and studio after I signed in. Then led the way. Frankie glanced around again, and I loved the way she looked at everything as though she needed to catalogue it for later. Once in the room, I set the guitar down and started getting set up.

"Before we dive in," I told her as she eased out of my jacket. I paused a moment because, hell yes, I liked seeing her in it. She'd worn Jake's a lot, and yeah, I'd been all kinds of jealous. Now we were going to have to make sure she wore mine as much as she wore his. "Mom invited you to Thanksgiving, and she promised Dad would be on his best behavior. I know you've already got plans or at least invites to Coop's and Jake's, but you're welcome at my place, too."

She turned those wide-eyes on me. "Um…"

"No pressure," I said, taking the jacket and hanging it up. "Seriously. None. It's going to just be the three of us." It was one of the first years we weren't going to visit family elsewhere. "And I'd love to have you there that day. Bring Archie, too." I know he didn't have anywhere else to go. He'd made it clear he'd rather drill his teeth rather than go to dinner with his parents, if they were even in the state.

"I have no idea what I'm going to do yet," Frankie said slowly. "Everyone has asked, but you're right I don't want Archie being on his own either."

"We'll figure it out," I suggested. "I just wanted you to know. And if Dad starts, we'll ditch and go grab Chinese food or something."

She laughed, which was the whole idea.

"Okay, now that we have that out of the way." I sat down at the piano and patted the bench next to me. "Come here, Angel. Come listen to me play for a bit and we'll go over that song."

The third song was one I'd written a *long* time ago. Long enough it was a little embarrassing. I'd tweaked it some, on and off, then reworked it the week after Halloween. I'd recorded it during my last studio time so she could hear it.

"Oh," I said sliding off the bench just as she sat down to grab my backpack. I pulled out the lyric sheets and the music. I handed her the first, then I handed her the big envelope.

She stared at it.

The label's name was on it.

"Ian?" Startled, she stared at me.

"I sent that demo you helped me make to a few different labels, scholarships, and contests." They'd called me the week before, and I'd had some time to get my head around it.

"Holy crap." Her mouth formed this delightful circle.

Settling back on the bench next to her, I nodded to the packet. "Open it?"

"Do you know what it is?"

"I have an idea," I told her. "But it's the kind of thing I need my green-eyed girl to help me with…"

Her hand was shaking as she slit open the envelope, and I helped brace it so she could pull out the thick wad of paper. There was a CD in the mix, too.

My CD.

I set it on the rack next to the music sheets, and she turned the packet right side up to read the cover letter.

Mr. Rhys,

Per our conversation, I've included a sample contract for your attorneys to look over. We think you'd be a good fit, and we would like you to consider working with us to develop an album. You've got a great sound, and we think you can do great things with it.

She jerked her head up and stared at me. "Ian, they want you to record with them."

I cleared my throat. "Yeah," I said slowly. "It's not a guarantee of anything. I'd have to write some new stuff and get it recorded, and they'd want to give me feedback and I'd probably have to go to them at some point. I don't even know if this is…"

She didn't let me finish the thought, her lips on mine burned the words right off my tongue. Packet dropped into her lap and half-forgotten, she had her hand in my hair, and I twisted to pull the rest of her right up against me and into my lap.

The clang of the keys broke us apart, and Frankie stared at me, almost glassy-eyed. "Do you want to do it?"

I hesitated.

"Don't think about it. Just first reaction. Is this something you want to do?"

"Only if you'll do it with me," I told her. That was my first reaction. I loved the music, I loved playing. I loved writing it.

I loved her more.

"You know I'll help you," she said, staring at me like I was an idiot.

"No, I mean, I want you to sing with me." I had thought about this. Especially after I caught her singing along one day, unaware anyone was listening. When she forgot about everything else, she had the most gorgeous voice. All she needed was a little faith in herself and a little practice. "I want you to help me pick the songs, tell me what you think. I want you."

Her eyes widened, and she said, "Ian…"

"No pressure," I promised. "We have time to think about it. And I haven't talked to anyone else about this either. Just you."

"Your secret is safe with me."

That hadn't even been a question.

With some reluctance, I settled her back on the bench and then turned to the keyboard. From the corner of my eye, I caught her staring down at the letter and then looking up at me. I meant it when I said I wanted her with me.

"Okay," I said, flexing my fingers. "I'll play it through a couple of times, and you follow along. Then when you're ready, jump in and sing."

"And when I butcher it?" She made a face.

I chuckled. "We'll fix it." I bumped her hip. "Trust me."

Even if she rolled her eyes, she moved the packet so she could look at the lyric sheet.

It took me three passes, but she joined me singing on the fourth.

By the fifth pass, her voice gained confidence.

On the sixth?

I let her do all the singing, and it was everything I could want it to be.

For Your Consideration

Archie

What are you guys doing for the
holiday break?

Jake

Next week? Probably spend it with
Frankie. Dinner with my mom and
the girls on Thursday.

Bubba

Pretty much the same. Mom asked
Frankie over to TDay too.

Archie

No, Christmas break. I know what
we're doing next week.

Bubba

Usually we drive to my grandparents.
Not going with them this year.

Jake

Nothing that I know of.

Coop

Why?

Bubba

Thanks for joining. Did we
wake you?

Jake

Considering he's got Frankie to himself? I'm surprised he's even on here.

Coop

She's asleep. Fuck off. What was so important you started texting at almost midnight?

Archie

I want to take Frankie away for Xmas.

Bubba

What?

Jake

Excuse me?

Archie

Keep your panties on. You guys are invited, if you can get away.

Coop

Details.

Jake

Yeah. Explain.

Archie

Still working it out. We get 2 weeks. She can't go back to work yet. Holidays suck as it is. Don't want to deal with her mom on top of it.

Bubba

Makes sense.

Coop

Following. Trips are expensive.

Archie

My treat.

Jake

…

Bubba

Explain.

Archie

If you can take the 2 weeks, It'll just be the five of us. Away from here. We can celebrate Jake's birthday and Xmas.

Jake

Not hating it.

Coop

Not sure Mom will go for it.

Bubba

I'm in. Who is convincing Frankie?

Archie

It's a surprise. Jeremy will watch the cats.

Jake

LOL

Coop

You like to live dangerously.

Bubba

Maybe. If we're all in. Maybe not.

Jake

I'll convince Mom.

Coop

Fuck, I'm not staying here for two weeks without all of you.

Archie

Excellent. Just remember, not a word. I don't want her stressing about it.

Jake

Yep. You want to live dangerously.

Coop

This will be all of us living dangerously.

Bubba

Yep. Wouldn't have it any other way.

Chapter Nine

5 COURSES, 4 BOYS, 3 MOMS, 2 TURKEYS, AND ME

FRANKIE

The best part of Thanksgiving break was just hanging out with the guys. We didn't date so much as just spend time together. Archie practiced new chores. Dishwashing? Nailed it. The night for experimental cooking?

Well, it turned out that we needed to air the apartment out, and we still hadn't been able to get the stench of burnt onions and garlic out of the kitchen. Coop and Jake decided that Archie and Ian were no longer allowed to cook anything but boxed stuff.

No way that could go wrong, right?

Fortunately, I had another skillet, because the last one was not going to survive. No amount of scrubbing could get the burnt residue off of it. Despite the various disasters—and yes, I totally took pictures of Archie cooking to send to Jeremy—I hadn't laughed that hard in a long time. The downtime also let me get caught up on homework and start my new delivery job.

True to his word, Ian backed me when I told the guys what I wanted to do. Jake and Coop immediately began to list the different services and the pros and cons of them. Signing up to do the job was a lot easier than I expected. Coop and Jake went with me the first time, then Ian jumped in to go on the second. Archie came along for the third.

His running commentary on the orders and the app nearly had me running off the road, until I told him he wasn't allowed to talk anymore.

By the night before Thanksgiving, though, I had earned about three hundred in tips from working several long shifts—well, long according to Jake and Coop, but the only thing in danger of hurting on me was my ass, so I didn't listen to their assessment. The three hundred would be deposited the following Monday, and there were bonuses if I continued delivering over the holiday weekend.

The only day the guys pretty much argued with me about was Thanksgiving itself, and I could handle that. I figured if I tried to work the way I had my Mason's shifts, that would be fair. They debated that, but we'd figure it out.

Ian and I did get more studio time on Tuesday—where he confessed he would be teaching kids to play instruments in the spring to help offset his studio use. I also got to learn a whole second chord on the bass, which was good because I couldn't actually hold it yet, but Ian braced it in my lap while I sat in his.

The night before Thanksgiving, Archie and I left to stay at his house. I'd be having breakfast with him and Jeremy. We'd worked out a whole schedule for the day, and I'd made a bet with the guys because they didn't think I could eat as much food as I was going to be offered. Particularly since I had plans with everyone.

Call me weird, but I was looking forward to the challenge. That, and being woken by Archie before the sun was even up, his hands on my thighs as he buried his face against my pussy. I was halfway to an orgasm before my eyes even opened, and my whole body curled up to the stroke of his tongue.

A string of curse words spilled out of me as he thrust two fingers into me and curved them upward at the same moment he locked his lips around my clit. The whole world fractured and split right down the middle as pleasure swamped me. I was still panting when he eased his way up to smile down at me, all kinds of proud of himself.

Not that I had any complaints. He cupped and teased my breasts, the stroke of his thumbs over the nipples making me squirm. "You back with me yet, babe?" The soft invitation in his voice added another caress to my senses.

Still looking for the words to answer, I let out a squeak when he pinched one nipple and bit down lightly on the other. My hips bumped up against his, and his cock left a damp stripe across one of my thighs.

"There she is," he murmured, nuzzling the tip as they strained tighter, then he sucked one against his teeth and anticipation pooled in my belly. I went from replete to desperate and needy as he took his time lavishing my breasts. "Good morning…"

I huffed out a laugh and carded my fingers into his hair. He answered the tug to rise up and kiss me. There was the barest hint of mint on his breath, but the rest of him tasted like me.

"Hi," I told him between blistering kisses that had my toes digging into the bed as I lifted my knees to cradle his hips against me. The weight of his erection pressed against my stomach, and I ground against him lightly.

"Hope you don't mind the early morning wake-up," he teased, sitting up abruptly and leaving me gasping as he reached to the side of the bed. "But you looked so fucking beautiful, and it's been forever since I had you in my bed."

A shiver went all the way up my spine, of desire and guilt. "I'm sorry…"

"Shh," he told me, his dark eyes fixed on me as he opened the foil and then rolled the condom on. "I'm not blaming you. I like sleeping in your bed, too." Then he dropped back down until his nose brushed mine. "I like sleeping with you." Kiss. "I like touching you, too." Kiss. "I really like it when I have you all to myself."

He stroked his cock against my pussy, slicking himself up. Then, holding my gaze, he lined himself up and pushed in, filling me in one relentless thrust that had my head tipping back. Oh, that felt better than I even remembered it. I dug my fingers into his shoulder and started to bring up my right hand, but he caught it gently and eased it back down.

"Let me do all the work, babe," he teased before kissing me again. I wrapped my legs around his hips, arching my back, and because I loved the way it felt to rub against him.

"Archie," I groaned and granted, I'd just woken up, but my voice sounded far huskier than usual. "I want to touch you, too."

"I promise, you can touch me whenever you want, babe. I just need you right now." The last six words broke me. No way I could tell him no, not when he strained into me and then locked his mouth over mine as his hips began to piston. The angle was perfect and he felt amazing, as did the way he hooked my shoulders and kept me from sliding as the tempo he rocked into me at increased.

My orgasm raced up at me at a startling pace, and all I could do was suck on his lower lip and dig my fingers in to hold on as he toppled right over the edge. I clenched down around him, and his hips stuttered, then he bit my shoulder as he came.

Still panting, we lay there in a tangle of limbs, and Archie pressed his face into my throat. "So," he said after several long minutes. "As I was saying…good morning."

Giddy laughter erupted through me, and he raised his head, his own lips twitching. His hair was tousled, and shadow of stubble on his cheeks had left a little burn on mine, but I seriously didn't care. "I think I said 'hi.'"

"You did," he agreed, still grinning. The twinkle in his eyes just made me laugh harder, though we both hissed as he eased out of me. I missed him almost as soon as he was off the bed. After disposing of the condom, he came back with water and offered me a drink.

"How early is it?" I managed after a couple of swallows. A stretch caught me on the last word, and I let out another satisfied groan, all deliciously achy and sore in the right places.

"Early enough," he teased, running his hand up and down my thigh. "Jeremy won't have your Thanksgiving Day breakfast ready for at least another hour."

I glanced at him from beneath my lashes. "Oh really?"

"Hmm-hmm," he said, setting the water next to the bed before gripping my hips and tugging me back down before settling himself between my thighs. Heat swept up through me. "But this is my time, and I know just what I want to be thankful for."

My laughter ended on a gasp as he buried his face against my pussy again, and coherent thought shredded a few minutes later. The overstimulation was almost too much, but I came at least twice more before he slid into me again.

I was going to feel him all day. When I told him as much, he'd grinned unrepentantly.

"Totally my plan, babe. I want you to know how thankful I am for you."

That almost made me tear up. Especially when he helped me into the shower. I loved him. No two ways about it, and he made me feel loved, too.

On our way down the stairs to eat—my breakfast, he teased, since he'd just had a few courses of his—I squeezed his hand. "I'm thankful for you, too."

"I know," he said with a wink. "'Cause I'm amazing."

That just made me laugh all over again.

Trina answered the door when I knocked, and she grinned at me. "Coop," she called over shoulder, eyes dancing. "Your *girlfriend* is here."

I bit my lip at the description, and she grinned wider as she beckoned me inside before giving me a hug. I was careful in how I returned it because of the cast.

"You have to save me," she said, even as Coop yelled from his room.

"From what?"

"Trina," Carly said from the kitchen, exasperation written all over her face. "You need to finish in here. Leave Frankie alone. Good morning, sweetie." She blew me a kiss. "I'll give you a hug in a second."

"Why can't Coop help you?" Trina argued, one arm still around me. "I want to talk to Frankie."

Carly rolled her eyes. "You can talk to her after you finish setting the table. And Coop did his part, now get in here."

"Ugh, she's such a tyrant," Trina muttered, and I gave her a squeeze.

"I won't leave before you talk to me," I promised. "How is that?"

"Thanks," she murmured.

"Sis, help Mom and stop holding my *girlfriend* hostage," Coop mimicked her tone perfectly as he wandered in from the hall. I grinned because his hair was damp and his cheeks freshly shaved. If I were to bet, he probably finished whatever his mom needed, then went to shower when I texted that Archie was driving me back. Archie was currently ensconced at my place with the cats and the video games.

I hated the idea of him being there by himself, but he assured me Coop would be over later, probably when I was at Jake's and Ian's, and he'd gotten me all night so he was pretty damn content.

Coop swept in to give me a kiss and not just a peck, but a full on tongue infused dance with my libido.

"Gross," Trina said with a cackle. "Get a room."

"Don't mind if I do," Coop told her wickedly as he wrapped an arm around me. Carly laughed, and my face caught on fire. Crap, for just a second, I'd forgotten his mother was right there. But she just waved us away.

"Go get the canoodling out of the way. We're eating in thirty minutes. I hope you're hungry." The last bit was to me. Coop smirked, since he damn well knew I'd had a big breakfast at Archie's. Even pacing myself, I'd had a fantastic helping of French toast and strawberry crepes.

"Starving," I promised. "What are we having?"

"You'll see," she said with a grin, then waved us away, and Coop didn't need telling twice. He tugged me through their living room, which was always so colorful right down to the Barbie dolls with their crocheted dresses over things like boxes of tissue.

I swore Carly knitted and crocheted for therapy. Newsflash, Erin mentioned that during my last session, but my broken wrist put a pin in that for now. Not that I was thinking about knitting. Though if I did decide to do it, I could ask Carly.

"And keep the clothes on," Carly called after us as we got to Coop's room, and Trina made dramatic gagging noises before both of them laughed.

Yep, my face was on fire. Coop rolled his eyes as he pushed his door closed and then tugged me over to his bed. He had a twin still, but I didn't care. At one time, there had been bunk beds in this room. Then when we were thirteen or so, one of the bunks vanished, so when I spent the night, I usually got the bed and Coop took the floor. Though spending the night also waned in there, too.

"Coop," I warned him. "It took me and Archie an hour to do my hair." Mostly 'cause Archie kept messing it up when he kissed me. "Do not make me look like I rolled out of bed to go and have dinner with your mom."

A wicked grin curved his lips, and he settled on the bed and leaned back against the wall, then patted his lap. Since I was wearing a dress, it was easy enough to straddle his lap with one knee on either side of his thighs.

"Do not mess up the hair," he murmured right before he kissed me. "Got it."

Ten minutes later, I was already regretting his mother's orders about clothes. Five minutes after that, he nudged my panties aside, and I slid right down on his cock. Awareness that we could be called at any minute only heightened the need. These guys were going to make me crazy as it was, but I couldn't stop kissing him, and he kept shushing my moans until he had to put a hand over my mouth. We were both laughing as we came.

Breathless, I bit his palm, and he grinned up at me. "You are so fucking beautiful, you know that?"

"You're just saying that 'cause I rocked your world," I teased, and he snorted.

"You always rock my world. Doesn't change the fact that you're beautiful and I love to watch you come." Heat and pleasure rushed through me. He eased me off of him slowly and then got up to take care of the condom. We didn't risk going out in the hall and made do with tissues to clean up.

"I wish I had more time," he told me as he teased a finger along my panties. I was so sensitive at this point, my hips bucked of their own accord.

Before I could respond, Trina thrust the door open and Coop turned easily, blocking her view as I smoothed my skirt down. She eyed both of us with a smirk. "Mom said food's ready."

"Don't you remember how to knock?" Coop went after her with hooked fingers, and she squealed more like she was seven rather than fourteen and raced away from him. I paused in the bathroom for a sec to wash my hands—well, hand—and check my appearance.

My hair was a little tousled, but not a lot I could do about that. The first sign of a hickey was showing up just below my collar, so I fixed the pullover sweater I'd worn. That with the flowy skirt weren't really dressy, but still nicer than usual. I had on my charm necklace underneath. Archie had slipped it into place before I pulled the sweater on.

Instead of turkey, Carly had made lasagna, and I goggled at it, garlic bread, and salad. The apartment had smelled great when I got there, but this wasn't what I was expecting.

"It's turkey lasagna," Trina told me, grinning at me. "So it kind of counts, but we wanted to do comfort food."

I could eat my weight in Carly's lasagna. "I love it," I told them, then smiled at Carly. "Thank you."

"My pleasure," she said with a careless laugh. "To be honest, this is easier than fixing up everything else, and I know for a fact the two of you will probably kill a pan on your own, so I made a couple more. Plenty for you to take home leftovers."

Right on cue, my stomach growled, and Coop held out a huge slab of garlic toast, then crossed it with another. "Hurry, we need to feed the beast."

I didn't even think about it. I just flipped him off, and a split-second later, I sent Carly an apologetic look, but her shoulders were shaking with laughter. "Sometimes, he just deserves it," she said as she poured herself a glass of wine. It wasn't quite eleven in the morning, but no way I was going to judge.

There were sodas for us, and we passed the dishes around, well, they passed them, and I helped brace my plate. "You know the fun part about this?" Coop said. "You don't have to worry about cutting your food." His gray-green eyes danced teasingly, and I wrinkled my nose at him, then scratched my ear with my middle finger.

Trina burst out laughing. "Dork, this is why you didn't have a girlfriend forever. You have to be nice to her."

"I am nice to her," Coop argued, winking at me. "I am always very nice to her."

Nope. Uh uh. I took a drink of my soda and gave him my best bland look. "I don't know, Trina. He's had plenty of girlfriends before. He's had lots of practice being nice. Look how that worked out."

It was my turn to get a glare. "Really?"

"Oh yeah," I said, smirking back at him.

"True," Carly piled on. "But he never had the *right* girlfriend."

Coop pointed at his mom. "What she said."

Carly patted his arm. "It's all right, dear. You'll figure it out sooner or later."

"Hey." He stared at her. "I think I figured it out in kindergarten. I wasn't the slow one in this relationship."

"Ooo, did you just call your girlfriend dumb?" Trina asked, and it took everything I had not to burst out laughing.

"Yes, Cooper, did you just call your girlfriend dumb?" Carly eyed him almost sorrowfully. "I did think I'd raised you better than that."

"He's a work in progress," I assured his mom. "And I think I'm up to the challenge."

"What the hell is going on?" Coop goggled at all of us. "No ganging up on me at this table. Frankie is on *my* side." He eyed me. "My girlfriend, my side."

"A good girlfriend doesn't let you get away with putting your foot in your mouth. Especially if you're going to pull something."

That set Trina off laughing again, and even Coop snickered as he shook his head. "Eat your food, Curtis, or I'm going to steal your garlic bread."

"Don't make me stab you." It was hilarious, and I laughed almost as much as I ate. There was even cheesecake for dessert, and my stomach was groaning, but Coop and I split a piece before he helped with dishes.

Coop walked me back to my place, after I checked with what Trina had needed—she wanted to borrow a dress from me, and as soon as Coop heard the words 'date' and 'dress,' I had to drag him out of there and promised she could come over that weekend and pick from the four I had.

"She doesn't need to be dating," he grumbled.

"Yeah, and you keep growling at her and she'll start sneaking around, and then what will you do?"

"Figure out who it is and ask Jake to beat the hell out of him," Coop told me firmly as he opened the door.

Jake glanced up from where he was playing a game with Archie. "Whose ass am I kicking?"

Thirty minutes later and still stuffed, I got ready to leave again. Jake surrendered the game controller to Coop while Archie dug into the extra lasagna we'd brought back. I got two thorough kisses that left me tingling before Jake and I headed out.

"Hope you're hungry. Mom and the girls were making the whole thing, including pumpkin pie," he teased me, and I groaned.

"I will find a way to survive. Though you might have to wheel me out of your house when it's over."

He snorted. "Good thing I lift weights, right?"

I pinched him, and he laughed. "Ass."

"Well then, don't call yourself fat," he retorted and delivered a smack to my ass as I got into his SUV, then he leaned in to kiss me. "Or pick on yourself in any way, shape, or form. You're perfect."

It was my turn to snort, and I shook my head. "Not sure about that. Have you met my boyfriends?"

"Yep," he told me, his eyes heating. "One of them is tall, strong, determined, and more than willing to deliver beat downs when appropriate."

I grinned. "Also sweet, funny, and adorably nerdy when it comes to history."

"That, too," he agreed with a wink. Then he kissed me again, one large hand cupping my face as he tangled his tongue with mine. With a long sigh, he rested our foreheads together. "I wish we had time to just get naked and celebrate that way."

A shiver went through me, and seriously, you'd think I'd be more than fine after my day, but this was Jake and I bit my lip as I studied him. "How much time do we have?"

He raised his brows, then glanced at his watch. "We'll be late in about twenty-eight minutes."

"Know a quiet place to park?" Then I dipped my gaze to his groin and back up. His eyes flared.

"Fuck yeah, I do."

It took us exactly eight minutes to find a spot and less than one minute after that did I have his jeans open and his cock in my mouth. "Don't grab my hair," I warned him. "I can't fix it."

"I can," he growled, then fisted my hair. It was a lot faster and more frenzied than I'd imagined, and Jake didn't give me a lot of control this time as he thrust up against my mouth. Honestly, I didn't care. I kept swallowing around him, sucking against the tip and then stroking my tongue along the underside.

When I stole a look up, he had his gaze fixed on me, and my heart clenched at the heat and affection in his gaze. It sent a thrill of pleasure through me even more than his groan as he fisted my hair tighter and bounced against the back of my throat before he came.

And look at that, I didn't even gag.

Jake was shaking when he tugged me upward and kissed me. Panting, he glanced at his watch and then me. "I don't have time right now, but I am definitely paying you back later. Maybe tonight?" The last was more a question than a promise, and I grinned as he tucked himself back into his boxers and zipped up his jeans.

"Maybe," I told him. "Honestly, I really enjoyed the hell out of watching you get off." His face was still flushed, and he raked a hand through his hair before he dragged me back for another more thorough kiss, and my whole system hummed.

"Thank you, Baby Girl," he murmured before he helped me with my hair. My heart did another of those little flip-flop things. I was still buzzing on that when we got to his place.

The girls were thrilled to see me, and I got dragged into the dining room to help with the table setting—well, more I was there to get peppered with a dozen questions about Jake and me dating.

"He never brings girls home," Louisa told me almost primly.

"He's been bringing Frankie home for years," Blake countered. "She doesn't count."

Rolling her eyes, Becca snorted. "Of course she counts."

"Girls," Alicia said as she carried in a large casserole dish to set on the table. It was so formal and fancy. We never ate in here, at least not on any of the trips when I'd come over before. We usually ate in the kitchen. The dining room table usually had homework and crafts all over it. "That's enough, we discussed this. You're not to give Frankie a hard time, and you will behave."

Even I straightened up at the formal tone. Alicia glanced at me and winked where her daughters couldn't see.

"That's my job."

I stared at her as she gave me a hug.

"We'll discuss your intentions about Jake later…"

"Mom!" Jake said from the doorway, his eyes wide. "Leave Frankie alone."

Alicia laughed, wrapping an arm around my shoulders. "No, dear. A mother's privilege is to interrogate the girls after her one and only son."

Jake glared at her, and I laughed. One, I didn't want them to actually fight. And two, I didn't think Alicia was planning to interrogate me—I hoped anyway—but she was winding Jake up.

"I can handle it," I told them both with a grin. "Hit me with your best shot."

"Oh, see, this is why I like you." Alicia gave me another squeeze. "Girls, go wash up. Jake, put that turkey on the table."

After she headed back to the kitchen, Jake said, "Sorry, I didn't think she was gonna do that."

"I don't mind," I told him, giving his hip a bump. "After all, maybe I have nefarious intentions where you are concerned."

"God, I hope so," he said, then stole a kiss just as his mother walked back in.

"Jacob Elijah Benton," she said in a cool tone that had Jake jerking to attention, and I had to smother a smile. "Mind your manners."

"I was definitely minding them, Mom," he said, grinning slowly. "Frankie said something delightful and deserved a kiss for it."

I rolled my eyes, and she snorted. "Food," she ordered him. "Go."

No one would let me help, so I ended in a chair that was to the right of his mom, with Jake seated next to me. Louisa was on his other side, followed by Blake and Becca to complete all of us at the round table.

The sheer volume of food they'd set out had my eyes widening. Turkey and trimmings. Stuffing. Green beans. Sweet potatoes—with the marshmallows. Cranberry sauce. Hot fresh bread rolls—yes, those made my mouth water.

I was going to die.

Like at Coop's house, the food made rounds, and Jake helped me pass things to his mom. He also handled carving the turkey, stealing a whole leg for himself and leaving the girls to bicker over the other one. It was loud and noisy, and just about perfect.

Contrary to her earlier announcement, the only thing Alicia interrogated me about was colleges, and I was okay to talk about that. Becca jumped in to discuss the ones she wanted to go to—eventually—in between discussing the upcoming winter dance recital, and did I want to go?

The best part? Jake kept his thigh pressed to mine for the whole meal.

I managed to not only make a dent in the food, I ate some pumpkin pie. When it was all done though, I didn't think I'd be able to get up from the table to save my life. Eventually, and groaning, I tried to help with the clean-up, and even though they all told me to sit still, I could ferry dishes even one handed.

I had to do something, or I was gonna puke. I didn't think I'd ever been this full.

Alicia insisted on packing up leftovers for me to take home, and then she sent Jake off to take out the trash. Alone in the kitchen, she said, "Do you mind if I ask you a direct question?"

"Nope," I told her and braced for it.

A smile softened her face, and I could see where Jake got his charming smile from without even trying. "It's not that bad. I just wanted to know if you and Jake are being safe? He gets prickly when I ask him about these things."

Clearing my throat, I nodded. "Definitely safe. He takes really good care of me." Then, because I wanted her to know it wasn't one-sided, I added, "And I'm trying to take really good care of him."

After releasing a breath, Alicia nodded. "Thank you, and I know you take good care of him. He's been happier in the last few weeks than he was all summer." She winced. "Aside from…"

"It's fine," I told her. "Honestly?" At her nod, I continued, "Me too. This summer sucked, and there's been some really awful stuff this year, too, but… Jake's definitely one of the best things about everything."

"Good." Then she swept me into another hug that caught me off-guard. "I worry about you, sweetheart, and I'm glad you and Jake finally figured it out. You two have known each other forever." I hugged her back, eyes getting a little misty at the affection.

"Thank you for having me over for dinner." The backdoor slammed, and Jake edged into the room as Alicia gave me a quick kiss on the cheek before she let me go.

"Thank you for coming. The girls loved having you, and I meant it, I want you to come over more often. We all worry about you…" Then she tossed a look at Jake, who was scowling at her. "It'll also mean I get to see Jake more."

"Mom," he grunted, and she laughed.

I felt a little guilty about that, but maybe I could fix it some. "I'd like that," I told her. "I don't know when or how often, but I would like that."

"Then it's settled." Alicia gave Jake a smug look. "Told you, I liked her."

He rolled his eyes and wrapped his arms around me. "I like her more." After his mom left us alone, he nuzzled a kiss just behind my ear. "You might even say I love you."

My heart bounced up to my throat, and I tilted my head back to look up at him. "Yeah?" Not my most erudite response.

"Yeah," he said, grinning slowly, and I twisted carefully and wrapped my left arm around his neck as I set my casted right on his shoulder. He dipped his head, voice dropping low and sweet. "I love you, Frankie Curtis. Don't ever forget it."

My stomach bottomed out, and my eyes sparked with tears. "I hate you for doing this right here and now."

He chuckled at me and pressed a kiss to my nose. "Sorry."

"No you're not," I said with an exaggerated sigh.

"No," he agreed. "I'm definitely not. But I do love you."

"It's a really good thing I love you, too, or I'd be annoyed at you for making me want to cry."

His grin gentled, and he wrapped me up against him, face buried against my hair. I closed my eyes and held onto him. Against my ear he whispered, "The next chance I get, I'm going to eat you out until you're screaming, Baby Girl. Then I'm going to do it again."

A shiver raced up my spine, and my tears dried up at the tease. I groaned, and he chuckled.

"Better?"

"You are such an ass sometimes." But who was I kidding? There was no heat in that statement at all.

As much as I'd have liked to just stay there and snuggle him or more—especially after that pair of declarations—we had to go. Ian was supposed to pick me up for dinner at his place.

I groaned by the time I climbed in Jake's SUV, and he grinned at me. "I can find us a place somewhere to park and see if we can make it work in the car."

"Okay, now that's just mean." I thumped him. One, because it sounded awesome, and two, because we were already running a little late.

"Anything for you, Baby Girl."

I stuck my tongue out at him and got a kiss for my trouble.

Not so bad, really.

But I was so damn full, and Jake set the food his mom was sending with us into the backseat, pumpkin pie and all.

In the driver's seat, he glanced over at me. "I can carry you and hand you over to Bubba if you're having trouble."

I flipped him off, but Jake just laughed.

I really had *no* idea how I was going to eat the next meal. And I kind of didn't care, 'cause Jake just said he loved me and my whole system hummed.

This might just be the best Thanksgiving ever.

Ian's parents were going to kill me. The sheer volume of food they'd made rivaled that of what had been prepared at Jake's house, only there were far fewer people. When Sara brought out the sweet potatoes and started loading up my plate, I swore my eyes turned into saucers.

"I know how much you used to love these," Sara—she and her husband both insisted I call them by their first names, no more Mr. and Mrs. Rhys—said. "You do still love them right? If not, I've got other options. Joe and Ian are bringing the turkey in now."

"Bringing it in?" On the drive over, Ian had been playing his songs in the car, and we'd been singing all the way here. It had been fun, though honestly, I wanted to lie down so bad and just die from being stuffed. I think I'd officially discovered too much food.

"Yes," she said putting the dish down, then put a finger to her lips. "They deep fried the turkey."

Oh God. I was going to die for real.

"Stay put, I'm going to get the rest."

"I could help," I offered. It was weak, but maybe moving around would help.

"No, I insist. I've been dying to pamper you, and we haven't seen you in weeks." Well, three weeks—ish. The last time had been at the police station, but probably not a discussion we wanted to have.

"I don't need to be…" But it was too late, she was already on her way back to the kitchen. I leaned back in the chair, grateful as all get out for the skirt.

'Cause it had an elastic waist. The smell of the turkey hit me as Ian and his dad carried it inside, and the golden-brown color and the rich, savory scent teased me.

It smelled fantastic.

I was so going to die.

The smile on Ian's face sent a jolt through me, and I put a pin in my pity party. He'd been so delighted when Jake pulled up with me. He'd come to get me in his mom's car, even though I had offered to drive myself over.

Jake had carried our leftovers up to join the guys gaming, and it had been kind of weird to leave them all there while I went to Ian's, and at the same time, I loved the idea they were going to be there when we got back.

Sara was back with another dish as the guys set the turkey in the center of the table, both of them beaming with pride. "It's gorgeous," I complimented them.

"It is," Sara said, laughing as she kissed her husband on the jaw. "Now if it tastes as good as it looks, this is going to be your job from now on."

For his part, Joe just let out a mock sigh. "Yes, dear."

It wasn't long before the table groaned under all the food, and the carving of the turkey revealed not only was it perfect, it had this excellent crunch on the skin. The conversation stuck to safe topics—football, apparently whatever game had been on today was a point of contention between Ian and his dad—colleges, and Christmas decorating. The fact that they wanted to know if I wanted to come back the next day to help them put up their tree was kind of sweet, if a little overwhelming. I did my best to take bites, sometimes doing more pushing my food around than eating.

Whenever Joe or Sara focused on me though, I pushed through. I actually managed all of the sliced turkey, some of the cranberry sauce, a full helping of sweet potatoes, and the grilled brussel sprouts. Ian kept our feet entangled, since we were sitting across from each other. When it was time for dessert, I had to beg off.

"I really can't eat anymore," I said, almost pleading. "I'm so stuffed. It was so good."

Ian shifted to pull out his phone, and then he snapped a picture of me.

"What are you doing?" Sara asked him with a frown.

"Documenting the moment that we discovered Frankie can actually get full."

I blew a raspberry at him, and he laughed, so did his dad and his mom. Thankfully, they let me skip the dessert, though Sara said she was sending a pie home with me and more leftovers.

Never had I been so grateful that the guys were staying with me. The leftovers alone would take care of a third of my food budget without even trying. After cleaning up, Ian and I ended up in his room where I could flop on the bed and die in peace while he played with his guitar.

Both of his parents had watched us as we headed up the stairs, and never had I been so aware of their scrutiny.

"Stop worrying about them," he told me, while I was laying with my left arm over my eyes. "Mom loves you, and I thought Dad was pretty cool."

"They were great," I told him. "Beyond great." I dropped my arm to look at him. "But it's like they think we came up here to make out. And that's…weird."

He grinned slowly, still tuning his guitar. "They aren't going to be sneaking up to listen at the door."

Kill me, I did not need that mental image. "You suck."

A soft laugh escaped him. "And you're embarrassed."

"Not embarrassed, just… Your dad already had problems with me…"

He stopped playing with the guitar. "He *never* had problems with *you*. He hated the situation you were in, and he was worried about you. But you? They love you, Frankie."

I chewed my lower lip and then sat up slowly. I'd kicked my shoes off as soon as we were in the room. "I don't want to mess this up again."

"Neither do I," he told me. Then he glanced at his guitar, then at me. "Do you want to make out?"

My eyes widened. Um… "While they're downstairs?"

He shrugged. "If they already think we are, what does it matter?"

I opened my mouth to argue that point and then snapped it shut again. He quirked his brows and then began to set his guitar down. Rising, he pressed a finger to his lips and walked over to lock his door, and then he moved back to his stereo and turned it on.

The strumming of his guitar filled the room, and I bit my lip. He turned it up and then walked back over to the bed. When his lyrics drifted out of the speakers, I groaned. Okay, I didn't think he could write a bad song, but this was one of the first ones he'd ever played for me. His eyes were on me as I scooted to the end of the bed. He dipped his head to kiss me, and I sighed against his mouth.

I wanted… I wanted a lot of things, and when I fumbled with the snaps on his jeans, he lifted his head and glanced at me.

"Frankie?"

"I want you," I told him, and his smile dazzled me. "All of you."

He gripped my upper arms gently and pulled me to my feet, and for one second, my heart fell. The last time I offered, he'd turned me down.

Then he teased his fingers under the edge of my sweater and tugged it upward, over and off, leaving me in the much thinner tank top I'd worn underneath.

"Are you sure?" was the only thing he asked.

"Yes," I promised, all trace of hesitation gone. He swooped his head down, and then his lips moved over mine, hard, fierce, and demanding, even as he wrapped his arms around me and dragged me in close.

Oh.

Yes.

Exactly what I wanted.

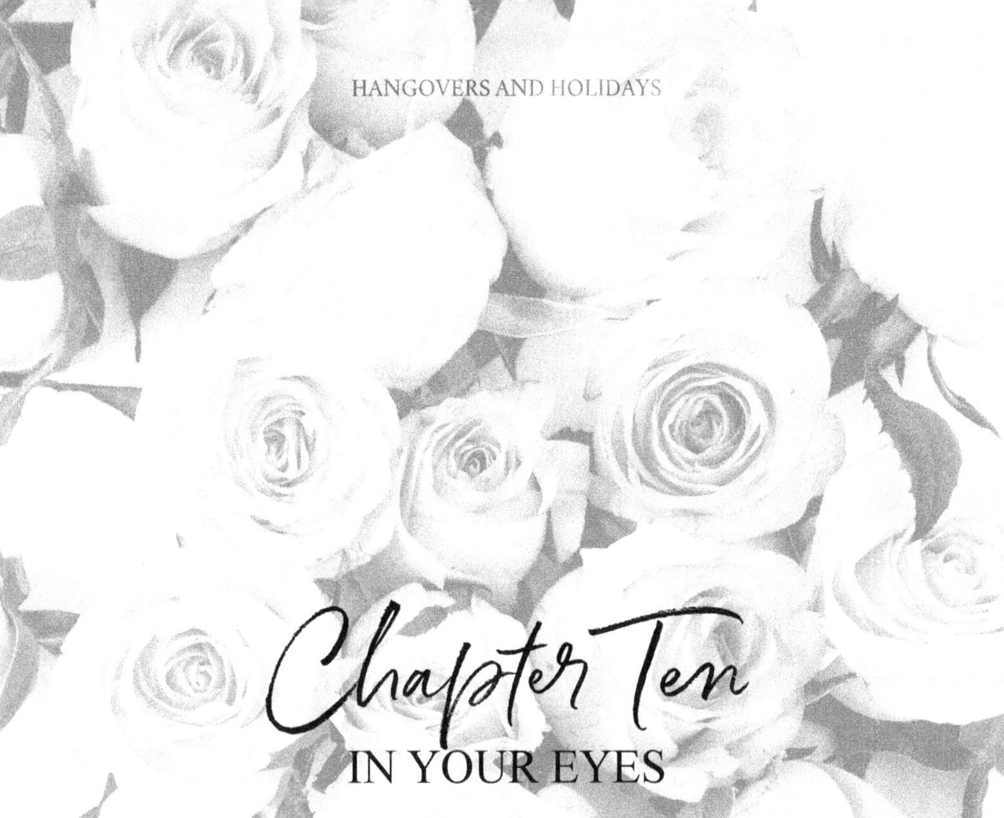

Chapter Ten
IN YOUR EYES

Locked against Ian was probably one of the best places I'd ever been. The ferociousness in his kiss demanded every ounce of my attention, and I was very much on board with that plan. The sharp bite of his teeth against my lower lip pulled a moan from me that I tried to swallow. Three facts burned in my brain.

We were at Ian's house. His parents were downstairs. And Ian had his hands under my tank top and the bra unhooked so smoothly I hadn't even felt it. Everything about his kiss was hot, demanding, and relentless. The only time he let up was to pull away and lift my tank top up. Between us, we got it up and off. The lacy bra slid right off my arms, and Ian's gaze locked on me.

Heat scorched over my skin. A part of me gulped. I was standing in front of Ian, shirtless and bare. The weight of my skirt was soft against my legs, but it had nothing on the way his gaze moved over me. I wanted this. I wanted him. I'd wanted him since that day in the pool when he'd kissed me. A real, proper kiss.

We stood there, hung in that moment, with his music playing as if our own personal soundtrack. The earlier threat of food coma all but fled. So did my worries about the fact that we were in his parents' house. How many times had we been tucked away in here with his guitar in his lap while I sprawled on his bed? Impatience crept through me, or maybe it was just the way he kept looking at me, adoring me, I pushed my fingers into the elastic band of the skirt and pushed it down my thighs until I could wiggle and step out of it.

Then it was just me in a pair of lace panties that Archie had picked out that morning. The bra matched it, not that I gave a damn at the moment. Beads of perspiration glistened on Ian's forehead, and a muscle ticked in his jaw. The weight of his hands settled on my hips, and I licked my lips slowly. When he tracked the motion of my tongue, almost riveted, joy bubbled through me.

It wasn't just me.

"Ian…" I didn't get to finish the thought. It was like saying his name just unleashed him, because his hands spasmed against my sides, and then he picked me up and pulled me right to him. I managed to get my arms around his neck before his mouth slammed down on mine. Coherent thought shredded as he dug his fingers into my ass. I curled upward, pressing my thighs to his hips, as desperate to be closer to him as he seemed to be in me.

The sleepy rope of tension inside of me grew taut. The rub of his shirt against my breasts teased my already taut nipples, and I ached for him. No words escaped, not that I could even form them with the way he held my mouth hostage. He kissed me like he wanted to gobble me up. And I didn't care how much I'd eaten today, I was starving for him.

When he slid a finger under the seam of my panties, I pulled my head up. Not far, because I didn't want to break the moment. So many broken moments along the way littered with misunderstandings and cracked by our own personal histories and family dramas.

Ian stared at me as he traced his finger along the curve of one butt cheek. It was hardly the most intimate touch, and at the same time, it was everything. His eyes blazed with a kind of intensity I didn't think I'd ever seen in him before. A shiver worked its way up my spine at the promise in those deep blue eyes.

"Angel," he whispered, his voice hoarse like it took real effort to squeeze my name out.

Oh, did I know how that felt.

Not quite trusting my voice at this point, I raised my eyebrows and hoped like hell he wasn't about to back us off again. I mean, I'd understand. I had kind of jumped him—literally as well as figuratively. Pressuring him would be as dickish as if he were pressuring me.

"I don't know," he said slowly, as if each syllable cost him personal effort before he swiped his tongue over his lips. I couldn't help but track the motion. From the last few minutes, I had three thoughts about that very talented tongue. I'd always loved the sounds he made with it when he sang. He kissed me like he wanted to own me. And I couldn't wait to feel what that tongue would be like on other parts of my body.

"You don't know?" I prompted when no more words were forthcoming. His breath brushed my cheek as he brushed his lips against mine. Okay. I was good with more kissing, but he stopped just short of actually kissing me, and I hesitated.

"I don't know—*you* don't know how badly I want this," he admitted, and my stomach bottomed out. I bit my lower lip to hold back a moan of complaint. I was already plastered to him, mostly naked. I didn't think I could make it much more clear how much I wanted him unless I painted a sign on my abdomen with an arrow pointing down that said 'put your dick here.'

The absolutely inane thought burst through the hazardous to my mental health sexual tension clouding my brain, and I had to bite my lip harder to keep from laughing.

Mostly because it would be inappropriate, but also because then I'd have to explain it. And I was having the worst time focusing at the moment, with his lips this close to me and the feel of his hands cupping my ass when I wanted him to do so much more.

Swallowing, I turned his statement over in my head and then rolled my hips to grind against him. Maybe this was one of those places where actions spoke louder than words. The thickness of his erection was right there, and my panties soaked with the first grind. A vein pulsed in his throat as he tightened his hands on my ass, and the finger along one of my cheeks became all of them. The lace ripped as he swallowed, and I let out a little laugh.

Heat burned up through me, and I kissed him this time while fisting the fingers of my left hand into his hair. The world twisted, and then I was on my back on the bed with all of his weight pressing into me. The grind of his hips rasped the denim right against my pussy because he yanked the lace away.

Somewhere between one kiss and the next, he muttered, "Sorry."

"I'm not," I gasped as he caught my arms, unhooking them from his neck and then pushing them back against the bed. He was so damn careful with my right one, it made my heart ache. But he also broke the kiss to push up and look down at me.

The way he stared at my breasts had me squirming. The vein in his forehead had begun to throb, and his pupils dilated enough to almost drown out the blue. When I arched my hips again to get him to move, he suddenly moved his free hand to my hip and locked me in place.

"Angel," he told me in a ragged tone, as if the words had been torn out of him. "I need you to let me do the moving, 'cause I don't know that I have it in me to be gentle right now. I've wanted you for a really long fucking time…"

"Anything you want." Not a difficult promise to make. Just sign me up. "I don't want to pressure you…"

He laughed, and it was a rough, sexy, and altogether captivating sound. "Angel, you're not pressuring me for anything. Fuck me." He touched his tongue to his teeth, and then he dragged his gaze down to my breasts. "I've pictured this moment a thousand times. I've probably jerked myself off to it at least that many, and let me tell you…my palm has nothing on your body."

The shiver working its way through me now sent goosebumps over every inch of my skin, and my nipples tightened even further. It was like his perusal alone was a caress, and I began to squirm a little as he roved his gaze over me. He moved his hand from my hip, then cracked it back down lightly and my back arched. It was just at the curve, and it didn't hurt so much as shock me.

"Lay still," he said. "I want to look. That bikini hid all these parts, and I want to see."

I swallowed as he bumped my thighs until I loosened my legs. The blush I'd resisted earlier flushed across my skin, leaving a trail of fire in its wake everywhere his gaze settled.

"You're so beautiful, Angel," he whispered, stroking my hip where he'd smacked me. "And I mean it, I don't have gentle in me right now."

"I can handle it," I promised, and he snapped his gaze up to mine. The hunger flaring in his eyes settled all internal arguments and worries. I could handle it. "I know you won't hurt me."

"Never," he promised. "Never." He tilted his head back for a moment and gulped in air like he needed it. "Keep your hands there." It wasn't a request, so I just nodded, and he let go and tugged his shirt off and tossed it behind him before he stood. As much as I missed the weight of him, I stared as he pulled his belt free, then shucked off his jeans. His boxers swept down with them, leaving his cock in prime view.

Everything about Ian was cut—his shoulders, his pecs, his hips. He had an Adonis belt to die for. Even if I didn't know he'd played football, you could hardly miss it. Nothing spare anywhere, and all of that gorgeously golden tanned flesh—well, except around his groin and hips where his swim trunks usually rested.

The nest of blond curls around the base of his cock even managed to look sweet, and I rolled my eyes internally at that bit of monologue. His cock was thick, just like the rest of him, and the tip was almost rosy it was so red.

He ran his hand from the base to the tip, and I might have whimpered as he gave it a couple of hard pumps, his fingers flexing around it. Then he paused, so still, and I sucked in a breath.

"Fuck," he said, then cut his gaze to his dresser and back to me.

"What?" Hot and cold blitzed me at the same time, leaving me dizzy.

"Fuck," he repeated, then reached over to his nightstand.

"Ian." I started to sit up, but he pointed a finger at me.

"Don't." The predatory look in his eyes when he riveted them on me held me far more captive than that single word. "Condoms. They're in my bag. Downstairs." He cursed again.

And a laugh escaped me, more from delight at his intensity than any real humor. At the same time, I couldn't adore him more at the moment. He was so worried. "We don't need them," I told him softly.

This wasn't exactly how I'd planned this conversation. In fact, I'd shied away from it a couple of times already. Not because I didn't want to tell the guys, but more that I wasn't sure how to approach it without sounding like I'd turned into some kind of sex-crazed, horny teenager.

I had a few years of being a horny teenager under my belt. The guys wouldn't care. I knew that. Intellectually. After that near slip with Coop, I damn well knew he'd be all in. Knowing it in my head wasn't the same as knowing it in my gut.

That said, Ian didn't need one. And he sure as hell didn't need to tear himself up about it.

"What?" He pinned me with a look, and I squirmed again. He wasn't even touching me, so how was he managing to make me feel like he had his hands all over me?

I licked my lips, then met his gaze steadily. My voice was pretty wrecked from wanting, but I didn't care. "You don't need one. You're clean. I got tested… and I asked the doctor for an implant." I shifted my arm this time—the left one, so I could half-turn to present him the upper arm, and it meant kind of rolling on my side. Ian studied my arm and then dragged his gaze down the length of me.

If my nipples got any tighter, they might break off. I was so damp, the slickness had to be painting the inside of my thighs. Still, all I got was a thrill from the way he kept devouring me with his gaze. I was not a coy person and I'd never pretended to be a sexpot, but if he kept looking at me like that, I needed to practice.

"It's effective. No pregnancy. And…that was why I asked you guys about getting tested. I don't…" Fuck, I was going to bring this up, and I could only mentally cross my fingers it didn't end this before we even truly got started. "I didn't want to be the reason any of you got something if the others had it."

I braced for his reaction, but the sudden blinding grin was not what I expected. "You are the fucking *best*," he swore, then he crawled back up the bed and his mouth was on mine before I could even process the words. The searing kiss stole every ounce of breath. He stroked his hands up my arms and positioned them above me again. The smooth coolness of leather slid over my arm, and I tilted my head to find him threading his belt around my left wrist, then looping it before I glanced at him.

"I really need you to keep your hands to yourself." He looked so damn serious, I nodded. "Is this okay?" He gave the belt a little tug, and I wasn't saying no, so I just nodded. He hooked it through the slats of his headboard before he slid it over my cast. "This is just a reminder. Don't pull, I don't want you to get hurt."

That wasn't a request. More than a little turned on by the prospect, I just nodded and watched him as he turned his attention back to me. Then he kissed me again, another blistering capture of my mouth as his tongue swept inside. The weight of his cock was right on my thigh, and I squirmed a little, wanting to move. He stroked his hands down, and this time, he pinched my ass.

"Stay still," he ordered. Then he was kissing my jaw and my throat. A moan slipped out of me when he closed that hot mouth on a nipple, and I forgot about the not moving thing. That earned me another slap, and the groan that hot sting elicited should have embarrassed me. It might later.

I didn't really care. He cupped one breast, massaging it as he sucked hard on the other. My back arched, trying to get closer to him. The hand on my hip slid between my thighs, and I let out a hiss at the first brush of his fingers.

"Fuck," he groaned. "You're so wet." He didn't leave me room to respond before he stroked my clit. And I was too primed, the tension in me snapped, and I thrust my hips up. He moved to the other breast, and I swore I felt his teeth this time as he pushed me ruthlessly.

Already too sensitized by the day, it didn't take me long. The orgasm crashed through me and left me almost soundless, even if I wanted to scream.

He bit along the underside of my breast, and I hissed at that, then he pushed a finger into me, quickly followed by a second, and my thoughts melted. This was everything I'd hoped, but not enough of what I wanted. At my protest, he lifted his head and eased a third finger in. I clenched down on him as he stared up at me.

"Like that, Angel?" he whispered. "Are you going to like it more when it's my dick and not my fingers?"

"Yes." Was that even a real question?

"How badly do you want me in here?" He pumped his fingers in, and the hard thrust of them as he curled to stroke my g-spot had my eyes rolling.

"Ian…"

"How badly?" There was a bit of a cruel streak in him. One I hadn't expected. "You're going to have to tell me."

I rocked my hips up to meet him, and he pulled his fingers out. Then I got another slap on the ass for my trouble.

"Dammit," I swore, and he grinned.

"I told you not to move."

"You're killing me," I complained. Not really. I just wanted…

"Then be still and let me enjoy myself," he instructed, and his voice had deepened, the husky notes darker and demanding. "Or I'm just going to come all over your belly, and that won't make either of us happy."

As if to illustrate his point, he moved his hand down to his cock so I could see the moisture glistening on the tip. He rubbed himself, his knuckles whitening as he fisted the base before stroking up to the tip.

I licked my lips. That looked fantastic, if a little painful.

"Can you be a good girl, Angel?"

I almost laughed again. It would be so cheesy, except my body responded to the tone as much as to the way he looked at me when he said it. "I can be anything for you," I promised. "Just don't stop."

"Not going to stop," he whispered. "Don't think I could right now." He eased me onto my side a little, then reached up to fix the belt until he had me almost rolled over onto my stomach before he fixed the loops. It wasn't remotely uncomfortable, though I didn't like losing my view.

At my little huff of protest, he chuckled and then he bit the curve of my ass. The bite stung, but he pressed a kiss over it and then traced his hands up and down my sides.

"Angel, you look beautiful no matter how you're lying, but I have always loved your ass." The admission almost made me preen as he massaged one cheek and then the other. "You have no idea what it does to me to see you in jeans, do you?"

"Um…" I glanced over my shoulder at him as he stroked down the backs of my thighs and eased them apart. You know, it would be worth whatever spanking he wanted to give me. I shook my ass at him, and Ian's mouth curved as he caught my eye. The moment held there, and then he landed a hard slap on my left cheek, the one he hadn't spanked earlier, and heat jolted all the way through me.

At my harsh breath, he kept me pinned with a look as he massaged the heat from where he'd landed it, then he cupped his palm as he landed a second, and I groaned.

"Fuck," he exhaled and moved, bracing my hips as he lined himself up, and then he pushed in, no pause for breath as he thrust deep. My whole body curled as I tried to push back into him, but there was no room for it as he draped over my back, and then his mouth caught mine as he began to rock his hips.

The feel of him was incredible, and I let out a sharp cry as he rocked into me. The slap of his skin hitting mine served like a damn metronome, and somewhere the fact that his music was still playing hit me and a laugh escaped me. His groans and harsh breaths punctuated our kisses. The belt came loose from my wrists, and he dragged me back up with him, mouthing kisses along my jaw as he kept slamming into me.

The shift in angle was everything, and every push made me cry out. I had to be quiet but I didn't want to be, and Ian was no quieter than I was. He skated a hand down my chest as his other arm kept me up with him as he increased his rhythm. When he began to play with my clit, I lost it and dropped my mouth to the arm he had braced over my chest and clamped my lips against him, trying not to scream.

Vision whiting out, I couldn't do anything but hold on as he rocked into me. Every stroke was like riding pure heat, and I only surfaced as he let out a long, low moan, hips jerking once. His orgasm was a lot quieter than mine, but the rush of heat pooling through me was so fucking different.

Somehow, he twisted to get us down on our sides, and he cradled me to his chest. Slowly, the fact that my whole body trembled registered, as did the slow strokes of his hands along my sides and up to my breasts, more soothing than stimulating. He was kissing me, too. Against my neck and along my shoulders.

I shuddered as he eased out of me. Oh, so much messier. That thought drifted from somewhere as he nudged me onto my back, and then he cupped my face before nuzzling a kiss so gentle, it brought tears to my eyes. I lost track of time, just lying there drifting as we kissed. This time when I lifted a hand to run through his hair, he only caught it for a moment to kiss it, and then I was free to touch him.

Eventually, our panting breaths slowed, and he stared down at me from heavy-lidded deep blue eyes, pupils blown and his expression so possessive, it made me shiver all over again. "How are you feeling?"

Oh, yes, the wrecked tone in his voice made me smile. "I don't have words," I admitted. I could still feel him inside of me. The heat. The weight. No condom was great.

I never wanted to go back.

I could also feel him leaking out of me. I could live without that, but not enough to make it matter. He kissed me again, and the song on the stereo shifted over to one of the new ones, the one he'd said he'd written about me, and I traced my fingers against his face.

When he slid a hand down to catch some of his cum and trace it back up to rub against my labia, and I raised my brows. "Marking territory?" No idea where that came from, but his sudden blinding grin made me glad I'd said it.

"Just reminding myself this is real," he whispered. "That I'm not dreaming."

At that, I lifted my head and nipped his jaw, then kissed along his throat until I could find a spot to suck a hickey into place. He began to toy with my clit, and the overstimulation made me whimper, but I didn't push at him to stop.

"Definitely not a dream," I assured him as I dropped my head back to the pillow.

"Good." Then he did something I could never have expected. He not only kissed his way down my body, he nudged my thighs apart so he could settle between them. The hush of his breath over my pussy sent a fresh wave of heat through me.

Before today, I was pretty sure I'd pushed every limit.

I was wrong.

"I hope you don't mind if we break your curfew," he teased, and I laughed. A laugh that turned into a groan as he ran his fingers down my labia and parted them before he pressed his face against my pussy and proceeded to eat himself out of me.

I didn't think I had it in me to come again.

Trust me, I was wrong about that, too.

It was late when he slipped out of his room to the bathroom and came back with a washcloth. He helped clean me up from our next round, and I shuddered through every touch. I was too sensitive now. When he tried to apologize, despite his smug grin, I pinched him.

As much as I'd love to never move again, I had to get dressed. He helped me, including getting the charm necklace back into place, though I did go home without panties. The scraps of mine were tucked away in his drawer. We slipped out like thieves—thank God his parents had gone to bed and I didn't have to look Joe or Sara in the eye after fucking their son five ways from Sunday. Or I should say, after their son fucked me five ways from Sunday.

My ass was still a little tender, but not in a bad way. Everything was. And at the same time...

"Ian?"

He glanced at me as he started his mom's car. We'd had about forty text messages from the guys that we'd utterly ignored. It was almost midnight, and we were finally heading back to the apartment. Jake's sarcasm had echoed through his *Well, thanks for the update, asshole* that he'd sent to Ian after Ian answered him.

"Yeah?" The possessiveness was still there in his eyes.

I licked my lips. The intensity, the day, all of it... It was too much and perfect at the same time. "Don't think this lets you off the hook for those dates."

He stared at me a beat, then burst out laughing.

"I wouldn't dream of it, Angel."

I grinned and leaned back in the seat.

"You hungry?"

I considered his question. "I could eat."

I'd definitely worked up an appetite again.

Chapter Eleven
MERRY MAYHEM

I startled awake to the soft weight of a hand on my cheek and two fingers pressed against my lips. It was dark as hell, save for a crack of light let in from the hall.

"Archie?"

He motioned for silence, then beckoned me out of the bed. I'd been sandwiched between Jake and Ian, so he had to help me climb out. Coop was right there at the door, and he had clothes for me in his hands.

It wasn't until I was in the hall and Coop was helping me put on a pair of yoga pants while I braced one hand on the wall, that I said, "What's going on?"

"We're going Black Friday shopping," Coop told me in a hushed voice, and Archie rubbed his hands together gleefully. He was way too awake for what was—I caught Coop's hand to look at his watch—three-thirty in the morning?

"What the hell? We just went to bed a couple of hours ago." If that. No wonder I was so groggy. Not even the cats had stirred, and they were usually the first ones to pounce when I got up, no matter what time it was.

"Hands up," Coop said as he tugged my tank top up and over. Then he had a bra that he slid me into, and I stared at him a beat. Wait, why was he dressing me? But he had it hooked on and then tugged a sweatshirt over my head. It was all slouchy, comfy clothes, so I wasn't going to complain too much.

In the living room, Archie held out one of my reusable coffee mugs filled to the brim, and I downed it gratefully as Coop pulled on my socks.

"I'm not five," I told him. In fact… "I tied *your* shoes when we were five."

He shot me a grin. "Then call this making up for it."

"Why are you two so happy?" And why weren't we waking up Jake and Ian?

"Because we are going to hit the sales, we're going to see what there is to see, and we're going to people watch," Archie said, his eyes dancing. "This is like the first Christmas in forever that I've been excited for… We need to get you a tree."

"Um, we usually get one like the week before—"

"Yeah, that doesn't work for me," Archie said, grinning. "I want to do a tree, we can pick out any color you like. You can get a rainbow one."

"Then we're going to set it up in here," Coop picked up the thread. "And we'll all decorate it."

They were certifiable. "When did we make this plan?"

"Last night, while you and Bubba were ignoring our text messages." Archie told me with a grin, then dropped a kiss on my nose. "I asked Bubba if he wanted to go when you were getting ready for bed. He said if he woke up on his own, sure. Otherwise, he was going to sleep."

"Jake would rather have his teeth pulled than go shopping today," Coop said as he snagged a jacket and pulled it on. "So that means it's just us."

And apparently, I didn't get a vote. Then again…they were both so adorably enthusiastic.

"I demand more coffee."

Archie's grin widened. "And you will get it."

Thankfully, their enthusiasm proved contagious, because there was a freaking line outside our first stop. Even bundled up, I huddled between Coop and Archie as they began "observing" the crowd.

Oh, hopefully no one heard us, because by the time they did open the doors, I was giggling so hard I was almost crying.

Coop snaked a cart, and they began *wandering*, almost idling as others around us dashed madly. Thankfully, the store had a coffee shop and they opened early. Archie put an order in on the app as we made our way through electronics and the guys debated the latest new gaming systems.

Then another sweep through clothes, and they both paused at the ugly sweaters.

I cracked up.

The first one had a reindeer on it and said *Dat Ass Doe*. They got progressively worse from raunchier to funnier and to just pure groaners. "We should get matching ones," Archie said, giving me a speculative look.

"Sure, why not?"

"Because I think you'd look cuter in this one," Coop argued holding up what looked like an oversized hoody sweater in brown and white. He twisted it so I could see the little tail and the ears. It was a *doe* sweater that would cut off at mid-thigh. He waggled his brows playfully at me.

Maybe it was how early it was or the lack of caffeine, or the fact that I was still high on all the endorphins from the day before but I grinned. "If you're daring me to wear it, I will."

Both boys gaped at me for all of thirty seconds before Archie snagged it from Coop's hand, checked the size and dropped it into the basket.

"Sold," he declared. Though we weren't done. We ended up with ten ugly Christmas sweaters, some for me, most for them, and at least two I had every intention of stealing at some point.

It was absolutely ridiculous.

We split up while Archie went for the coffee, and Coop directed me back to the Christmas decorations. Then the crazy shopping really began. When

Archie joined us with the coffee, I settled in to be entertained as they debated every single Christmas tree on sale.

"I don't really need a seven foot tree," I'd argued. Not that either of them listened to me. I don't think I'd ever had a large tree.

"All the more reason you *should* have one," Archie pointed out.

"Besides," Coop said, siding with him. "When we all get that place for school, we're going to need a tree there, too. Consider this an investment for future Christmases."

Uh huh.

Still, while they argued the differences between the fake fir trees and the blue spruces, green or white—there was also a dark blue one that was really pretty—I kept looking at a pure white one that had multi-colored lights that alternated with soft golden ones. It was pretty and sweet.

"That one," Archie and Coop said at the same time, and I snapped my gaze to them. They were both staring at me.

Face heating, I shook my head. "It's too much, and it's huge."

"That's why we brought my car," Coop told me, then pressed a kiss to my forehead. "C'mon, Arch, put your back into it."

They got the box and wrestled it over to the cart, then glanced at the decorations. We were spending a fortune, and I was trying to do the mental math when Archie nudged me.

"Stop," he told me. "This is my treat."

"You can't pay for everything," I argued, and he slid an arm around my shoulders and pressed a kiss to my temple.

"I can do whatever I want, it's Christmas. Now don't be a Scrooge."

Hey!

"I'm not a Scrooge!" I elbowed him just before he danced away, laughing. He came back with a Santa hat and tugged it onto my head.

At my glare, his smirk grew.

Boys.

I grunted, and he laughed. They finally settled on some colored balls—blue because they actually were the prettiest colors—a couple of ornaments with the year on them, and though Archie hesitated when he spotted the *Wizard of Oz* ornaments, I grabbed them anyway.

And I was paying for them.

That was a fun argument all the way to the front of the store.

The coffee helped, because after we left that store, we headed over to the mall and from there to another electronics store. Archie swung through another drive thru for coffee and breakfast when I started to flag. It wasn't even eight in the morning, and we'd been to eight different places.

They were insane.

But their good mood was contagious. They almost had me convinced to do a picture with Santa, but thankfully, none of those places had their Santa's open yet.

Jake and Ian were both awake when we got back to my apartment. Ian's very thorough kiss had me grinning as Jake swooped in to pick me up for one of his own. "I love the hat," he teased. Yes, I was still wearing the Santa cap. Archie and Coop both insisted.

They helped Coop and Archie bring in the bags, giving us hell over the sheer amount we bought. I had splurged, a little. I'd found some mugs for the guys that I wanted to add to my kitchen, different ones with different sayings for each of them.

I'd also managed to sneak away in the mall while Coop and Archie were checking out the new games display and found boxers. They were goofy and maybe a little corny, but since I had managed to now steal a pair of boxers from each of them—I needed to grab some from Ian, but he didn't wear boxers as much—I wanted to get them special pairs of their own.

Since they also had bags I wasn't allowed to see, I kept hold of these two and carried them off to hide somewhere in my room. Except, there was literally nowhere in my room the guys didn't go or have access to.

I ended up stashing them all with the cleaning supplies in the hall closet behind the vacuum. The little robot of Archie and Jake's was still motoring around the apartment, and the one in the closet hadn't been pulled out in days.

Fingers crossed, I'd find somewhere else to hide the stuff when they weren't looking.

Ian caught me in the hall and slid an arm around me before tugging me in close. "Hey," he murmured before giving me another slow, toe curling kiss. "How are you doing?" Palm spreading over my ass, he rubbed a slow circle over the part he'd given more than one solid spank the night before.

The yoga pants and panties might as well have not even been present for the intensity of sensation sweeping through me at the light contact.

"I'm good," I said, biting my lip. "How about you?"

"I'm amazing," he said, then the corner of his mouth curled up. "I would rather have woken up to you than Jake, but Archie told me they planned to steal you this morning. Did you have fun?"

"I did."

Whatever else I was going to say evaporated as he closed the distance between us and slanted his lips over mine. I sighed into the kiss as he stroked his tongue along mine. Every hard muscled inch of him fit right up against me, and the squeeze of his hand on my ass had me thinking about the night before.

"Ahem," Archie said. "Not to intrude, but I'm going to intrude. Can the canoodling and come help with the tree."

Ian lifted his head and said, "Five minutes," before he swooped back down to take my mouth again. A groan wound up through my throat when he picked me up.

"Well, I'm going to guess things are working out," Coop said.

"No shit?" Jake retorted.

"I'm timing this because she'll need air eventually."

At Archie's comment, laughter burst through me and Ian lifted his head with a grin before he made a face at them. "Thank you for the comments from the peanut gallery."

"You're welcome," Coop said with a small bow.

"Tree," Archie reminded us. "Kissing later."

Ian grumbled a noise of disagreement, and for a second, my chest tightened. But when he glanced at me and turned his back on the guys, he winked. Relief swarmed me, and he gave me another peck on the lips. "To be continued?"

Oh most definitely.

For the next two hours, the guys got the tree out and set up, then fluffed it. I'd never seen so much debate over "fluffing" before. It was enough that I actually filmed some of it and sent it to Rachel, who sent me back a series of laughing while crying emojis.

The ornaments we'd bought barely covered the tree. Ian and Jake had a similar reaction to the *Wizard of Oz* ornaments I'd picked up that Archie and Coop had, but I refused to be dissuaded. "I had fun that night… You know we had good memories, too. I'm choosing to remember the good ones. Besides, breaking Sharon's nose was a good one for me, too."

There was a beat, then they all started laughing and the worry over the ornaments went away. I had another box with some of the more meaningful ornaments to me socked away. Some I'd made in elementary school. There was one that Coop had made me when we were in first grade, and I had another that Jake had made in third.

Their faces were priceless.

"You kept that?" Jake asked as he stared down at the lumpy blob of clay with a hook in it. It was supposed to have been a train engine, but pieces had broken off and the paint had faded. I could still see it though, just the way he'd made it, and my name was still inscribed on the bottom.

"I liked it," I told him.

"I could probably make you a better one," he mused, and I snagged it back from him.

"That's fine, but I'm keeping this one."

"Don't argue, man," Coop told him as he held up the smashed face cat ornament he'd made me. "We'll just call it less than modern art."

Still. The tree seemed kind of barren.

"Okay, I've got some stuff at my place," Ian said. "Some ornaments and gift ones that I have set aside that are mine. I'll go grab them. I know where they are."

"Ditto," Jake agreed.

Before I knew it, they were all splitting up, and I got a series of quick kisses before they took off. In the silence after they left, Tiddles wandered out to stare at the tree with me. He glanced at me like all the noise and interruptions to his routine were my fault.

"Hey, they haven't decorated you yet," I teased him. At the same time, the tree warmed the whole living room up. It made it feel cozy in a way I didn't think it ever had. More, despite the absence of the guys, it didn't feel so empty.

Coop wouldn't take long, so I headed back to grab the presents I'd managed to get and found the wrapping paper stored in the back of my bedroom closet. The wrap job I did was pretty awful, but the wonders of tape and bows helped.

I'd just finished wrapping the last one when the front door opened.

"I'm back," Coop called. "You are not going to believe what I found."

"Yeah?" I gathered up the hastily wrapped packages and managed to balance them. Coop turned from rummaging in a box on the coffee table and stared at the presents before he hurried over to help me. "I got them."

"Yeah, yeah," he grumbled, then gave me a kiss with a little nip on the lip. "But I'm here to help, and it gives me an excuse to see if any of these are for me." He always was a little impatient with presents. Not that it stopped him in the slightest from giving each one a shake before he slipped them under the tree.

I laughed and wandered over to the box. "What did you find?"

"Oh," he said, and reached in to pull out a series of three oversize round ornaments that were definitely handmade and shedding glitter. In the center of each one were pictures—of us.

"Oh my god," I exhaled and stared at them. "We were so tiny."

"And buck-toothed," he teased, nudging the one I took. "But you still have the best smile."

I rolled my eyes. "And you couldn't believe I'd kept the ones you made me." I stuck my tongue at him.

He gave my ass a squeeze. "I think that was Jake. I know what a sentimental sap you are, even if you try to hide it."

"Pfft, I'm not a sap. I barely like hugging most days."

"Not true," he argued, sliding his arms around me and pulling my back to his chest. "You do like hugging. You just like hugging the right people." When he rubbed his cheek against my hair, I melted a little and leaned into him.

"You give great hugs."

"Exactly," he murmured. "I'm the right people."

Eyes closed, I just let him hold me for a minute. "I'm not freaking out."

"I know you're not," he agreed, and at the same time, I didn't want him to let go. "This is not a 'freaking out' hug, this is a 'damn, you're hot and I want to rub my dick against your ass' hug."

Laughter bubbled right up through me, and I snort-giggled. He licked his index finger and made a sizzling sound as he marked an imaginary point. When I glanced up at him though, his gray-green eyes were warm, if a bit concerned.

"Well, your dick gives great ass hugs," I said, waiting until we'd pulled apart and he went to take a drink. Water sprayed out of his nose, and I grinned, marking my own point in the air. We were still laughing when the guys got back.

They brought with them treasures each. Among Jake's stash were a pair of ornaments he'd picked up during the time he'd lived in Germany. We didn't talk about when he was gone so much, but Coop and I had both felt his absence. As sorry as I was for his parents, I was so glad that his mom had moved back.

Ian had a bunch of sports and music ornaments, including some cartoon characters playing instruments. Archie had these crystal snowflakes and teardrops. They were fancy as hell, and I had a feeling they belonged to his grandmother. He also had some light up ornaments and action figures.

To say the tree had a most eclectic theme when we were done would be understating it. It was a little lopsided, and we didn't have anything for the top of it. I had Jake put my Santa hat on it for now.

Archie passed out the sweaters and told everyone to change. After, we got together in front of the tree, and he worked it out with his phone to do a group selfie of all of us in front of our crazy ass tree.

He even managed to get one where Coop and Jake were both kissing my cheeks, which meant we had to do another with Archie and Ian doing the same thing. I loved the snaps he got and made him send almost all of them to me. I'd also noticed a couple of other presents had been snuck under the tree while we'd been decorating, not that I commented.

I'd save my shaking for later.

After we'd cleaned up, we settled in for leftovers—of which we had *tons*—and movies. First up, predictably, was *Die Hard*. It definitely qualified as a Christmas movie. I dozed off during one of the next films, curled up against Jake, and woke up snuggling Coop.

"Had to pee," Jake told me with a grin. "Then he wouldn't give you back."

"You wizz, you lose," Coop chortled, and that had Archie rolling his eyes.

Still, it was an awesome day, and by the time we wandered off to bed, I was full, the house was Christmassy, and I couldn't believe our week of freedom was almost over.

Oh, and the guys were going running in the morning.

No, thank you.

"Don't worry," Coop whispered against my ear. "I have other workout plans."

I was definitely *not* worried.

Chapter Twelve
YOU CAN TELL ME ANYTHING

"I can't say I really did the homework," I admitted. I wanted to apologize, but at the same time… "It was the holiday, and I got distracted by a lot of things."

"Good distractions?" Erin asked.

It was Monday, and I had three appointments this week since I'd had none the week before. I wasn't sure how I felt about that. The last appointment here had just been kind of brutal. I supposed that was the point, right?

"I think so," I told her, leaning back on the love seat and sitting cross-legged. I'd slipped out of my boots. She'd told me on my very first visit that I could make myself comfortable. The weather had turned a little balmy after the cold storms of the weekend. But it wouldn't last.

"Do you want to talk about the distractions? What made them good?"

"The guys," I admitted. "Thanksgiving was amazing." A smile pulled at my mouth. Thanksgiving had been more than amazing. The only place it might have been better was if all five of us had been together all day. "But…for starters, I got a new job because my old one wants me to take more time to heal and to get through the holidays."

That still stung, no matter how well-meaning Marsha was.

"I'm delivering food. Coop and Jake both do it, and I've gone with them while they work. It's not bad, and I get to drive and I kind of like it. The guys took turns going with me, in case I needed help to carry stuff. They're also really great about just hanging out."

"That sounds nice," she said.

"It was, it is. I'm going to work tonight, probably after we do our weekly 'where are we all at on homework.' Semester finals are coming up, and I will hopefully be out of this cast before then." More and more, I just wanted it off. It itched. At least I didn't need pain meds hardly at all. I barely noticed it, except for the stupid cast.

So that was something, right?

"The school is making accommodations for you, though, right?"

"They are," I said with a nod. "But it's… I like being able to do things for myself."

"Understandable. How was your Thanksgiving?"

A flush warmed my face. "It was fantastic. Probably the best Thanksgiving I've ever had." No probably about it. "Usually, it's just me and my—me and Maddy. We'd get some fried chicken and the sides, and maybe watch a movie. This was different. This was a really big breakfast with some of my favorites, then dinners at the guys' houses with their families, and it's kind of cool to see how they get along with their moms and in Ian's case, his dad, too."

There was all the making out and all the sex, but I wasn't quite ready to tell her about that. If anything, my body spent the weekend humming. The guys stayed, splitting time and rotating who slept with me. Coop and I were beginning to really enjoy the weekend mornings after the others took off to run.

Ian jumped in to help me with showering. If how late we were getting back from his place on Thanksgiving hadn't tipped them off to the change between us, that had.

A shiver traced up my spine. The demanding side of him that popped up when we were alone and naked was…wow. Not that I was complaining. They all had their possessive tendencies, but I'd never have imagined this side of Ian.

I couldn't wait to get to know it better.

"I'm glad to hear that. Did you do anything special?"

I grinned. Did I?

"You could say that. When we got to the weekend, Archie insisted we get up early to go hit the Black Friday sales." I laughed.

"Have you done that before?"

"No, but he wanted to people watch, and it was…funny. We got breakfast and picked up a tree for my apartment. It's an artificial one, but Maddy never really wanted to do a tree, except maybe the week before. Always a real one, which I kind of like, too. But the lights on the tree are gorgeous, and the guys went a little crazy with decorations."

"How so?"

"Um, everyone went home and grabbed a random box of their own and brought it back. Then we all put our kid ornaments on it, the kind of stuff you make when you're in elementary school or got when you were younger. I had a small box in my room of some of my favorites." Things I'd set aside over the years or snuck out the other box.

I was glad I had.

Maddy had taken that box with her.

Yeah. I shoved that thought away.

"It's neat, Coop and I have had Christmas stuff together before and sort of with the guys but, it was always the stuff at their houses or at mine. Never ours. This one…this is ours."

"Are you excited about Christmas?"

I kind of was, but I didn't want to admit it. Maybe if I didn't get my hopes up, they couldn't be dashed. "I still have to figure out presents, that's going to be hard." And kind of exciting. Of all of us, Archie and I were most likely to get

Christmas together. The other guys would have to be with their families. Then again, Archie might want to see his grandfather.

We'd figure it out. Though I had a feeling they'd want me to rotate between the houses. That was kind of a headache, but I wanted to see them, too. We could make it work.

"How are you balancing your time between them?"

I stared at Erin. "It's difficult, and at the same time, the easiest thing ever."

"How so?"

Why did I know she was going to ask that? So far, we hadn't delved too much into my relationships. I guess that was where this was headed.

Yay?

Chapter Thirteen
MAKING ARRANGEMENTS

JAKE

"I can't believe you intend to go out of town for two whole weeks, including your birthday, much less for Christmas itself." Mom stared at me. I hadn't expected her to be thrilled, but the flicker of hurt in her eyes crushed me. At the same time, the thought of staying here while they were all gone?

No, I couldn't do it.

"I knew you probably wouldn't be a fan," I told her. "Normally, Christmas with you and the girls? That's awesome. But I want to spend this one with Frankie."

Her expression troubled me. I couldn't read it. "Frankie is more than welcome to join us, I think I made that clear over Thanksgiving. I would never turn that girl away."

"And I love you for it," I assured Mom. "But Archie is right, Frankie deserves something special. To be away from all of this, from that apartment, from the shadow of her mother, and from where everything has gone bad. Senior year was supposed to be a blast, and it's like she just takes knock after knock. We want to do this for her."

Arms folded, Mom leaned back in her chair. "Where are you planning on going? Can you just come back for Christmas Day?"

"Mom." I sat forward and held my hands out to her and waited. I'd picked a time when the girls would all be at their activities and it could be just the two of us. Coop and Bubba had to talk to their parents, but they were both eighteen. Even if their parents weren't thrilled, they could just go.

I wasn't quite there yet.

Relenting, she took my hands. "Jake, Christmas is for family."

"Frankie is my family. The guys are my family." How did I explain this without upsetting her more? "Mom, in a few months, I graduate and I'm going to college. You know I'm going out of state."

She frowned. "I know, and that's coming way too soon as it is."

"You're going to be fine. You've got the girls. Becca starts high school next year, another year after that, and she'll be driving. If she picks up any boys you don't like, just tell me, I'll hot foot it home and knock them out."

That got me a smile.

"This is our last Christmas though, baby," she said. "The last one before you really start moving out and on."

Okay, that was a little melodramatic. "It's not like I'll never come home for Christmas again. But this is what I want for me. I don't want to make this a fight with you." If I had to wait until my actual birthday to pack and go, I would. I'd fucking hate it, but I would.

"You're going to go regardless, aren't you?"

Maybe I'd failed to keep the obstinance off my face. Or maybe Mom just knew me. "It's Frankie," I told her. "I want to be where she is."

Mom sighed. "Have you considered talking to her? Maybe adjusting the plans a little?" That was a reach, and we both knew it.

"We haven't told her yet," I cautioned. "It's a surprise. Largely 'cause Archie is funding the whole thing and she'd say no in a heartbeat. She hates when we spend money on her."

"But you plan to do it anyway," Mom said, her tone wry and a hint of amusement on her face as she squeezed my hands.

"If I had the money? Hell yes, I would pay for it myself." I had paid for a couple of things. One of which was currently burning a hole in my pocket, but I saved it. I was giving it to her on my birthday. "You know…ever since we came back, she's where I've wanted to be."

"She was where you wanted to be when we were gone," Mom reminded me gently, and I gave a little shrug. When they'd uprooted us to Germany, I'd been pissed. I hadn't wanted to leave Frankie or Coop to go to the other side of the world. It had *sucked*. Worst, I hadn't wanted to write to them. And say what? *Having a shitty time, wish I was there?*

I'd had the emotional depth of a teaspoon, and I didn't have the words to express why I was mad that I was there and they weren't. Mad that I'd left her behind and Coop got to be where I wasn't. That day when I saw them again after we got back here…it had lifted everything off me. The crap with Dad, the worry about Mom and the girls.

I was where I belonged.

They slotted me back in like I'd never left. Then I'd met Bubba, and he was a part of us, too. I shook my head. "Yeah, she was. I'm not trying to hurt you," I promised. "I get that you want us all home. I'm sure the girls will be less than thrilled that I'm gone—then again, they might enjoy not having me there to give them crap."

"Don't start," Mom said before she squeezed my hands and releasing them. Standing, she moved to the cupboard and got out a wine glass. "I could wish you weren't going," she told me. "I hate the idea of you being far away on both your birthday and Christmas." Maybe especially Christmas, but she didn't have to say that. I got it.

Still, the way she was talking sounded like she had reconciled herself to the idea. I crossed my mental fingers. "If it helps, I'll miss you, too."

She paused as she pulled the corkscrew out of the drawer and gave me a droll look. "No you won't. You'll probably call us on Christmas Day, talk for fifteen minutes, and then hang up. I'll be stunned if you remembered me on your birthday. After all, I only went through eleven hours of labor."

I bit back a smile. "I'll always remember you, Mom."

"Hmm-hmm." The snort of disbelief only made me smile wider. She got the wine bottle opened and poured herself a glass. Not looking at me, she said, "Frankie told me you take very good care of her, and that she is trying to do the same for you."

"She does," I promised. "Mom, she…she just does."

"I'm glad." Wine glass in hand, she turned to face me. "Understand that before you're twenty-five, I'm not ready to be a grandmother."

I opened my mouth, then snapped it shut. Wincing, I raked a hand through my hair and then stared at her. "Okay, Granny, I wish you'd told me that earlier."

That earned me a dark look, and I laughed.

"Joke." I was quick to raise my hands in surrender. "Trust me. Not ready to be a dad either, and I know Frankie's not interested in being a mom. In fact, other than making sure we have birth control covered, that's really the farthest thing from our minds."

She let out a sigh and then gave me a little nod.

"Mom…"

"It's fine, Jake," she told me before I could continue. "I get it. I always knew you were going to be the first one out the door. That you were going to do fine building a life away from us. I just…didn't think it would happen so soon."

"Want to do a family Christmas before I go? Just one for us?" It was an olive branch, and the look she gave me said as much.

"One present each for you and the girls," she told me, meeting my concession with one of her own.

"And one for you," I argued.

She snorted. "Fine. Frankie is welcome, and if she comes, we'll add one in for her. All other presents, including your birthday present, you can get when you get home."

I grinned slowly. "Sounds reasonable."

"Hmmph," she grumbled and took another sip of her wine.

"Thanks, Mom," I told her as I stood.

"I haven't said yes," she warned me.

"But you're not telling me no." That mattered.

"No, baby, I'm not telling you 'no.' I get what it is to be young and crazy about someone. You've loved that girl for so long. I just really hope she knows how much you care and appreciates it."

"I'm the lucky one," I told her and snuck in a hug. Mom thwapped me once, then returned it before giving me a light shove away. "I am, Mom. She's…"

"Yes, yes, I get it. She's perfect, and you're going back over there tonight, aren't you?"

I grinned. "Yep. Want me to go get the girls and bring them back so you can enjoy your wine before I go?"

"You, Jacob Benton, are sucking up."

"I'm just being a good son," I teased, and her absolute snort just made me grin. "I'm the best son you have," I continued, and she laughed.

"Yes, Jake, yes you are. Off. Get your sisters, and I'll order pizza from the place. Pick it up with them and bring it home, since you are a good son, then you can go spend the night with your girlfriend because I am literally the most understanding mother on the planet."

"You are the best." No arguments. No lie.

On the way out to my car, I called Archie.

"Mom's on board," I told him when he answered.

"Yes." I could almost picture him fist pumping. "Coop talked to his mom.

Just waiting on the nod from Bubba, and I'll lock in the tickets."

When I started the SUV, the phone transferred over the Bluetooth to the speakers. "We're flying?"

"That's the plan. We could drive, but I'd rather just fly and rent a car there. Already made the arrangements for the place we're staying."

"And you're being cagey as fuck about it," I told him as I backed out of the spot. "I get that it's a surprise for Frankie, when do the rest of us find out?"

"When we're all locked in." Smug fuck. "Don't bitch and just let me enjoy spoiling her and you guys by extension. This is the first Christmas in a long fucking time that I'm actually looking forward to."

That killed any argument I could make, even if I wanted to give him shit. I still didn't really know his parents, but based on recent experiences and that bullshit with Frankie's mom and his dad in the park? Yeah, I'd pass.

"Fine," I told him all aggrieved. "But I reserve the right to claim Frankie on my birthday and have her all to myself if I want."

Archie snorted. "Birthday boy always gets what he wants. That's always been the rule."

It had been. "Just making sure we're clear there, Daddy Warbucks."

"Bite me," came his response, sans any real heat. "You know what, just let Frankie bite me."

Then we both laughed. "Fair deal." Still chuckling, I continued, "I'm on my way to get the girls and pizza before I drop them back at my mom's. You at Frankie's tonight?"

"Nope," Archie said. "I want to be, but Grandpa is back in town and I'm going to have dinner with him. It might run late, business stuff."

Yeah, no comment on that.

"You might have her all to yourself. Bubba was talking to his parents tonight, so he may or may not get out of there depending on their reaction." Considering Bubba had been *attached* since Thanksgiving, I was okay with that, too. When they ran so late, I'd figured it out. I wasn't the only one, and on the one hand, I was glad for them, but on the other—we were back to having to divide her time four ways. I'd discovered I was a bit of a greedy bastard. Bubba helping her shower cut into *my* time with her.

Then again, he looked fucking deliriously happy, and she'd *relaxed*. So at least it cut some of the tension, and that was good for everyone. I didn't have to be a dick about it. "Cool. If that's the case, don't make it over tonight. I'd appreciate it."

Archie laughed at me. "Yeah, yeah. Gotta go. Grandpa is here."

"Take care, man."

An hour later, I finally got to Frankie's to find Coop there but no Bubba. That was fine, I could live with Coop. He gave me a quiet thumbs up as he raised his brows at me. I nodded. His near silent yes didn't go unobserved though.

She was sitting on the sofa looking absolutely adorable in her tank top and boxers—mine, and I never wanted them back—her laptop balanced on her knees and her hair tousled like she'd just pulled it out of the braid and let it fall in kinked and curly waves.

"What are you two plotting?"

I grinned. "What we're going to do with you now that we have you all to ourselves."

Coop straightened, then shot me a speculative look before he grinned at Frankie. "Bad things."

"Very bad," I agreed.

"If either of you says something like 'math homework' I may throw this laptop at you. Not that it will hit, because my aim currently sucks."

I snorted and toed off my shoes before moving over to slide behind her on the sofa, and then I dragged her onto my lap, easily balancing the laptop so it didn't fall. "Well, it might involve an equation and some variables," I teased. She wiggled her ass a little to get more comfortable, and I just sighed. That little wiggle had become one of my favorite forms of torture.

The words on her screen leapt out at me and effectively killed the beginnings of my hard-on.

...Mitch...

"What are you working on, Baby Girl?" It came out a lot harsher than I meant it to, and she snapped the laptop closed before I could read the rest of the sentence.

"Nothing."

Bullshit.

Coop moved to sit next to us, and he dragged Frankie's legs over his lap so we were sitting cozy. "Easy," he warned me before he looked at her. "We're not being nosy."

"Oh, I'm being fucking nosy. She's writing about Mitch. If we're writing about that asshole, I want to know why." I didn't want that asshole anywhere near her. Not even in non-verbal communication or as a sentence in a word program.

She squirmed a little under my focus. "It's nothing, just something I'm working on."

"If it's nothing, then you can tell me what it is—"

Coop jabbed his elbow into my ribs, and I grunted. "Don't be such a dick," he ordered me.

"I'm not being a dick." But I shut up at his nod toward Frankie. Her expression had tightened, and she'd gone a little pale. "Okay, fine. I'm being a dick." Blowing out a breath, I pressed my forehead to her shoulder. "Sorry, Baby Girl. I do not like that asshole. I do not want you to ever have to think about him again."

I'd still like to bury the son of a bitch.

After I broke every bone in his body.

The rush of anger had me grinding my teeth, and I didn't miss Coop's worried look. Forcing myself to relax, I smoothed a hand over her bare thigh. She was here. She was fine. The cast on her arm seemed to make a liar out of me, but that went in another week.

Then we'd work on building the strength up in that arm, and I was going to work on her right and left hooks. No one was putting her in that position again. Another breath, and she relaxed back against me, tilting her head until it rested against my shoulder.

"I'm okay," she reminded me. Something she shouldn't have to do.

"You're better than okay," I told her. "You're fucking amazing."

"Yeah, you are," Coop added when she scrunched her nose. "No arguments. We're right. You sit there and just accept that we are."

That got a huff of laughter, and I pressed a kiss to her temple, fucking glad Coop was there and I hadn't just dragged her into some fight she didn't need to be in. Goddamn, I needed to put a muzzle on my temper.

"Erin wants me to journal some of the stuff that happened to me. Just… what I'm feeling or what I remember. Even what I think happened versus what I know."

Why the fuck would she want her to write about it? But I bit back the question as Coop nodded. Okay, he got this part. Good. I eyed him.

"Is it helping?" was all he asked. Okay, I could use a little bit fucking more than that.

"I don't know," she admitted. "Sometimes, when I talk to her, it's easy and it's kind of fun. I told her about Thanksgiving." Her smile made me smile.

Thanksgiving had been amazing. "That reminds me," I murmured. "I do believe I owe you at least one orgasm or two."

The flush moving up from her chest continued to delight me, but nowhere near as much as the way her ass tightened and clenched up. Oh yes, that woke my dick right the hell back up.

Coop chuckled. "I'm sure arrangements can be made."

Damn straight they could be. "You in?"

The little catch in her breath and the way her lips parted as she dared a glance from me to him had me stroking her thigh gently. I wasn't the only one, Coop was rubbing her calf. There were a lot of things I wanted from her and couldn't wait to discover. Sharing her was just another fabulous item on the list.

But we weren't rushing anything. I'd rather ease her into wanting it. Better, I wanted to ease her into asking us for what she wanted. The blowjob in the car had been amazing, even more when she'd seemed so damn delighted about it.

"That's a stupid question," Coop answered with a grin. "I'm always *in* and *up* for it."

It took me a beat, but I wasn't the only one groaning at him. Frankie poked his side as she grinned, then she glanced up at me. "Anyway," she said, pulling us back to the topic at hand. "I don't know if it's helping. Some things are harder to talk about than others. The stuff I have a hard time with, she wants me to journal. See if I can work out the feelings there and then talk to her."

She pursed her lips, then looked from me to Coop and then down at her laptop. When she flipped open the screen, I put a hand over her left one to hold it still for a moment. "Baby Girl, you don't have to show us. I'm not that much of a dick. Really."

"You're not a dick," she murmured, twisting and brushing a kiss to the corner of my mouth, and damned if that didn't make me want more instantly. Ignoring my own dick for the moment, I focused on her. "You really aren't. I get it. You guys are all protective. You more than some."

"Hashtag fact," Coop drawled, and she grinned at him. Sometimes it annoyed me that he always knew exactly what to say to her. That he could make her smile, even when tears flashed in her eyes. But that was the selfish prick in me. The majority of the time, I was damn glad for him. "But Jake's job is to be the biggest, baddest one of them all."

Another laugh escaped her. "Yeah, yeah. The point is…these are things I've had trouble talking to you guys about, too. So maybe I should let you read it. Maybe I can share it that way."

"Frankie, do you want us to read it?" Coop asked her, and I threaded my fingers through hers.

"No," she admitted with a bit of a wince. "Not really."

In that case, I reached past her and closed the laptop again. "Then we won't." Coop nodded at my words. "When I'm being a nosy prick, just tell me to fuck off, okay?"

She snorted. "When was the last time you listened to me when you thought I was holding back?"

Not an unfair assessment. "We'll work on that," I promised. "You tell me not to be a prick, and if I get bossy, tell me I don't get sex. That will shut me up."

Coop's eyebrows climbed, but Frankie half-twisted again and ground that gorgeous ass against my cock. Yep, definitely torture. "Bullshit."

"True, but I will wait until after sex before I grill you again." I grinned, and she rolled her eyes. But she also laughed, which had been the point. Speaking of distractions, I glanced at the clock on the DVD player. "You hungry, Baby Girl?"

"No," she said, shifting as though she planned to get up. "I might be peckish later, but I had a sandwich when we got home."

"Damn," I murmured. "I'm starving."

"What do you want?" Thank you, Baby Girl, for walking right into that. Coop just rolled his eyes as he grinned. But he also snagged her laptop as I scooped her up and stood.

"You," I told her. "Coop can watch or you can blow him. Or he can wait his turn." I didn't much care which, but first, I was eating her out until she came a few times.

"You're so gracious," Coop said drily, but the little shit was right behind me and Frankie was laughing.

"I try," I told him and settled her on the bed. Between us, we had her naked in under a minute, and I had her thighs over my shoulders as I looked up to where Coop was already stroking her breasts. Damn that was a sight. "You are all done with homework right, because I don't plan on you leaving this bed for the rest of the night. Good? Good." I didn't wait for her answer, just buried my face where I wanted to be.

It took me under five to have her back bowed and hips arching as she came.

That was one.

Chapter Fourteen

GNO

FRANKIE

"So, when are you going to tell me which one is the best in bed?" Rachel asked in that oh so blunt manner, eyebrows waggling. "Inquiring minds are dying to know."

I didn't slow down, taking a bite of the Monte Cristo and just flipped her the bird. My session with Erin had been late today. I'd have had all of ten minutes in my last class, so I just texted the guys that Rachel and I were going to have some girl time and I'd see them at home. Three sessions in one week was not a good idea. Even if we hadn't had one the week before.

My eyes were sore from the crying, and my nose was shiny. Thankfully, blunt-as-fuck across from me hadn't made a single comment, other than to hand me a wet wipe to clean up with and some tissue. When I mentioned going to do something distracting, she went straight here. The little bistro in the strip mall made the best sandwiches, and they had one of my favorites.

Ensconced in a booth, I dug right in and loved every powdered sugar and melted swiss cheese with turkey and ham minute of it. Rachel studied me, and I could almost see the wheels ticking behind her eyes.

"Can I guess?" The spark of laughter in her eyes softened the teasing comment.

"Does it require using knowledge gleaned from gossip from aforementioned bed partners?" I was rather proud of how I phrased that.

Rachel considered it a moment, then wrinkled her nose. "Fine. I'll shut up. But I do reserve the right to bring it up again. You can tell me one thing though."

"What's that?" I snagged my drink.

"Did Archie take my tongue advice, and do any of the others need it?" Apparently, our girl's night was going to double as embarrass the fuck out of me.

"I'll tell you," I began, enjoying her sudden grin, "*if* you tell me what Skylar thinks of your technique and does she reciprocate?"

Yep, that was me, fighting fire with fire.

Smile dimming a fraction, Rachel sighed. "Skylar and I broke up."

I was officially an ass. "I'm sorry."

She shrugged. "No biggie. She's still gorgeous and that ass, but… Alas, it is what it is. I'm not ready for anything long-term anyway." Though she made light of it, the look in her eyes went a little too far away.

"Do you need to talk about it?" Not want. Need. Something Erin had brought up like four times now. I listened. No one ever *wanted* to talk about their problems. Wanted implied some kind of desire. Need, however, was an entirely different kind of beast. I *needed* to talk about mine. I'd needed to for a long, long time.

Course every time we scraped crap off the top, it was like a pressure cooker, it freed it up for more to bubble to the surface. I shoved all that away for a moment. This wasn't about me. It was about Rach. I reached over and put my hand on hers.

"You don't have to," I said, squeezing her fingers, and though hers had been icy at first, she turned her hand over and grasped mine. "But, you always listen to me, so the same goes for you. Whenever, however, you want."

A faint smile tugged at her lips. "However?"

"You're about to be dirty, aren't you?"

She laughed. "A little bit." But she squeezed my fingers again before letting go with a sigh. "And there's nothing really to talk about. Skylar and I were having fun. Then we weren't. It's no biggie. I got orgasms out of it, and she was fun. Now she's doing her thing and I'm doing mine."

That seemed just a bit too glib. "I'm sorry. I liked her."

"Me, too," she murmured, before taking a bite. We were quiet, maybe too quiet. That, or she waited for me to take a drink on purpose. "Course if you really want to make me feel better, you can tell me which one fucks the best. It's Coop, right? He seems like the type to make sure you come a lot before he gets off."

I swear, I could taste the damn bubbles in my lungs for how much soda just came out my nose.

Absolutely unrepentant, the bitch laughed at me.

"I always thought Archie would be a greedy fuck, he seems the type. Jake's probably intense as hell, but he's got stamina." At my dour look, she grinned. "What? I've seen him play football. I guess the big question is *Bubba*." There was just the hint of a wicked gleam in her eyes.

I groaned, and she let out a delighted cackle.

"Yes, I *knew* it. When?"

"Do we have to do this now?" I mumbled around the sandwich, hurrying into another bite to not have to talk about this. Admittedly, I didn't mind Rachel *knowing*, but I could live without sharing the salient details in the middle of a bistro that was half-packed with people snagging food before going shopping or grabbing something to eat mid-shopping. Weekends were gonna suck at most places while the countdown to Christmas was on.

"Well, no," she intoned with a little sigh. "But it would make me feel better."

"I hate you," I told her with absolutely no heat, and she reached over to boop my nose lightly.

"No you don't, I'm your favorite. Spill. At least tell me when and where. After the shit that went down at Halloween and everything the last few weeks, I knew you and Bubba were going to get there. You've been more than a little sappy about him, and all the hurt in your eyes when you look at him is gone."

That sobered me a little. "We talked." I'd told her a little about that. But not any real details. "Halloween, you know, before the guys tried to jump us." Well, technically, they did jump us, but whatever. "He was really honest, and we talked and…he told me he wasn't going to make decisions for me anymore or assume. And he really wanted another chance." I picked up one of the fries and gave her a small smile. "So far so good."

She studied me, the intensity in her gaze promising she was trying to use x-ray vision to see straight into my brain. "You're happy?"

I thought about Thanksgiving. The weekend after it. The whole of this last week. I'd gotten alone time with all of them…and some time with all of them. I didn't think too closely about Jake and Coop right now, because then I'd be on fire. They were both pushing in this slow, subtle way. Okay, maybe not so subtle. I wasn't blind. The point was, they both seemed to enjoy watching me get off with the other, and when they worked together…

Well, my body started humming just at the thought. So far, the most we'd done was me kissing the other one and some light petting while I was actively getting fucked or…well, fucking the other one.

A ripple of hot cold raced over my scalp and that was enough of that.

"I'd pay money to know what you were just thinking about," Rachel said. "It was dick, right? All the dick? Did you have to be into dick? Couldn't you like just a little vag in your life? Like one vag?"

I groaned. "I'm sorry. If I did, it would totally be you."

She mock sighed, a long and forlorn note. "I know. But once you go vag, you'd never go back and those boys would be so jealous."

Snorting, I grinned at her. "I'm happy, Rach."

"Good," she said with a decisive nod. "That's how it should be. So, you and Bubba…?"

Eyes rolling, I shook my head. "Fine, but only because I feel bad for you."

"Hey, I take pity." Her smirk was a little too sharp, but I got it. "So, spill. When? Where? How many?"

I snorted at the last question. "Thanksgiving," I admitted. "His house. His room."

Sipping her drink, Rachel mimed wide eyes at me and motioned me to go on.

"And that's all I'm saying," I informed her sternly. "Except…" I paused, replaying aspects of that evening over in my head. His belt. The spanking. The way he felt when he kissed me like I was his last damn breath.

"Except?" Rachel prompted.

"It was amazing," I told her. "He was amazing."

"How many times was he amazing?"

"Oh my god," I groaned. "What is it with you and the guys, and how many?"

The corners of her lips curved a little higher. "Because guys get off every time, they just do. It's mechanics. But to get a girl off is an art. So, tell me—are they mechanics or are they artists?"

I nudged my plate away and balled up my napkin before I threw it at her. "Artists." Face hotter than hell, I still grinned. "Definitely artists."

"Yes," Rachel said while toasting me. "That's what I wanted to hear."

Thankfully, we abandoned the topic before she got into how many orgasms I'd scored since, and I skipped out on the more salient details of my Thanksgiving Day trysts. To be honest, it was hard enough to believe I was currently balancing four relationships—four very active relationships. It stunned me how perfect Thanksgiving had been and that the guys were all okay with each other.

Even Ian.

Maybe especially Ian.

More than okay. They were conspiring about something. I'd caught them plotting more than once. Quiet conversations that cut off when I came out of the bathroom or into the kitchen. Sly looks when they thought I wouldn't see.

Text messages.

All the messages that were flying. Texting even when we were all in the same room like they were answering other people.

It irked me, but then I'd see their smiles and catch them laughing with each other, and I didn't want to rock the boat. So, whatever they were plotting, I let it go.

For now.

We paid for dinner, and Rachel hustled me out of the bistro and down three stops to the same spa where we'd gotten our nails done for Homecoming.

Ice fisted me in the gut when she pulled open the door and it jingled a welcome. It didn't matter that it was a lot colder or that the sun had already set or that holiday jingles rolled out of the overhead speakers, all at once, I was standing outside the shop talking to Maria. She'd warned me. Told me what happened to her, and I'd felt so fucking bad for her.

And a few hours later, I was waking up at a hospital to find out if it happened to me, too. Rachel let the door close after waving to the people inside and narrowed the distance between us. "Hey, you okay?"

I rubbed my arm and nodded. But I wasn't okay. "Yeah," I lied. But suddenly, I didn't want to be out here. I just wanted to go back to my place and curl up and hide.

The second that thought took root, I hated it. I didn't want to fucking hide. I shouldn't have to hide. I forced myself to look up at the shop signs. They had Christmas lights twinkling in the windows. They'd sprayed faux snow on it, too and painted a Christmas tree side by side with a Menorah.

It was the closest we would get to snow for the holidays. We might get an ice storm.

Maybe.

Probably rain.

Could even be sunny and in the seventies.

But snow?

Pfft.

"We can skip this," Rachel offered. "Head over to the mall? Do some shopping? Or just go find a place that's warm to talk. I think the picnic table at the lake is out. Definitely too cold for that."

"I'm okay," I said, meaning it this time. "Just was thinking about the last time I was here." My nails looked terrible, and I still had a cast. That was coming off on Monday, fingers crossed. We had finals most of the following week, then like three days of the week after that to get through before the holiday break kicked in and I didn't have to think about school for a couple of weeks.

"You sure?" She eyed me like she could tell I was shining her on a little. "I want you to have fun tonight."

"I am having fun. I'm with my best friend."

Rachel narrowed her eyes at me and then blinked them before she half-turned away. "Right, okay. Let's go make our feet beautiful. I'll save my hands for when you can get yours done, too."

Inside, we got set up and they pampered our feet. It took me a hot minute to relax, but by the time they were painting my toes, I had. Then I let Rachel talk me into that face waxing thing again. That turned into a leg waxing thing, because hey, who didn't want to skip shaving for a few days?

When she suggested a Brazilian though, I was out of there. Nope.

Not happening.

'Cause dude, *ow*.

"Trust me, clean shaven vag…it's a turn on." She gave me a knowing look.

"I'll take your word for it." I trimmed. That had to be enough. Hell, the guys had helped me shave my legs the last few weeks, and no, I wasn't telling

Rachel about that. It had been embarrassing enough the first time Coop offered.

"If you change your mind, let me know." We were heading for her car, her arm looped through mine. "I know a great lady, barely feel it—well, after the first time. First time kind of sucks." She made a face. "But I would totally buy you ice cream after."

Laughter eddied up, and I shook my head. "You are a terrible influence."

"Lies," she cackled. "Lies."

Our next stop on girls' night out was indeed the mall. It was packed, but we weren't in a hurry. If anything, Rachel seemed more interested in window shopping.

"Rach," I asked as we wound through one of the candle stores. The place reeked, but Rachel paused periodically to sniff different ones. How the hell she could tell them apart, I had no idea. All I could smell was *everything*, and it made my eyes water. "What are you planning to do for the holidays?"

"Eh," she said with a shrug. "Probably go to my aunt's house where I have to deal with the cousins and the extended family, including my great-grandfather who is probably the coolest one who will be there. He's like a hundred and fifteen years old and spry as fuck." The quirky grin she wore promised me she was only half-kidding. "It's in Ohio. So there will be snow. And a lot of boring shit and football."

She made a gagging noise.

"There will also be Mack Morgan to deal with, but Mack and I are like this." She crossed her fingers. "He'll happily play my beard for the more conservative half of the family while the other half rolls their eyes at us, and depending on my mood, I might let him get lucky."

Her beard. That sucked.

Wait…what? I snapped my head around to stare at her, and her shit-eating grin made me glare. "Just checking to see if you were paying attention. Trust me, even if I decided I wanted to check out a dick, it would not be his. He doesn't like vag. But he grew up there, and gay is a four-letter word. I do know that college has been *very* good for him.”

All of a sudden, her face turned thoughtful. “What?” ‘Cause that was a dangerous look.

“I don’t know, but I think he’s the only person I know who gets as much dick as you do. Maybe a little more.” The sly smile and twinkle had me groaning.

“Ugh, you suck.”

“Nope,” she said. “That’s the whole point.”

I was still groaning when she dragged me out of the store after buying two candles.

“What are you doing?” Rachel asked as we headed into the game store. It was crowded as hell, so I just shrugged.

“Nothing big. Probably working and hanging out with the guys.”

She hummed and just got in line rather than browsed. I scanned the walls and then looked at the rack of new games.

“I’m gonna go see what they have.” Maybe there was something the guys didn’t have. Good fucking luck with that. Archie had everything, and what few he didn’t have, Jake, Coop, or Ian had surely picked up.

Rachel gave me a nod. “Just stay where I can see you.”

I cut a look over my shoulder at her. Was she for real?

“You heard me.”

Ugh. As much as I wanted to complain about the protective note, it warmed me that she cared enough to snap at me. I studied all the new titles. Three-quarters of which were already loaded on the game system the guys had brought to the apartment. Yeah, I couldn’t buy one of these, not even as a present, because chances were they already had it.

But what about…?

I checked where Rachel was, she still had two more people in front of her, so I headed over to the other wall where they had accessories for game systems. They had the drums and guitar pieces. All the stuff for playing musical band games. I used to think Ian hated them, but I figured out why he didn’t play them.

Because he actually knew how to finger a guitar, so it made just mashing buttons a little different.

They had some of the fancier accessories though, including an actual guitar with strings. Would that be better or worse to play on? I squatted down to ease the box out and flip it over so I could read the back. It took a little balancing, because the crowd had thickened in the store. These places were always so tiny. The accessory had a couple of different settings—and apparently, it had also been designed for players who could actually play.

Oh hell yes.

I grimaced at the price. It was a lot. But Ian would love it, and the guys would get a kick out of playing a different set of games. I could get them the regular gaming guitars. The mental math was a kick in the crotch to my wallet. On the other hand, if I got them a couple of games to go with it, we could spend a huge chunk of break just doing this, especially if I got my cast off.

"There you are," Rachel snapped at me, and I nearly fell over as adrenaline flooded my system.

"Holy shit," I said, glaring at her.

"I couldn't see you," she snarled, glaring right back. "I told you to stay where I could see you. There are too many people in here, and I don't want anything to happen to you."

And my irritation dried right up. "Sorry, I just…" I motioned to the guitar. "I was looking for stuff for the guys."

Her own expression softened, and she squatted down next to me. "Bubba?"

I nodded. "And then regular ones for the other guys and some music based games. Maybe drums and something else to do the whole band effect."

"Aww, you could have your very own boy band," she crooned, and I tipped my head back and stared at the ceiling.

"Yep, my own boy band, and I'll be their personal groupie."

"Pfft, you'll be the lead singer, and they can be your backup boys." She elbowed me and then handed me the two huge bags she'd been lugging. "Do you want to get this now?"

"What—you didn't have anything when you got in line!" I stared at the big bags.

"I know," she told me smugly. "I had them pull my stuff ahead of time because it's a zoo in here. Come on, what am I carrying?"

I pointed out the different pieces and she stacked them up, and then we snagged three different games and a couple of spare controllers for when the guys broke something. Because boys.

Back in line, I bumped Rachel with my hip as she stood uncomplainingly with all my crap. "Thank you."

"Yep," she said. "But you can buy the pretzels."

Oh. Pretzels. "Deal."

My bank account wept after I paid for all of it. So much for the money I'd made this week, but at least I had the job, and now I had something fun to go with the kind of goofy gifts I'd gotten them.

We made our way out to the big fountain where Rachel set me up with our stuff, and even though I was supposed to pay for the pretzels, she went and got them. When she was back and we were both getting cinnamon all over ourselves eating the oversized hot pretzels, I asked, "What do you want for Christmas?"

"Nothing," she told me. "Or whatever you want to get me. I'm not picky."

I groaned. "I need a little more than that. I could get you a book of poetry…" She made a buzzer noise like we were on a game show.

"Strike one," she teased, then took a bite of her pretzel and eyed me.

The problem with Rachel was she really didn't talk about herself. I chewed my own pretzel as I sifted through various memories. Music was a given, but we liked a lot of the same things, and she had an almost exclusively digital collection. We didn't always buy whole albums, just the songs we wanted. Books were the same way, and books could be cool presents.

Hmm.

A flicker of a memory tickled the back of my mind, and I grinned. "I have an idea."

"What would that be?" Rachel eyed me curiously.

"Not saying," I said with a grin. "But I think what I have in mind will work."

Rachel liked art. Sketches. Painting. Crafts. But it wasn't something she advertised. She used to be really good at it.

"Fine, then I won't tell you what I got you either." Her smug little grin just made me laugh.

"You know you don't have to get me anything."

She mimed her fingers talking. "Your mouth is doing this. But I'm not listening. Now, you up for more shopping, or do I need to take you back to your boys?"

I eyed the stacks of bags around us, then stared at her. "How much more shopping do you have?"

"I have eighteen cousins," she told me with a straight face.

Holy shit.

"Exactly."

"More shopping it is."

We actually made a side trip out to her car to drop off the first round of stuff. Then a second round. Somehow, I got shanghaied into trying some stuff on, including snow jackets—why did they sell those in Texas?—and a snow suit because I was the same size as her cousin. I had to admit, the outfits were cute. By the time we finished, the mall was closing and the guys were blowing up my phone. Rachel cackled as she sent them a text, and I stared at her.

"What did you do?"

"Told them if they kept bugging you on my time, I would keep you overnight."

I snorted. But my phone stopped blowing up and hers started.

She was still laughing as she started the car. "Feel better?" she asked, giving me a side-long look.

"I do," I admitted. I really did. Even though tonight was my normal date night with Archie, he hadn't protested in the slightest when I headed out with Rachel. Even told me to have fun. "Thanks."

"Anytime," she told me. Then, as we were heading back to my place, she said, "You know, you could tell me who has the biggest dick if you wanted to make it up to me."

"You don't care about dick," I said with a groan.

"Nope," she agreed. "But you do, and I want to know you have all the dick you need."

I was still laughing when we got to the apartment, and Rachel helped me get the giant bags inside without them seeing what was in them. Course, she did that by telling them I was exhausted and hurting.

Bitch.

Archie

I have a car picking us up to take us
to the airport. It's an early flight.

Jake

When are we planning on telling her?

Bubba

I still can't believe Rachel got her to shop.

Coop

Rach is good. I wanna know how
you bribed her into doing it.

Archie

Told her no way she could pull it off.

Jake

LOL

Coop

Yeah, I see that.

Archie

Anyway, car picks us up early at Frankie's.
Takes us to the airport. We're flying first
class, early flight. We have a car waiting
for us on the other side.

Jake

We renting one?

Archie

I would, but they prefer drivers to be 21. So I hired a service. We'll have a car whenever we need one.

Bubba

Holy crap, man. I wanted to help pay for this...

Archie

Nope. My treat. The lodge will be stocked.

Jake

Lodge, so your grandfather came through?

Archie

Yep. We'll be close to good skiing. But we're also going to have privacy. The staff will give us space.

Coop

The staff.

Jake

Archie

You guys want the details or do you want to be asses?

Bubba

They can do both. Keep talking.

Archie

The staff is there to facilitate, but it's basically the five of us and that's it. We're going to have a live tree delivered. There's also going to be one just like the one we put up at her place.

Jake

I know we're packing Frankie. Do we pack the presents she already put under the tree?

Archie

Nope, Jeremy is going to ship everything up when he comes to pick up the cats. He'll also have someone in to deep clean the master while we're gone.

Bubba

So, we just add our stuff and he ships that up, too?

Archie

Yep. Jere will get it there. I also arranged for a couple of skiing lessons. I've been.

Jake

I know how.

Bubba

Ditto.

Coop

Never been. Never seen more than like four inches of snow that melted the next day. She's going to lose her mind.

Archie

Good. Now, last bit of business…

Jake

LOL Business.

Archie

The lodge has several rooms. We've all been sleeping with her, so I'm making sure she gets the largest, but I think we should each get our own rooms.

Bubba

Because we're all going to want our own time.

Jake

Definitely.

Coop

So a schedule?

Archie

Yes and no. I want options. I like having her to myself some nights.

Jake

Agreed.

Bubba

Fair.

Coop

So, last question. When does the screaming orgasm count begin?

Chapter Fifteen
LEAVING ON A JET PLANE

The last day before holiday break was always a half-day. This year, it also served as an unofficial senior skip day. The principal had announced no seniors would be reported if they didn't come to school. Unsurprisingly, my phone blew up with texts from Jake, Coop, and Archie.

Archie

Skip day!

Coop

No brainer.

Jake

Freedom, Baby Girl.

I bit back a grin and cast a glance over at Ian, who had his own phone in his lap. He'd rolled his eyes and snorted, but we both skated through math class without paying a lot of attention. The last few days before the holiday were such a waste. The only things really happening this week were class ring and

Letterman jacket pick-ups.

Since I was getting neither, no skin off my nose.

Coop and I went out to do deliveries in the evening when I'd pulled a longer shift than normal. I'd finally gotten the cast off earlier that week, and the doctor wanted me to take it easy. I had exercises to do, but he didn't think I'd need actual physical therapy. We'd revisit it in a few weeks. Best news he could have given me, really.

Even better was the make-out time with Coop. I never thought I'd be the girl in the backseat, but we made it work. With the guys all waiting for us at the apartment, the alone time wasn't going to happen there. It took a little wiggling, and Coop slid on a condom before we had a chance to talk about the rest.

I needed to talk to them still, but then he was in me and I was riding him, and fuck, I just forgot the rest of it. At least it made cleanup simple. I didn't think the guys would notice, but Jake took one look at me when we came in and grinned. He insisted on helping me shower, even if I didn't need the help, and that turned into a much louder set of orgasms that left me shaking.

No way to hide the fact I'd screamed. For his part, Jake just grinned at me as he helped me wash up. Thankfully, neither Archie nor Ian said a word until we were getting ready to crash. They kicked Jake and Coop to the pallets on the floor and climbed in with me.

It was hysterical and a little embarrassing. I never thought I'd get to sleep, but I was out in minutes after they settled hands on me…one on my waist, the other on my hip. Ian snuggled against my back, while I pressed a hand to Archie's chest, right over his heart. He traced a heart pattern on my hip, and I smiled as the cats picked their way onto the bed and found their spots.

That was all I knew until Archie nudged me awake at way too fucking early in the morning. "There cannot possibly be sale shopping today," I complained, curling up tighter and pressing my face into the pillow. Seriously. I was sleepy. It was dark. We didn't have school, and it was warm and toasty in the bed.

Why did we have to get up?'

"C'mon, Angel," Ian coaxed as someone tugged away my blankets and he lifted me up and out of the bed. I blinked bleary eyes at them. Why the hell was everyone dressed?

"What is going on?"

"You'll see," Archie told me, looking far too awake, and his expression practically radiated smugness. I adored him. I really did.

But I would cheerfully punch him in the nose right now because I also liked sleep.

"Coffee," Coop said, holding out a disposable to go cup. "Hot, fresh, and sweet. Just like you."

My scowl was not sweet, but he'd brought me coffee, so I let that protest go, especially when he dropped a kiss on my lips.

"Drink the coffee," he teased. "Clothes are laid out for you. Something comfy and warm. Car will be here in thirty minutes."

"Fine," I agreed, more interested in the coffee than anything else. Jake turned to make the bed, and the cats were staring at us in varying levels of disgust. Well, two of them, anyway. Tory had vanished back under the bed.

I downed a big gulp of the coffee. It was just the right side of not scalding my tongue, yet perfectly hot. Ian guided me over to where they stacked my clothes as Coop made short work of the pallets. Archie had vanished, oh wait, there he was. He'd come back with coffee for everyone else. I took another swallow before shimmying out the boxer shorts.

It took a moment for the dead silence to register, and I glanced over my shoulder to find four sets of eyes on my bare ass. Getting naked around them had obviously happened. They'd all seen me naked, either in bed or the car or the shower. But not at once with all four of them in the same room.

And you know what? "You've seen my butt before, boys. Move on." I flicked my fingers at them and reached for the panties. I was so not awake enough for this. Coop chuckled softly, but it was Jake who snagged the boxers and then my tank top as I tugged it up and over. Out of habit, I just fastened the bra and pulled it over my head rather than try to hook it in the back.

"Damn," Archie murmured before pressing a kiss to my shoulder. "I was going to offer to help."

Yep, too damn cheerful. At least they hadn't been kidding about comfy clothes. The yoga pants and sweatshirt—Coop's, I thought—went well with the tennis shoes and heavy socks. I carried my coffee with me to the bathroom and drained it before brushing my teeth and putting my hair up into a braid.

Finally, I walked out to the living room where all four guys waited, their grins so wide, they looked almost painful.

"You all look very pleased with yourselves." I glanced from one to the other and then registered the suitcases.

Suitcases.

There were suitcases. They'd been plotting something for days, I focused on Archie. "What did you do?"

He had the temerity to look surprised and maybe a bit offended, playing it off in mock innocence. "Why did you automatically leap to it being me who did something?"

"Because you're Archie," I answered almost in perfect sync with Jake and Coop.

Chuckling, Ian shook his head. "She has your number, Arch."

"She's always had my number," he agreed before closing the distance and sliding his arm around my shoulders. "Frankie, we're about to jet off to adventure. Well, not so much adventure as a holiday retreat for five."

What?

But he wasn't done. "We're taking you to Colorado, near Aspen, where Grandpa has a lodge available for us to use. There will be snow and fireplaces, Christmas trees and presents. Ski lessons and snowman building. And just the five of us—no parents, no school, no annoying bitches or assholes allowed."

"You think he realizes he might be cutting himself off there with that last one?" Jake asked in a not-so-quiet voice.

Archie ignored the teasing as he studied me.

"You're serious, right now?"

"Absolutely. Everything is planned. You're packed. Our car will be here in…" He checked his watch. "Seven minutes. Jeremy will be by in a few hours to pick up the cats, and they will be pampered like royalty at my place. He will even take daily pictures and share their antics with you."

Shock held me mute for a second, but a glance at the guys told me not only was Archie serious about this, so were they. Then I looked at the tree and the presents.

"All taken care of, Baby Girl," Jake murmured.

I chewed my lower lip, and my stomach bottomed out. We were going… "Jake, your birthday."

"Yep," he said, still smiling. "Mom already signed off on it. Those three didn't need permission, and neither do you."

Until he said it, I hadn't even gone there. But he was right. I had the temporary emancipation order in place.

Holy crap.

"We're going away for Christmas?"

"We're going away for Christmas, and we're not back here until next year," Archie promised me, and I stared into his brown eyes, even as I had to blink back tears in my own. "And you're getting snow, babe."

Oh fuck.

The shock twisted with this fresh ripple of surprise, and I whipped around and hugged him. He laughed, wrapping me up tight. "Okay," he whispered, rubbing a circle between my shoulder blades. Oh hell, I was shaking. "It's okay. Good surprise?"

I sniffed once as I pulled back and then gave him a mock punch in the shoulder. "It's an amazing surprise! I can't believe you guys…"

Realization hit.

"You told Rachel! That's why I had to try on all those snow clothes for her to get her 'cousins.'" I was torn between admiring the sneakiness and wanting to smack her for tricking me.

"Pretty much," Coop said. "Okay, let's get the bags outside, boys. We can get this trip started." He tugged me away from Archie long enough to cup my face and give me a kiss. "It's going to be the perfect holiday."

He snagged three bags, including shouldering my backpack. Then Jake stole a kiss before he grabbed another three. Ian winked at me, and I rose up on my tiptoes to kiss him because he already had an armload of bags and his guitar case.

There were two left, and when I went to pick one up, Archie clucked his tongue at me. At my raised brow, he caught my right hand in his and raised it to press a kiss to my palm and then to my wrist. It looked so much skinnier and paler than the other one. "We're still treating this like spun glass. Besides, I have something else for you to carry."

Cool metal brushed my wrist, and I glanced down as Archie slid my charm bracelet on. There were new charms affixed to it, and he closed the catch gently.

"You got it back." It was a morning for surprises, and the sun wasn't even up.

He smiled. "Damn straight. I've been after them for weeks. Finally got them to release it, and I got the charms fixed on it." Next he hung the necklace over my head with its own charms. "Now that's better."

There were new letters on my wrist. One for each of them—including an I for Ian rather than a B for Bubba. Fuck, I really was going to cry. The brush of Archie's fingers against my cheek pulled my head up. "Happy tears, right?"

I blinked hurriedly and then nodded, before I sniffed again. "I just… This is a lot."

"But good?" The concern in his eyes was real.

"Car's here," Coop called from the back door. "You guys good?"

"Yeah," Archie said. "Give us a minute, and we'll be right down."

"Okay." The door closed, leaving us alone.

"It's okay," I promised him, even as he enfolded me into another hug and I burrowed in close. The weight of the charm bracelet on my wrist was like a whole second kind of gift in and of itself. I'd missed it. Missed the meaning behind it, even if I'd had Archie the whole time and zero doubt where he was concerned. "I love you," I whispered. "I love this and the fact that you guys did all this."

I loved that he was sharing the credit, too. His arms tightened around me, and he pressed a kiss to my neck, half-lifting me, and I just leaned into the hug. Coop's words about them being the right kind of people floated across my mind.

He wasn't wrong.

Archie didn't let me go until I wasn't sniffling. Then, and only then, did he set me on my feet. With a wink, he gave my ass a squeeze, and I chuckled. "Let's go, babe. We have a limo ride waiting for us and a plane to catch."

Holy shit.

I was getting on a plane.

"You know I've never been on a plane, right?" A thousand different thoughts collided as I grabbed my jacket, and Archie took it from my hands and held it up so I could slide one arm in and then the next.

"Yep, and you haven't had real snow before either," he teased before giving me a little nudge. "Or a vacation with your boyfriends. Or a Christmas like we're about to have." The indulgence in his smile just made me laugh again. "Trust me, babe, we're going for a lot of firsts and real experiences here."

The lick of dark promise in there sent a shiver up my spine, and from the look on his face, the sensuous place my brain went was exactly what he intended. I gave the apartment one last glance. The tree lights were off, and Tiddles sat on the sofa watching me, like he knew exactly what I was doing.

Glad one of us did. I blew him a kiss, and then headed out and locked the door after Archie passed through with the last two suitcases. As promised, there was a freaking limo waiting for us, and even with the butterflies and the nervousness, I was half-giggling as I skipped down the last two stone steps.

Archie threw me a look over his shoulder, and his grin widened. Yeah, I wasn't fooling anyone. I still couldn't wrap my mind around this. My phone buzzed, and I dug it out of my jacket pocket. I had no idea which one of them made sure my phone was in there and my wallet in the inner pocket, but I would have to kiss them all later.

Rachel

> Have a fantastic holiday, you lucky bitch.
> I want to hear all about it.

I laughed at the message.

Me

> IDK, you were in cahoots with them. Maybe you should get your deets from them.

The driver had taken the bags from Archie, and Coop beckoned to me from the open door. I slid inside and let him and Jake sandwich me between them on the front-facing seats. That left the rear facing for Archie, where Ian was already leaning back, an amused smile on his face.

"Having fun, Angel?"

"Yes," I said, wiggling back into the seat. The bracelet was hidden under the jacket sleeve, but I could feel it. That was enough.

Rachel

> Ha! Because I know you love me. Tell the boys they better enjoy the ski pants, I made sure they looked fantastic on your ass.

I rolled my eyes, but Coop snagged my phone and typed out a quick message and hit send before I could get it back.

Me

> Her ass looks fantastic in everything. Talk to you next year, Rach. - Coop

Then Archie slid inside, and the door closed. "Let's get this holiday started!"

Rachel's only response was a heart emoji followed by a middle finger followed by another heart. Fuck off with love.

I snort-laughed.

Perfect.

Airports kind of sucked. Airport TSA lines at six in the morning weren't much better. At least we checked most of the luggage at the curb. Archie had a frequent flyer pass thing that would have gotten him right on through, but he waited with us. When it was my turn to go through the scanner, I got picked to get a pat down.

That was fun, with the four of them giving hard stares at the male agent who pulled me aside. Only he didn't do it, it was a chick. She was fine, she was even nice about it. When I asked, because well why wouldn't I want to know why I'd been picked, she just said sometimes it was random.

Once we were all clear, Archie took lead and I walked, hand in hand, with Ian to pick up coffee, and then we settled into the first class lounge—swanky. Not that we had long to wait. I still couldn't get over the fact that they'd pulled this off.

"How long have you been planning it?"

Jake shrugged. "Thanksgiving-ish?"

"Not long after," Archie admitted. "Thought about it before. We've talked about trips." We had.

When it was time to board, I was a bundle of nerves and excitement. Or maybe my excitement was from my nerves. It was anyone's guess. Of the five of us, only Coop and I hadn't been on a plane or a trip like this. The pair of us had a lot of shared life experience on this particular aspect. Fortunately, it gave me a partner-in-crime to make faces with. Archie wasn't alone in laughing at us either. Both Ian and Jake kept shaking their heads and chuckling, though they all wore indulgent smiles, so I wasn't going to let it bother me.

First class was kind of fancy with huge seats. I had a window seat—score!

Coop had the seat next to me. Ian and Jake were behind us, and Archie in front. My only complaint was that would make it harder to talk to them, but really? We'd manage.

I totally took a picture of myself and then a picture of me and Coop, and fired it off to Rachel. It took a beat to realize Ian and Jake photo bombed. Archie grumbled so we had him do a selfie with all of us in the background and then the flight attendant gave us a not so indulgent look, and we planted our asses in the seats.

The butterflies in my stomach turned to hornets though, right about the time the plane hurtled down the runway as it prepared to take off. Coop held my hand, fingers threaded together as we both stared out the window. It was the craziest thing I'd ever done. I really didn't want to see the landscape racing by, and then suddenly, the roaring noise of the wheels on the tarmac gave way to just the engines as we were airborne.

I swore my eyes had to be saucers as I glanced at Coop and found him grinning like an idiot, too. He leaned into my shoulder as we stared out the window. The sun wasn't up yet, so it was all lights in the darkness twinkling, and at the same time, it was absolutely gorgeous.

This was even better than a roller coaster.

After we achieved altitude, the flight attendants offered us coffee—which we declined because Archie just shook his head with wide eyes, good to know— and juice or soda. Caffeine was vital, so I went for the soda. We also had a warm breakfast. Nothing fancy, despite the swank of where we were sitting. But hot biscuits that actually tasted like biscuits, scrambled eggs, and bacon? Yes please and thank you.

In no time, we were landing and it was still dark outside, but we'd been time traveling, so that was weird enough. The real difference hit me after we collected our bags and headed out to meet the car waiting for us.

The air outside was *cold*. Holy. Shit. Cold.

I clamped my teeth together as the wind cut right through me. Thankfully, it wasn't far to the car and the driver had been right there at luggage claim to meet us. Jake nudged me into the—thankfully, heated—back before handing over the bags. One by one, the guys slid in, and I was sandwiched between Archie and Ian this time, while Coop hooked his foot around mine.

Ten minutes later, we were pulling out of the airport. While it was getting lighter outside, it was definitely not getting sunnier. Maybe that was why it took me a hot minute—or ten—to realize it was actually snowing.

A couple of snaps pulled me out of my stare to find Coop and Jake both pointing their phones at me, both wearing shit-eating grins. "You look adorable," Jake told me, and Ian slid an arm around my shoulders and tugged me close to him.

"Be nice," he chided, then added, "But totally send me a copy of those pics."

"We need to set up a cloud account," Archie murmured, rolling his thumb in circles against my thigh. "That way we can all get all the pics, all the time."

"Well," Jake said, a sly grin curling his lips. "Maybe not all of them."

At that, I just snorted. "You first."

"I have no problems if you want nudes of me, Baby Girl," he said with a grin.

Ian raised his hand. "Not on the cloud account."

"Agreed," Archie added, but Coop just shrugged.

"What?" Coop said when Ian and Archie both stared at him. "Nothing I haven't seen before. If it gets Frankie to volunteer some, I'm all in."

There was a beat of silence.

"Count me in," Archie volunteered, and I groaned.

"Sorry, Angel," Ian told me. "I'm going to side with them. But we'll save that for later."

"A lot later," I muttered. The last thing I planned on doing was posing for any nude photographs. I darted a look at the privacy panel, but it was closed so we didn't have to worry about the driver. My face heated as Coop bumped my leg.

"Okay, we've all seen you naked, so why not naked pics?"

I stared at him. "Because."

Jake chewed his lower lip, his facial contortions doing nothing to hide his laughter. "Thank you for clearing that up for us."

"You're welcome." I groaned and tipped my head back. I had two weeks of *this* to look forward to, didn't I?

Even as I made a face, anticipation coiled in my stomach. Two weeks with just us. Nobody else. No one to judge. No one to ask questions. No one to have to impress or answer to. Just…us.

"Heads up," Archie nudged me, and I sat forward as the limo wound through the snowy landscape, and it really was just snowy with pine trees and mountains and white stuff everywhere. It was like a damn postcard.

It was close to perfect.

When I scooted closer to the window, Archie unlocked my seatbelt and hauled me right over into his lap.

"Hey," came the complaint from the other three.

"Keep your panties on," Archie told them, then rehooked his seatbelt over both of us, and I stared out the window as the lodge came into view.

It was a big wooden structure, like some massive, yet elegant log cabin. It looked like something right out of a book, right down to the smoke rising from the chimney, even as the snow continued to fall around it.

"What do you think, babe?" The hint of smug arrogance in Archie's voice echoed cleanly, but so did the real curiosity. A glance at him, and I met his hopeful eyes and twisted to kiss him. Not just a peck, but a full, open-mouthed, tongue tangling, delving deep kiss that had my whole body humming and his fingers digging into me.

"I'm going to guess that's girlfriend for she really likes it," Jake mused, his tone dry.

"I'm thinking loves it," Coop argued.

Ian snorted. "Looks more like she's totally turned on by it."

When I leaned back a little and broke the kiss, Archie's grin looked every bit as crazy as mine had to be. "Yes?"

"Oh yeah," I said, not even caring that we'd had an audience. Even better, when I scooted back around and just leaned into Archie, I reached back and Ian took my hand. A sigh escaped me as Jake winked and Coop just looked pleased.

It wasn't almost perfect.

It was perfect.

This was the kind of day I already wanted to capture in time and keep forever.

Then we were there and the doors opened, and I let out a squeal.

Yep, still cold.

Only this time, I didn't care. It was snowing, and the flakes were hitting my face.

Absolutely perfect.

Chapter Sixteen
LET IT SNOW

"**B**aby Girl, your lips are turning blue," Jake scolded me.

"Five more minutes," I called. Yes, my hands were stuffed into the pockets of my jacket and my sneakers were not at all waterproof. The wind sliced through my yoga pants like they weren't even there. I couldn't feel my nose. But there were snowflakes on my eyelashes and the whole world was covered in white.

It was downright magical.

Perfect.

Jake's shoulder pressed into my stomach, and I went from being upright to over his shoulder. "Hey!"

He slapped a hand against my ass, and it barely registered against how numb my skin was, except for the fact that I *heard* the slap more than felt it. That might be bad. But still. I struggled to get my hands out of my pockets, but Jake was already marching over the snow and up the steps to the *lodge*—this gorgeous, oversized, sexy log cabin of my dreams.

Feet stomping, he slapped my ass again when I wiggled. "You're freezing," he gritted out through his teeth. "Inside, warm up, and put on some fucking layered clothes. Then you can play in the snow all you want."

The heat hit me as we crossed the threshold, along with the scents of wood smoke, cedar, and that fresh, clean scent things get when they've been polished and dusted. I swore I could still smell the snow in there. The scent of coffee and sugar struck next, along with a rich scent of pine. The blood was also rushing to my head, but Jake didn't slow in the front room or by the fire I caught from the corner of my eye.

Oh, was that a hand-thatched rug on the wooden floors?

He took the stairs two at a time.

"Dude!" Coop yelled after him.

"Of course he is," Ian muttered.

I didn't really catch the rest of it. Or see Archie for that matter.

Oh, the stairway was pretty. Someone had wound green garland around the railings, along with lights and bows. It was all kinds of festive. Not that Jake's tight ass stopped long enough for me to enjoy it. I had one arm free, so I smacked his ass in retaliation as he strolled down the hallway, and he chuckled at me.

A minute later, I was flipped up and over, and landed on my back in the middle of an enormous bed.

Holy crap.

It was bigger than a California king. Pretty sure anyway.

Jake tugged one of my shoes off, followed by the other, and then he stripped down my wet socks.

"Hey," I said, yanking my foot away, only to have him catch the ankle and haul me back to him. "I'm not five."

"No, but your feet are blocks of ice, Baby Girl. So we're getting you warm and then into warmer clothes. Strip."

I frowned, then scooted to the end of the bed and glared at him. Jake motioned to me to stand up and then glared back when I didn't move. Arms folded, I continued to stare at him.

"Frankie…"

"Don't you *Frankie* me." It came out more heated than I intended, but at the same time…nowhere near as angry as I really was. "I'll grab a shower and warm up. If you guys would put my bags in here, I'll also take care of undressing and redressing myself."

He paused, eyeing me.

"But what I won't do," I continued, dropping my folded arms as I stood and poked him in the chest, thumping him once for each item on my list, "is be given orders, hauled around like a sack of potatoes, or be *snapped* at because I was having fun." He backed up a couple of steps but I wasn't done, so when he opened his mouth, I hurried on. "I adore you, but you are *not* the boss of me, nor do you get to just demand I comply because you've been looking after me. Thank you so much for everything, but I've got it right now. There's the door. Don't let it hit you in the ass on the way out."

The last few words came out shaky, but my whole body was trembling, and I wasn't sure if it was from adrenaline, the cold, or just me being pissed off. Either way, I needed a break. I'd been having a great time, and Captain Caveman here had gone too far.

He hesitated, and I tapped my chilled foot and tried to ignore the pins and needles sweeping through it as I glared at him. Movement in the hallway—the shuffle of a step—warned me before Archie stuck his head in. "We okay in here?"

I never looked away from Jake. The confusion wasn't hard to read, but right now, I didn't have it in me to explain what had ticked me off if he couldn't see it.

"We're fine," I told Archie, trying to punch up my tone. "Everything is beautiful. Jake was just going to leave me to some time by myself while I shower before I put on warmer clothes to go out in the snow."

Archie stared at me long enough that his gaze seemed like a tangible weight. I didn't want him to push right now. And I really needed Jake to back the fuck off.

"Cool," Archie said after a beat. "C'mon, Jake, I'll show you your room and then we'll grab Frankie's stuff. Bathroom's right through there." He pointed somewhere to my right. "Everything you need should be stocked, and we'll set your bags just inside."

When Jake didn't move right away, Archie hooked his arm and tugged him back.

"We'll see you in a few?" Archie continued as Jake took one reluctant step after another backward and away from me.

"Yep," I said, not moving to follow them because now my feet were really starting to hurt. The carpet was thick on the floor, and probably very plush and nice, but the cold had done a number on me. Once they were clear of the door, Archie pulled it closed and I let out a long breath.

Once alone, I hobbled into the bathroom, wincing with every step. Oh, cold shouldn't hurt when you warmed up. Though as soon as I was in the bathroom, I just *stared*. There was a huge picture window looking out onto the snowy landscape. It was *gorgeous*. An oversized tub that reminded me of the one in Archie's room occupied one corner, while a shower stall big enough for three or four people occupied the other. There were *three* showerheads.

Everything about the bathroom cried out luxury. One hand braced against the doorframe, I glanced back into the bedroom. The massive bed was the centerpiece, but the room also had a fireplace of its own, fat, cushy chairs, a television and all the amenities, and another gorgeous picture window where I could see the snow coming down.

The tears burned in my eyes again. It was really fantastic. I groaned. At the sound of the door opening, I hurried inside and closed the bathroom door. A minute later, I figured out how to get the water on, and it wasn't long before steam began to fill the bathroom.

I stripped out of the jacket and clothes. The trembling grew more pronounced because I was actually shivering. I clamped my teeth together rather than let them chatter. Bracelet and necklace set aside, I slipped under the hot water and groaned. It was almost too hot and not hot enough. I just let it beat on me for a few minutes.

The last thing I wanted to do was fight with Jake or spoil our first *hour* here by getting mad. At the same time… I huffed out a breath. The bossy thing was sexy to a point, but I wasn't a child, nor did I require manhandling, and maybe it was time they remembered that.

Maybe what I needed to do was *remind* them. Decided, I helped myself to the shampoo and the conditioner. It was the pricy stuff and smelled fantastic. Coconut and vanilla—wow. The soap was equally divine and a bit on the spicier side. It reminded me of the crisp air, and I had to wonder if I'd end up smelling the alpine lodge.

The thought was enough to make me giggle. By the time I finished and shut the water off, I'd warmed everything up and the tension bunching my muscles eased. Guilt had also begun to nibble at me. I toweled off my hair and debated using the dryer or just letting it air dry. My intention had been to run back out into the snow, but maybe we should all talk first.

"Here for two weeks, Frankie," I reminded myself. "Now is not the time to piss on everyone's fun."

I cracked open the bathroom door after I hung up the towel to find my suitcases waiting, as promised. The bedroom was also empty. It wasn't until I'd dragged one of the suitcases over and set it on the bed that Archie's earlier words registered.

He was showing Jake to *his* room.

The guys had their own rooms.

I had this giant room and giant bed all to me?

My stomach bottomed out. I mean, it made sense, we were all staying in this huge house. We didn't need to be crammed into one room. Having our space was important, and I'd just gotten irritated with Jake for invading my space and being all bossy.

Even if he was sexy and growly when he got all overprotective.

Ugh.

It took me a minute to locate panties and a fresh bra, but once I had them on, I dug out another pair of thicker leggings and an oversized t-shirt. Fuzzy socks completed my sexy ensemble. I eyed the suitcases and then the dresser. I should probably put shit away, but the disagreement with Jake nagged at me.

I slid back into the bedroom to grab my necklace and bracelet. Once I had both on, I left the suitcase open on the bed. I'd put shit up before I went to sleep, later. Or maybe I'd live out of the suitcase.

Probably not, that would drive me a little crazy.

But only a little.

Pulling the door open, I paused to study the hallway. There were big ass windows on either end. The views were incredible. There were other doors along the way, a couple open, a couple closed. I had to wonder if the closed ones were where the guys were.

The weird feeling bubbled back up. There was a reason for them to have their own rooms, I told myself. Hadn't we all been kind of on top of each other at the apartment? It wasn't always easy to get alone time with any one of them when it was all of us.

Jake and Coop didn't seem to mind.

A shiver went through me. They really didn't seem to mind. And the less I focused on that, the better. Better to resolve the issues we had before I worked out how to steal away with one of them because I got horny.

Halfway down the stairs, I had to snicker at myself.

Horny.

My life had gotten so strange.

And more than a little wonderful.

But definitely strange.

The stairs were even better than they'd been when I was upside down on Jake's shoulder. Christmas music played softly from somewhere. A huge tree stood center in the living room, lights twinkling on it. The fire burned merrily in the huge stone fireplace, surrounded by a half circle created by three oversized sofas. I didn't see a television anywhere, but I knew the guys—there would be at least one. I stole a look at the ceiling as I hit the last step.

The crossbeams were amazing. This whole place was awesome. The only problem so far—the living room was empty.

Maybe all the guys were upstairs?

My stomach grumbled. Maybe I was a little hangry. Following the scent of coffee, I promised myself I'd go up and dig them out from wherever they'd gone—Jake in particular—after I got at least a cup of coffee.

Trusting my nose, I headed down the hall away from the living room and paused at the closed door when Coop said, "Did you seriously have to just pick her up like a sack of potatoes? Seriously, man…"

"Yeah, yeah. She was fucking cold and her lips were turning blue and she had zero intention of coming inside."

"Still," Archie countered. "You managed to take her from being enchanted and delighted to fucking furious. Thanks for that."

"Bite me, Archie."

"Guys," Ian said with a sigh. "The point is, she's annoyed. Apologize."

"I'm not going to apologize for caring." Aggravation discolored every single word.

I sighed, a sound Coop echoed almost perfectly. I could picture him, even with the door closed. He would be standing there, arms folded with one hand up as he pinched his brow. "Why don't you apologize for being a dick then?"

I could live with that apology.

"So you're saying I should have just let her freeze?"

"I'm saying maybe not just tossing her over your shoulder and spanking her as you carry her up the stairs and then ordering her to *strip* like she's property," Coop drawled. "You know, maybe talk to her instead of *at* her? Maybe that could work."

The lack of actual verbal response didn't mean there wasn't any kind of response. I chewed my lower lip. I could sit here and let them continue to debate it, or I could just walk in there and resolve it.

Yeah, that was a no brainer.

They had coffee.

I pushed the door open and found all four of them staring at each other as they framed the island in the kitchen. The coffee smell wrapped around me like a siren pulling me in. Now that I was also in the kitchen, there was no mistaking the smell of biscuits.

All four heads turned, and the weight of their stares settled. As uncomfortable as it might be with tension prickling the air, some of my earlier unease of their noticeable absence in the room fled. They were all right here, and this was our holiday.

"I was a jackass," Jake said abruptly. "I shouldn't have just…picked you up and dragged you inside like that."

I paused to consider him for a moment. A muscle ticked in his jaw, and his lips thinned and then released like he was actively compressing them to keep from adding any more.

"Do you actually think you were a jackass, or are you saying that so I'll stop being mad?"

Those pale blue eyes were unflinching as he met my stare. "You were freezing," he half-growled. "Blue lips. Wet feet. Your socks were soaking when I got them off, and your feet were really cold."

"I was there," I told him. "But I return to my question, do you actually think you were a jackass?"

He cut a look to the ceiling as he sighed. "No, I think you were too caught up in how gorgeous it is out there to be safe and I didn't want you hurt. I tried to coax you, but you didn't want to listen, and these assholes were too delighted with your delight to say something."

"But you're never afraid to call me on my crap," I pointed out helpfully. Coop's eyes widened. Smart boy recognized my tone. Archie raised his brows and then turned to the coffee maker. Apparently, he wanted no part of this action.

Ian was the only one who didn't seem to react. If anything, he had his arms folded and his legs rigid like he was planted in that spot.

"No," Jake agreed with me. "I'm not afraid of calling you on your crap." Coop, groaned, but Jake ignored him as he continued, "But that wasn't crap out there. That was adorable, and I hated pulling you away from it. At the same time, I'm not risking your health. You're too damn important, and we made sure you had the clothes and gear you needed so you could play out there to your heart's content. That only works *if* you bring that beautiful ass inside before it freezes off."

He scowled, and I chewed my lower lip. To be fair, he wasn't *wrong*.

"So, if that makes me a jackass," Jake added when I didn't say anything, "so be it. You're warm, your cheeks are pink and your lips are, too." The fact that he fixed on them as he said it sent a wave of real heat through me. "I can live with being a jackass."

Archie held out a mug of coffee toward me wordlessly.

"So can I," I said after a beat, and that earned more than one blink of surprise. I took the coffee and wrapped my fingers around the mug. The warmth was glorious. I mouthed "thank you" to Archie before I looked at Jake, then swept my gaze over Coop and Ian to include them, too. "But I think you all need to stop treating me like spun glass or just picking me up when whatever I'm doing doesn't suit you. Yes, I got carried away out there, I can admit that. I've never seen snow before like this, and it's *awesome*."

That earned me an indulgent smile from everyone except Jake. "I know you haven't, Baby Girl. But I also know just how dangerous it can be if you get too cold. So, I'll try to dial it back, but if you are risking yourself, no way am I backing off."

"Wow, you can't just let her have the win and back off," Coop muttered with a groan.

"I don't need him to *let* me have anything," I informed Coop, and he grimaced. "I need you guys to just listen, and I'll try to do a better job myself."

"Angel," Ian said before Jake could speak. "We get it, and I think you're both right. Jake was right to get you out of the snow, but maybe not the rest. You were right to get pissed with us for being too protective, but we're not wrong to want to protect you."

"Agreed," Coop said after a beat, even as Archie nodded.

"Definitely agreed." All three of them looked at Jake, then at me.

I raised my brows and the corner of Jake's mouth twisted up into a smile. "I wasn't totally wrong."

"No," I agreed with him. "But I wasn't totally wrong *either*."

"So, we weren't wrong," he said slowly, and a spark lit his eyes. I rolled mine and shook my head.

"It kills you to admit it, doesn't it?"

"Nah," he said slowly. "I just don't like being wrong where you are concerned, and I am never letting anything happen to you again. Not if I can stop it." The ferocity there made me smile, even as I snorted.

"You're impossible."

"No, I'm infinitely possible," he told me drily. "I'm just not built to let you get hurt."

"But we have a compromise," Coop interceded eyeing both of us. "Or do you two intend to keep this crap up?"

Jake and I both stared at Coop. I stuck my tongue at him at the same time Jake snorted. Then we all cracked up.

But the tension in the room dropped several notches, and I took another sip of my coffee. "Do over?" I suggested.

"Fuck yes," Archie said. "Sold."

Before Jake could open his mouth, Ian wrapped his arms around him and

Coop clapped a hand over his mouth. "Yes," they both said, and I grinned. Jake rolled his eyes and then winked at me.

Laughter bubbled up again, and the last of my unease floated away. "I reserve the right to go over rules again."

"Done, babe," Archie told me as he slung an arm over my shoulders. "Allow me to show you this place. Then we'll grab some food, and you can get on the warm gear and we'll build a snowman."

Almost immediately, I hummed the song, and it was Ian groaning. The house was huge, but it was still cozy. Sure enough, there was a television in the living room, and it slid out from behind a panel. It was very James Bond, if he went rustic. In addition to the living room and kitchen, the downstairs boasted an office and a 'den,' but that was where all the games were set up. There was also an enclosed porch that was cold as hell, but you could be outside and dry.

The metal mesh around things confused me, but Archie just shrugged. "Bears wander by. Trash is stored out here and picked up periodically, so we don't have to worry about them knocking it over."

Wait.

Bears?

But he was already leading us back into the house and then up the stairs. Yes, there were indeed five bedrooms.

"You have the big master," Archie told me. "There's a smaller one down the hall. That's mine. Coop's in the room next to yours, Jake and Bubba are across the hall."

I glanced from one door to the next, then back to him. "So…everyone has their own beds."

"Yes," he said slowly.

"Archie suggested it, but we all agreed that yes, we all like sleeping with you. But sometimes, we all want alone time. So your room is communal for sleeping if you don't mind, but our rooms aren't. You're the only overnight guest in those rooms with us."

"Or something like that," Jake said, but I didn't miss the look he threw Coop, and I was both thrilled and a little nervous.

"The point being," Ian cut in. "We want everyone to be comfortable, but you most of all."

Archie rubbed his cheek against my damp hair and murmured, "And we all want to get laid."

Heat swept up my face, and I let out a little laugh before taking a quick swallow of coffee. You know, we were here…maybe we should just grab that bull by the horns. "Are we actually going to discuss the fact that I'm having sex with all of you?"

"We can," Jake told me. "If you need to. We all know. No one here is in the dark."

I pursed my lips and glanced from one to the other and then blew out a breath. "Okay, well…I'm starving. I need some fortifications if we want to get any uncomfortable parts out of the way." Yep, totally chickening out.

They chuckled, but thankfully, none of them called me on the delay. In fact, I passed my empty coffee mug to Archie.

"Do you guys mind giving Jake and me a minute? We'll be right down."

"No problem," Archie said, then gave me a gentle kiss before running his hand down my back and turning toward the stairs. From the corner of my eye, I caught him giving Jake a hard look. Then Coop swept into my view and gave me a kiss. Ian followed him. And they both cut a look at Jake, who just stared right back at them.

After they disappeared down the stairs, I focused on him. "Which one was your room?"

He backed up a couple of steps and nudged open the door across the hall. "May I?"

With a gentle snort and a smile, he held out a hand. I took it wordlessly and let him pull me into the room. He nudged the door shut, and I wrapped my arms around him. Jake banded his arms around me and picked me up, but I just hugged him tight and ignored the fact my feet were off the ground.

"I'm sorry," he murmured. "I don't like pissing you off."

"Won't stop you from doing it though," I answered him in an equally soft voice, even as I pressed my nose against his neck and inhaled his scent.

"Nope," he admitted. Rubbing my back gently, he lifted his head and then pressed his lips to mine. It was a simple kiss, a gentle apology, and offer of truce all in one. "I love you, Baby Girl," he reminded me, and I smiled.

"Even when I'm a brat?"

"Do you still love me when I'm a jackass?" he teased.

I grinned. "Most of the time."

He pressed his lips to mine and then paused again before he jerked his head back. "*Most* of the time?"

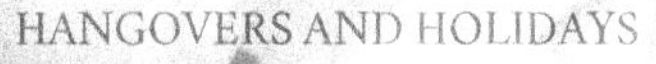

Chapter Seventeen
FOUR TO TANGO

After we made it back downstairs, Jake had grumbled a bit more but settled after I curled up in his lap. The temptation to stay in his room and keep making up had been overwhelming. But the others were waiting, and I wasn't ready to test how willing they were to wait if making up turned to sex. I just wasn't. Not yet.

The heady feeling accompanying the unspoken but natural follow up thought that I would test it eventually made me dizzy. Heat rolled through me, and I forced my mind away from Speculation Avenue. With fresh coffee in hand and the fire burning merrily, it was hard to believe it wasn't even lunchtime. Still, the snow fell outside, and I had a hard time tearing my gaze away from the windows.

"You know, I never thought I'd have competition from the weather," Coop drawled, but I just shot him my middle finger.

"Like you're not staring at it, too," I huffed, but Jake just chuckled and pressed a kiss to my shoulder. While I still wasn't thrilled with the caveman tactics from earlier, I'd forgiven him. I probably overreacted. Maybe.

Firm maybe.

"True," Coop said, then fixed his gaze on me. "But I'd rather stare at you."

Ian laughed as he leaned back on the sofa he'd claimed. They'd all gotten one really, except for me and Jake. He'd sat down not far from the fire and I wanted to be next to it, too, ergo, his lap was now my chair. I also wasn't too proud to admit I needed the comfort. Arguing with them wasn't new. But fighting like we had earlier had a way of catapulting me back to the previous spring and that gut-wrenching feeling of betrayal that they'd warned all the guys off of me and had for years.

It just... Ugh. I shook my head. Better not to think about that. Feelings, as Erin had admonished me during that last session, were complicated. Fuck, I needed to email her and let her know I wouldn't be at my sessions the following week.

Putting my coffee on the hearth, I wiggled forward to grab my phone from the coffee table. Yoga pants did not have pockets.

Really, the only problem with them.

Jake gripped my hips, whether to steady me or keep me from grinding on him, I wasn't sure. I also didn't ask. When I leaned back against him and stretched my legs out, he slid one arm around my middle and tucked his head against my shoulder.

"I didn't really book us plans for today," Archie said. "So when you're ready, we'll totally head back outside to play."

I grinned, even as I opened the email on my phone. There was a Wi-Fi available.

"Password for the Wi-Fi?" Jake asked.

Archie rattled it off, and I typed it in. Man, it wasn't until I had both thumbs flying as I logged in to the Wi-Fi, then opened my mail and wrote a note to Erin, that I realized how much I missed having both thumbs. If Jake read what I wrote over my shoulder, he didn't comment. Instead, he just asked, "When are we going skiing?"

"Day after tomorrow," Archie said. "Then I have a few ideas for the weekend. We can go skiing again after that."

"Wait, so you don't have us all scheduled and time-clocked booked right down to who gets Frankie when?" the teasing note in Coop's voice kept the question from being harsh, but it was a little on the nose.

I cut a glance toward Archie, who sprawled back on the sofa, feet up on the fat, square coffee table that looked like it had been carved out of some huge tree trunk. Seriously, I loved everything about this house. He smirked. "If I'm the one making that schedule, you should probably consider being nicer to me."

Ian laughed. "Nope, not biting. The only one who makes that schedule is Frankie."

My face heated, but at the same time, I let out a little sigh. "Maybe we should talk about that." The weight of four stares settled on me, and I lifted my chin. At least Jake was mostly behind me so I only had to face three of them. That wasn't fair, though. So I uncurled myself from Jake's lap, despite his protests, and moved to sit on the hearth and cradled my coffee cup. Now I could see all of them.

"Okay," Archie said, meeting my gaze. "What's up?"

"We're all okay talking about this with all of us at once? I can have this conversation individually, too." Please don't make me do that. Still, I stole a look at Ian. Of the four of them, he'd been the most reticent.

"I'm fine with it, Angel," he told me almost gently. "I thought the fact that I didn't protest after Jake made you scream for three minutes yesterday would have told you that."

"They aren't really quiet," Archie admitted with a wry grin. "Then again, Frankie is a screamer, and that's kind of nice."

"Kind of?" Coop snorted. "It's *excellent*."

Oh. My. God. I rubbed a hand over my face. It was probably redder than Rudolph's nose. Yes, I was a screamer. But these four all had ways of just turning me inside out. Just sitting here talking to them had me squirming a little and the tension coiling my belly. *"Anyway…"* I stressed the word as I balanced the coffee mug and glanced down at the charms on my bracelet. They steadied me. Every single one meant something.

"I've been meaning to have this conversation, and I think it needs to be a conversation. At the same time, it's kind of embarrassing." I made a face, but Coop just met my gaze steadily without a trace of teasing or humor. Archie and Ian wore similar expressions, and a glance at Jake said he was on board, too. Okay. I could do this. Licking my lips, I pressed on. "Ian knows this, but I talked to you guys about getting tested and stuff. I got tested, and I got an implant." I motioned to my arm. "So…the whole condom thing is okay now since we're all clean."

The intensity in Coop's eyes went up a notch. That shiver of anticipation tickled its way up my spine.

"And," I hurried on, "we're talking about a schedule, do you guys really want one? Like we were doing for homework and dates?"

"Can't hurt," Archie said after a minute when no one else said anything. "But sometimes, you want what you want—when you want it."

"And sometimes, we're feeling creative," Jake suggested. "Or adventurous."

I glanced over at him and grinned. Yeah, *that* was another part of this conversation.

"I think," Ian said slowly, "whatever you're most comfortable with is going to work for us. I mean, am I probably going to be envious if you disappear upstairs with one of the guys and spend a couple of hours screwing around? Not going to lie. Probably."

My gut tightened.

"But it's not going to chase me off. Because I know they will be too when it's my turn."

I almost dissolved into a puddle of relief. This sounded almost too good to be true.

"Coop's not said anything," Archie pointed out.

"Coop is fine," Coop stated, stretching his arms over his head and letting a bit of his abdomen peek out as the hem of his shirt rose. "Coop wants Frankie. Coop has Frankie. Long as Frankie is happy, Coop is happy."

"He's also apparently talking about himself in the third person," I murmured, eyebrows raised.

He winked at me. "That's because Coop is happy right now. He's got his girl, his friends, no parents, no responsibility, snow as far as the eye can see, and a chance to just be. I'm delirious." The words squeezed my heart so tight, it pressed the air out of my chest. "My only request is that if you're in your room, even if one of the others is there, I can come and sleep with you, too."

"Fuck, dude, come sleep with us if we're in my room," Jake said. "I don't mind."

"I don't mind," Ian said slowly, but he did look thoughtful.

"Just be aware that you might get booted if a good morning wake-up call is involved," Archie told him. "Coming back to the smell of sex all over the room after a run is one thing. I don't necessarily want to share the fun that early."

"But you're not opposed to later in the day?" Coop asked, a faint smirk on his lips.

Archie shot me a considering look. I gave up on pretending I wasn't blushing. It wasn't so much that this whole conversation was embarrassing—I mean, it was—but it was more that we were talking about this so openly and they were all be so relaxed about it.

Rubbing his thumb against his lower lip, Archie said, "If Frankie isn't opposed—I'll try anything once."

All the breath whooshed out of me at that admission. Coop's grin just grew. He'd made his desires more than clear. He and Jake both for that matter. I had a feeling it was only a matter of time before we dove into the next step, and as nerve-racking as it might be, I grew more curious with each subsequent day.

"I'm open to it," Ian said slowly, and I tracked my gaze over to him. The intensity in his eyes was like a pair of candles burning hot. They scorched me as he swept me from head to toe. We'd only had a handful of times alone together, but he'd easily become the most demanding of the four of them in very specific ways. I hadn't realized how much I'd like being tied up or spanked.

Though the latter was something both Jake and Archie liked to do, but not the way Ian did it.

Or maybe they just hadn't worked their way up there.

Fuck. A delicious shiver raced over me, and Ian's smile turning knowing. "But I want the caveat that if anyone is uncomfortable, we shift the plan," Ian continued.

"Agreed." The swiftness of the word spilling from the others left me as the last one.

"Absolutely," I said.

"Then we just figure out what we all like," Archie mused, then he grinned. "Any more tough topics, babe?"

I groaned. "I don't know if I could survive any more at the moment." All the blood was in my face, but at least there was no fear of my cheeks getting cold. Probably not any time in this century.

They chuckled.

"Cool," Coop said, bouncing to his feet and holding a hand out to me. "Let's get changed and go play in the snow."

I clasped his hand and let him pull me to my feet, but he picked me right up and kissed me. His tongue delved against mine, twisting, twining, tasting, and stroking until I was shaking.

"You think he's going to remember she wanted to go play in the snow?" Jake's dry question made Archie and Ian both laugh.

Lifting his head, Coop winked at me and thankfully didn't put me back down on my rubbery legs. "I just wanted to have my first kiss on the mountain," he said. "You know, a real one."

A laugh escaped, especially when he quirked a brow as he set me on my feet. I gripped his arms for balance as I got my wobbly legs under me.

"Anyway…last one outside has to sleep in their own room tonight." Coop bolted for the stairs before the last word left his lips.

"Fuck," Jake swore and tore after him with Ian right behind him. Archie stared at me with a bemused expression, and I had to wonder if I wore the same one.

"Do you think he knows I'll be the last one?" I had to ask, and Archie threw his head back and laughed before he offered me his arm. Threading my arm through his, I bumped his hip with mine as we headed for the stairs.

"I don't know," he said as we ascended the steps. It wasn't hard to hear the guys laughing and shit talking each other across the halls as they changed. "I could take my time and then all I have to do is lure you to my room tonight."

He paused at my door and pressed me right up against it.

"Thoughts?"

"Um…" I said, flattening my hand against his chest. Fuck, I really did like having my wrist out of the cast. "I win?"

His laughter echoed up the hall and carried just enough wickedness that Jake stuck his head out the door. "What are you two plotting?"

"Nothing," Archie denied before brushing a kiss to my lips and opening my door to nudge me inside. I bit my lip, but I couldn't stop the laughter from bubbling up. He made a shooing motion, and I blew him a kiss. Closing his fist over it, he carried to his heart. "See you in a minute, don't forget the waterproof boots."

"I won't."

The door closed, and I let out a little laugh and danced in a circle. Pressing a hand to my stomach, I took a deep breath, but the smile on my face wouldn't go away. I had no idea how I got lucky with all of them. For that matter, I wasn't sure how crazy we were to try and do this. "But so far, so good," I whispered to myself, then crossed my fingers. Closing my eyes, I gave myself a moment to get it together.

Laughter and thumps echoed from beyond my closed door, and I swore my smile widened. My cheeks hurt from the force of it.

"Okay," I told myself. "Let's do this."

It took me ten minutes to change, because I had to make sure I shimmied into the right pieces. I'd tried these on in the store, but it was still different to slide into the black ski pants with their suspenders and high waist that did great things for my ass and my boobs—thank you, Rachel. Next came the moisture wicking socks, then the heavy boots. I joked they felt like moon boots when I first put them on, but they added a scant inch to my height. I was in no way at risk of catching up to any of them.

Pausing, I checked myself in the mirror. The red top cut nicely with the black. It was a Henley, warm enough but also breathable. Layers, Rachel assured me, were the key. Also the best part of the ski pants, I decided, was how they hugged my ass but showed zero panty lines.

Score.

I put my hair up and pulled the earmuffs on. They looked adorable. The jacket was last, and it was red and black with gold piping. I paused long enough to take a picture of myself to send to Rachel, then I shoved my phone in the pocket and zipped it closed. The opportunity for pics was too great, I wasn't going to miss them because I left the phone up here.

Gloves in hand, I opened my door to find Archie leaning against the wall, looking devastating in his own pair of ski pants, boots, and open jacket. Instead of earmuffs, he had a knit cap pulled over his head, and he looked both adorable and hot in equal measures.

"Wow," he exhaled as he gave me a once over, and I did a little pirouette so he could get the full effect. His eyes were full of heat and approval. "I owe Rachel."

"So do I," I teased. "Your turn."

He gave me a little spin after he pushed away from the wall. He stalked over to me, and I had to bite my lip again. "You think they'd notice if I decided to keep you inside? We could watch the snow fall, naked and in bed."

"Tempting," I admitted as he hooked the front of my jacket together and began to zip it up, despite his teasing invitation. "But I don't think we'd see much snow if we were in bed naked."

"No," he agreed, laying one flap over the top of the zipper and tucking it in. "We definitely wouldn't, but I'm throwing my hat in right now. You and me, my room tonight. Any night, really."

Another shiver skated up my spine as I returned the favor and zipped him into his jacket. "You guys are going to make choosing hard," I warned him.

"Maybe," he murmured, then gave me another kiss before he tugged the top of the jacket up to shield my nose and mouth. "Gloves, babe."

Bundled in, I pulled the gloves on, and he gave me an approving nod.

By the time we reached the bottom of the stairs, it wasn't hard to guess the guys had beaten us both out there. A flash of movement by one of the windows had me laughing. "You should let me go first, if you really want to be the last out."

"And let them hit you with all those snowballs?" Archie eyed me like I was nuts. "Not happening, babe. Besides, the reward is infinitely worth the challenge."

I snorted, then grabbed his arm when he would have kept going. "Is there a back door?"

His deep brown eyes gleamed as he gave me a slow smile. "Frankie, you're a bad girl."

"It's your terrible influence," I retorted, and his grin grew.

"This way."

Two minutes later, we ducked out through the kitchen onto a closed in porch, then down two steps into deeper snow. It was awesome. Archie took my gloved hand in his and lead me around the lodge. We pressed against the side, and he snuck a peek around the side.

"Any minute now," Jake called. "They're going to come out. Don't hit her."

"No shit," Ian said. "Any other advice you wanna give?" The thump of snow and a grunt had me clapping a hand over my mouth to keep from laughing.

Well that, and the fact that Coop had just come around from the back corner of the house and stealthed toward us, snow crunching under his feet. There was the sound of scuffling from out front, and Archie's shoulders were shaking.

I tapped his back as Coop gave me a look. I could read *traitor* in his eyes quite clearly. No, I wasn't choosing between them.

"One sec, babe," Archie said, distracted. "Trying to figure out where Coop is hiding. Then we can leap out and pelt them."

Yeah. About that. Coop was almost to us, and when I raised my eyebrows at him, he balanced a rather hefty snowball in one hand, and he motioned for me to duck with his free one.

"Archie," I said, because truly, he deserved another chance.

"One more sec, Bubba and Jake are re-arming."

Okay. Coop shot me a look and then glanced down like was I going to do it or not?

Uh huh. I ducked, and Archie pulled back from looking around the corner in time to take the snowball right in the chest. The spray of snow spattered me, but it was hilarious as Coop let out a war whoop. Even funnier when that whoop echoed from the others. The snow started to fly, and it was every man—and in my case, woman—for themselves.

Grabbing handfuls with my gloves and packing them together, I flung them at the guys with no small amount of joy. Some of the snowballs shredded apart before they even made it to their targets, but others had sweet little poofs as they hit their backs or their chests.

Jake toppled Ian into the snow and the two tumbling damn near took out Archie. Coop snagged me and dragged me backwards as the pair kicked up more snow. I couldn't tell if they were fighting or wrestling or snow swimming. It was even funnier when Archie pelted them both and they turned on him.

Gray-green eyes dancing with laughter, Coop tugged me away from the battle. "Snowman," he whispered. Yeah, I could definitely go for that.

Except, building a snowman was a lot harder than it looked like on television or in books. First we had to pack the snow and try to roll it into a ball. It didn't always cooperate. Coop and I broke the first one by falling on it together while trying to get it to keep rolling. Then massacred a second one because he shoved snow down my back.

Fuck that was cold.

I was so getting him back for it.

"You know, it's easy to tell who are *not* the engineers in the group," Jake drawled, and Coop and I turned as one and shot him the bird. He just laughed and started packing snow together. "C'mon, Baby Girl. I'll show you how it's done."

"Oh, I don't think so," Archie called, and I twisted to find him with the base of a snowman already started as well. "This is at least decent enough packing snow. It could be much worse. How about we leave this to the experts? In this case, me?"

Ian snorted. "Where did you get certified in snowman expertise?"

"Every winter for ten years," Archie declared. "You Texas folk are out of your depth."

Oh, that was so the wrong thing to say.

The race to build the better snowman was on. Ian joined me and Coop as Archie and Jake went a little crazy. "C'mon," he said, giving me a nudge. "Let's finish this one you two started."

Between the three of us, we got the base set, then the body, and I was working on the head while Ian cut toward the woods to find arms and Coop headed back to the house for something to make eyes and a hat for its head.

I glanced over to where Jake was actually shaping his in the snow. It wasn't so much three balls stacked together as a squat looking dude that might resemble Santa when he was finished. Archie was doing something similar. They were packing and shaping the snow so they had features. They were amazing. I pulled my phone out and snapped a couple of pics because we'd been too busy playing to take pictures. But they were both so serious and intent. How the heck were they…

"Got 'em," Ian told me as he came back holding up two spindly looking branches. He joined me in watching the other two while I kept smoothing the head in circles to make it nice and round. "I think they want to impress you," he murmured against my ear.

A warm glow spread through me. "Well, it's definitely working." Tilting my head, I glanced up at him and made a kissing noise. He chuckled and tugged my jacket collar down to free my face and then brushed his lips against mine. His were much cooler, but I didn't care. I just leaned into him as he teased my lips to part and then groaned when he stroked my tongue gently.

He tasted like coffee and chocolate. Hmm, chocolate sounded really good.

As if on cue, my stomach grumbled, and Ian lifted his head. He fixed the collar so it shielded the lower half of my face again. "Let's finish this up so we can feed you."

"Okay."

Coop returned with stuff for the head just as I finished it. The body listed a little, and the hat had to be stuck on with a stick 'cause the wind kept tugging at it. The eyes were mismatched, but he'd found some rocks that were about the right size. He used an actual carrot for the nose and made me laugh.

"And done," Archie called.

"Me too!" Jake declared, and all three of us turned to look at their masterpieces.

They really were stunning and so utterly beyond my league as far as snowman building went. Jake's definitely had a Santa feel, and Archie's looked more like a pirate, but they were adorable.

I started bowing, and Coop and Ian joined me as we declared, "We are not worthy!"

More pictures, this time, me getting shots of all four of them with the different snowmen, then they insisted of pics with me, and it was a challenge, but we managed one hysterical selfie with all five of us crammed together around the snowman Coop, Ian, and I built.

I never wanted this vacation to end.

Chapter Eighteen
MORNING WAKE UP CALL

After building snowmen—well, attempting to anyway—we escaped back to the warmth of the lodge. Our attempts fell apart about an hour after we were finished. Only Archie and Jake's remained because they'd used water and stuff. I didn't ask, they had a whole explanation they gave to Coop and Ian when we'd all clomped back into the house and stripped down out of the snow gear. I cradled my hot cocoa while they debated it and stared at the fire.

Dinner had been in the oven and waiting for us, not that I ever saw anyone preparing anything. When Archie said we wouldn't notice the staff, he hadn't been wrong. I didn't even know who picked out the movie, it was a comedy and the guys' laughing was the best sound. I curled up with Ian, but I was half-asleep and not even following the film.

I must have fallen asleep because I went from being warm and toasty on the sofa, to being carried with my nose planted firmly against Ian's neck. Right, I needed to change into pajamas or something, was the very last thought I had. Maybe. Then I woke sandwiched between Ian and Archie, legs tangled and my head pressed against Ian's chest, while Archie's hand was firm on my hip and his morning erection was pressed against my ass.

For a moment, I completely forgot where we were. The light in the room came from the wrong direction. The warmth all around me was nice. Ian smelled good, and the muscle beneath my cheek flexed as I started to stretch. The fingers on my hip tightened, and I went from being plastered against Ian to rolled back to chest with Archie.

The stroke of his thumb along the edge of my panties had me squirming, until he tightened his fingers in a silent admonishment to be still. His breath whispered over my throat as he kissed his way up to my ear. "Shh," he murmured, the vibration more than the actual words. I didn't really get a chance to respond because he slid his fingers under my panties, and I swore my eyes rolled back as he glided his finger right along my labia, unerringly to my clit.

His teeth scraped my earlobe, even as I bit my lip to keep from moaning. There was absolutely no patience in Archie as he massaged my clit in short, swift strokes, circling it with two fingers, until he hit just the right pressure and I shattered.

My breath came in sharp, explosive little pants, and Archie twisted, turning my head so his mouth could clamp down on mine. It barely smothered my cry, but I was trying. It was almost impossible to contain my writhing though as he slid his fingers away and let me turn. He rolled us away from Ian with a kind of practiced ease, and then I was sprawling over Archie as he kissed me like he could consume me.

Not that I wasn't lapping up every stroke of his tongue. The stiffness of his erection pressed against me as I rolled my hips and ground against him. Reaching between us, I began to stroke him through his shorts and his teeth scraped over my lower lip before he sucked on my tongue.

Still writhing from the aftershocks of my first orgasm, I sighed at the silken heat of his dick in my hand. He let out a hissed breath, fisting my hair to keep me in place, even though I had zero intention of moving. The fabric of my shirt against my nipples just added another layer of sensation to the rasp of his stubble on my cheeks, the bite of his teeth, the stroke of his tongue.

When he hooked two fingers of his free hand to tug my panties to the side, I needed no further encouragement. Between us, I maneuvered and then rubbed his cock against me, slicking his head, and I lifted my head, breaking his kiss. I was braced on my left arm, and he moved both of his hands to my hips. Whether I rose up or he lifted me didn't matter, but I positioned him and then sank down as he thrust upward with one push.

Back arching, I tilted my head and bit my lip. The force of his gaze on mine was almost too much as he filled me. The heat of the connection was so much more intense. He didn't give me long to adjust to the sensation, not that I wanted it before he lifted me and began to thrust. I rolled my hips on instinct, the faintest of rotations that had him gasp out a harsh exhale, and my gaze snapped down to meet his.

His flushed cheeks and dark eyes promised me he was every bit as affected as I was. The angle of his thrusts stroked against the spot that always made me see stars, and I flexed around him. When he moved his hands under my shirt to massage my breasts, we ground together until moans spilled from my throat with increasing frequency.

The slap of our flesh coming together pushed me, as did his soft grunts. When he reared up, hips slamming into mine, I forgot all about being quiet, and then his mouth was on mine again. One light tug had us pulling apart as he ripped my shirt up and off, and then he kissed down my throat until he reached my breasts. His mouth closed over one nipple.

The tension circling tighter and tighter within me fractured, and I split apart. I dug my nails into his shoulders, desperate to hold on, and then his mouth swooped back up to take mine as a scream ripped out of me. I don't know if it was my clenching around him or he had just been that close, but he came in a rush, and the flood of heat bloomed inside of me, then we collapsed together in a twitching, shaking mess.

Or maybe that was just me.

Wrecked.

I was wrecked and so intimately aware of where he still rested inside of me, my inner walls fluttering around him. A soft groan to my right pulled my head up, and I met Ian's heated stare where he watched us, his blue eyes so bright against the darkness of his blown pupils. He ran his tongue over his lower lip, and I stared at him fixedly until a faint motion dragged my gaze downward.

He had his own dick in his hand, palming it from base to tip and back down. The faintest smear of dampness marked his fat tip, and it was my turn to lick my lips. Archie still shuddered below me, and I flicked a look up to find Ian still watching me. How much had he been awake for?

Excitement threaded through my veins at the idea he'd watched us. It collided with the relief that he hadn't just rolled out of the bed and left us. His gaze shifted, and I knew he and Archie had locked gazes. Some wordless communication passed because Archie eased me upward as he slipped free, and we both hissed at the loss of connection. He pressed a kiss to my throat, a scrape of his teeth, and then another kiss to my jaw, and when I turned to him, he brushed my lips.

"I'm going to shower and get the coffee started," he murmured. "Good morning."

Then he smoothed a hand over my ass and rolled us until I was on my side with my back to Ian. When Archie slid out of the bed, he'd already adjusted his boxers. Another kiss to his fingertips before he brushed it over my lower lip wordlessly.

Then he was striding out of the room.

Before the door even fully latched, Ian's breath whispered over my shoulder and his arms came around me to drag me back to him. The sucking kiss was going to bruise on my throat, and I didn't give a damn. Still shaking from orgasm, I just gripped his hands where they spread over my chest. He flicked my nipples, then rolled them as he kissed his way to my ear.

"Don't even think about moving," he said in this low, dark tone that had me shivering all over again.

We were okay.

I closed my eyes at the flood of relief and desire pooling together. A sharp slap against my ass had my eyes snapping open again, and I found him staring down at me. "You going to be a good girl for me?"

"I'll be anything you want," I answered honestly. The fact that he was here and wanted to be here where I wanted him? Not a hardship to offer at all. A slow smile curved his lips, but his eyes were all heat, want, and demand. He massaged my ass, easing the sting before he delivered another slap, jolting me with a fresh wave of lust.

"Anything?" Was he teasing right now, or did he really want to know?

Maybe I had lost my mind, or maybe these guys just melted my brain. "Anything," I said. After all, he'd said he was willing to try, and he'd just watched Archie get me off and the evidence of that was still damp on my thighs and leaking out of me.

The one drawback to no condoms, and at the same time, I couldn't complain about that fact.

"Angel?"

Oh, right. I needed to answer. I grinned up at him. "Anything," I promised. "As long as it doesn't hurt them."

He nodded once and then nuzzled the corner of my mouth. "But this is all right?" The weight of his hand on my ass vanished for a split-second before another sharp crack of it landed, and everything in me went liquid.

"Fuck," I exhaled the word against his lips. "Yes. That's all right."

I swore his eyes brightened before they darkened with a promise of all the things he wanted to do, and a shiver stole through me. I couldn't wait to discover what all those things were. He massaged the heat out from where he'd slapped me, and one ass cheek definitely felt like it was glowing from the sharpness of those stings. The warmth stole through me and kept me liquid as he slid away from me.

My protest died on my lips as he circled the bed and shed his own boxers. The tight ripple of muscle across his ass as he strode into the bathroom had me panting. For the few seconds he was out of sight, I tried to pull myself together. I'd literally just had back-to-back orgasms, I shouldn't be this wound up, and then Ian strolled back out of the bathroom.

The thickness of his erection pulled my gaze. The tip was red and swollen, as was the underside. It looked almost painful. Everything about Ian was gorgeous, and it was hard to put into words sometimes, especially when he walked across my room like he owned it. He paused at the door to the bedroom, and the soft snick of the lock had me partially rolling over to track him.

Then he was back at the bed, and I rolled onto my back as he gripped my panties and tugged them off. It was a little embarrassing how messy I was, but if it bothered him at all, he didn't let it show. Instead, he ran a warm washcloth up the inside of my thigh, and I let out a little gasp.

"Too much?" he teased, not remotely slowing as he wiped me thoroughly from anus to clit and back again. He cleaned my thighs and urged my legs apart so he could study my pussy, and there was something so exposed about lying there while he cleaned up the evidence of the last guy I'd just been with.

But the moment his gaze lifted and the naked lust in his eyes became visible, all my qualms crushed under an answering wave of heat.

"We're okay," I whispered.

"Yeah, Angel," he said, smiling so gently, it wrenched my heart. "We're more than okay." He did another pass with the washcloth, then leaned down to press a kiss to the inside of each of my thighs. "We're okay." He tossed the washcloth aside and then began to run his hands up and down my thighs as he studied me.

Head tilting, I had to fight the urge to lift my hips at his caresses. Ian stroked me like he owned me, and right now, I thought he just might.

They all did.

Owned pieces of me, and I didn't plan on taking any of them back.

"What are you thinking?"

"Thinking about all the ways I could do this," he told me, his gaze leaving fire everywhere he trailed it over me. "I wish like hell I had some silk ties or this bed had slats in the headboard."

Like his.

I swallowed. Maybe it was playing with fire, or maybe it was the fact that this side of Ian really did turn me inside out, but I stretched my arms above my head and then locked the fingers together. "I can keep them here if you want."

His eyes flared, and he leaned down to bite the underside of my breast. It was just a hint of teeth, and then a long, deep suck that had me squirming. Hickeys were really becoming a way of life at this point.

"Yeah?" he asked, sliding one hand under my thigh and pushing my leg up until my ankle was against his shoulder.

I nodded.

"You can keep them there?" It was like the question warned me a second before he cupped his hand against my ass and delivered a firmer, more stinging slap that had my hips arching upward. Fuck, that hurt and felt so good at the same time.

I had to be white knuckling my hands to keep them still, but I nodded, a little breathless as he massaged the heat out. "If you want," I told him, then licked my lips. Ian's gaze never left my face as he urged my other leg up, and then he was kneeling in front of me, my toes almost touching behind his head as he began to run his dick up and down along my pussy.

"I have one question for you," he said, teasing me, or maybe teasing us both as he rubbed the tip back and forth, but always skating around my clit like he had to know I was already on edge.

"Okay." I mustered out the two syllables with some serious effort. Considering the fact that I'd woken up to mind-blowing sex and kisses and now faced more and I hadn't even had a drop of coffee, I thought I was doing damn good. That, and I was faced with all that golden muscle on his chest and shoulders.

He really was just awesome to look at, and I'd always thought he was good looking, but he was so much more than that.

His smile lit me up as he murmured, "You paying attention to me or my dick, Angel?"

"I can multitask," I whispered, and he laughed as he nudged inside of me, and I sucked in a breath. I was almost too sensitive, and at the same time, I wanted more. I would have pushed my hips up, but he pinned me with one hand on my hip.

"Yes, you can," he agreed, then his smile faded and his expression sobered. The rawness in his eyes had me holding my breath. "You know that I adore you, right, Frankie Curtis?"

My heart squeezed as I stared up at him. "I love you, too." It was almost impossible to ease the words past the lump in my throat, but Ian stilled so utterly at the admission, and then he pushed into me with a relentless thrust as he dropped down to cage me in and his mouth was on mine.

There were no words. There was barely a breath, and I wanted desperately to put my hands in his hair or to hold onto him the way he did me, but I told him I could keep my arms up there, so I did. As it was, I met his kisses and held on as he pounded into me. Every thrust just lit me up. He shifted to wrap my legs around his waist, and I arched my lower back, pushing up until he was striking that sweet spot every single time.

"Scream for me," he beckoned in between sucking on my tongue. It didn't take long for me to completely unravel, and when he slid his hands up to clasp mine, I held on, anchoring myself as I fell apart.

The scream that ripped out of me didn't even sound human, but he felt so damn good, and when his whole body shuddered and he came, his fingers threaded through mine as he slammed home and stayed there. Heat bloomed deep within me, and we were both shaking. The taste of his breath was on my lips, the kisses breaking up for each of us to gulp in oxygen, and then he'd kiss me again.

A knock on the door rifled across my consciousness, but I was boneless and pure liquid, held together only because he was gripping me. Ian kissed me again, slower and deeper.

At the second knock, he lifted his head long enough to say, "Fuck off," before he captured my lips again. A laugh eddied up through my languor, and I could almost feel him smiling in between little licks of his tongue as he sought entry again.

"Dude," Jake called, amusement echoing in the single syllable. "Breakfast is almost ready."

Ian ground his hips against mine. Even if he was softening, I was still fucking sensitive, and my back arched at the contact and a little hiss escaped me. He chased it with another kiss.

Another knock.

"Seriously, Jake," Ian growled. "I will kick your ass. Go. The. Fuck. Away."

Coop's laughter joined Jake's, and I couldn't help giggling. They were being all of twelve. "We have coffee," he taunted.

Head raised, Ian stared down at me, and some of the rawness in his eyes had relaxed, but there was a kind of glow there I wanted to capture forever. He freed one of my hands as I tugged on his, and I lifted it to cup his face. When I skated my thumb over his lower lip, his smile grew.

"There's breakfast burritos, fried potatoes, and some clever bastard made sure there were fresh baked bear claws and apple fritters." Coop was the devil. My stomach rumbled.

"And coffee," Jake added, I could almost picture them snickering and elbowing each other.

Licking my lips, I pressed my fingers to Ian's mouth and raised my brows.

He gave me a slow nod, curiosity sparking in his eyes.

"Boys," I called. "I have a mouthful right now, so it'll have to wait."

The dead silence that greeted that declaration had Ian burying his face against my neck as he began to laugh.

"*Fuck*," Jake swore, but it was more a groan than anything else. "Baby Girl, find me if you're still hungry after."

Ian's shoulders shook even harder, and there was a pair of thumps in the hallway before the guys moved away.

When he finally lifted his head to look at me, he smiled so hard, it actually made my heart hurt for how happy he seemed. "A mouthful?"

"Well," I told him, "I definitely need a shower, and from everything else I've felt, you'd be more than a mouthful."

The heat in his eyes burned vibrantly. "Is that an offer?"

"No," I told him slowly, then rubbed against him, and his cock twitched against my thigh. It might take some persuading, but I had it in me, even the boneless mess I was in. "It's a demand."

He kissed me again, slow and sweet, and I gave into temptation and twined my arms around his neck. A minute later, he dragged me upward, then scooped me into his arms as he walked us both toward the shower.

It took a minute to get my wobbling legs under me, and by the time we stepped under the hot spray and I pushed him back toward the tile to kneel down, he said, "You don't have to…"

But I glanced up at him, even as I wrapped a hand around his semi-hard stiffness. "Who said anything about have to?"

I didn't wait for his answer before I closed my lips around his tip. Ian's groan was a beautiful thing, and he leaned his head back as his whole body tensed. I had the best view in the house.

It definitely took some persuading and we were late to breakfast, but Ian looked far more wrecked than I did by the time we finished washing up and dressed to go downstairs. The bed was definitely messed up, but he helped me fluff out the sheets and leave the blanket back so the very damp spots could dry.

I made a face, and he laughed.

Downstairs, the guys were still in the kitchen, and the knowing looks coupled with the good morning smiles and kisses just left me feeling warmer rather than embarrassed. Jake tugged me over onto his lap, while Coop bounced up to grab food for me.

"I can do it," I argued, but Jake chuckled.

"We know, Baby Girl, but we want to spoil you."

The plate Coop made me was piled high with all my favorites, including the apple fritter. Archie brought me coffee, and Ian just grinned at all of them as he got his own. "Not feeling the love here, guys."

"Not gonna get bent over a table by us either," Archie told him. "I gracefully bowed out and left you with Frankie this morning. I think I did my fair share."

Ian chuckled. "*After* you two woke me up."

"I didn't hear you complaining," Archie snarked back, and I followed the byplay with fascination. Jake rubbed one of my thighs, just petting it in a slow soothing motion. It was sweet, but Archie and Ian weren't fighting. Not really.

"Nope," Ian told him as he poured his own coffee. "Definitely worth waking up to watch that." He tracked his gaze over to me, and I clenched up at the heat in his eyes. "Even better to play after."

And that did it—my face flamed, and I stuffed food in my mouth.

The huff of Jake's laughter before he pressed a kiss to the back of my neck helped. So did Coop's wink. They were really all okay with this.

I needed to stop freaking out or worrying. We were all on the same page.

We could do this.

Relaxing, I dug into my food and just soaked up the conversation as they kept teasing each other.

I reiterated my earlier opinion. I never wanted to leave this place.

After breakfast, we decided to decorate the trees, and then the guys wanted to check out the video games. I was fine with that. Archie had us booked for skiing the next day, and there were other plans in the works. I caught more than one secretive glance. The boys were plotting, and I was content to let them.

The game room also boasted a fireplace, so while they got set up for whatever marathon session, I curled up in the chair nearest the fire with my e-reader. Rachel had texted that she sent me an early present and to check my email. Sure enough, there were books waiting for me to download.

She was getting on a plane today to head off to deal with her family, but she insisted I needed to read all four books in the series.

Trust me, you can thank me later.

With the crackle of the fire and the guys snarking at each other as my soundtrack, I delved into the world of the Wolf and the assholes she went to school with. By the time I got to the end of the first one, I didn't want to pause for lunch. The guys had to drag me into the kitchen, and after a quick round of kisses, I buried myself in book two.

At the end of the second book, I was laughing aloud and texting Rachel—even if she was on a plane.

Bitch, I know why you wanted me to read this. But I'll take it. Ride or die.

She didn't answer, but I didn't expect her to, and I definitely needed to know what happened next. Coop quirked a brow at me as I cackled, and I waved him away. Jake wasn't so easily put off, but when I promised him a blowjob later if he'd let me finish the next two books and keep the others off my back, I got a series of protests from the others.

I tuned them out and went back to reading.

I had to know what happened next.

Chapter Nineteen

RUNS

"**W**edge," Jake ordered as he glided along beside me like king the hill. I didn't mind. Archie, Ian, and Jake were more than comfortable on skis. Thankfully, I had Coop to share my skill level at the lesson all *five* of us took. Well, technically, only Coop and I were taking the lesson. The other guys came to hang out with us and *supervise*. Jake's incredulous look accompanied by Ian's easy grin and Archie's teasing smirk had been great, right up until the instructor, Josh, showed up.

Maybe a couple of years older than us. *Maybe*. He was easily as big as Jake and Ian, with a laughing smile and an easy demeanor. And he was an outrageous flirt. His walking me through my first lesson on how to wedge and position my legs and subtle adjustments to my hips lasted for maybe all of five minutes.

Archie and Jake sent him away to help Coop, and *they* took over my ski instruction. So far, I could go down the hill without landing on my face. I called that a win. I glanced over to where Josh had Coop going a lot faster. He didn't make him wedge all the way down the hill.

"Eyes front," Jake reminded me. I snapped them ahead to where Archie waited for us. They took turns going down the hill, not that they even needed the stupid poles. I thought those looked sexy on television. They were irritating as fuck in real life while trying to figure out where to put my hands and how to hold them without whacking myself or them. "You don't worry about the people behind you. You worry about who is ahead. You have to avoid Archie, so how do you do that?"

I did a plough-turn. Almost like I knew what I was doing, and it slowed me enough that I angled away and around Archie. The bunny hill was not that long a course. An hour ago, it seemed to take forever to get down, but I was getting faster.

Coop hit the runout before I did, and he glanced back at me as I skidded and turned. Only instead of coming to a stop, I pivoted and used the momentum to get me back to the rope tow. My least favorite part of this whole thing. There'd been some definitely uncomfortable humiliation the first time I'd attempted to use it. The idea was to grip the rope and let it pull me up to the top of the bunny slope where I could ski away from it and down.

Yeah, it hadn't really worked the first time. Even in gloves, I couldn't grip it for crap. Jake had skied right up behind me and pushed me up the hill as it towed him. That happened the second and third time. On the fourth, Archie suggested I shift my grip, which helped. Still needed one of them shoving me.

It kind of sucked, but they never complained, and the humiliation wore off. My wrist was still a little weak, and Ian had scolded me when I bitched.

Okay, that wasn't fair. He hadn't scolded me so much as given me a sympathetic squeeze and reminded me I had been out of a cast for like a week. Then murmured I needed to be nicer to myself or I'd get a spanking.

I had to admit, the grin I gave him was probably not remotely discouraging. Particularly with how his eyes had lit up. Playing with fire was apparently my new hobby.

This time, I grasped the rope tow, left hand right on the rope just above the knot and my right hand in front of it, and I kept my skis parallel as it tugged me to the top. Thrill skated through me as I skied away from it at the top like I knew what I was doing. I didn't even mind the seven-year-old who bypassed me and shot down the hill like an Olympic-level skier.

You go, girl.

Josh and Coop were right behind me, but to my shock, Ian, Jake, and Archie stayed at the bottom.

"Looking good," Josh complimented me. Then he nodded to Coop. "You two ready to do this on your own?"

An hour of instruction, and we were experts? The sun was out today, and I'd started out in my ski pants, zipped up snow jacket, gloves, a fuzzy knit cap, neoprene facemask and goggles. I'd felt ridiculous, but the guys kept grinning at me, so what did I know?

I'd already unzipped my jacket because despite the cold, I was hot. The neoprene mask was in my pocket. I kept the hat, the gloves, and the goggles. Exhilaration fountained at the idea of making the run down the slope all by myself. Well, as by myself as I could be with the kids blowing past us like we were tree stumps and the other novice skiers who seemed to be taking to the task like a duck to water.

Thankfully, Coop had fallen almost as much as I had in the beginning, even if he'd done at least two of them on purpose. I didn't feel like an idiot. Glancing at Josh, I raised my eyebrows. "Together or individually?"

Coop chuckled.

"You guys can go down together," Josh told me with an easy smile. "You both have the hang of it. Contrary to what a lot of people think, sixty percent of this is learning to stop. You can stop. You can turn. You have control. Everything else is at your own pace."

Snorting, I said, "Right." But at the same time? If I graduated from the bunny slopes, that meant we got to ride on the ski lift. It would probably be more fun for the guys if they weren't trapped with us here, too. Not that they'd complained once. With that in mind, I glanced at Coop. "Race?"

"Winner gets?" Coop asked as he adjusted his grip on his poles, but the gleam in his eyes was impossible to miss, even with the sun shining on the snow.

"Winner's choice," I teased with a wink, and he whooped, but I was already pushing off.

I'd learned more than just how to stop. During one of my first runs, I'd learned how to go so fast, I'd ended up crashing into the barriers at the bottom because I hadn't quite mastered stopping.

Time to test the theory of whether Josh was right about stopping being the key to everything.

Shouts of encouragement and cheers came from the guys as I whipped down the hill. The tension and the low-grade fear bubbled in my stomach. As with every other time I'd done this, I worried I wouldn't be able to stop. Images of skiing accidents would dance across my brain. The idea that I could tumble and break something didn't fill me with a lot of confidence.

But halfway down the slope, all of that melted away. Earlier, a kid had zipped past me, arms out wide as he skied past yelling, "I'm flying!"

I was flying.

Riding that adrenaline, I zipped right down to the runout and wedged, then plough turned to a stop mere feet away from the guys, with Coop reaching me and performing a similar stop seconds later.

A wild grin stretched my lips, and I held up my hands. "I win!"

"Yes, you do," Coop said with a laugh. A second later, Josh joined us, and he gave Coop a high five before he turned to me. I smacked his hand, though to be fair, I hadn't really gotten to work with him much.

"Thank you, Josh," I told him, because he deserved that much. "You helped make this very easy." In more ways than one.

"My pleasure," he said. "You guys stick to the greens this morning, but I think between you, you could do a blue before the end of the day."

Yeah. Nope. Green sounded good to me.

"And if you guys want a little advice," he continued, glancing from me to where Jake and Archie stared at him like they wanted to punch him. Really, the guy was being nice. Ian had a gloved hand over his mouth, but I swore it was just to hide a smile because his eyes were sparkling. Coop snickered next to me. "They've both got good control, but she seems like a risk taker… Take chair two up. Then follow the sign for the Little Dipper. It's a longer trail, nice views, takes you right to the Big Dipper, and it's the perfect thirty-minute ski down, nice and gentle slopes, clearly marked edges, no moguls. Easy peasy."

Okay, he winked at me with that one, and Coop's laughter dried up and he joined Jake and Archie in the glaring.

Rolling my eyes, I said, "Thanks again, Josh. I appreciate it."

"Yes," Jake said with far less enthusiasm. "Thanks again."

After he skied off, chuckling, I glanced at the guys, and Ian just let out a laugh. "You were flirting."

"No," I argued. "I wasn't."

"You *thanked* him," Jake snarled at me. Granted, there was no heat, but he was not a happy camper.

"I thanked him because he gave us a lesson and stayed really nice, even when you guys were being asses to him."

"Sorry, babe," Archie said with a shake of his head. "You might not think you were flirting, but you were flirting."

"And *Josh* was definitely fucking flirting." Coop was almost scathing. What the hell?

"That, and he was looking at your ass," Jake continued, glaring after Josh, even if the instructor was gone.

"Wow, so I shouldn't be nice or polite?"

They all looked at me like I'd missed the point, and I threw my hands up.

"You know what? Let's ski." Because that had to be easier. I was having fun, and I refused to have a fight.

They grumbled, but some of the pissiness seemed to evaporate by the time we reached the ski lift. A new thrill bubbled up through me.

"Dibs," Archie said, cutting ahead to join me. "Okay, the easiest way to get on the chair is to get ahead of it and then just relax and sit down. We'll be in position before it gets here, but I've got you."

The nerves were back. I hated heights. But I would gladly stab myself in the foot before I admitted it. Especially right now. Archie took my elbow as we got in position, and then we were seated and he pulled the safety bar down and we were off. Whoops from behind us had me twisting to see Jake and Coop taking the next one. Then Ian was on his own.

I needed to ride up with Ian next.

"Having fun?" Archie asked. He had both of his ski poles in one hand and slid his arm around me. There were way too many layers to really enjoy the contact, but I liked it anyway.

"Yes," I told him and grinned. I'd put the goggles up on my head, and I kind of wished I had sunglasses. At least the goggles had tint so it helped to shade my eyes. "This is awesome, and if I haven't said thank you for kidnapping me for Christmas, *thank you*."

His eyes warmed. "My pleasure."

"It's certainly been mine," I teased, and he threw his head back as he laughed.

The views from up here were breathtaking. My stomach dropped when I found myself looking down at these huge pine trees, but Archie gave me a squeeze.

"It's totally safe," he said.

"Yes, I know. Only about thirteen people have died from ski lift malfunctions since the early seventies."

Archie loved me. He didn't say a word about the fact that I'd researched that. He just hummed an agreement.

"And it's beautiful up here," I admitted. I kind of wanted to dig my phone out and take some pictures. I also didn't want to rock the ski lift chair and end up falling out. Was falling out really a threat? Probably not. Still, better safe than sorry.

"It really is," Archie said, and I caught him staring at me.

Laughing, I elbowed him gently. "I'm all bundled up like a bank robber in bubble wrap. Don't make those eyes at me."

"Maybe," he murmured, and rubbed his nose against my temple just below the knit cap. His skin probably should have been cold, but it was warm to me. "But you're still beautiful, and there's this lovely idea of unwrapping you like a present."

A shiver of want went through me, and I sighed. "That's dramatically unfair."

"So is the boner I've had since you shimmied your ass into those pants this morning," he said with a grin. "But I'm managing."

"Is that why you were growling at Josh and didn't want him giving me a lesson?" I arched my brows.

He scowled, but the expression didn't touch his eyes as he shook his head at me. "He was flirting with you, babe."

"The girl at the ski shop was flirting with you," I pointed out. "I didn't get all growly and snarl."

Archie chuckled. "You feel free to stake your claim on me whenever you want. They can flirt, but I won't be touching any of them."

I leaned toward him. "Exactly. Besides, apparently, I'm very dense when it comes to flirting."

His whole body shook with laughter, and it colored his words as we were almost near the top. "See how they are leaning forward? Just as you get to the end, you're going to push off from the chair and ski away from it, using the momentum because the lift doesn't stop. Then we'll swing out to the side and slow and wait for the guys. Got it?"

It was almost our turn. I should be way more nervous, but I just laughed. "Got it."

I could feel his stare for the longest moment, and then we were up. I leaned back as he pushed up the safety bar, and we both scooted forward, and zoom, we were off. I wobbled a little as I skidded to a halt with far less grace than Archie, who skidded to the side like an expert. He and Jake were pretty awesome to watch on skis. I hadn't really gotten to see Ian in action yet, but I was waiting.

One by one, the others joined us. Coop was a damn natural. I stuck my tongue out at him as he slid to a stop and turned so he landed right next to me. He chuckled and then wrapped a hand around my nape and kissed me.

For one second, my heart stopped and alarm rang through me. We'd been so careful about public displays, and then it fell away as his lips firmed against mine. He gentled the kiss only when I relaxed and sighed into it.

"If they weren't both green, I'd leave them," Jake drawled with more amusement than anything else.

A faint snap pulled my head back, and I glanced over to find Ian aiming his phone at me and Coop. "Just adding it to the collection," he explained, but the smile on his face and the ease around us relaxed me even more.

"Hopefully, I don't look like I have fish face." All four of them laughed at me, and Jake cut close to give me a kiss and then he tugged the neoprene out of my pocket and secured it over the lower half of my face before setting my goggles where they needed to go. "I do know how to dress myself."

I wasn't really that irritated, but the habits they'd formed while I'd been hurt seemed to only be getting stronger. He messed with my knit cap and then winked at me. Ass. "I'm doing this to save us from the distraction hazard."

"Her lips are a hazard?" Ian's dry tone had me snickering. We also had other skiers moving around us as they came off the ski lift, but our little group didn't get more than a few passing looks. Nobody here cared, other than we were kind of in the way.

Coop opened his mouth, and I stared at him. He gave it a beat and then closed it with a shake of his head. "Nope. That's a trap."

That made me laugh my ass off.

It took us another good minute to sort ourselves out. The green felt a lot steeper than the bunny hill, and I could see the other swerve away from the trail we were going to follow, and that just made my stomach hollow out.

"That's a blue," Ian told me. "We're not taking you down there your first time."

"Uh huh." I didn't say they weren't taking me down there at any other time, either. We could save that argument for some time between *nope, I don't think so*, and *never*. I was good with that.

It took us even longer to sort ourselves out. Ian took point with me, and Coop followed with Archie, while Jake showed off, moving back and forth between us like it was nothing.

When he started skiing backwards down the hill though, I considered slugging him. When Archie and Ian joined in on the antics, showing off, I let out a little sigh and Coop moved closer to me. We were zig-zagging lazily, and the other three were easily ten yards ahead of us. I couldn't even stay irked at them, because they were being adorable.

All three of them kept glancing back to check on us, but Coop didn't seem to be in anymore of a hurry than I was.

"So," he said. "I believe you won earlier. Have you decided on your choice?"

I grinned, even if he couldn't see it behind the mask. While I hadn't been thinking on it, I had kind of decided. "Yep."

"What will it be?" He eyed me, and I was torn between watching him as I spoke and paying attention to what I was doing. I was still getting used to shifting my weight inside the ski boots and not picking my feet up to move.

"I don't know if I should tell while we're up here."

Our erstwhile escorts had pulled away farther with their clowning around. But I was doing okay, and Coop and I seemed to be matching pace really well.

"And can I say that this is tickling the hell out of me? How many times did we wish for real snow at Christmas?"

"Too many," he said with a laugh. "You can tell me anything anywhere.

Don't be coy. Especially after the instructor hit on you."

"He did *not* hit on me."

"He totally checked out your ass, and he was hitting on you." Coop pointed a finger at me. "You miss that shit. We don't. Hence why Jake and Archie wanted you practicing with them."

"Uh huh."

"What?"

"Nothing," I told him over my shoulder. "You guys are adorable."

His snort just made me grin harder. "You didn't used to think it was so adorable."

The grumpy grumble didn't help his case.

"Well, before, I couldn't get a date 'cause you wouldn't let other guys near me."

"Yeah, well, it worked out for me," Coop said, a little cockier again.

"Worked out better for me," I teased, and his eyes flared.

"What did you decide you wanted?" He circled us right back to where we'd started.

"You remember what we discussed on your birthday?" I didn't look at him. "All the things you wanted?"

The half-strangled, "Yes," did a lot for my confidence.

"I think I want to test one of those out."

I wasn't really certain what happened, but we went from cutting back and forth neatly to Coop crashing into me, or maybe I crashed into him. We went down flailing, and one of my skis snapped right off the way it was supposed to, and we lay there in a lump of limbs, staring at each other.

Breathless, I burst out laughing, and he followed. There were shouts from ahead, and when we tried to get up, my other ski got caught under his and we both pitched into the snow. I lay there for a sec, laughing too damn hard to get up, and Coop was no help. It was like some damn sitcom.

Only better.

Jake got to us first, but Ian and Archie were right behind him. They were all carrying their skis because they'd jogged back up in the snow. Or whatever.

I flat out giggled when Jake popped the lock on my ski and picked me up first, and then they got Coop up.

When they asked what happened? We busted out laughing all over again. Thankfully, neither of us were hurt, and we got our skis back on and resumed our leisurely pace with all three babysitters in attendance.

The rest of the day went like that—easy with the laughter. I was almost an expert on taking the lift up. We'd returned to the top three more times before we took a break for lunch. The lodge food wasn't anything special, but it was filling and I was starving. I was also ready to strip out of my coat and just ski with the long sleeve shirt on because I kept getting hot.

Both Archie and Jake nixed that, but conceded I could probably unzip and take the neoprene off.

Score.

After lunch, we hit a different set of greens. The resort had quite a few. We'd do them once or twice, then switch to another. The views were always spectacular. The last one we hit also had what they called a black-rated run as well as a blue that forked off from it, and yeah, that looked like I'd be falling off the cliff. Jake and Archie kept looking at the blue, and I said, "You guys should do it. You know what you're doing, and Coop can keep me company."

Coop slung an arm around me.

"I can hang out, too," Ian said when Archie and Jake still hesitated, but I poked him.

"I saw you look at that run just like they did. Go, we'll be *fine*."

"And if we're not, that's what ski patrol is for," Coop offered up cheerfully, earning three death glares from the others.

"Go," I ordered them. "I'm getting tired anyway." That was the truth. "So maybe we'll go grab hot cocoa or coffee or something if we beat you to the bottom."

We were so not beating them to the bottom.

Archie pulled out his phone and sent a message before stowing it away and pulling his gloves on. "The car will be waiting for us when we get down there. Back to the lodge where we can soak those tired muscles in the hot tub and have dinner?"

Yes, please.

Coop and I waited for them to set off. The minute the guys started moving down the blue, I read the envy and the longing on Coop's face.

"Do you want to try it?"

"Nope," he lied through his teeth. "Because you don't want to, and I'd rather hang out with you anyway. There will be other opportunities. Archie made more than one reservation for us to go skiing."

He had, hadn't he? I glanced toward the blue again, ignoring the people who hopped off the ski lift and either took off down the blue or the green. I didn't mind just standing here staring out at the view.

"Coop, what if I can't ever choose?" The question had been right there in the back of my mind for weeks.

"Then you don't choose," Coop said slowly. "And we adjust."

That simple. I glanced over to find him staring at me steadily.

"Is that what's worrying you?"

"It's a little unusual." It was more than a little unusual. "Let's be real here."

"I thought we've been real from the beginning." The reproach in his voice had me lifting my chin a little.

"We have been…I guess. I just… You guys all agreed to date me, even if I was seeing the others, and I knew I'd have to choose eventually." And the idea of choosing between them? No. I didn't even want to entertain the idea. Call me greedy and selfish, I didn't care. I wanted all of them. Nearly losing Ian the way I had cemented it. I wouldn't risk any of them now. "The last few weeks…"

"Have been good," he said softly, then pressed a kiss to my temple. "Stop worrying. Talk to the guys about it. Talk to them individually, or talk to us as a group. But I can tell you my answer right here and right now."

I lifted my gaze to meet his.

"I'm in this for the long haul, Frankie. Cradle to grave. That hasn't changed."

There had never been a point in my life that I could remember where Coop wasn't a part of it.

"I can share you with them," he continued in the same soft voice. "I know how much you love me, and I'm secure in that. I hope like hell you know how much I love you, too."

The corners of my mouth curved, partially in disbelief and partially in delight. He just took the words right out of my mouth. Literally. "You really are my best friend."

"And I always will be," he said with a wink. "Now, no more worrying. Those assholes adore you, and no one is here under duress. Talk to us. We'll sort it out."

"Oh, I might need to get drunk for that conversation." Especially if it was all of us.

Coop's grin turned wicked. "Or something."

I raised my brows.

"Later," he said. "Let's go before they think we got eaten by the mountain."

I laughed, but followed him, and yeah, I left some of the worry I'd been carrying behind and I was a lot lighter on the way down. I hadn't even admitted to myself how much I'd been worrying. But we were having a blast.

I really didn't want anything to go wrong.

"Stop worrying!" he called to me over his shoulder as he cut back and forth in the snow and I followed him. As tired as I was, this had somehow gotten a lot easier, or maybe the motions just made sense now. I didn't care. "Frankie, I can *hear* you thinking."

"Yeah?" I yelled. "Can you hear what I'm thinking now?"

"Yes," he said with a laugh. "And I'd rather play with your ass than mine, thanks."

I damn near tripped as I laughed and blushed.

But I did stop fucking worrying.

Chapter Twenty
ALL FOUR ONE

Somewhere between leaving the slopes and riding in the car back to the lodge, my legs had begun to stiffen and my back protested. I refused to complain, even if I was exhausted. It was late enough the sun had already begun to edge down, and the temperatures promised to drop a few more degrees. The forecast called for more snow, and I couldn't wait. All the way back to the lodge, I had my head tucked against Coop's shoulder and my eyes half-closed. I didn't even realize I'd fallen asleep until I roused to Jake carrying me in the house.

"I can walk."

"Uh huh," he said, slanting an amused look at me. "You still want to hot tub?"

Oh. That sounded amazing. "There's the one out on the deck, right?"

"Yep." He bumped the door open with his hip and then paused as we both stared at my bed. Not only had it been made—something I knew we hadn't done that morning, but there was a fresh coverlet on it, this one a deep green, and there were roses on every single surface. Red roses. White roses. Yellow roses. Pink ones. There were blue and violet ones. Every color I could think of, including rainbow roses.

Jake set me on my feet, kissed my forehead, and gave me a little nudge before he withdrew and closed the door on his way out. None of them followed me into the rose-perfumed and bedecked room. I turned in a slow circle, some of my exhaustion fleeing. There was even a mini-Christmas tree with roses affixed to it. I searched each bouquet, pausing to sniff them. There were no cards, no notes, nothing, at least not on the ones on the dresser. But I moved slowly as I padded around the room. I'd stripped out of the snow gear before I slipped into the car.

Someone had stacked the fireplace, but it wasn't lit and that was okay. The warmth in the room was more than sufficient for me to strip off the socks. The only note present was next to what had to be four dozen red and white roses on either side of the bed. It was a simple white card with silver thread along the edges.

We wanted to get them for you.

Right next to it was a new charm for my bracelet—a simple pair of skis and poles. Tears flooded my eyes, and I bit my lip as I swung my gaze over all the roses. They'd wanted to get them for me.

My heart thumped almost painfully. I snatched up my phone and did a quick video sweep of the roses, and then hesitated. It seemed almost too personal to send to Rachel. And at the same time…

You know what, I'd figure that out later. I dropped the phone on the bed, even as it began to vibrate with updates to the cloud account. The guys were uploading pictures, and some of the images danced over my screen and I grinned. I hadn't even realized the guys had taken snaps of me on the ski lift. There was one of me and Archie with me grinning up at him like he was everything, and that thump in my heart double-timed.

As I stripped off my clothes to leave on a stack next to the chest at the end of the bed, it hit me. I didn't bring a bathing suit, did I? I checked my suitcase, which had been emptied and put away into drawers. The staff had been busy while we were gone. Archie insisted they were going to be discreet, and he'd been right. I hadn't seen them yet.

In the top drawer, I found a new strapless bikini in red waiting for me. The tags were still on it. I debated it, but I wasn't sure I was brave enough yet to go down there naked. Not even if they'd all seen me naked and wrecked. Then again…

I chewed my lower lip as I held the scraps of cloth up and glanced at the mirror over the dresser. My cheeks were flushed, and my eyes shone. Was I nervous or excited?

Possibly both?

Well, I could always take them off. Not that they left much to the imagination once I had them on. The heat to my face had spread down my neck and to my chest. I darted into the bathroom to run a brush through my hair. I'd had it braided for most of the day, but it felt good to let my scalp relax, so I settled for piling it on my head into a messy bun.

It was stupid how much something like doing my own hair filled me with a measure of glee after weeks of having to rely on the guys to help me. Not that they'd ever minded or complained, but still…

I kind of wanted to put my charm bracelet on, but not in the water. Finally, after having delayed enough, I grabbed my robe and tugged it on before sweeping my gaze over the room again. The roses were amazing.

Flat. Fucking. Amazing.

I half-expected the guys to be waiting for me in the hall, but they weren't. Taking the time on the walk downstairs and out to the deck to get my shit together, I tried not to focus on how giddy I was or how the muscles in my legs were caught in that in between state of sore and stiff, but also wobbly and overtired.

Downstairs, a fire burned merrily in the fireplace and the Christmas tree twinkled with all its assorted lights, and those were the only sources of illumination. A note with my name on it waited on the coffee table, and I paused to snag it. Flipping the card over, I laughed.

We'll be back in to enjoy the lights. C'mon out to the hot tub, drinks and food waiting.

I kissed the note and set it back down. I'd steal it later and add it to the card about wanting to get me flowers.

Sure enough, the guys were outside. Darkness had fully fallen, and there were twinkling lights all over the deck. It had been mostly cleared of snow, and the hot tub steam rose up invitingly in the air, even if the chill out there made me shudder before I even opened the door.

Even better, my favorite four people were waiting for me, and they all glanced over or twisted to see me as I slid the door open. The cold air was bracing after being inside, and the wood was cold against my feet. Yeah, I should totally have grabbed slippers or something.

"Hey, guys," I called, hurrying the door closed and not hesitating to make a run for the tub. I dropped the robe and slid in without taking a pause. Jake caught my hand as I stepped up and in to offer me some balance. "Holy fuck, it's cold out here."

The water was blissfully hot, and I sank right into it.

Archie chuckled, but his heated stare did almost as much to warm me as the water. "I like the bikini."

"I debated whether to wear it or not," I admitted as Jake tucked me under his arm and pulled me right against him. The smoothed seats were comfortable, and the water bubbled as the jets surged it. Four harsh inhales greeted that statement, and I had to bite my lip to keep from laughing. I didn't dare glance down in the water to see what they'd gone with, but I was pretty sure Jake had on trunks of some kind.

"Well," Archie said, recovering first. "You can do whatever you want. No one here will judge."

"Nope," Coop said, and I caught him studying me, a small smile playing on his lips.

I wasn't going to leave them in suspense. Before I could say anything more, Ian handed me a glass of wine and paused long enough to give me a kiss before he settled on the bench on my other side.

"Smooth," Jake complimented him, and Coop snorted.

"He was just faster."

"You snooze, you lose," Ian said cheerfully, and his thigh pressed against mine. Another shiver worked its way up my spine that had absolutely nothing to do with the cold. The varying grins held nothing of recrimination or jealousy or anger.

Another tense band of worry relaxed, and I took a sip of the wine with a sigh. The snow falling overhead was magical because it seemed to evaporate before it got to the water. At the same time, it was like we'd been transported to another world.

"Dinner's inside," Archie told me. "Ready for whenever we are, but there's also snacks and fun." He motioned to the covered trays around the edge of the tub. I hadn't really paid that much attention to them.

"Fun?" I asked, glancing from one to the other.

"Well, we are in Colorado," Archie said. "All the rules are suspended for the next couple of weeks, agreed?"

"I don't see why not." Jake stretched his legs out.

"Or something," Coop teased, eyeing me. "Technically, most of us are legal adults."

I wasn't alone in flipping him off. Jake gave my shoulders a squeeze. "Fine, then Frankie and I will be over here in our youth while you old fogeys be legal."

Ian snorted. "Technically, Frankie's emancipated, Jake. So you're the 'baby' for the moment."

"Fuck that," Archie dove in to it before the two could start sniping at each other. "The point is, I had some treats picked up for us, and since we're not worried about random drug tests with the season over, I don't see why we can't enjoy them."

Drug tests? My eyebrows climbed, and I wiggled away from Jake to twist and pop open one of the silver lids. Chocolate waited for me, and I blinked slowly. "You got us edibles?"

"Guilty," Archie murmured, and I stole a look over at him.

"Um…before we dive into whether this is wise or not," I hedged. "I really need to do something first." I put the lid back on and took another swallow of the wine. Between the heat, the alcohol, and the company, more of the tension bled away. At Jake's curious look, I cupped his face and kissed him.

He was closest after all.

Then one by one, I moved around the circle, giving each of them a long, if gentle kiss. Coop caught the back of my head and deepened it until I was half-panting when he let me go. Apparently, that was all the encouragement Archie needed to drag me onto his lap as part of his kiss, and the sudden déjà vu to our first night sent a thrill through me as his fingers slid right under the seam of my bikini bottoms to stroke my ass.

I bit his lower lip, and he groaned before he sucked on my tongue, and I was definitely not even a little chilled. With reluctance, I pulled away and moved back to Ian, and he set his beer aside to kiss me deep, dirty, and raw. This Ian took my breath away every time. It was like any restraint he'd held on himself since our first kiss had all but disintegrated. The erection rubbing against my ass was a reminder that I wasn't the only one getting turned on.

Gulping in air, I sank back into my spot for all of two seconds before Jake dragged me over into his lap, and the gentleness in the kiss gave way to something far fiercer. I wasn't just playing with fire anymore, I'd definitely lit the blaze.

"Better," he murmured before tracing my lips with a finger. "I was trying to be polite, I should have known better."

A giddy laugh escaped me as he settled me back on the seat between him and Ian. When Ian handed me my wine, I grinned at them.

"Not that I'm objecting to the kiss, Angel, but was that for something in particular?"

"Because I wanted to," I told him, and then glanced around our little circle and met each gaze one at a time. "And because I loved the roses, thank you."

The smirk on Archie's face was perfect, as was Coop's and Jake's deep laughter. Ian just nodded at me, then winked. "You think we don't always listen, but we do."

"No," I told him softly. "I know you do. I'm just as guilty of being dense, you know."

"Truth," Coop announced. "But you're with us now, right?" The look in his gray-green eyes made my heart stutter, the conversation we'd had on the mountain so close and fresh in my mind.

"Yes," I said, then drained the last of the wine. He chuckled at me and moved to grab the bottle, and I passed him my glass. Jake tipped up his beer and took a long swallow. It was hard to look away from the motion of his throat.

Honestly, it was hard to look away from any of them.

"As I was saying," Archie cut back in. "Before I was so gloriously interrupted."

I laughed.

"I got us some edibles to try. There's gummies. Chocolate. Cookies. A little bit of everything. But I thought it might help some of us relax and experiment as we like." The last had to be directed at me, but then he focused on me as Coop returned my newly filled wine glass. "There is absolutely no pressure."

"Well, I'm definitely curious," Jake admitted, and he pressed a kiss to my temple before shifting to grab the chocolate from the tray I'd been looking at before. He took a bite, and we were all watching him as he chewed it thoughtfully. "Peanut butter," he admitted, and then washed it down with his beer.

At my face, he chuckled and tugged me close for a kiss.

Beer and chocolate, ugh. I smacked his chest, and he rumbled with laughter. "Want to try a bite, Baby Girl?" He held up the second half of the piece he'd eaten, and I pursed my lips.

"Are we going to get stupid and say ridiculous stuff?"

"Maybe," he said with a shrug. "We're all safe here, right?"

I trusted all of them, right? That was the unspoken question. "I have never been high," I admitted. "Except for like, the pain drugs, and then I was just asleep."

"You were adorable, even when you were sleeping," Coop told me. "But you don't *have* to." He popped a couple of the gummies, and Archie had a cookie in his hand. He locked gazes with me as he took a bite, and even Ian had stretched past me to snag one of the pieces of chocolate.

"What the hell," I said. "You only live once." I opened my mouth and Jake fed me the chocolate. It was very peanut buttery, and I had to scrape it off my teeth with my tongue before washing it down with the wine. I didn't know what I'd expected to happen, but it was just good. There were other snacks, too. Not just loaded ones. Like, there were brownies, sans the THC, and there were hot wings under one of the trays on a heated plate, even.

I giggled at the feast of it all, and *dinner* still awaited us. Leaning back against the tub, I stared up at the sky. "I really love this," I admitted.

"Me too," Coop agreed. "Skiing was a lot of fun."

I grinned at him. "It was. And we're going again, right?" I glanced at Archie.

"We can go as many times as you want," he promised. "We rented skis for this, but if you end up loving it, babe, I can totally buy you your own pair and we'll make ski trips a regular thing."

"There's skiing on the East Coast," Jake told me, before pressing a kiss behind my ear. "Good places in Pennsylvania and Maryland that I know of."

"And we can always come back here," Ian suggested. "I have a feeling Archie's grandfather wouldn't mind it."

"Nope," Archie said. "Grandpa will let us visit whenever we want. Open invitation."

I smiled. I'd already grown super fond of this place. "I can't believe you set all this up," I murmured. "Just made all the arrangements so we could all steal away together. It's such a you thing though." I glanced at Archie, and he grinned at me.

"Did you think I'd be more likely to steal you away by myself?"

"Maybe," I mused, but not so much anymore. "You guys were all so specific about parceling my time. Making sure I didn't ignore you and keeping me so busy, I barely had time for anything else."

"You make time for what's important," Coop reminded me. "And to be fair, you didn't notice it as much until this year."

"That's not totally true," I pointed out, still mellow. The absolute lack of tension was just kind of profound. Was I always so wound up? "I noticed before, just…figured it was what friends did. You were kind of greedy when we were kids, too."

He snorted, even as Archie let out a soft laugh. "I'm still greedy," Coop informed me. "I pretty much want everything with you. But I told you that earlier when you asked me."

Oops. That got some interested looks. "Asked him what?" Ian nudged me. "Um…"

Jake had taken out one of the chocolate pieces and snapped it in half, then he offered me the other half, and I studied it and him a beat. It was a good excuse to not embarrass myself. Then again, I took it and held the piece of chocolate before I glanced around at them. Coop gave me a soft, if encouraging look, and I sighed.

"I asked Coop what happens if I can't choose." I really didn't want to ruin our trip or this evening or anything. We were all here and we were all having fun and I was going to ruin the mellow.

"You're not ruining anything," Jake told me and nudged my hand to my mouth. Oh, good idea. Better to eat the chocolate and shut up. I was almost done with my second glass of wine, and maybe I should go for a third.

Maybe that would let me hold onto the mellow floaty sensation.

"What happens with all of us if you can't choose?" Archie clarified, shifting in the water to get fresh beers for the guys. He drank wine, too. He'd had wine with me. But when they were together, they enjoyed their beers. I wasn't going to complain. I could drink beer, but I preferred the wine.

At my nod, Ian curled one loose tendril of my hair around his finger. There was still peanut butter on my teeth, so I was licking at it and keeping my mouth shut for the most part. "Then you don't choose, Angel."

Just like that, and my eyes rounded.

"Am I for real?" Oh, look, he could translate my expression. I nodded dumbly.

"Yep," he said slowly, and then tugged the curl, and I leaned toward him automatically. "I had a lot of time to think about this. What it's like to be without you, I got a taste of that too. Not a fan. And I've had a taste of being with you and even watching you with all of them." He gave me a considering look. "And I'm a little selfish, I'm going to want you to myself more than I want to share, but that doesn't mean I am going to make you choose."

Holy shit. "Really?" My stomach seemed to be flip-flopping between bottoming out and filling with a thousand butterflies.

"Really," he promised. "I know I have a long way to go to make sure you trust me again, Angel. So I'll reassure you anytime you need it."

He didn't have to go that far, but I just… "I don't want to mess this up." It was easier to just say it to him. Like it had been to Coop. But I'd told Jake that in the beginning, and I swept my gaze over to include Archie. "I never imagined this. All of you, and now I can't imagine it without you. I don't want to." Anytime I tried to, everything just seemed bleak. "And I'm selfish, too. I don't want to have to."

"Okay," Jake told me, pulling me back against him. "It's okay, Baby Girl. You don't have to imagine anything. I stand by what I said. I'm okay with these three idiots. No one else."

"Agreed," Archie told me, locking his gaze on me. "I know you love me." My face heated. "I told you I love you, and I meant every word." There was absolutely no shyness in him. "Would I leap at the chance to have you to myself? Yes. But can I share you with them?" The corner of his mouth curved. "Not in bed, and not all the time. But the rest of it? Yeah. I can. For some reason, I like these assholes, and I know you need them."

Not just want them. "I need you, too," I reminded him. "And I do love you. I love all of you." Ian was the only one I hadn't really admitted it to. I mean, I'd danced around it some. Said it in the heat of the moment, but this was different. I thought it might even be hard to say. I laughed and shook my head. "This is crazy, right?"

"Maybe," Coop said with a shrug. "But the only people who matter are here." The smile on his face was gentle. "Don't be afraid of it. Or of us. If we were gonna kill each other, we probably would have when Bubba pulled his shit."

I winced, but Ian ran his knuckles down my cheek. "He's not wrong. I'm surprised only Jake tried to kick my ass."

"I thought about it," Archie admitted. "But Jake was always better at just doing it. So next time, I'll make sure I get my punches in."

Coop snorted, but his grin was unflagging. "Let's not let there be a next time. We can all settle things with our words."

Jake let out a little sigh, then kissed my temple before passing me to Ian. I saw it coming and so did Coop, 'cause he put his beer bottle on the edge and then Jake grappled with him and water flew everywhere.

It was hilarious. Ian looped his arms around my waist and kept me in his lap as we all lost it laughing. Only after the two settled and Jake reached for me did Ian scoot to the side and shake his head. "Not happening. Mine now."

That generated more laughter, and I leaned my head back against his shoulder. Coop pointed at Archie. "Okay, spill. What are our plans for the rest of this two weeks, Mr. I'm Playing Everything Close to the Vest?"

Archie snorted. "Just enjoying surprising all of you. Can't a guy just be nice to his friends and our girl?"

"Yes," I told him. "Absolutely." The smile on my face hurt. "But I kind of want to know, too."

"Yeah?" He grinned slowly. "Do you want to know enough to come sit on my lap while I tell you?"

"Hey!" Ian tightened his arms. "That's cheating."

"No, that's just playing with style." Archie lifted his wine to toast us, and the giggles hit me. It was ridiculous and fun.

"I'm with Bubba," Jake said. "That's cheating. But I'd totally do it if I had something sneaky for Frankie, too. Oh wait…" He eyed me. "I do." He patted his lap. "Wanna know what it is?"

With a snort, Coop said, "Come sit with me, Frankie. I won't cheat or try to use blackmail. We all know I'm your favorite, anyway."

"Longevity doesn't make you the favorite," Jake countered.

"It does when she told me she wanted to help me make some wishes come true." He waggled his eyebrows, but three sets of very speculative eyes turned on me, and I made a face.

"Wow, Coop, did you really just do that?"

"Oh yeah," he said. "We're all one big happy little family right here. I'm not shy."

I wasn't either, but…

"Tell you what," Archie offered. "What wishes of his are you making come true? You tell me one, and I'll tell you one of my plans."

"Girl wants to see the cookies before she gets in the van," I retorted.

Not missing a beat, he opened the container with the edible cookies, and I burst out laughing. Even Ian was chuckling, and he spread his hand over my stomach as he pressed his lips to my shoulder. "You're all cheating."

"Hey, you have her, *why* are you complaining?" Coop challenged him.

"I do, don't I?" Ian's hand dipped down to my bikini bottoms, and my eyes opened wide. Was he really going to… When he stroked his fingers against my pussy, I let out a little gasp and my face heated, and at the same time, the laser focus from Coop and Archie had the tension tying me up in knots.

When he cupped his hand and applied just a little bit of pressure, I clamped my thighs together. This was a little…

"Too much?" he murmured against my ear, and I shifted a little.

"Maybe." I didn't sound certain.

I wasn't certain.

"Okay." And just like that, he rubbed his hand on my thigh as he freed it and then back over my stomach. I was burning up now, and I was pretty sure it had nothing to do with the water.

"No rush," Ian said, but there was just a hint of smugness in his voice, and when I glanced up to meet his gaze, he kissed me soundly, and the little flare of self-consciousness slipped away as I groaned.

Eventually, pruney as hell, we had to get out of the water. Thankfully, I was hot enough that even if my nipples pebbled at the icy air, I wasn't freezing. Coop scooped me up gallantly after wrapping me in my robe, and the guys gathered up the wine, my glass, and some of the food to carry back inside. We toweled off just inside, but nobody bothered with going to change. Instead, we ended up in the living room, around the fire, eating pizza.

That was what Archie had meant about dinner. I was also in Archie's lap, since he never got a turn in the hot tub, and they laughed and teased each other as much as they did me. I was still smiling when Archie whispered in my ear, "Tell me what wish you're giving Coop."

I glanced at him and shook my head, then leaned over to whisper my answer. "Why don't you think about what wish I can give you?" Maybe it was the wine or the edibles or the company, but even if I flushed at making the offer, I wasn't remotely embarrassed by it.

Not even when he said, "You already did," and kissed me until I was gasping and needy.

"Keep it up, Arch," Jake murmured. "She's going with me and Coop tonight."

"That's okay," Archie said against my lips as he stared down at me. "We have lots of time."

Wow.

All for me.

All four of them.

Chapter Twenty-One
TALK LIKE LOVERS, LAUGH LIKE FRIENDS

It was late when I finally dragged myself up from the sofa and headed upstairs. We'd talked for hours. Talked. Laughed. Teased. Devoured pizza. I finished the wine bottle. I was definitely floating, but I wasn't…out of it. I kept expecting to be drunk, but I was just effervescent. Maybe it was the edibles. Either way, I gave each of them a sound kiss before going up. My body hummed from each one. They all kissed differently, and I didn't really think about it that much except…

Well, I'd kissed them all a lot tonight. I went from being curled up with Coop, to sitting in Ian's lap, to sprawling across Archie, and finally, sitting on the floor with Jake. The crackle of the fire and the twinkle of the Christmas lights and all my guys in one place hanging out. We'd debated a movie, but ended up just muting some random action flick for the background while we talked.

About so much.

My head was kind of full from all of what we talked about. The topics ranged from the inconsequential to the important. I drifted into my room and danced in a small circle as I stared at all the roses. It was even better than it had been when I'd first discovered them. Shedding my robe, I padded into the bathroom.

I could probably fall on my face as I was and sleep. But the fact that I still had chlorine from the hot tub on me would leave me itchy in the morning. I paused to brush my teeth as the shower warmed up and used the toilet. Some things were just better in private, thank you very much. Then I stepped under the hot water and let out a sigh.

The sound of the shower door alerted me to the arrival of someone. Yeah, no way I would be sleeping alone. That much had been made clear over the course of the evening. They all had their own rooms, too, but they liked sleeping with me.

No complaints here. I liked sleeping with them.

Warm hands settled on my hips and drew me back against his chest.

"Hi, Coop," I murmured, and his soft chuckle rolled over me.

"What would you have done if I were Jake?" he teased, taking the loofa out of my hands and beginning to run it over my chest.

"Said 'oops,'" I teased, and then sighed as he massaged my breasts. I didn't know if he was trying to help me get clean or just using it as an excuse to touch me. I didn't really care either. Especially when he flicked both nipples with his thumbs. "But I know Jake's hands," I continued. "Just like I know yours."

I knew all of their hands. The callouses on them were different. Archie's had more scars along his fingertips from soldering iron burns. Ian's were as familiar with the different calluses from playing guitars. Jake's were work hands, his calluses from weights and from working on large parts. Coop's hands were softer in some ways, smoother maybe, yet still rougher than mine, but his hands were probably the most familiar of all.

He pressed his lips to my throat as he skated his hands down from my breasts to my stomach. "You feel good," he said as he rubbed his erection against my ass, and I chuckled.

"So do you." I twisted to steal the loofa and began to soap him up. He ran his hands up to my face and then tilted my head back so that my hair got soaked. I closed my eyes as he began washing it, the gentle scrape of his fingertips over my scalp almost more intoxicating as the wine. "If you keep that up," I warned him, my whole body going languid. "I'm going to fall asleep on you."

As if to make a liar out of myself, I wrapped my hand around his cock and stroked it. The soap made my hands slick, and Coop's breath huffed against my cheek as he tipped my head back to rinse it, and then he kissed me until I half forgot what we were doing and it was just me sighing into his lips. He rubbed the conditioner through my hair and rinsed it before pulling us both under the spray.

I might have swayed a little when the water shut off. The door opened, and I belatedly realized we weren't alone as a damp haired Jake took me from Coop and wrapped me up in a towel. "Hi," I said, giggling as he grinned down at me.

"Hi," he murmured before kissing me with a kind of thorough slowness that melted my bones. He lifted me like I was nothing and perched me on the cool marble counter. Not even the chill could really jolt me out of my happy place, though it did wake me up a little. "How are you feeling, Baby Girl?"

"Pretty good," I told him. Not even the earlier muscle soreness was an issue. I didn't think I'd been this relaxed in like, ever.

"Yeah?" He was dressed in a pair of black pajama bottoms and nothing else, which left me all of his chest to play with as I ran my hands over him. "And how sober are you?"

I burst out laughing. "Not drunk," I told him, then peered up at him. His pupils were huge against the pale blue. "Pretty sure we're high though."

"Yeah," he agreed, that crooked grin on his face making my heart do flip flops as he toweled me dry and then squeezed the dampness from my hair before pulling a comb through it. Coop watched us from where he leaned against the wall, a towel around his hips and seeming not to care about the water droplets chasing over his chest. I cared.

I kind of wanted to trace the path with my tongue.

Jake tucked his finger under my chin and nudged my mouth closed before tilting my head so I was looking at him again. The amusement on his face made me grin wider. "Coop said you were interested in experimenting, but…"

"But?" I raised my eyebrows. You know, this should be a really embarrassing conversation. *Especially* after the hot tub talk, but it wasn't. I was more curious than anything.

"But I don't want you making any euphoria-infused decisions," he warned gently, and I swore my grin grew.

"You're always trying to protect me," I told him, and ran my fingers over his cheek. "Oh, smooth. You shaved."

"Yes," he said with a chuckle, bracing his hands on the counter on either side of me. He wasn't really touching me at all now. "I shaved."

"See, protecting me." I leaned forward and nipped his lower lip. "Wanna know a secret?"

Coop laughed softly behind him, and I caught the amusement in his gray-green eyes as we locked gazes. "Jake loves your secrets," he teased me. "He loves knowing everything about you."

"That's so he can protect me," I agreed solemnly. For the most part, Jake just studied me, and I let out a little sigh. "You don't have to protect me all the time," I chastised him.

"Yes, I do," he disagreed. "I protect what's precious, and you're the most precious thing in my life."

Just like that, and my heart squeezed so tight, I wasn't sure I would be able to take a deep breath. Which would suck if I stopped breathing because, you know, oxygen. "Jake," I said almost sighing, because really, these guys made me feel so damn cared for. "I told Coop this on the mountain, and I promise, I was very sober. Right? Back me up here, Coop."

He chuckled. "She was very sober, and she was worrying about having to choose between us. So, I know this isn't the edibles talking."

"Exactly," I agreed, and then ran my fingers over Jake's chest. "But it's okay if you're not into it." I mean, it would suck, because Jake seemed to be really into it. "I get it. Well…okay I get it and I don't, because you really didn't seem to mind—"

Jake cut the rest of my statement off with a kiss that robbed my breath. I wrapped my arms around him, and he slid his hands under my thighs and lifted me. The heat of his chest against my breasts had me sighing as I sucked on his tongue. The soft huff of Coop's laughter followed us out of the bathroom into my rose-bedecked room. Not missing a step, Jake sat on the edge of the bed, and I straddled his lap.

Was it possible to be writhing in anticipation and utterly relaxed at the same time? Coop smoothed a hand down my back as Jake fell backward and pulled me with him. Not once did Jake let go of my mouth as he fisted my damp hair to keep me in place. When Coop stroked a hand over my ass, I let out a little whimper and ground myself more firmly against the stiffness of Jake's cock. The pajama bottoms added to the friction, and his groan vibrated through him.

When he ran his hands down my sides, Coop gripped my hair and then tugged, and I arched up to kiss him. The angle was awkward, but then Jake sucked a nipple against his teeth, and I stopped caring about angles so much as touching.

"Any preferences?" Coop asked against my mouth before tracing my lower lip with his tongue.

Drowning in sensation, I stared at him a little blankly. "Preference?"

"Hmm," Jake murmured, then eased two fingers into me, and I let out a little whimper of sound. Oh, that felt so good. "Yes, Baby Girl. Preference on who fits where."

On who fit… Oh.

Oh.

A shudder raced up my spine, and I leaned back a little to glance from Jake to Coop as Coop pressed a finger against my anus. It was slick and warm as he pressed it into me, and my whole body seemed to ripple at the dual intrusion.

Oh.

"Did we break her?" Jake asked, a smile flirting around his lips as he curled his fingers to stroke inside of me, and I was torn between pushing back against Coop and writhing at the pace Jake set. They were both different.

"Nah," Coop murmured as he nipped a kiss to my neck. "She's just wrapping her mind around where she wants our dicks to go."

A groan tore out of me as Jake scraped his teeth over the nipple he neglected earlier. "Should we make it for her?"

"We could," Coop debated as he eased a second finger in, and the burn had me fighting to catch my breath. Okay. I never imagined anal. I'd read about it, sure, but this was… I really couldn't bring my scattering thoughts together. "But I really think she needs to tell us…"

I really didn't catch the last of that as Jake curled his fingers and brought his heel up to rub my clit. My vision whited out, and a cry tore out of my throat. They didn't slow their touches. If anything, Coop added more slickness to my ass, and it hit me that it was lube.

That thought just sort of floated out there and back. Lube made total sense. Right. As soon as I grasped that thought, it splintered along with the rest of my focus. I gripped Jake's shoulder and fisted the bed covers. They were wrecking me in all the best ways, and I'd barely gotten to touch them.

"Shh, Baby Girl," Jake murmured, smoothing my hair back as he eased his fingers out of me, and I let out a whimper at the loss. Coop's fingers were still in my ass, but he'd gone still, and like Jake, he sought to soothe me, running his free hand up and down my back. I trembled and then flicked my eyes open—when had they closed—to find Jake smiling at me. "There she is. Back with us?"

I kind of nodded dumbly. At least I think I did. I didn't really trust myself to speak.

"It's okay," Jake continued. "You're okay."

"I know," I told him, suddenly aware of the tears on my face and my breath coming in sharp, fast pants. It was too much and not enough. "I am." The last came out more like I believed it.

Coop bit down on my shoulder where it met my neck, the feel of his teeth grounding as my pulse continued to race. "We can ease off here," he told me. "Do it like we did before…"

"No," I rushed out, swallowing hard and then licking my lips. I met Jake's gaze, and he gave me a soft nod, almost encouraging. But the warmth in his eyes was the only promise I needed. This only went as far as I wanted. Maybe he was overprotective, he always had been. I was very much aware of that. But it also made me feel treasured. "I want this," I told him, and then tore my gaze up to look at Coop. I pressed back against his hand, and his smile grew. "I want both of you."

I could do this. I wanted to do this.

"How do you want us?" Coop asked again, and there was no doubt in my mind this time. I glanced at Jake, then at Coop.

"Do either of you really care who goes first?" I licked my lips. "It was your wish," I reminded Coop.

"I care," Jake said in the same breath Coop released an amused, "Not even a little bit."

We both looked down at Jake, and his eyes fixed on me, his face flushed.

"I care," he repeated. "I want that first if Coop doesn't care."

"It's a little early for your birthday, man," Coop said with no small amount of merriment. "But I think if Frankie is willing to let you have it, I'm definitely not getting in the way."

With that, Coop eased his fingers out of me, and the emptiness struck me a moment before Jake surged up to kiss me. "Won't be the last time," he said before he devoured my mouth. Coop moved behind us, and then Jake stood, his hands under my thighs again as he lifted me with him. The handoff happened so smoothly, I giggled in delight as he passed me to Coop. They traded with Coop settling back on the bed, his head on the pillows, and between them, they maneuvered me to straddle him.

Oh. Yes.

The stretch Coop always caused as I sank down on him had me rocking. We had to ease him in, but at the same time, little explosions detonated in my system as he pushed in deep. The bed dipped as I dropped down to kiss Coop, and they were both pushing my ass up a little, tilting it. More lube was spread over my ass, and I let out a groan and a shudder as I sank all the way down on Coop, only to have Jake press a couple of fingers into me. No hesitation, and the burn intensified.

But I didn't hate it.

He added a third finger as I fought to not rock my hips. I lifted my head, needing to pant for air. Coop rubbed his hands over my ass, before spreading the cheeks as if to help Jake. I stole a look back at him, my chest heaving, and he smiled at me. "You doing okay, Baby Girl?"

I didn't know how much more I could take, but I nodded. The burn intensified as he moved his fingers, and Coop kept us both dead still. Little tremors still rioted in my system, the aftershocks of the earlier orgasm. I dragged my gaze over Jake. He'd shed his pajama bottoms, and I could look at him all day. Licking my lips, I glanced back at Coop.

"Have you guys ever done this before?" Probably not the time to bring this up, but Coop shook his head.

"Not like this we haven't," he promised.

"Trust me, not into their junk enough to have to see it on the regular," Jake told me as he eased his fingers out. There was that sense of loss again, and I strained around it and shifted against Coop. He pumped up once, then twice, and suddenly began to hit just the right angle with each thrust. I shook from it.

Jake wiped his hand, then he was urging me forward again, and Coop dragged me down for another kiss. I rubbed my breasts against his chest, writhing at the different sensations, even as he kept rocking his hips up into mine as they kept me still. Then he eased back as Jake pressed the tip of his cock against my anus.

We were doing this.

Goosebumps spread over me as Jake murmured, "I love you, Frankie." The soft words settled me in a way I hadn't realized I needed.

Coop sucked on my tongue for another long moment, preventing me from answering before he let me go long enough to say, "I love you, too."

Then Jake pressed in, and there was the burn, and I let out a hiss of breath as I fisted the covers. Everything shook. It was too much. He didn't slow down, just rocked his way in, until the burn gave way to something more shuddering as my whole system fluttered and Coop let out a grunt.

They both muttered, "Fuck," in the exact same breath, and laughter bubbled out of me.

"Pretty sure that's what we're doing."

There was a beat as we all sort of hung there, Jake's fingers biting into my hips and Coop's resting on my waist, and while I couldn't see Jake, Coop was right in front of me. Sweat trickled along his jaw, and I dipped down to lick it from his throat to his ear, and he let out a shudder of his own.

Their strangled laughter was the best sound I'd ever heard. Then they started to move. What few thoughts I'd held onto shredded all over again. The feel of them, rocking me between them as we fumbled and then found our pace took me apart.

It was all friction and heat and want, and I couldn't breathe. Jake wrapped his hand in my hair and turned my head back for a kiss. A vein throbbed in his temple, and his face was flushed. The rawness there tore me open, and he only let me go when Coop tugged, and then I was kissing him. I'd never been so full, and even adjusting to it wasn't enough, as every stroke eddied me higher and higher until I broke.

Coop swallowed my screams, and I don't know which one of them came first. They'd pushed me right through one orgasm into the next, and then we collapsed together in a sweaty pile of limbs. At some point, the thought we might be crushing Coop surfaced, but he mumbled against me when I tried to move.

"Gimme a minute."

I huffed a laugh against his throat. His pulse raced against my lips, and then Jake groaned and shifted. The single motion had all three of us shuddering as he eased out of me. I ached in all the right ways—sore as hell, but so loose and languid, it was like my limbs had been melted.

"Hang on a sec, Baby Girl," Jake said, his voice hoarse and wrecked. I had zero plans of going anywhere, so I just gave a wave. That was about the full extent of my physical reserves at the moment. He wasn't gone long, though the water came on in the bathroom and then off again. A minute later, he smoothed a warm washcloth along my ass, and I let out a little sigh.

Definitely sore.

Not unpleasantly so, but I swore I almost whined at the contact. He chuckled.

Ass.

Then between them, they eased me over, and Coop and I both let out a sigh.

"This whole no condom thing is freaking messy," I complained, and that just made them both laugh.

"But worth it," they both stated in almost the same breath, and I groaned as Jake nudged me onto my back and then he ran that washcloth up between my legs. A fine tremble took me everywhere as he cleaned me up. Then Coop dragged himself off the bed. By the time they stripped the cover off the bed and tucked me under the blankets and fell in on either side, I was already half-asleep.

I didn't want to just pass out though. "I feel like I should say something profound," I admitted as Coop rested a hand on my stomach, and Jake rolled onto his side. They'd killed the lights, but the flickering light from the fire danced over his features.

"Yeah?"

"Uh huh, but all I can come up with is wow."

A smile cracked across his face, and he nuzzled a kiss to my jaw and then pressed a light one on my lips. "Wow works."

"Agreed," Coop said, his voice still thready and a little out there. I turned my head to look at him, but he had an arm over his eyes and he looked mostly asleep. If not for the way his fingers traced against my skin, I would think he was. "Definitely wow. Wow fits."

A giggle escaped me. "We're so erudite."

Groaning, Jake nipped my ear. "You don't need to use SAT words in bed. Fucking awesome and blissed the fuck out work, too."

True words. "Definitely blissed out." A random shiver raced through me. "We can do that again, right?" Maybe when I could pay more attention instead of just falling apart.

Silence greeted my question, they both looked at me like I was a bit of an idiot.

"So that's a yes," I said, and then smirked as I stretched. Oh, there was that ache again. I wasn't so sure how I felt about Coop taking my ass now that we'd done that, because he was definitely bigger than the other guys. I leaned over and kissed his cheek. "Wish granted."

His shoulders and chest shook with his laughter.

"Mine, too," Jake told me, and I gave him a soft kiss, too. "But I have other wishes."

"Yeah?"

"Hmm-hmm," he said, tracing his fingers over my collarbone. "I think I'm going to get a tattoo on my birthday."

That didn't surprise me. Jake had mentioned wanting to get one before.

"We could do that," Coop said. "I've been thinking about what I would like."

"What do you want to get?" The idea of a tattoo fascinated me, but it was permanent art that wasn't going anywhere, and I had no idea what I wanted. At least not yet.

"I have a few ideas," Jake murmured as his voice thickened with sleep. "How about I get your name tattooed on my ass, Frankie? Make sure everyone knows who I belong to.”

“If you’re showing people your ass before they find out, you’re gonna get in trouble,” Coop teased, and I grinned.

“You should get something pretty,” I mused. “Or badass.”

“You’re pretty,” Coop quipped.

“And badass,” Jake agreed. “But really, I was thinking about a dragon maybe.”

“Oh, I like dragons. Eastern or Western?”

“Wings,” Jake said after a beat. “So western. Got a color preference?”

I chuckled. “I’m not picking out your ink, you have to do that.”

“But I want you to like it.”

I smiled at him, meeting his gaze in the low light. “I’ll love it because it will be a part of you.”

“You can’t go too complicated though,” Coop said around a yawn. “Those take time. Maybe something simple at first, then we go find a place at home and get the complicated ones done.”

“What are you getting?”

“No clue.” Coop snuggled up against me. “What about you Frankie? Would you get a tattoo?”

“I don’t know… Though, if I tattooed all of your names, it could take a while.”

Silence followed, then there was a hum of sound from Jake, and I flicked him a look.

“You’re thinking about it, aren’t you?”

“A permanent mark that tells others to fuck off, you’re ours? Hell yes, I’m thinking about it.” Possessiveness filled his tone.

“Fuck,” Coop exhaled. “Now I’m thinking about it, too.” He traced his fingers up my side. “I’d want it somewhere everyone could see it.”

I rolled my eyes. “I’m not getting a ‘property of’ tramp stamp.”

Another beat of silence.

"It could be small," Jake said, and then Coop added, "We could even put it in French. Then I could get really turned on every time I saw it."

Another beat, then they both snickered like they were twelve.

"Do I want to know?"

"I was thinking about tattooing your ass," Coop admitted. "Where only we got to see it."

"No," Jake growled. "To tattoo her ass, some dude will be looking at it. *And* he'd have to touch it. I think not."

"Then what were you thinking about?" Coop challenged him.

"I was thinking she could be a little more discreet and just get a four tattoo."

A four.

"Oh," Coop said, then snickered all over again. "Fantastic. I love it."

They were both cracking up, and the joke finally sank in. I sat up, grabbed my pillow, and began beating them.

We didn't get to sleep for a while.

Not until I got pinned to the bed by both of them again. Then I was too boneless to care about their *fantastic* dick jokes. Or much else for that matter.

Chapter Twenty-Two
MORE HEARTS THAN MINE

ARCHIE

The sound of Frankie's laughter drifted up the hall when I went to bed. I wasn't too proud to admit how long I'd lain there and just savored the sound, even as I envied the hell out of the fact it was Coop and Jake in there with her. Admittedly, I couldn't quite wrap my head around the idea they shared her so readily between them. I'd given it half a shot with Ian right there, but I couldn't say it would be a regular occurrence.

And here she thought *she* was the selfish one. I got her wanting all of them, too. I could do that. I could share her with them, but I wanted *my* time, too. Seeing her kiss them or cuddle with them, that was fine, but if there was active sex going on…well, I wanted it to be my hands on her and her hands on me. That was why I left her when it was Bubba's turn. They needed their privacy, too.

Still, waking that next morning, I reached for her first thing and she wasn't there. That part sucked.

No lie.

I dragged myself out of bed, threw on some sweats and shoes, then headed down to the gym. Grandpa didn't build this place, but he'd added a few amenities. The lodge had been designed to be more of a cozy escape, and it was absolutely perfect for the holidays. When I'd told him I wanted to bring Frankie here for Christmas, he'd teased me this might be a bit of a too romantic getaway, but that had been it.

Her room was quiet as I passed it, and the temptation to stick my head in was mitigated only by the fact that I didn't need to see Jake's or Coop's naked asses. Downstairs, I grabbed water from the kitchen and checked the spread. The housekeeper and the cook had both been by. It was almost ten. Breakfast was set up to stay warm, and all I had to do was turn the coffee maker on.

Today, I'd try my hand at the espresso machine. But I wasn't waking anyone. We had big plans tonight.

They needed their sleep.

Bubba found me in the gym when I hit the second mile of my run on the treadmill. He grunted a morning and then hit the second treadmill. Normally, I'd have my headphones in, but since it was indoors and the sound wouldn't carry upstairs, I had music blasting from the speakers. We just ran.

Five miles was a good distance. I could go longer, but I didn't need it. I'd started running to clear my head when I'd been at boarding school. I fucking hated living in the back pockets of all the other kids there. It was better than living with Edward or Muriel, but the urge to run had started there, and it was a good way to just get out from under the rest.

Jake and Bubba ran for other reasons. Me? I ran for my sanity.

I left Bubba to his run and moved to the weights. I wasn't gonna do much of a workout. The skiing yesterday had left me decently sore. But that was almost all legs and running was legs. I needed to do arms.

"Hey," Bubba said, joining me when I grabbed a pair of twenty-fives to warm my biceps up. "What's on the agenda today?"

"Concert," I told him, and then checked the doorway to make sure she hadn't drifted in when I hadn't noticed. Not that it was possible. I *always* noticed her. "Got us tickets to Torched. They are doing concert in Denver, and the car will pick us up at five." Gave us plenty of time to get there without rushing.

"Fuck me, seriously?" Bubba gaped at me. "I know you said you were checking their schedule."

I grinned. "Seriously. She loves them."

"I know she does," he said, grabbing weights of his own. "Hell, I love them. But she's gonna freak at you for spending the money."

Shrugging, I said, "Maybe. Then she'll be too busy enjoying them. When that last song dropped, she couldn't stop singing it."

Bubba laughed. "She's getting better at it than she thinks."

"Why the fuck does she think she can't sing?"

A scowl tightened his brow. "Three guesses, and the first two don't count."

Her cunt of a mother. "Fuck, I hate that bitch."

"Ding. Ding. Ding. We have a winner. She's got a voice, she just needs to believe in it and to train it."

"Whatever you need to help her," I told him.

"I got it," Bubba said, giving me a firm look. "I'll take care of her."

Message received. I nodded. We were both quiet, until I was done with the weights and ready to hit the showers. Only then did he clear his throat.

"Hey, Arch?"

I eyed him and couldn't help it, I braced. We were all a little raw from the recent pass. "What's up?"

"Thanks."

I raised my brows.

"For yesterday. For letting me and Frankie have the time without…"

"Oh," I snorted a laugh, then waved a hand at him. "No biggie. I get it. I'd rather you hadn't been there, but I like waking her up, too."

"Same," he said slowly.

"Bubba," I told him. "Let's be clear. Jake and Coop are a lot more comfortable sharing than we are. I think we're fine with where we're at. I'm not in any hurry to change that."

The guy actually looked relieved. "I'm a bit of a greedy bastard where she's concerned."

No shit. "So am I. As long as we understand each other, we're fine."

That was that.

Frankie didn't emerge until early afternoon. She moved slow and more than a little gingerly, and I was in the middle of checking our reservations for the weekend when she made her way down the stairs. Tracking her steps, it hit me why she was walking like that, and I had to hide my smirk behind the coffee. The smile on her face and the relaxed look in her eyes, coupled with the flush on her cheeks, told me everything I needed to know about whether she'd enjoyed it.

Well, that and the enthusiastic cries from the night before.

Fuck, I really did love that she was a screamer.

Even better than all of that was the way she kind of floated over to where I was sitting, and I shifted my tablet so she could sit on my lap. At her plaintive look, I passed her my coffee, and she smiled. The happiness there resonated within me and a sense of contentment I didn't think I was capable of settled in my bones.

"What are you doing?" she murmured after another swallow of the coffee.

"Just making my list and checking it twice," I teased her. I'd closed the tablet screen when she'd appeared on the stairs. I set it to the side and then just wrapped my arms around her.

She smiled. "Are you naughty or are you nice?"

"Which do you prefer?"

Her laugh was soft, but very warm. "Both."

"Me, too." I nuzzled a kiss to her cheek, and she snuggled back into me.

The fire crackled merrily, and the Christmas lights were on. The shipment of presents should be in today, I'd already had a word with the housekeeper. She promised that her husband would make sure they were delivered and arranged by the next day at the latest.

One by one, the guys wandered out. Jake brought us more coffee, and Coop brought out the food. Frankie seemed utterly content to just doze in my lap. Bubba came down with his guitar and treated us to an impromptu concert as he toyed with some songs. I'd always known he enjoyed his music, I just never realized how serious he was about it.

I just hadn't paid attention.

Frankie had. She'd gotten him that lyric book and sheet music for his birthday. It had seemed a weird present at the time, but I saw it now. She saw us. The different parts of us we didn't always show each other.

Making a mental note to follow up with Bubba's plans at some point, I decided I had to do some research in investments for the musical business. The more I listened to Bubba, the more I realized this guy needed to do something with it. Especially since he even got Frankie to sing for us while he was playing.

Yep, music was going on the list.

"Why can't I know where we're going?" Frankie asked, her gorgeous green eyes glittering as she stared at me. She was dressed in ripped jeans, a dark green long-sleeved shirt with the shoulders cut out, and a pair of calf-length boots that just added to how long her legs seemed. Even better, she had on her charm bracelet and the necklace. I had more charms to add to it for the holiday, not just the skiing one.

The microphone would be ready for it after tonight.

"Because it's a surprise," I told her as we waited for the guys to join us. The best part of a concert—there was no dress code. But I had a feeling Frankie would have at least two new concert shirts before the evening was over.

Admittedly, being able to have the car service bring us nice limos for the trips was a perk I'd never regret, but I missed having our own cars. I liked being able to steal away with her. The ride there, we ate snacks, drank sodas, and laughed. It was a game of twenty questions with Frankie, each one growing more outrageous than the last.

Bubba knew where we were going, and I clued Jake and Coop in when Frankie went to get ready. They'd both gaped at me and then Jake swore. "She's going to lose her mind."

That was the plan.

I wasn't the only one enjoying her increasingly outlandish asks though, so it was kind of a win for all of us.

When we reached the venue, it was hard to disguise what we were there for. Speechless, she'd glanced from the sign to me, then back to the sign. Was I grinning like a damn cat? Hell yes, I was.

Speaking of cats, I'd shared the video Jeremy sent me of all three of her little pets being cosseted in style at the house. Jeremy had even invested in a series of cat trees and toys. The video had all three of them stoned out of their minds on catnip.

It had been hysterical.

Frankie flung herself at me, the hug so fierce that I almost missed the flash of tears in her eyes.

"Hey," I said, cupping her face and thumbing away the moisture. "No tears unless they sing some gut-wrenching sad song." They better fucking not.

"These are *happy* tears, you ass." She sniffed, then grinned at me. "I've *never* been to a concert."

I smirked, then dropped a kiss to the tip of her nose. "I know."

"And this is *Torched*!"

"Funny," I teased. "I thought you might like them." Her pinch just made me laugh.

She tucked herself right up under my arm as we strolled inside. I'd been to concerts before, nothing big really. But I'd never been crazy about a band or a group the way she was about Torched. She ended up getting three shirts. I really liked the sleeveless one with the roses in the center. Those were a big deal to the band. One of the singers had roses tattooed along her arm, and Frankie mused that maybe she could do that.

"What do you think? Should I dye my hair blue?"

That would be a negative. Thank fuck all three of the others were on my side in that argument. The thought of all that golden blonde disappearing? Fuck. No. Her laughter was worth a little bit of ribbing though.

Bubba took point as we headed to our seats with Jake behind us. A move I appreciated, considering the number of dicks checking out Frankie's ass. The jeans did great things for them, but Jake looked like he was making a list.

"I got the bail covered," I told him with a clap to the shoulder as we put Frankie in the middle, two of us on either side. This time, I took advantage of grabbing the one to her immediate left as Bubba took the one to her right. That put Coop and Jake on the outside.

We'd grabbed water bottles from a vendor on the way in, and I wasn't the only one checking the seal. No one was giving her another damn drugged drink. Not on our watch.

But all of that faded when the music started and Frankie lit up. I had to admit, Torched gave a hell of a performance and the music was great. But Frankie dancing and singing along with them elevated it to a whole new level. Damn, she could move, and I knew for damn certain she had no idea how good she looked rocking her hips, hands up, as her body went loose and fluid.

The guy behind us checking her out irked the shit out of me. But when he caught me looking, he shot me an apologetic wave and dragged his eyes off her. Good decision, since I wasn't opposed to siccing Jake on him or punching him myself.

The girl group gave a badass concert, though 'girl group' seemed almost too patronizing a description. They were a band—all three of them played instruments, and they swapped them out. They had backup players, too. Bubba kept pointing things out to Frankie about the guitars. I'd have to get him to fill me in later.

Their first album, *Party Girl*, was one of Frankie's top five favorites. That much I knew. When they segued from their new stuff to that album, she'd kissed me right in the middle of the second song, and fuck if I didn't want to find a way to fuck her right then and there. I could wait.

Her excitement was worth a little pain and suffering.

The concert only lasted about three hours from start to finish, but we were all hot and sweaty by the time we, along with the masses, began to make our way out. Frankie's eyes glittered, and she needed to hit the bathroom. We found one without a hideous line and parked ourselves to wait for her. As soon as she was inside, I let them know that when we got back, Frankie was sleeping with me. No one argued. Look at us, being all mature. Only when she was back with us—ha, and changed into one of her concert shirts and looking sassy about it—did we take turns hitting the restrooms ourselves.

Yep, some things we were just gonna be paranoid about.

Burgers, fries, and shakes waited for us in the car. I'd asked the driver to grab dinner for us when he picked us up and to grab something for himself to eat while he waited. I'd wanted to score backstage passes for us, but they weren't doing them for this part of the tour.

That was fine. They were gonna be in Dallas right after graduation.

And I already had tickets *and* passes.

Was I smug as fuck about that? Yes, I was. But I'd save that reveal for later.

Hoarse from singing and flushed from dancing, Frankie's joy flooded the interior of the car. Of course, we had the music on and she half-danced to it while eating her burger. It hit me as she darted her attention between Coop and Bubba that it had been a long time since I'd seen her really happy.

To be honest, I wasn't sure I'd ever seen her this happy. It made stark the shadow she'd been living under for so long and me more determined than ever to cut that cunt of a mother out of her life for good. It wasn't my call, yeah yeah. But Frankie *flourished* without her. I sprawled back in the seat, head tilted back with my eyes only half-open, but I didn't miss a move she made.

Four months.

In four months, she'd be eighteen. Even if we only ever had the temporary order, we just had to make it last.

Then goodbye, Mrs. Curtis. May she and Edward rot in hell together.

She nudged me with her elbow as she shifted over to sit closer to me. "You okay?"

I smiled down at her and then pressed my lips close to her ear. "Just thinking about all the ways I want to make you come later."

Her shiver and flush made me smile, and her swift inhale told me more about her interest than anything else.

It took no convincing to steal her away as soon as we got back.

Waking to Frankie was nearly as good as taking Frankie to bed. Who was I kidding? It was mostly equal and sometimes better. Like the fact that she woke me this morning with the hot suction of her mouth, and fuck if I wasn't coming in nothing flat. It was almost embarrassing.

It was only fair I repaid that favor after my brain stopped melting. Her joy tasted as sweet that morning as it had the night before.

Round two, we took our time. So much, we hit round three before we finally dozed off for a nap. We didn't get up until lunch.

The presents arrived when we hit the slopes the next day. Frankie was a damn natural, but she was so wary of the blue, even if she insisted we could split up so we could check out the different ones. Of all people, it was Coop who convinced her by the end of the day to try one. Not because he'd done it, but because he'd do it if she would.

Excitement sparkled in her eyes, but she kept chewing her lower lip. Heights were not her favorite thing. Course, Coop got her to go on a rollercoaster. She could handle the blue. We'd do the easiest one. Finally, she said yes, and it took everything I had not to cheer out loud.

No problem, Jake did a fist pump and a very enthusiastic yes. That covered it for all of us.

At the top of the blue, she stared down the hill with huge eyes and then looked at us. "If I break anything, as soon as I'm healed, I'm coming after you."

"Deal," Jake said, all confidence and ease. "You're not going to break anything. You can do this."

"Slow and steady," Bubba advised. "We're not leaving you. Promise."

"I'll even go first," Coop told her. "You can follow me. That way I can take all the pratfalls."

Her snort made us all grin, but when she glanced at me, all I said was, "Whatever you want to do, babe. We can cross back over to the green about a third of the way down if you want to try something else."

Lips pursed, she adjusted her hat and then pulled down her goggles. It was sunny as fuck today, which was great, except the snow was blinding when we first got up there. The goggles helped. "I got this. And if I tell myself that enough," she insisted, "I'll be right."

I chuckled. "You have this."

Despite the bravado, she blew out a couple more breaths and resettled her feet before facing the downward slope. None of us moved, letting her take her time. Then she said, "Fuck it. You only live once," and pushed off.

Heart clenching, I was a second behind her. Jake was right behind me. That left Coop and Bubba to follow. Bubba would keep an eye on Coop. Between the three of us, we had them covered. She zigzagged her way, wedging if she picked up too much speed, but you couldn't miss the moment she relaxed and her confidence actually bloomed. She did a perfect cut, and instead of wedging to slow, she turned and used the momentum to execute a perfect parallel turn.

At the bottom, she was laughing when we caught up to her.

This trip was the best idea.

It was blues for the rest of the day. Easy blues. But still blues.

Back at the lodge, the presents filled in the underside of the tree until it was near full to bursting. Frankie was torn between looking at that and heading up to change. We were hitting the hot tub again. One foot on the stairs, she paused to eye me, then the guys. "Any more surprises waiting for me up there?"

I smirked. "Wouldn't be a surprise if I told you, would it?"

Besides, the next big surprise was scheduled for Jake's birthday. He'd already signed off on the idea because he'd seen Frankie watching those videos, too. Should be a good night.

"Uh huh."

I made a shooing motion, and she stuck her tongue out at me.

"Promises, promises," I teased, and she laughed before heading up the stairs at a swift clip. Damn, that made her ass sway when she walked that way.

Coop let out a breath and so did Jake. Bubba laughed.

"What?" I glanced over at him.

"Just glad I'm not the only one who makes like some cartoon dog with his tongue lolling out."

No, he definitely wasn't the only one. "Hard not to," I admitted. "Never giving her up." In case that wasn't absolutely clear.

I slanted a look at the other three, and Jake just shrugged. "No argument, but I'm not either."

"Ditto," Coop said, grinning. "Besides, weird as this shit might be, it works." All three of us cut a look at Bubba, and he held up his hands.

"I have already choked on my own stupidity. When I said I was in, I meant it. Besides," he continued, heading for the stairs himself, "she needs you guys."

"She needs all of us," I reminded him.

He paused at the top of the stairs with Coop and Jake not far behind. Meeting my gaze, Bubba nodded. "Yeah, she does. I'm just glad you guys saw it a hell a lot clearer than I did."

I followed them, but slower. I was still the first one downstairs, and I gathered up the edibles and the wine. Tonight, we'd soak, eat, play, and laugh. That was what these two weeks were about.

The five of us finding a real rhythm and convincing Frankie that not only could we work, we would work.

Would I keep her to myself if given the chance? Hell yes. But this worked, too.

The fact that she strolled out in that barely there bikini for the second time without an ounce of her shyness from the first night? Win.

The smile on her face? Win.

The idiots splashing into the hot tub around us, making her laugh and smile?

Fuck it.

Win, too.

I took a bite of a cookie and stretched back after she took the glass of wine.

This was the kind of life we could all get used to.

If I had my way, we would.

Chapter Twenty-Three
NEVER HAVE I EVER

FRANKIE

"This is a terrible idea," Coop said as he lined up the shots. A storm had blown in early in the morning with blizzard-like conditions and promised to make the roads hazardous, so our plans for sightseeing and shopping had been delayed for a day at the lodge. Archie sent a message to the staff to let them know we would fend for ourselves.

Fending for ourselves included video games, movies, books, and a crock pot with pot roast and all the fixings. It had all been prepped, I just got it started, but it would be ready for dinner. In the meanwhile, we had the most ridiculously piled high sandwiches for lunch and cereal for breakfast. We hadn't even bothered to get dressed. A fire burned merrily in the fireplace, and I had put on fuzzy socks to keep my feet warm while I was dressed only in one of my new Torched t-shirts that hit me mid-thigh. I wanted an oversized one on purpose, so I'd gotten one that would fit Jake or Ian.

"Possibly," Archie said, giving me a slow smile as I snagged one of the blankets. I hadn't bothered with pants since it was just going to be us, but the sound of the wind made me cold. "But it could be fun, too."

I snorted. "You just like playing with fire."

"Yes," Archie agreed with a wink. "I do. So do you."

Also true. We were all sitting in the living room with the whiskey—wow, that crap was strong—bottle in the center of the table and five shot glasses filled and passed around to each of us. Ian and I had one sofa, Jake and Archie were on the opposite one, and Coop took the floor with his back to the fire. Between the isolation of the howling wind, the crackle of the fire, the twinkling of the lights, and the soft huffs of their laughter, it had been a fun way to spend the day.

"I still think strip poker would be more fun," Jake argued. "Or we could do strip combat."

"The only one we all want to see naked is Frankie, and she's not playing," Coop said with a shake of his head.

"Speak for yourself," I told him. "You could all strip for me, and I wouldn't complain."

"Yeah?" Jake rose and Ian threw a pillow at him.

"Sit down."

All of us laughed.

"*Anyway*," Coop said, motioning to the whiskey. "Never have I ever is on the table, who starts?"

"Age order," Archie declared. "Bubba, you're the oldest."

"Frankie's the youngest," he countered.

"Uh huh." I slanted a look at him. "By a few months. But you've been an *adult* longer than the rest of us."

"Impossible," Ian teased me. "You've been an adult for as long as I've known you."

I poked him with my toes, and he wrapped a hand around my foot. The flash of amusement in his eyes promised tickling, and I just stared at him. If he started that, there would be no drinking game and we'd end up breaking something in here.

"Fine," he said with a mock sigh. "Never have I ever gotten a ticket."

"Lame," Archie said. "Dude…"

I groaned and reached for the shot glass and suddenly had four sets of eyes staring at me. I chuckled at the absolute shock in Jake's eyes and the curiosity in Archie's, but it was Coop narrowing his eyes at me that made me smile widest.

"*When* did you, Ms. Safer than Sex Driver get a ticket?"

"Week before I got the restrictions off my license," I told him, and then downed the shot and grimaced. Holy crap, that stuff was awful. It burned all the way down to my belly and had my eyes watering. "Smooth," I coughed.

Archie snickered. "It can be, you're just a lightweight."

"Then it's so good we're starting with whiskey." I licked my lips and put the shot glass back on the table.

"The week before you got the restriction taken off?" Coop pressed. "You didn't say anything."

"'Cause it was embarrassing." I blew out a breath. The heat detonated in my belly and definitely chased away even the illusion of chill. "And it probably would have pissed you off."

That earned me a look even more intense than the first half of my answer. "Explain."

"Dude." Jake flung the pillow at him that Ian had tossed earlier. "Chill with the 'tude."

Coop ignored him and pinned me with a look. "Fine, it's not a big deal now, I just… Maddy was gone, again, doing whatever, and Tiddles was sick. I had to take him to the vet, and my license said I couldn't drive without a licensed, over eighteen driver in the car, and I hadn't had a chance to hit the DMV 'cause…" I made a wave with my hand. Maddy again. No need to get there. "So I took him. Got pulled over on my way back for a rolling stop because I was tired. Got a ticket, went and got the restriction off my license that weekend, and got the ticket dismissed. They cut me a break. But yes, I've had a traffic ticket. If we're going by age, then you're next."

He glared, at the shot glasses not me, and sighed. A muscle ticked in his jaw, but he clearly needed a distraction.

"Probably wouldn't have gotten it if I'd dared to flirt with the cop. He was cute."

Now he glared at me, and so did the other guys. I swallowed a smile. Goal achieved.

"Never have I ever *not* noticed when someone was flirting with me." Damn.

"Wow," I said as I reached for my shot glass. "Rude."

Archie snickered. "You tried to make him jealous."

"No, I succeeded." I tossed back the shot, and that wasn't as bad as the first one. Exhaling, I slid the glass back to the table for Coop to refill. "But you guys may have to tuck me in shortly, because holy crap, that's strong."

"We'll look after you," Jake promised, then elbowed Archie. "You're up."

He studied me a beat and said, "Never have I ever had a good day with my dad." The darkness in his eyes promised every single word was true. Archie may have made his peace with what a piece of shit his father was, but that didn't mean I had to like it.

"Suck up," Jake teased, and it helped, lightening the mood a fraction as he, Coop, and Ian all took their shots. My hand didn't even twitch toward my glass. Couldn't have a good day with a person who didn't exist.

"Can't help it if it's the truth," Archie said, sprawling back and rubbing a finger along his lower lip. But when I raised my brows, a little worried about him, he smiled. It was the barest curl of his lips, but it told me he was okay.

The guys shook off their shots, and then Coop refilled the glasses.

"Never have I ever," Jake began and then considered his answer, before smiling at me, "wanted someone the way I want you."

No one reached for a drink, and the silence in the room swelled with everything that statement held.

"And you called *me* a suck up," Archie mused, alleviating some of the tension, and laughter rippled through the room.

"Your turn, Baby Girl." Challenge twinkled in his eyes, amusement that dared me to get them back for their teasing.

I could totally do that.

"Never have I ever gone down on a girl."

The rich baritone of his laughter as the guys groaned buoyed me. But all four of them did their shots.

"You asked for it," Ian told me. "Never have I ever gone down on a guy."

Yeah, I could have seen that one coming. I did my shot, and wow, my lips were tingling. And around we went again.

"Never have I ever…cheated on a test."

To my utter shock, Archie did a shot, and we all stared at him. He smirked. "I went to boarding school. It wasn't about needing the answers so much as seeing if I could get away with it." He grinned. "Never have I ever not been on the honor roll."

Jake flipped him off and so did Coop. Ian grinned as he squeezed my toes, because neither of us needed to drink. Honor roll had been right up there with getting into Harvard. Yes, I might have overthought that need to get to college *a lot*.

"Never have I ever stood in line at midnight to get the latest game," Jake said, and it was Coop's turn to glare. Because yes, he had, and I'd stood in that line with him so I picked up a shot.

I was going to be so drunk.

"When I start puking," I told them, "I don't want to hear any complaints."

"I'll hold your hair," Ian promised. "But let's throw some snacks down."

"On it," Archie said as he bounced off the sofa. "Hang on a sec for your turn, babe."

He came back with chips and salsa. And despite our earlier lunch, I was starved. Archie also brought out water.

"Never have I ever taken a class I didn't want to in order to be with someone else."

"And just like that, you go from being the sweetest girl in the room…" Coop mused, then winked as all four of them tossed back their drinks.

"Though I'm a little hurt. You could have taken a basic engineering course just to hang out with me."

"And me," Jake piped in.

I laughed. "Seriously, guys, you always asked me what I was taking when it came time to pick classes. You had me pick first. How was I supposed to match my schedule to yours?"

"And this is why you are the smartest girl in the room," Coop said, slurring a little. Not that I could really talk. My tongue had joined my lips in numb land, and my fingers and toes were tingling. I had also started in on the water.

It was Ian's turn again, and he stretched his legs out before dragging both of my feet into his lap. Oh, he was massaging my right foot, and just like that, I wanted to purr. "Never have I ever…" He mused for a long time.

"Getting lost over there?" Archie asked with a grin.

"Just trying to decide what I haven't done," Ian answered with a shrug. "Fine… Never have I ever had sex somewhere public."

Dammit.

Jake and I both reached for our glasses.

"Wait…" Archie leaned forward, looking from me to Jake and then back. "When?"

"Thanksgiving," Jake said, grinning at me as we saluted, and I giggled at the sudden stares from the other three as I knocked back my shot.

"Though technically…"

"It counts," Jake told me.

"Fair enough."

"Technically?" Coop asked, and I pushed his face away from me, even as he grinned. He rescued my shot glass as I settled back on the sofa. Ian was doing wonderful things with my foot. And a yawn stole through me.

"And on that note," Jake murmured. "Switch it up."

"On it." Coop stood, then braced himself a moment like he had to keep from swaying, and vanished toward the kitchen.

"Eat," Archie ordered, nudging the basket of chips toward me.

"I will," I told him. "You know I can eat, but I'm floaty as hell right now, and this is kind of nice. It's not even embarrassing to think about the fact that I've had sex with every single one of you. Sometimes, with two of you at the same time"

And it wasn't.

"It's actually kind of nice," I continued as Coop wandered back in with fresh glasses and another huge bottle of water. He half nudged me up, and then I was in his lap while my feet were still in Ian's, and Coop offered me some of the water.

"It's more than nice," Coop told me. "I doubt you'll hear any complaints."

"Ha," I said, and then took a long drink. Oh, that was cold and good, too. The chip was really salty. "Aren't we still playing?"

"Pausing," Jake told me. "You're smashed, Baby Girl."

I squinted at him, then held up my thumb and forefinger together. "Little bit. But feel free to keep going, I just won't do any more shots."

"We're good," Archie said.

"Aww, c'mon, it's kind of fun, and I don't wanna be a party pooper."

"You're not a party pooper," Ian soothed. "But go ahead, Angel. What have you never?"

"Hmm…lots of things. Though that list is getting smaller." Then again… "I mean, I would have said never have I ever been on a date, but that wasn't entirely true, even before this year." I pointed accusing fingers at them. "You guys kept trying to take me on dates, especially Archie, I just didn't see it."

"Very true," Archie said. "Apparently, we just sucked at dating."

"Fuck," Jake said. "That's true, isn't it?"

Coop laughed, the vibration of his rumbling chest making me smile. "Yup. So it's all our fault, Frankie. We should have gotten better at it."

I sighed. "Guys, how do we make this work?"

I didn't mean to get maudlin but…

"I love this. I love all of us, and you said I didn't have to choose, but… how do we really make this work? Archie and I don't have to worry about what bad meatloaf thinks because—you know—fuck them."

"Atta girl," Archie said with a wink.

"But Ian, your parents…"

"I don't care what they think." Despite the shine in his eyes and the whiskey he'd drunk, Ian sounded stone cold sober. "They're my parents. I love them. I respect them. They can love and respect me. But they don't make my decisions. I'm where I want to be."

"Ditto," Coop and Jake echoed.

"But still…how do we make it work?"

"By doing what we are," Archie said. "We're making it work right now. We're all on the same page." He flicked his gaze to Ian briefly, then back to me. "Finally. We all love you enough to work, and we get along. We know how to share."

"And when we don't," Jake said with a shrug, "we know how to settle that, too."

"What are you worried about?" Coop asked me, and I focused on him because sometimes, it was just easier to talk to him about this stuff. Not that I didn't or couldn't talk to the others, but Coop just seemed to roll with stuff. He never judged me. "I don't judge you. Fuck, if I did that, you'd have to judge me, and let's be honest, I'm way more judgeable."

"That's not even a word. Also did I say that out loud?"

"Yes," came three other answers in varyingly amused voices.

"Oh." I winced. "You guys aren't hard to talk to…"

"We get it, Baby Girl. Answer Coop. He's the voice of sanity in the room anyway."

"True," Ian agreed, and Coop scowled.

"Wow. I'm not sure I want to be stuck with that job."

"Too bad," Archie chided. "Now hush and let her talk. What are you worried about, babe?" He repeated Coop's earlier question.

I ran my tongue over my lower lip and Coop groaned, but at my questioning look, he just shook his head and offered me another chip to eat. Hmm. Food was good. "I tried to talk about this the other night," I admitted. "About what happens if I don't choose. And…you said it was fine, you all still wanted one on one time with me—not complaining about that at all."

Archie chuckled. "Good to know." Despite his smile, he studied me with such intensity, it was like he stared right through me.

"I'm thinking about what comes next. We're—we're going steady or—I'm going steady with all of you?" Was going steady even the way to put it?

Jake pushed up off the sofa and stalked away through the house. My heart sank.

"Yes," Ian said quietly. "As far as I'm concerned, you're my girlfriend. But you're also Coop's, Archie's, and Jake's girl, too. We're your boyfriends. Weird?" He gave a shrug. "Maybe, but the idea has grown on me. Especially over the last few weeks."

"Because I broke up with you?"

"Partially," he conceded. "But you need all of us, and we work really well together where you're concerned."

"Besides," Jake said as he reappeared. "There's something that seems to keep escaping your grasp, and I want to make it as clear as possible." He nudged stuff aside on the coffee table and sat in front of me before tugging my hand over and sliding a ring right onto my middle finger.

I stared at it for a beat, and it took my whiskey-soaked brain a hot several seconds to catch up. It wasn't just a ring. It was a class ring.

It was the class ring for our year.

I glanced from it to him. "What…?"

"I knew you wouldn't order one. You always weigh the practical versus the frivolous. The ring would be frivolous to you. The fact that you've been weighing your decisions like that for years will never fail to piss me off, because you shouldn't have had to do that. So I ordered this for you…"

"You're doing this now, asshole?" Archie asked, an edge to his words.

"You shower her in gifts. Fuck off, Arch, and listen."

I stared wide-eyed up at Coop, and he rounded his eyes in return, so we both looked at Jake. Those pale blue eyes were anything but cool as he locked his gaze on mine.

"I thought…" Ian began, then held up his hands when Jake glared at him.

Yeah, okay. I squirmed to sit forward, and Coop helped because my limbs were still on the floaty side. I cupped Jake's face to bring his attention back to me. "You ordered this for me?"

I hadn't really looked at the ring, but it was hard to miss with my hand against Jake's cheek.

"Yep. See the four stones on the corners?"

There were four stones there, one big one in the center and four stones on the edges, smaller but definitely there. Our graduation year was etched on one side, and on the other, it had my name. Below our year was a rose, and below my name were hearts intertwined.

"Those are our birthstones. Green for Bubba. Pink for Coop and Archie. Blue for me."

Coop chuckled. "The only pink I like."

And I couldn't help flashing a grin back at him before focusing on Jake again.

"The diamond is you," he said. "Right in the center where you belong." He covered my hand with his. "*That* is how we make it work. We make it what *we* want it to be. Not promising easy. Not even promising I won't beat the crap out of these idiots if they get stupid with you. But what I do promise is that I'm in. All the way. Whatever shape it takes, however we make it."

"Me too," Archie said. "Even if I could have lived without the pink. I'm in. For all of it."

"And me," Ian repeated. "I meant it, I'm here. Whatever shape this relationship takes. I'm here."

"You heard my answer on the mountain," Coop said against my ear, but my gaze remained locked on Jake's. "They're right though. We will figure this out. We're not perfect. Any of us, but we want to make this work. For you. For us."

"The question," Jake continued softly, tracing a finger over the ring, "is do you want this to work with all of us? Because I think we can do it. And I don't give a rat's ass what anyone says about it. I'll take out anyone who tries to make you feel bad about it."

Flushing, I took a deep breath and then looked at each of the guys. Was I a little drunk? Oh yeah. Was I feeling floaty? Definitely. But they were all stone-cold serious and sober. They wanted me. "I want it to work," I said slowly, then licked my lips before finishing, "I want us to work. Whatever that looks like."

Jake's smile lit me up, and he cupped my face and dragged me down for a kiss. The only one not touching me at the moment was Archie, but I could feel the weight of his gaze, and when Jake let up for a breath, I exhaled.

Okay.

We were doing this.

I glanced at my ring. "You know I should yell at you for spending money on me. I should yell at all of you."

"But you're not going to," Coop said. "Because spoiling our girlfriend is our prerogative."

I laughed. "Only if I get to spoil my boyfriends."

"You can spoil me, or despoil me, anytime you want," Archie said. "I totally volunteer as tribute."

Jake snorted. "Yeah, but it's my birthday here shortly, and the birthday boy…"

I grinned at him. "Gets whatever he wants."

"I can't wait for it to be my birthday again," Ian said idly.

"Speaking from experience," Coop said. "I'm pretty sure we can't wait for it to be all our birthdays, though at the moment, I'm thinking about Frankie's."

And just like that, I flushed, and I was pretty sure it hit my toes with how hot my body went as all four of them focused on me.

Their soft chuckles promised they hadn't missed it, but they also let up on it, and some of the ragged emotion eased as Ian went to grab his guitar and Archie cleaned up the shots.

"I think it's time for terrible action movies."

I could do terrible action movies.

I could do just about anything.

I glanced down at the ring on my finger. Coop thumbed a tear away from my cheek before I even realized it had fallen. "Happy tears, right?" he asked against my ear.

"I'm kind of an emotional drunk," I admitted, and he pressed a kiss just below my ear before tightening his arms around me.

"You're not drunk," he said softly.

No, not on alcohol. Tipsy? Sure. But I was more drunk on all of them.

"Never have I ever been this happy," I said when they cued up the movie and passed out the popcorn.

No one reached for their drinks, and I grinned before tucking my head against Coop's shoulder. I thought the trip couldn't get more perfect.

I was wrong.

Chapter Twenty-Four
HAPPY HOLIDAZE

The tattoo artist eyed all of us as we stood at the counter. Coop had a couple of sketches out, and Archie had some images up on his phone. Jake and Ian were studying the pics on the walls, and I was studying the layout of the shop. This place was by appointment only. You were supposed to do a consultation on one day and then come in on another to get the work done.

I didn't want to ask how much money Archie had thrown at them to change the rules. He didn't say a word about it either. It was just Archie. Always fixing things. But it was also Jake's birthday, so I would not make a big deal out of it. As it was, I woke to Jake curled around me this morning and full of affection. Not sex, just cuddling and kissing and petting. It had been nice.

Sex would have been good, too, because apparently, I had an insatiable appetite for these four, and maybe it was a good thing I'd waited so long to discover this. I didn't know how we would have managed before now.

A shiver raced up my spine at the very idea, and Jake slid his hand over my lower back, then around my middle before pulling me back against him. "Cold?" he murmured against my ear, and I snuggled into him. I'd had a coat on when we got here, but we'd all shed them inside the warmth of the shop.

"No," I told him. "Not anymore." He chuckled and tightened his arms around me as Archie and Coop glanced over at us in between their conversation with the artists.

"You guys going to jump in here?"

"I know what I want," I told him. It had been simmering in the back of my mind for the last few days, ever since Jake and Coop brought up tattoos.

"Care to share?" Ian asked, and I stroked the back of Jake's hand to get him to let me go. He still followed me over to the counter as I pulled out my phone.

"I want a combination style tattoo, if that's okay." I tabbed over to the pictures I'd saved. I'd spent some time skimming the web in between hangovers and drinking and edibles and making out. What did I do over my winter vacation?

Had a *hell* of a lot of fun.

The first image was a heart with an infinity symbol looped through it, and the second was a fancy block number with images inside of it. The artist leaned over my phone and then eyed me.

He wasn't a bad looking guy, but I didn't think there was an inch of skin on him that wasn't decorated. It was beautiful in its own way, but really distracting because I wanted to study each piece and not stare at him at the same time. "Can you do this as a number five, then the infinity symbol weaved through it with their names on each loop?"

"That shouldn't be too hard," the guy said. "You want colors?"

"Or something prettier?" Jake asked carefully. When I glanced up, they wore varying looks of neutrality.

"I think this could be really pretty," I argued, then glanced at the sketchpad the guy was drawing on. The lines he made were flowing, and curvy. The five was pretty.

"Names?"

He added them as I spelled them, and I kept it Ian and not Bubba. When he was done, he turned it around to show me, and I grinned. Simple. Elegant.

"What do you think?"

The guys stared at it a beat, and then Archie rubbed the back of his neck. "Tattooing our names is pretty permanent."

"So is our friendship."

No matter what else, I wasn't giving them up. Even if I had to fight tooth and toenail to hang onto them in the long-term as friends, if we didn't work out. But I wasn't thinking about the future beyond that. We'd just decided that we were making this a real relationship—they were my boyfriends, and I was their girlfriend. The five of us.

Coop rubbed his jaw. "I want the same thing, but just Frankie's name on the loop."

"Ditto," Ian said.

Archie chuckled. "C'mon, you guys don't want to tattoo my name on you forever?"

"Nope," Jake said. "Frankie's, yes. I love you guys like brothers, but I don't need it tatted on me somewhere."

The second artist joined the first, and they glanced at us with more than a hint of speculation. My ears had to be on fire, but thankfully, my hair covered them, and I didn't shy away from the looks. The second artist was also older, and he tapped the sketch. "You want to personalize these a little more, you've got room in here. We could add something inside the five or even in the loops themselves."

I chewed my lower lip.

"Roses?" Archie suggested, and I laughed.

"Cat pawprints. Books." Coop nudged me. "Graduation cap…"

"Roses," I decided. "I want roses inside mine. Then I can get them colored in later." They had come to mean a lot to me, besides being my favorite flower.

The artist was already sketching in an idea.

"Musical notes for you, Ian?"

His eyes flared as he met my graze, and he grinned. "I like that."

"Tools for Archie," Coop suggested.

"Eh, I was thinking more this." Archie held out his phone, and the second artist peered at it.

"We have a book for those," the guy said before slipping away, when he came back, he flipped it open to the page for Chinese symbols.

"These three," Archie said. He tapped the ones for love, loyalty, and friendship.

"Me too," I said abruptly. "I want those instead of the roses."

"Make that three of us…"

"All of us," Jake said as Coop nodded. The artists chuckled, but they finished the design. Next, we just had to decide where we wanted them. I went for my shoulder blade. The guys weren't a fan of me shedding down to my bra, but they were all right there, and the only other people were the artists and they weren't flirting with me.

If anything, they were solicitous in making sure I was happy with what they sketched out and making minute changes. I loved that he'd added a hint of a heart to the upper curve of the five. It was subtle, but perfect. The guys' names would be in calligraphy. I was going to have to get a picture of it when I was done.

The guys decided to get theirs in the same place. Which meant it would be prominently on display whenever they were shirtless.

All the moisture in my mouth fled as I settled on the chair and leaned forward to relax. The artist talked me through the steps and explained everything he was going to do. Jake was going at the same time I was, since he wanted to get his first.

Birthday boy always gets his wish.

We stared at each other as they got started. The minute the cool gel hit my back, I tensed a little, but the artist just started rambling on about the different tattoos he'd done over the years and I focused on Jake's eyes.

It didn't hurt so bad.

Okay, I lied. It hurt like a bitch. I swore it was like they were literally carving the symbols into my back and not just using a little tiny set of needles. But after a while, the hot pain just kind of all washed together and faded. It helped that Coop was right next to my head and Archie and Ian were also there, both of them watching critically.

All too soon, it was done, and then it was Archie and Ian who were up. Coop waited with us and helped me pull my shirt on after they'd treated it. He also took a picture. It was red and blotchy and inflamed and kind of perfect.

"Guess that's that," I told him, as I inspected my name now tatted on Jake's back. It was about to be tatted on all of them. A possessive thrill skated through me.

"Guess it is," Jake murmured and then kissed me lightly, murmuring, "Mine."

"And mine," Coop said, giving me a wink.

"Stop hogging Frankie," Archie complained. "Or at least hog her where I can see her. We're over here bleeding for her."

Laughter burst out of me, but I grabbed a chair so I could sit between he and Ian, splitting my attention between them. All in all, it took three hours to get it all done. But by early afternoon, with instructions in our pockets and all of us sporting new tattoos, we headed out for the car. It was partially sunny, and the guys had reminded us to keep the tats out of the sun—not going to be a problem—and it would probably take a week or so before the scabs fell off—didn't that sound charming—and we had all the supplies necessary.

Three steps out to the car, Ian clapped Jake on the back as they laughed and we all winced.

Yeah, that would take some getting used to.

"Frankie's mine for the afternoon," Jake called as soon as we were back at the lodge. "You guys fuck off and do whatever."

Then he had my hand in his, and we headed up the stairs.

"Car picks us up at six," Archie called.

"We'll be ready!"

That was a few hours off. "Picks us up for what?" I asked as Jake pulled me into *his* room and closed the door. He turned the lock and leaned against it, grinning at me.

"For a surprise," he said, and I raised my eyebrows. The ring on my finger had seemed so heavy when he'd first slipped it on, but now I loved the feel of it there.

"Why am I getting a surprise? It's your birthday."

"Exactly," he told me as he stripped off his coat, then reached for his shirt and tugged it off, even as he toed off his shoes. "My birthday."

I went to unzip my coat, but he caught my hands.

"Nope."

"No?"

He shook his head once, then unzipped his jeans, and I got to enjoy watching him strip those off and the boxers with them. I would never get tired of looking at Jake or the way his muscles rippled as he moved.

"No," he said, narrowing the distance between us. "My birthday remember?" Tugging the zipper, he peeled it downward and shivers raced over my skin. "I want to unwrap my present."

"So now I'm your present?" I teased, but who was I kidding? My nipples were two stiff peaks straining in his direction, and the tension coiling in my belly had already pulled taut. I wasn't even close to naked, and I was already so turned on, I didn't know what to do with myself.

Fingers under the hem of my shirt, he traced a path against my abdomen. "You're the best present I ever got."

I swallowed around the lump in my throat as he tugged the shirt up with extreme care as he got to my shoulder. With gentle urging, he turned me around and slid his hands down my arms.

"This is going to sound really sexist, but I love the fact that you have my name on you," he half-growled the words. "Ours. Our names. Our girl. Right there, and if any asshole gets too close to you, there is no mistaking who you belong to."

Yep, the possessive edge to those words sent another shudder through me as he dipped his hands to my pants and rolled them down. Unlike the guys, I'd just gone with stretchy warm pants rather than jeans. They peeled right down, panties and all. He paused to press his lips to the curve of my ass and then dragged his teeth along before he bit me near my hip.

I didn't even have to ask what he was doing as he sucked on the skin. They loved to leave little love bites on me. I had a whole pattern of them, and they'd been on display during the tattoo session. Thank God, the guys there hadn't said a word.

"Hands on the bed," Jake ordered, and I pressed my palms to the end of it, to brace myself as he tugged off my boots and tossed them behind him. They landed with a pair of thumps. Then he had me stepping out of the pants. My socks went next, and that just left my bra.

Glancing over my shoulder, I found Jake sitting back on his heels staring up at me. "I love that my name is on you, too," I told him. "I can officially say you guys are mine. No one else gets to touch."

"Not again," he promised. "No one else will touch me again." With light fingers, he traced a path down my thigh and up again. "Frankie…do you have any idea of all the things I want to do with you?"

I could think of a few. I smiled. "Well, we've done a lot of things we've never done before…or at least, I haven't."

His pale blue eyes lifted to lock on mine as he dipped his fingers between my thighs, and I shifted my stance to widen it. The drag of his fingers along my labia, the promise of his callouses as he stroked the dampness waiting for him and spread it around. It wouldn't take long for me to soak his hand. Not once did we look away from each other as he played.

"Did I say thank you for that?" The depth of emotion in his eyes was almost too much but I wouldn't turn away from him.

"No," I whispered. "But I'm pretty sure it was implied. Especially when we couldn't move."

He chuckled. "How's your back?"

"Fine," I promised. Sure, it ached, but I didn't care about it right now. "Yours?"

"Not even a blip." He pressed two fingers inside of me, and I let out a sigh. "Fuck, I just want you, Frankie."

"You can have me," I told him, and he withdrew his hand, then caught my hips and tugged me back toward him. I turned and then straddled his lap there on the floor and sank down. Together, we gripped his cock and angled it so I could just impale myself on him, and he echoed my shudders.

The friction of his erection pushing into me lit me up. Hands on his shoulders, I locked my gaze on his as we lingered there, connected, but still. With one hand, he cupped my face and then pushed my hair up and away.

"Do you remember when you left for Germany?" I asked him softly.

"Try to forget it," he murmured, nuzzling a kiss to my jaw. "I hated leaving you and Coop."

"We hated it, too."

"Then why are we discussing it?" He mouthed kisses on his way to my ear, and I rocked my hips, the barest motion, and it had him hissing. There was something really empowering about knowing how much I affected him.

God knew he had an amazing effect on me.

"Because," I said, beginning to ride him slowly, no rush, just a gentle up and down. It seemed like I took him deeper with each downward push. Or maybe it was wishful thinking. "If you hadn't come back…I think I would have tried to find you someday."

Lifting his head, he snapped his gaze to mine and dropped a hand to my hips, helping me move but not rushing me. "Even after I didn't write?" The rawness there echoed something in me.

"Maybe especially because you didn't." It didn't seem so weird to vocalize this. "Jake, I missed you so much when you were gone, I think Coop got sick of me bringing you up."

He chuckled. "I missed you, too."

"But I didn't have the words for it. I tried to write you, you know."

A frown. "No…"

"I didn't know where to send it, and I nagged Maddy to death about helping me find an address." He thrust up to meet me this time, and the jolt sent little shocks through my system. "Probably pissed her off."

"I never got any letters," he admitted. "I didn't write because I had no idea if we would be back. Dad went where the assignments took him. It might be that I would never see you again."

Every arch of his hips as I sank down delivered a stroke to that spot that had me tilting my head back and groaning. "I wouldn't have let that happen." My breath came in shorter bursts, and Jake was panting. "I would have figured it out. Internet…it's a great thing."

Jake surged upward, and then I was sprawled back on his bed without ever losing him as he pressed my thigh higher and deepened his angle. "Friend me somewhere?"

"Oh yeah." The second word rode a whimper as he slammed his hips forward, and I dug my fingers into his shoulders. We were touching everywhere, and where I might have been chilled earlier, I was burning. "You'd have totally stalked me on Instagram."

A huff of laughter, and then he sucked a spot on my throat before kissing it gently and laving his tongue over it. "Yeah, I would have. Probably road tripped if I saw some of those bullshit posts giving you a hard time."

"See…" Fuck, I was so close, and the tension corded tighter and tighter. Jake hadn't slowed for an instant, every push and grind sending another delicious wave through me. "We would have found each other…maybe reunited for your birthday."

Another laugh, this one harsher. "That's a nice dream," he said, pinning me with a look. My back rubbed against the cover, but I didn't care. The little stings added to the pleasure spiraling out in my system. He framed my head with his hands, keeping me in place as he began to piston his hips. A muscle ticked in his jaw, and the strain showed in the lines of his neck.

I wasn't the only one who was close. I stretched my hands down to dig my fingers into his ass, encouraging him to go faster, even as I hitched my thigh higher for him. The stretch burned so good.

"But I'm really fucking glad I didn't have to wait years. I'm glad I came back. And you're never getting rid of me again."

It was my turn to laugh. "You're damn right, I'm not." Then I wrenched my hands up to cup the back his neck and drag his face down to me. "Mine, birthday boy. All mine."

I bit his lower lip before I kissed him, and he began to thrust his tongue against mine in time with his cock. He dipped his hand between us and stroked once over my clit, and I splintered. The orgasm didn't so much rush up to swallow me, but spill over like a spring storm. He swallowed my cry with his kiss, and his hips stuttered as he followed me over.

After, we just lay there, kind of floating together. Gradually, the sting on my back let me know that it wasn't thrilled with my position, but I still couldn't be bothered to move. The rest of the afternoon, we spent like that—naked, lounging on his bed, and just talking.

We talked about everything and nothing.

We even debated our favorite history videos and argued over which one was better.

It was ridiculous and sweet and perfect.

I glanced down at my dress and then over at Jake where he sat on the edge of the bed waiting for me. We'd eventually had to get up and shower so we could get changed for the night. The dress, like a lot of my other clothes, had been picked out by them—but this was a new one, and I kind of liked it.

Also, I had no intentions of asking how they got it fitted. It was a solid body contouring dress with a mini skirt that cut off at mid-thigh. The midriff was open, save for two crisscrossing straps in the front and the back. The top may as well have been strapless, because it hugged my breasts and I didn't have a single bra that would work with it. The halter strap that wrapped around my neck was more for show than anything else.

It was also a stunning holiday green. If it weren't cut so sexy, I'd say it was the perfect holiday outfit. I did a spin for Jake, and he stared at me with a faint look of strain.

"Maybe we get you something else to wear," he suggested. "Or I'm going to be hard all night."

I grinned at him. "But you get me tonight. Just feel bad for the boys, they don't."

A wicked grin curved his lips. "This is true. If I asked, would you give me a blowjob in front of them?"

"Jake!"

"Hey, birthday boy gets what he wants."

"And you want to torture them?"

"No," he said. "I want a blowjob. But, the other is a perk."

I laughed. "I am not tormenting them. Though…Coop would probably enjoy watching."

Turning, I glanced over my shoulder. "This is going to show the tattoo, and it's still really red and covered."

"Leave your hair down," he suggested. "And I don't care if they can see it. What I care is that you're comfortable."

I had to wear heels with this outfit, so I wasn't sure how comfortable

I would be. "Well, here's hoping I don't have to walk through snow to get in wherever we're going."

"I'll carry you if I have to." Nope, he wasn't revealing anything, and I couldn't even complain. Birthday boy got his way. The tux he wore had a straight tie rather than a bow tie, and damn, he looked gorgeous in the crisp white shirt and black suit, all freshly pressed. He'd shaved and styled his hair back.

For a moment, I just stared at him and licked my lips.

"You can unwrap me when we get home," Jake said with a wink. Before I could reply, a knock hit the door.

"Tuck it back in Jake," Archie called. "The car is here."

With a snort, Jake offered me his arm. "How about a blowjob in the car?"

I was still laughing as we headed out. The looks of appreciation I got from the guys chased away any sense of self-consciousness brought on by the outfit. I had on my ring and my charm bracelet, but I skipped the necklace because of the straps.

It was a fairly long ride from the lodge to Denver, but the guys remained mute on our destination. After the Torched concert, I knew that we were going to some show, but I had no idea what.

The car pulled us right up to the front of a theatre, and the sign on the marquee told me the rest. Holy crap. Emersyn Sharpe was headlining with the Spitfire dance troupe and the Fly by Night show. I'd only ever seen them on YouTube.

Tears threatened again, and I glared at the guys.

"Birthday boy gets his way," Jake informed me, then pressed a finger to my lips. "Archie asked if I wanted to take you to this for my birthday, and I said hell yes."

I laughed. "You guys…"

"It's Christmas," Archie reminded me before he slid out of the car and held out his hand to help me out. "And Jake's birthday. It's all about having fun."

This was the kind of performance that I had always wanted to see. Like going to the Torched concert, but so very different. Not only was I getting to see it, I was getting to see it with all of them looking devastating in their suits.

Thankfully, there was no snow to walk through. Inside, we were shown to a table—not to just seats—and there was a supper being served. We didn't have long after we were seated that the food was brought out and the drinks, and then the show was starting. When the lights plunged down, Jake found my hand and held it, Coop had his free hand on my thigh, and the music started as two dancers appeared out of the shadows.

Emersyn Sharpe was unmistakable—lean, muscular, and powerful. Her dance partner was Aaron or Erin or maybe Rick something. I didn't pay as much attention to him, though he was huge by comparison to her, and he threw her into the air and caught her and moved her around like she was nothing. It was like she danced on the air, and that was when they were on the stage.

When the silk fell and she began to use that to climb and dance, it really was magical.

A glance around the table when the lights changed showed me the guys were as rapt as I was, and that let me relax and really enjoy the show.

Jake didn't complain once when I squeezed his hand at some maneuver she did as she danced. Nor did they comment when I had to dab at my eyes afterward.

What a magical life she had to perform like that.

What a magical life I had to get to see it with the guys.

After the show, the night wasn't over. The car took us to a club that let us in, even if we were only eighteen. And while we couldn't drink, we did dance.

Holy hell, did we dance.

Chapter Twenty-Five
GREEN-EYED GIRL

IAN

Ihad to give credit where credit was due. This vacation was everything Frankie needed. From the skiing to the Torched concert to the evenings sprawled around the lodge playing video games. Christmas crept up on us like the cherry atop the sundae of this trip. I'd have been jealous, but we were all making a concerted effort to not hog her time. Sure, Jake stole her on his birthday. I respected that. One of us, sometimes two of us, was always in her bed, but she didn't push anyone away.

The morning of Christmas Eve, I slipped into her room where she and Coop were a tangle of limbs. The latter lifted his head and peered at me, then yawned and rolled back over as I slid in on Frankie's other side. Drinking in the sight of her, I smiled at her as I cupped her cheek. Her eyes danced beneath her closed lids. I almost hated to rouse her from dreams, but then those perfect green eyes fluttered open to focus on me.

A smile curved her lips so easily, I let out a soft sigh. Carefully stroking her hair back from her face, I mouthed the word "coffee" and lifted my eyebrows in question. She stretched and the sheet dipped over her nakedness, and she smothered a yawn as she glanced toward the windows. It was still early, but I wanted her to myself for a bit.

Scooting toward me, she murmured, "Shower?"

The sex smell in the room told me why, and I lifted the blankets and scooped her up. She smothered a giggle against my shoulder. I hadn't bothered to pull on anything other than the pajama bottoms, and I carried her into the bathroom. A pillow bounced off my back, but Coop laughed as I ignored him and it.

Nudging the bathroom door closed, I turned on the light with my elbow. As much as I'd like to keep holding her, I set her on her feet and flipped on the water in the shower for her. Frankie stared up at me sleepily when I faced her, and when I would have kissed her, she widened her eyes and clapped a hand over her mouth.

"Morning breath," she muttered, and I chuckled, then nuzzled a kiss to her jaw before I turned her around to her sink. I had brushed my teeth, and I contented myself with rubbing her back gently as she cleaned her own. Those green eyes kept darting up to look at me in the mirror. My dick was wide-awake and straining toward her. When she backed into me, I didn't try to hide it, and then Frankie just leaned into me and closed her eyes. Wrapping my arms around her, I buried my face against her neck.

Everything about her was beautiful, and the relief coursing through me each time she settled into my arms couldn't be denied. The clench of her ass against my cock had me groaning. Skating a hand over her chest, I began to massage her breasts, and she ground her ass against me. Fuck, I wanted everything with her. The possessiveness she aroused in me was undeniable. I loved pinning her down, and I wanted to tie her up and let her ride my tongue until she came.

Dropping my hands to her hips, I pressed my thumbs against the curve of her ass and nudged her forward. The tattoo on her shoulder had scabbed, but I could still make out my name there, and that sent another bolt of lust straight to my already straining cock. Meeting her gaze in the mirror, I ran a hand down to cup her pussy. The wetness coated my finger, and she let out a sigh, even as steam began to rise in the shower.

Frankie grinned and braced her hands against the counter without any urging from me, and I groaned. I'd had plans to steal her down for breakfast and to play with her for a couple of hours before the guys woke up.

We could still do that.

I shoved my pajama bottoms down, and her eyes flared.

Tongue tracing over her lower lip, she never let go of our eye contact as I fisted myself once or twice. Fuck, I ached for her. With the lightest pressure from my free hand on her hip, she arched her back and pressed forward until those peaked nipples were just above the cool counter.

I teased my cock against that beautiful pussy and began massaging her ass. Then she wiggled her butt at me in invitation. Cupping my hand, I landed the barest of slaps against the roundness, and she bit her lower lip.

Oh, she was muting herself.

That would not do.

All thoughts of a quick shower fled.

I wanted her moaning.

I wanted her crying out.

I wanted her to fall apart.

The second strike of my palm was more stinging for me, and her cheek reddened as I began massaging out the heat. The flare of her pupils as they dilated sent a pulse straight to my dick. Nudging my dick forward, I breached her with just the head. The hot slickness beckoned me to lunge forward, but I fisted my control.

Frankie wrapped around my cock was way too damn perfect. I wanted to blow every time I slid into her, and it took every ounce of concentration to rock into her before I dragged her back and slid my hand up her chest to her throat. Then she was pressed back against my chest, and I was balls deep in the loveliest vise.

Her sigh answered my own. That she enjoyed everything from the spanking to the pinning to the surrender was a gift I would never not treasure. She began to rock her hips, and I let her control the pace as I pressed my lips to her ear.

The fogging mirror hid her from me, but I had every inch of her memorized. I began to hum, and the jolt seemed to go through her as she recognized the first couple of bars. That was my girl. I couldn't match the accent from the film, but singing "Christmas is All Around Us" had her clenching beautifully on my cock.

When I bit down lightly, she bucked against my grip and then just went all lax and liquid against me as we rocked together. No hurry. No rush.

Well that was a fucking lie. I could pound into her with how hard I was, but having her fall apart around me was the second best feeling in the world. The absolute best came when my name fell in a strained note from her lips.

When she dragged her hand up to wrap around my nape, I dipped my head and met her minty kiss as my thrusts became sharper. The soft mewling sounds escaping her had me chasing her tongue with my own.

Cupping her pussy again, I traced a circle around her clit. The little shocks had her clenching and flexing around my dick, disintegrating my control. Applying real pressure, I gave her that last nudge, and she screamed. There it was—the throaty cry that had my balls dragging up tight, and three pumps later, I came as she fluttered around my cock and sagged into me, trembling.

Fuck.

"Oh yeah," she whispered against my lips as we both panted, and then she dropped her head to my shoulder. There was a mess sliding down her thighs, but it was hard to care when she was so soft and trembling against me.

"Good morning," I managed to exhale, and her laughter boosted me higher.

"It is now," she said, her grin wreathing the words. The bathroom was filled with steam, and we both hissed as I eased out of her. I let her catch my hand as she turned, and then her lips were on mine and we swayed as I kissed her. Cupping her chin, I nudged her head back to change the angle and then savored every stroke of her tongue as I maneuvered us into the shower. The water hit us from three sides.

Rich people and their amenities.

I didn't think I'd ever complain again. We took our time, soaping each other up, and I sighed as she ran her hands all over me. Most of the time, I was too intent on pulling her apart to let her explore, and there was something enormously satisfying every time she glanced at me as she traced a muscle line. Even more when she took care to wash my cock, and I was more than happy to return the favor.

It was less about groping and more about just savoring. I savored her breasts, her hips, her throat and her ass in equal measure.

When she dropped to her knees though, I wasn't ready to have her mouth on me, and fuck, I went from relaxed to hard as a stone between one pull and the next.

I fisted her hair, and as much as I wanted to let her have that control, it was eating away at mine. Still, I didn't drag her closer or try to set the pace until I bumped the back of her throat and glanced down to find her eyes on me.

She relaxed her mouth at my tug, and then I was fucking into her with care, watching to make sure she wasn't gagging, and I spilled like it was my first time as my body went boneless. Her smile after was so worth it.

We finished the shower, eventually, and I checked her tattoo. The scabbing looked good. It was already falling off in places, leaving the dark lines in sharp relief against her soft skin. Pressing a kiss to the side of it, I whispered, "Do you have any idea how hot it is that you have my name on you?"

My *name*. Ian. Not Bubba. I had been Ian to pretty much family only for years.

Until Frankie.

For her, I was Ian.

She grinned and twisted to glance at me. "Probably as sexy as it is for my name to be etched on you."

I dragged on my bottoms as she sauntered out of the bathroom—and I did mean sauntered. The sway of her hips had me wondering if we needed to go downstairs at all.

"Fuck, you're beautiful," Coop said with a groan, and I chuckled.

"Thanks," I told him as I scooped up the pillow he'd flung at me earlier and sent it careening back to him as Frankie laughed. She was utterly unabashed in her nudity as she went in search of clothes, and something I hadn't even realized was tense settled within me. No artifice had ever clung to Frankie, she'd always been herself. The shy parts. The bold parts. The warmth. The affection. Hell, even her hostility when we were dicks.

But over the last few weeks, right in front of us, she'd blossomed. The woman glancing at me as she pulled on a pair of dark green panties and a matching bra was the result of that.

"Is it possible I can convince you to come back to bed?" Coop asked, and I glanced over to find him staring at her with the same raw emotion that was probably on my face.

The flush of pink to her cheeks as she laughed beckoned we join her. "Hmm, I would," she promised. "But I'm starving."

Flinging himself back against the pillows, Coop grumbled.

"You don't have to get up," I told him as Frankie dragged on an oversized shirt that was definitely one of mine. No complaints here. I almost hated the leggings as she tugged those on and hid those sexy legs away, but it was freezing outside, and while it was warm up here, who knew about downstairs yet.

"Yeah, yeah, you just want her all to yourself."

No lie. "Yes, I do." With her socks on, she slid Jake's ring on her finger before facing me. Her hair was still damp, her face rosy and her eyes sparkling. She really was edible. I was still staring at her when she tossed a shirt my way.

Oh look, another one of mine. Apparently, I'd been leaving a lot of my clothes in here.

"Fine," Coop muttered, dragging the blankets up after Frankie blew him a kiss. "You get an hour."

I tugged it over my head and grinned at her. "Food?"

"Food," she agreed with a swift nod. "And coffee."

Yeah, I saw that one coming.

At the door, I glanced back at Coop. "Two."

"Ninety minutes," he yawned. "Final offer."

Breakfast awaited us downstairs. Archie's very silent staff had already crept in and delivered it. The counters were clean and sparkling. The coffee maker just required flipping on and it began bubbling. Frankie eyed the espresso machine and gave me a playful look.

Why not?

It took four attempts, but we managed a mocha with two shots of espresso each, whip cream, and she went hunting for sprinkles. The amused look on her face was worth it. Food stacked on plates and coffee in hand, we headed out to the living room. I got the fire going, and then she settled next to me with a blanket thrown over both of us. The tree lights gleamed, and the wood crackled.

"So, wanted me all to yourself, huh?" she teased as she took a sip of her coffee. The little foamy, whip cream mustache was adorable, and I grinned at her.

"I always want you," I reminded her, and she grinned. "But yeah, just for a little while. This has been…"

"Amazing," she finished for me. "And we still have another week here, Ian." Yeah, we did. "I still can't believe you guys did all of this."

"A lot of it was Arch," I admitted. "The guy really loves you."

Her expression softened. "I love him, too."

Yeah, I knew that, too. Even trying, I couldn't find the earlier jealousy over the idea. She loved all of us. She was more than capable of loving all of us. And I loved her too much to let that ever be an issue again.

"I found a karaoke place about forty minutes from here…" I began.

"Yes," she said, grinning. "When do you want to go?"

I laughed. "Whenever you want? I'm thinking not on New Year's."

"Probably better if we don't. People get crazy on New Year's."

Yes, they did.

"But any other time?"

She nodded. "Whenever you want."

"That was only half of what I wanted to talk to you about," I admitted as she tore into her bacon. She'd downed half of her espresso, and that was after the cups of coffee we drank while we were figuring the machine out.

"What's the other half?"

I glanced toward the stairs. It was quiet, and if the other guys were awake, they were giving us this time. I'd done the same when I'd spot her curled up with one of them. No one wanted to make a schedule per se, not while we were here. We'd have to do that when we got home, there was no escaping it. For now, I shoved that out of my head.

Here, we made time for each other to spend time with her. That didn't change how much I enjoyed the time we were all together, but right now…

"I had an email from the producers."

All at once, she curved to sit sideways, her whole focus on me. "And…?"

"And they want those new songs by the end of January."

"Holy crap."

"I know," I admitted. The advanced timeline had caught me off guard. It was a lot of work, but I wanted to do it and I really wanted…

"What do you need me to do?"

The open offer had me grinning wider. "Sing with me on it."

"Ian…"

"Trust me?" I asked her. She glanced to the side and then back at me. "Just sing with me on it. Let me record it, and if you really hate it, I won't use it." But no way she could hate it if she would listen to herself uncritically without the voice of that woman in her head. "Help me pick the best tracks."

As she chewed her lower lip, I had to resist the urge to push. That she would sing with me at all was a big deal. The first time, I had to tease her into it, and getting her to record that piece for Archie had been a break through. But I wanted everything for her. Music might be my dream, but Frankie was every bit a part of that dream.

"I trust you," she told me, and a grin pulled at the corners of my mouth. "I just don't want to torpedo your chances."

"Not possible," I promised and brushed a kiss to her lips. "You're my muse, and everything I do is so much better because you're here. You singing with me? That's icing on the cake."

She laughed. "You make it hard to say no."

"Then don't say no."

Head back, she stared at the ceiling for a long moment. "If I hate it, you won't use it?"

"You have my word." And my word to do everything in my power to convince her that she was exactly what my music needed.

"Fine," she said with a groan. I nearly spilled our food with the force of my kiss as I captured her lips and savored her agreement.

"You won't regret it," I promised her.

"Let's hope so," she whispered under her breath, but I let that go. For now. I had enough faith in her for both of us…for now.

By the time the guys began to descend the stairs, I'd grabbed my guitar and we were working our way through one of the songs I wanted to use. I only had about half of the lyrics written, but "Green-Eyed Girl" wasn't hard to verbalize.

It encapsulated every complicated feeling I had for my girl—our girl—and I caught sight of Jake on the stairs, pausing to sit as she joined me in the second line.

His grin mirrored my own.

He didn't continue down to join us until we paused for me to grab a pencil and add a couple of new lines.

"Baby Girl," Jake said as he leaned over the couch to kiss her good morning, "that was awesome."

A startled laugh escaped her and she flushed, but the pleasure in her eyes just made me smile. When she threw a look at me for not warning her, I just shook my head.

"You sing like an angel," I repeated. I'd say it over and over again if I had to.

"A sexy as fuck angel," Jake agreed. "Do it again…and do you want more coffee?"

"Water for me," I told him, and Jake nodded as he headed for the kitchen.

Archie and Coop weren't far behind.

The biggest win of the morning?

She kept practicing with me as the guys filtered into the living room to join us with their breakfasts and coffee. The red tint to her cheeks faded only some, but she pressed on, and the guys? They soaked up every note right alongside me.

Music was my thing with Frankie, but I'd share this part of her, too. Right now, I'd share it with these guys because they believed in her every bit as much as I did.

If I had my way, I'd share it with the world.

Christmas Eve was a blast. We'd gone out in the afternoon for some skiing, more for fun than anything else. Frankie loved it, and I'd forgotten how much I enjoyed it. Coop and Frankie still fumbled some, but they were never short on laughter or teasing.

We headed back before it got dark, and everyone changed into the pjs Archie had left out for us.

"Dude, it's a good thing I like you," Jake called from his room. "This has got to be the corniest thing we've ever done."

"We have matching tattoos," Frankie countered from her room, and I leaned against the doorjamb to mine, waiting for the others.

"Matching tattoos are *sexy*," Coop said as he appeared in his doorway, wearing an identical set of pjs to me and probably the others, too. The red bottoms were covered in little Santas, while the white tank tops just said *ho-ho-ho*.

I'd seen dumber things. At least they were comfortable.

"Stop your bitching," Archie said. "It's fucking Christmas. Show some spirit."

Jake snorted. "That should be a goddamn jingle. Work on that, Bubba."

The pair stood in their own doorways, and yep, we were all wearing identical outfits.

"You guys are adorable," Frankie drawled as she stepped out of her room, hands on her hips. "And apparently, we're not matching one hundred percent."

She had on the exact same bottoms and a white t-tank that did nothing to hide her nipples and the fact that they were peaked and stiff against the fabric. But it was the words on the tank that had me swallowing a guffaw.

Coop didn't even try, and Jake shot Archie a look like he was pissed, but his eyes danced too merrily to make it seem real. Archie just grinned and strolled right for her. "Don't mind if I do," he teased, as he wrapped an arm around her and pulled her to him.

Her tank top sported a spring of mistletoe in the center with the words *Kiss Me* and arrows pointing up and down.

Raunchy.

And hilarious.

Only Archie.

Then again…I wasn't complaining.

Without question, Frankie was the best present we could have gotten.

You Get Me

FRANKIE

"Which one of your assholes sent me the cactus?" Rachel eyed me through the video chat. The quirky grin and raised eyebrows had me cracking up.

"That would be me," Coop yelled from the other side of the room. "But really, it's from all of us."

"Well, fuck you," Rachel replied. "I have no idea how I'm getting a condom cactus home."

A condom… "A *what?*" I asked, staring at her, and she turned the camera to the cactus sitting on the table. It was indeed a phallic-shaped cactus that looked like it had a condom on it, with little spines sticking out. Laughter escaped me, and I clapped a hand over my mouth.

"Yeah, yeah," Rachel snarked as she reappeared on the screen. "Merry effing Christmas to you, too."

It was kind of adorable, and I'd seen the card attached to it. I didn't know if she'd meant me too, or not. But the guys were getting a kiss for that.

From a set of pricks to the prickly bitch, thanks for sticking *it to us and with us.*

"Is it really that bad?" I asked, but before she could respond, there was a sound behind her and she twisted.

"Get out, Mack," she said. The guy must have responded because she huffed. "Get out before I throw this cactus at your eyes, and you need to protect those things. They're the only balls on you."

I snorted another laugh, but the door closed and Rachel stared at me with wide eyes that she then crossed.

"Ugh, please tell me all about how miserable you are and that you have gotten tired of all the dick," Rachel said, but at my expression, she sighed. "No, you look ridiculously happy, which is good. It means I don't have to stab any of them. Tongue lessons working out for you?"

"I think they've got it covered," I managed to splutter without blushing too much. Actually, the blushing had dialed down some. There was a freedom to being here. "We got tattoos."

"You got…" She gaped at me. "Pictures or it didn't happen."

"I'll show you when we get home." Then, because Rachel really did look kind of miserable… "How much longer are you stuck there?"

"We go home day after Christmas, thank fuck. I'm tempted to bedazzle some horns and wear it to dinner tomorrow, because if I'm going to Hell, I might as well get a full scholarship."

Poor Rachel.

"Girls' night, as soon as I'm back," I promised her. "Anything you want to do…"

"Anything?" She waggled her eyebrows.

"Watch it, Manning," Jake called from across the room.

"You're just bitter 'cause you want to watch," Rachel said and winked at me.

I rolled my eyes, and she burst out laughing 'cause Jake went quiet. I glanced over to find all four of them staring at me.

"So…" I said, trying and failing to contain my smile as I looked back at the screen. "Tell me you've done *something* fun while you were there."

"Drove out to Amish land to get away from the fam," she said. "That was a *good* time."

I shouldn't laugh.

I really shouldn't.

But her expression was hilarious.

"So, all done with me, tell me what you've been doing. I know who…"

"Don't hate me," I began, and she gave me a gimlet stare. "We saw Torched…"

She swore at me in French.

For ten minutes.

It was epic.

Chapter Twenty-Six

DAYS LIKE THIS

Christmas morning dawned with a pinkish-hued sunrise that I watched through the huge picture windows in the living room with my head tucked against Coop's abs. Instead of choosing who got to sleep with me last night or me going to sleep with one of them, we dragged out sleeping bags and gathered all the pillows and crashed together around the tree. With the soft glow of the Christmas lights and the fireplace crackling to set the mood, Ian had strummed Christmas carols on his guitar and we'd sung them, sometimes really badly, and laughed.

So much laughter.

Archie insisted we each open one present. He also picked out the presents for each of us.

Jake got actual boxing gloves that had all of us laughing, but then again, Jake had just grinned.

For Ian, there were a series of different guitar picks that had my face on them. Wow. Ian loved them, but I died at Archie's utterly serious, "Now you can finger her whenever you play…" comment.

The guys loved it, though.

For Coop, it was an amusing Dr. Freud therapy ball. Kind of like a Magic Eight Ball with a twist. That, and a bunch of inkblots that made no sense until he held them up with a delighted grin and said, "They're you. He used your face to map inkblots."

Archie smirked. "We see her everywhere, there must be a diagnosis for that…"

And that had my face burning. My gift though… I'd assumed it would be a charm, but it wasn't. It was a photo of all five of us from ninth grade. I barely even remembered that day, just that we had all been laughing. I was hanging off of Jake's back for some reason, my arms looped around his neck, as Coop and Ian flanked us, and Archie was in the front with his arms spread wide. We all had these wild grins on our faces.

Oh.

"We were getting ready to go camping." The four of them convinced me camping would be fun. They weren't wrong. It also involved bugs. But I could live with that. Jeremy had driven us out to a campsite, made sure we had everything, and then given the guys this stern lecture out of my earshot.

Thank. God.

I hadn't really paid attention then, but I knew exactly what it had to entail now. It had been right at the beginning of our first summer together that bridged freshman and sophomore years.

"I love it," I'd told him, and the guys laughed at me.

Archie didn't intend to open a gift, but screw that. I dug around until I found one of the ones I'd gotten for him and thrust it in his hands. Thankfully, the guys had backed me up. He eyed the package and then me. He shook it once. "A card redeemable for sex whenever I want it?"

I rolled my eyes, and Jake hit him with a piece of popcorn. Still laughing, Archie opened it. Considering what he'd just gotten me, I thought it was on the appropriate side.

"You utter sap," Archie mumbled, before chewing his lip as he stared down at the framed photo I'd wrapped for him.

"But I know how much it meant to you," I teased him, and he turned it around to show the guys. It was me and Archie at our first mini-golf 'date' that I hadn't known was a date. We'd gotten in one of those photo booths and taken goofy pictures. There was a scrawled note included that he'd written when he asked me to go in the first place.

Don't ask me why I'd kept the note, but I'd tucked it away in my yearbook. So yeah, maybe I was a sap.

He dropped a kiss on my lips as he stared at the photo. "Don't think I don't know this means you want to go mini-golf again…"

The bubble of emotion around us swelled a little brighter. It was well after midnight before we went to sleep, but I hadn't been this excited to wake on Christmas morning in forever. Coop stroked his fingers through my hair as we watched the sunrise. Eventually, I climbed out of the pile of them and he padded after me.

While he started coffee, I made breakfast. Today, there would be no staff. It was just going to be us. The food for a Christmas feast was also stocked and ready to go. The cook had even left instructions. Pretty sure those were for the guys, but we'd manage. I'd already seen pumpkin pie secreted in the back, along with a couple of other kinds. Cans of whip cream, too.

There would be so much food.

Coop wrapped his arms around me from behind and nuzzled a kiss behind my ear. "Are you having as much fun as you look like you're having?" The murmured question made me smile.

Tilting my head back, I grinned at him. "More."

His eyes softened. "Good."

We worked together easily. He passed me coffee and traded it for the huge platter of bacon I'd fried. Then he got the biscuits in the oven and traded off with me when I got the eggs started. When he pulled out the salsa for the eggs and raised his brows, I grinned. I'd added some sausage, peppers, and other veggies, too.

Jake stumbled into the kitchen first, and thankfully, Coop saved the pan of eggs as Jake swept me up in a kiss. It was all good, until he stole my coffee and I threatened him with a spatula. Ian and Archie shuffled in after, and Coop saved Jake's life by getting me more coffee.

After breakfast had been consumed, Coop and I made mochas for everyone before we spilled back out into the living room. There were so many presents. I swore that more had appeared overnight. Some came from *Santa*, and I elbowed Archie and he bit my neck lightly.

"What's the point of having the money if I can't spoil my family?" he asked against my ear, and a shiver overtook my whole body. Love. Loyalty. Friendship. That was our family.

The game controllers I'd gotten them were a hit. So were the boxers. Apparently, I wasn't the only one who had that idea, as they'd made a box of boxers for me, too. I found the Christmas charms in one box. In another was a copy of one of my favorite books of all time. Mine had fallen apart years earlier, and it was out of print. Jake had found it for me.

There was a guitar under the tree for me, not for Ian, and I'd been stunned at the gorgeous piece done in red. The acoustic guitar had been sized for me, and I stared at it and then Ian. He gave me a shrug. "You keep saying you want to learn to play more. Now, no more excuses."

Okay, that delighted me more than it should. Archie and Jake got each other design books and plans. Even funnier, the schematics were for similar yet different items, and it launched them on a discussion of what they wanted to build first. Coop enjoyed the notebooks and reference materials. Not to mention a stack of games they accumulated between them.

When the guys disappeared to call their families, Archie and I wrapped around each other and just made out. There was no hurry to it and no demand, just long, leisurely kisses and cuddling. Not that it didn't give me ideas for later, but I savored this time, too. From the presents to the food to curling up and napping together in front of movies—and then save me, football, thankfully I had books to read—the day was almost idyllic. It was just us.

The week following Christmas maintained the pattern set by our first week. We went skiing. We went out to sing karaoke. Archie tracked down a place to go out dancing. It was like being on a week-long date with all of them, and we still rotated who slept with me. Invariably, someone extra showed up in the bed before dawn if I only went to bed with one of them, and I didn't mind in the slightest.

The approach of New Year's brought only one regret—we were flying home the day after. I would miss the skiing and the lodge, but I thought what I'd miss most was the freedom we'd found here. The guys had taken to holding my hand or wrapping me up in hugs and kissing me whenever the mood caught us. More than once, I'd be hauled out of one lap and into another, only to be kissed soundly. More than once, Jake or Coop had pinned me against the other.

And still, the need for them could hardly seem to be satisfied. Instead of hitting a club or a venue, Archie arranged for champagne, edibles, and freaking fireworks right where we were. I couldn't even find it in me to give him grief for the cost. It was…magical. They even drew straws for kiss order, and it was hysterical and adorable.

"Making a resolution?" Archie asked as I leaned back against him and watched the fireworks, my lips still tingling.

"Gonna focus on my music full time now," Ian said, then slanted a look at me. "And hopefully, my partner will be all in."

I grinned.

"Locking in that school decision," Coop said. "I really don't give a damn where we go as long, as it's got a program for all of us."

"And we're all there," Jake added. "Splitting up is not an option."

No argument from me. Even if it meant letting go of Harvard.

"That's not a resolution." Coop flicked popcorn at him, and Jake just flipped him off.

"I'm making plans, not resolutions."

I grinned as they sniped at each other.

"What about you?" Ian asked me, and I lifted my shoulders.

"I like all of yours," I told them. "Finish senior year, we have what? Ninety days or so left? Pick a college that wants me. Turn eighteen. Pass my AP exams. Graduate. Try not to screw this up with all of us. Mine are pretty basic."

"You're not going to screw this up," Archie said, nipping my ear, and the warm and somewhat warning looks I got from the other three added to the weight of his statement. "If anyone does that, it'll be us."

"No one is screwing it up," Jake said, then cracked his knuckles.

"Or you'll what?" Coop asked drily. "Beat the shit out of us?"

"Damn straight." Jake nodded once. "Pretty basic. We work this out. We worked too long and hard to get here, so we keep right on working."

"That's almost poetic," Ian told him. "I should put that in a song."

Jake just lifted his middle finger, and we all laughed.

New Year's Day was spent alternately packing—Archie was having most of it shipped back to us, but some things none of us wanted to wait on—and just spending the time together. I baked, because I really hadn't since we'd been there, and I wanted to make cupcakes. That night though, after the food had been eaten and a movie had been watched, I slipped away with Archie as the rest went to beat on each other in one last gaming session. The car would be getting us early.

In the room still filled with roses, though some had been consolidated, Archie pulled me over to the bed and wrapped his arms around me. The soft kiss he feathered over my lips had me sighing as he tugged off my clothes. I helped him pull them free before I went to work on stripping him, but after we were naked, it was just about curling around each other.

"Thank you for letting me spoil you the last couple of weeks, babe," he whispered against my ear before pressing a kiss behind it, and I chuckled.

"That should be me thanking you." I sighed as he traced patterns against my shoulder with his thumb. "I would have said no if you'd asked me before doing all of this." Guilt nibbled at me over this admission. "I'd have worried about the expense—which doesn't mean I'm still not—but I would have also worried about the cats, the time away, and…"

He pressed his finger to my lips. "I know, babe. That's why I didn't tell you. Sometimes, it's just easier to ask for forgiveness than permission. I want to spoil you with everything. You *needed* this trip."

"You needed it, too," I murmured, scooting to lay more firmly over him, and he balanced me easily as my legs tucked on either side of his and my breasts crushed against his chest. It was comforting and erotic in equal measures. He stirred against me, but it wasn't about turning each other on, not right now. I traced a finger along his jaw.

Spreading his palm against my ass, he smiled. "Yes, I did. I needed this time with you. We all needed the time to figure this out. And if I haven't made it perfectly clear to you yet, babe, I'm in. For all of it. The five of us work, and I don't give a fuck what anyone else thinks about it. The only people who are important are in this lodge."

He trailed his fingers up to my shoulder. It didn't sting anymore. Yet the lightness of his touch sent goosebumps rippling over my skin, and my nipples pebbled.

"We do," I admitted slowly. "But it still scares the hell out of me. So much could go wrong…"

"And so much has and can go right," he said, his tone firm. That caressing hand on my back began running up and down my spine in a petting motion. "Are you happy, babe? Right now?"

"Yes." No hesitation in my answer.

"And you're scared you're not going to be when we go back?"

When we went back… "Maddy. Eddie. School. The stuff with Mitch. Sharon. There are so many things that we have to deal with…"

"Fuck Maddy and Edward," Archie said, and I couldn't help but smile at the disgust in his voice. "Grandpa is working on dealing with Edward. Wittaker and I can hold Maddy off to get you to eighteen. We cut them off. They aren't us, and we don't need them." He trailed his fingers up to my hair and began to brush it away from my face. "I mean it, Frankie. We don't need them, and we're not giving them an ounce of control over us."

I sighed, then nuzzled a kiss to his jaw.

"As for the rest? We'll deal with it as it comes. I don't care about anyone else, and if they give you a hard time, you let us know. We'll take care of it."

"What are you going to do?" I teased. "Send Jake to beat them up?"

"I won't have to send him," he said, his tone almost smug. "Or have you not noticed that Jake is very much hit first and ask questions later where you're concerned?"

I laughed softly and then kissed him. It was a slow press of my lips to his. He wrapped his hand around my nape as we dueled with our tongues. There was no hurry in the kiss, more a savoring. Chocolate lingered on his tongue from our earlier dessert. I carded my fingers through his hair as he rolled us so he was on top. The kiss remained leisurely as he stroked his hands over me.

No hurry pushed us, it was all about tasting and kissing. When I nibbled away from his lips, he would drag me back for another kiss that took my breath away, each one deepening in intensity. When I snaked a hand between us to stroke his dick, he let out a huff of laughter before sucking on my lower lip and spearing his fingers into me.

Fuck, I hadn't even felt his hand on my hip. I shifted to kiss down his jaw and he let me until I started to squirm off his fingers. Then he pinned me back to the bed, and between us, we lined him up and he pushed into me as he braced a hand against the bed. Hooking my legs around his hips, we both sighed as he sank all the way to the hilt.

There was something different about the way he touched me tonight. Light caresses interspersed with tight grips as he adjusted our position. The possessiveness in his kiss demanded an answer. A rush, then a slow. It was like we were dancing, but he only let me take the lead so far before he took it back.

Every stroke and touch eddied me higher, and I swore tears sparked in my eyes as my vision whited out. We kept edging toward orgasm, only to slow down again and work our way back up. Instead of being frustrated or teased, I felt…loved.

A smile would turn his lips as our mouths met, like he couldn't help but smile, and when we tumbled over the edge, it was as natural as breathing. The harsh shout pulled from his throat buoyed me higher if possible, and the rush as we collapsed together, panting, left me shaken. He rained little kisses down on my face and interlaced our fingers together as he cradled me closer.

This.

This was what I never wanted to lose.

"We're not leaving anything important behind," he murmured after a while as if in answer to that earlier thought I hadn't spoken aloud. "We're all still going to be together. No matter what I have to do to make sure of it."

"Hey," I soothed. "What *we* have to do."

This wasn't all on him.

Another curve of his lips as he brushed them against my forehead. "We. I like the sound of that."

I did, too. "Boyfriends," I said slowly.

"Yep. You're not getting rid of us now, babe." He rubbed my shoulder. "Regrets?"

"Only that it took so long."

"It took as long as it needed to," he whispered. "It's always been you since the day I met you, Frankie. I've always been yours. Now you're mine, too."

Eyes closing despite my best attempts, I burrowed into him, and his arms tightened. We weren't leaving anything behind when we went home. Nothing important, sure. Didn't mean I was eager to leave. But I couldn't fight against the exhaustion swarming me, so I let the sound of his heart and his steady breathing lull me to sleep.

Thankfully, we didn't have a flight at crack of ass so there was time for coffee and last-minute rushing to search for anything we might have forgotten. Archie urged us not to worry, the staff would send anything missed on down. Then again, he checked that I had my charm bracelet and necklace on while Jake checked my ring. My new charms were safely tucked away in my backpack. We'd get them put on the bracelet at home.

"Did I stick my tablet in your stuff?" Coop asked, and I gave him a blank look.

"You've been sticking a lot of your tabs in her stuff," Jake said with a wicked grin, and I rolled my eyes, even as I flushed—just a little.

"Yeah, yeah," Coop said. "Fuck off with that. You snuck into her shower and locked the damn door."

I tried to hide my laughter with a cough, but Ian and Archie weren't so kind. "He didn't sneak into her shower," Archie countered. "He snatched her right out of the bed."

"You snooze, you lose," was all Jake said before winking at me.

Terrible boys.

All of them.

"I don't know," I told Coop, bringing us back around to the topic at hand. "Did you check my backpack?" They had all stuffed different things in there for the flight here because they'd done all the packing. Not that I'd seen Coop with his tablet the whole trip.

He brushed a kiss to my hair before he went to grab it where it sat by the door with our other suitcases. We seemed to have a *lot* more to take back than we'd brought, but I was with Ian. I was not leaving my new guitar here. We'd managed a couple of fingering lessons that tended to get distracted for other things.

"Got it," Coop called as he pulled it out of the front pocket. "Why do you have mail in here?"

I glanced over to see him holding a stack of envelopes. I frowned. I'd forgotten those were even in there. "Just put them back. I have to open them and figure out what they are later. Maddy was ignoring the mail, and I don't know if those are bills or not. I can wait to figure it out."

"Want me to take care of it?" Coop offered.

I made a face. "Later. We have an hour. I just want all of us to be right here together. We can deal with that when we get home."

He nodded once, but he stuffed the letters into his backpack instead of mine and ignored my look with a playful smirk. Tablet in hand, he rejoined us, and I leaned my head on his shoulder as he tabbed through his screen, looking for apps to play on the flight.

Jake, Archie, and Ian were arguing over some game, and it took me a while to sort out they were talking about an actual team sport and not a video game. At that, I tuned out and just savored having all of them there. I wanted every single last minute down to the last drop.

When the car showed up, I let out a little sigh, and Archie grinned at me.

"We'll be back, babe. I promise."

I believed him, but it still made leaving bittersweet.

As the car pulled away, I twisted in the seat to watch the lodge disappear behind us.

Reality left a lot to be desired, unless we could make what we'd had the last few weeks our reality at home.

A worthy goal, right?

Jeremy awaited us at the apartment when we got there. The guys carried all of our stuff inside, even Coop, who could have taken his stuff back to his place.

Even better, the cats were waiting for me. Tiddles was hilarious as he raced toward me meowing. It was like getting chewed out. Tory and Tabby both rushed out to see me and then promptly ignored me. Tiddles didn't bother with that, he rubbed all over me until I picked him up and cradled him.

The guys were filling Jeremy in on the trip as he poured coffee for us, and despite the obvious cleaning my apartment had undergone while we were gone, I wasn't prepared for the bed waiting in my room.

"Archie!"

His laughter robbed my tone of any threat.

"Surprise!"

It was huge, and it filled the room, but there was some space on either side of it. My dresser had been moved into the closet to create a walkway, and I didn't want to think about the fact that Jeremy had arranged this in our absence.

Even more, the closet had been organized and space created where the guys each had a spot for their clothes.

"Too much?" Archie asked from the doorway. He stood there alone, and the worry in his expression pulled at me. It hit me that I hadn't said anything after his surprise comment.

"Yes," I told him truthfully. "And no." I liked that they had a space here. "If you're mine, then you need a place here, too, right?"

His eyes warmed, and his smile grew. "Damn straight."

"Thank fuck," Jake said in a rush from the hall, and I laughed. The guys stuck their heads around the doorframe to look at me like a masculine totem pole of beauty and sex appeal.

"Would now be a good time to suggest you check out the other bedroom?" Coop asked. No one called it Maddy's anymore.

"Am I going to hate it?" Somehow, I doubted it.

"Well," Jake said, and he eyed Ian, who then looked to Coop, before all three of them looked at Archie and grinned. "If you do…"

"…we blame Archie," the others finished in tandem with him.

Archie just snorted and held out his hand to me. "You're not going to hate it."

It really was a good thing I loved them.

Chapter Twenty-Seven
SECOND FIRST DAY

"Frankie," Coop called. "We're going to be late."

"No, we're not," I yelled, digging under the bed for where my shoes got kicked when Jake and Coop started stripping me last night. They had a habit of clearing the floor, and this bed was huge, so I had to do some serious wiggling to reach my shoes.

"Nice ass," Jake said from somewhere behind me. "Keep that up, and we really will be late to school."

"No," Coop argued. "We won't. She is not having a freak out on our first day back about missing anything. Hands to yourself, Benton."

"Killjoy," Jake grunted. "C'mon, I can practically feel her on my dick as she moves like that."

I groaned. "Get out, you teases."

Male laughter filled the room, as did the sounds of wrestling as Coop dragged Jake out. After hooking my sneakers, I dragged them out and then sat back against the bed to put my shoes on. Tiddles eyed me from his favorite perch, and his tail twitched. They seemed no worse for wear from my absence, but why should they? They'd been spoiled rotten.

I bet they were just waiting for me to go away again so they could hang with Jeremy. But when I gave him a scratch under his chin, he purred his approval. Keys in hand, I snagged my backpack and then double-checked that my wallet was where it belonged. I'd repacked it the night before.

The bed was rumpled, the pillows askew, and there was no mistaking that we'd all thoroughly christened my new bed over the weekend. Everything else was spotless, well, except for the luggage that hadn't made its way back to the guys' places.

They really were moving some of their stuff in so they could stay whenever and for however long they wanted.

As much as it surprised me, I couldn't find a single complaint within me on that topic. I *liked* having them here.

"You get lost in here?" Coop asked from the doorway, his tone teasing but his eyes soft.

"Nope," I told him, following him into the hallway. The door to the other bedroom was open, and the pair of queen beds filled the room, along with more of the guys' things. Whoever wasn't sleeping with me had a bed they could use. It was warmer and cozier in there than it had ever been. The new carpet in the place was also softer. "I know exactly where I am." I made it as far as the doorway with my backpack before he lifted it off my shoulder with two fingers.

I drained the last of my coffee before rinsing out my cup, and then we were off. Archie and Ian were already outside. It was cold and overcast, but Ian was taking his bike and I'd dressed in a warmer sweater and pulled a coat on, because I was riding on it with him.

The guys could take their own cars, but they rode with Jake instead. We were all coming back here tonight to sort out the beginning of our last semester.

"It's cold," Ian warned me as he checked my jacket and then looped the scarf so that it tucked in.

"Compared to Colorado? It's practically balmy." It was in the fifties. "I'll be fine and don't make me wait. Please?"

I'd been dying to get back on the bike. If my wrist was up to skiing, then I was damn well up to the bike.

He chuckled.

"You be really fucking careful with her," Jake warned from where he stood by his yellow SUV.

"Really careful," Archie stressed.

"Leave off, guys, he's gonna drive like a little old man." Coop winked at me.

I grinned as Ian tugged the helmet onto my head and then did up the strap. Only then did he straddle the bike and get it started. I hopped on behind him and wrapped my arms around his waist. The vibration of the bike rumbled through me. The smile on my face almost hurt as he walked us backward. Jake had already pulled out, but I could see all three of them staring at us.

"He's going to follow us," Ian said over his shoulder.

I laughed. "I know."

Then we were off, and yeah, it was windy and a little cold, but it was perfect. Traffic was too heavy to really race along the roads, but I just soaked in the feeling of holding onto him, his hard abs flexing beneath my fingers and the strength in his back where I pressed against him.

The guys were right behind us, as promised, until they diverted to get the coffee. It was so weird to pull in and look at the school. It seemed…smaller somehow.

"Last semester, Angel," Ian said as I climbed off the bike. "You ready?"

A giddiness swarmed through me. Maybe that was it.

"Yeah," I said slowly and pulled off the helmet. "Four and half more months, and we are out of here."

He glanced at the school, then at me as we turned to head over to Jake's spot to store the helmets and grab our backpacks.

The guys weren't quite there yet, but I reached for Ian's hand as we walked and he clasped mine easily. Slanting a look down at me, he raised his eyebrows. "This is pretty close to a PDA," he reminded me.

It was. That was true.

Pivoting, I glanced around the parking lot. It was filling up gradually. Familiar faces were grabbing their crap out of their cars and heading in the building. Rachel's car appeared with the yellow SUV right behind it. We kept the PDAs off at school, we weren't advertising. I'd been hearing enough crap from the exes and the gossips and more.

"You know what," I said, glancing back to Ian and meeting his startling blue-eyed gaze, "I'm okay with it."

"With…?"

I rose up on my tip toes and wrapped an arm around his neck. He dipped to meet me automatically, and his lips smoothed over mine. They were cool and chilly, but his mouth was hot, and I opened to him easily. We clung there for a long moment, just teasing each other, before I slowly lowered to stand on my feet again.

"Angel?"

"I don't care who knows," I said flatly. "You guys are my boyfriends. That's all that matters."

No more hiding.

It was us.

His smile grew slowly, and then he nodded. "Damn straight, we are."

"Well fuck," Jake said as he wrenched his door open and looked over at me. "You sure about this?"

I glanced from Archie's bemused smirk to Coop's genuine curiosity to Jake's fiercely protective scowl.

"I've never been sure of anything more."

They were mine.

I was going to fucking own it.

"Well bring it on," Rachel said as she strolled up, and I grabbed a hug. She laughed against me. "I got your back."

They all did.

We'd have each other's.

"And look, I'm even happy to see these assholes."

Laughter bubbled up through me. "Look, they even brought you coffee."

"I could get used to this," Rachel declared, winking at me. "Ready to kick some ass?"

"That's my job," Jake declared, and he wrapped an arm around me before pressing a kiss against my temple. He laced his fingers together with mine and stroked his thumb over the ring. "Shall we?"

"Let's," Coop said with a mock accent. "We should probably get video of the dropping jaws."

"And the jealous looks," Rachel said with a hum. "So many jealous little bitches are going to cry."

"Be nice," I told her.

"What?" Rachel said. "You want me to offer them a fucking tissue?"

It was our last first day of high school.

It was going to rock.

* * *

Frankie and the boys will be back in *Brazen & Breathless*.

To keep up with Heather and all her series, join her reader's group:

Https://www.facebook.com/groups/HeathersPack/

Afterword

Whew. We made it. Halfway through senior year with five books under our belt and it's finally official, Frankie and her guys are in their relationship. Every one of them is on board. Every one of them is committed. More, Frankie is owning the relationship.

It's easy to look at them and wonder why this is a big deal, I get that. I see some of the comments I get and I read the emails who all want to know why it's taken so long. This book is part of the reason we took our time on this journey.

Building relationships takes time. Shifting a relationship, particularly ones founded in deep friendship, is nerve-wracking enough. When you shift the dynamics in a group with more, you run the risk that not everyone can handle the change.

At the beginning of the year, Frankie was not in a good place emotionally. She's still struggling. It's been a tough few months and yet, she's also got the guys at her back and the best kind of friend in Rachel. She's standing up for herself and she's owning her decisions. Owning up to the fact she loves these guys and wants it to work.

They love her enough and are close enough as friends that they are willing to make it work for her. Does that mean it's all sunshine and roses? No, relationships are effort. Happily ever after is always a work in progress. But we're seeing the progress now.

Best of all, they're a unit now and ready to handle whatever life throws at them.

So thank you again for being on this journey with me. I am so excited to see where we go next.

xoxo

Heather

About Heather Long

USA Today bestselling author, Heather Long, likes long walks in the park, science fiction, superheroes, Marines, and men who aren't douche bags. Her books are filled with heroes and heroines tangled in romance as hot as Texas summertime. From paranormal historical westerns to contemporary military romance, Heather might switch genres, but one thing is true in all of her stories—her characters drive the books. When she's not wrangling her menagerie of animals, she devotes her time to family and friends she considers family. She believes if you like your heroes so real you could lick the grit off their chest, and your heroines so likable, you're sure you've been friends with women just like them, you'll enjoy her worlds as much as she does.

Follow Heather & Sign up for her newsletter:

www.heatherlong.net

Also by Heather Long

UNTOUCHABLE

Rules and Roses

Changes and Chocolates

Keys and Kisses

Whispers and Wishes

Hangovers and Holidays

Brazen and Breathless

Trials and Tiaras

Graduation and Gifts

Defiance and Dedication

82ND STREET VANDALS

Savage Vandal

Vicious Rebel

Ruthless Traitor

Dirty Devil

ALWAYS A MARINE SERIES

Once Her Man, Always Her Man

Retreat Hell! She Just Got Here

Tell It to the Marine

Proud to Serve Her

Her Marine

No Regrets, No Surrender

The Marine Cowboy

The Two and the Proud

A Marine and a Gentleman

Combat Barbie

Whiskey Tango Foxtrot

What Part of Marine Don't You Understand?

A Marine Affair

Marine Ever After

Marine in the Wind

Marine with Benefits

A Marine of Plenty

A Candle for a Marine

Marine under the Mistletoe

Have Yourself a Marine Christmas

Lest Old Marines Be Forgot

Her Marine Bodyguard

Smoke & Marines

BRAVO TEAM WOLF

When Danger Bites

Bitten Under Fire

BOOMERS

The Judas Contact

Deadly Genesis

Unstoppable

Chance Monroe

Earth Witches Aren't Easy

Plan Witch from Out of Town

Bad Witch Rising

Her Elite Assets

Featuring:

Pure Copper

Target: Tungsten

Asset: Arsenic

Fevered Hearts

Marshal of Hel Dorado

Brave are the Lonely

Micah & Mrs. Miller

A Fistful of Dreams

Raising Kane

Wanted: Fevered or Alive

Wild and Fevered

The Quick & The Fevered

A Man Called Wyatt

Going Royal

Some Like It Royal

Some Like It Scandalous

Some Like It Deadly

Some Like it Secret

Some Like it Easy

Her Marine Prince

Blocked

HEART OF THE NEBULA
Queenmaker

Deal Breaker

Throne Taker

LONE STAR LEATHERNECKS
Semper Fi Cowboy

As You Were, Cowboy

MADISON, THE WITCH HUNTER
Every Witch Way But Floosey's

MAGIC & MAYHEM
The Witch Singer

Bridget's Witch's Diary

The Witched Away Bride

Mongrels

Mongrels, Mischief & Mayhem

SHACKLED SOULS
Succubus Chained

Succubus Unchained

Succubus Blessed

SPACE COWBOY
Space Cowboy Survival Guide

WOLVES OF WILLOW BEND
Wolf at Law

Wolf Bite

Caged Wolf

Wolf Claim

Wolf Next Door

Rogue Wolf

Bayou Wolf

Untamed Wolf

Wolf with Benefits

River Wolf

Single Wicked Wolf

Desert Wolf

Snow Wolf

Wolf on Board

Holly Jolly Wolf

Shadow Wolf

His Moonstruck Wolf

Thunder Wolf

Ghost Wolf

Outlaw Wolves

Wolf Unleashed